Quintin Jardine gave up the life of a political spin doctor for the more morally acceptable world of murder and mayhem. Happily married, he hides from critics and creditors in secret locations in Scotland and Spain, but can be tracked down through his website: www.quintinjardine.com.

Praise for previous Quintin Jardine novels;

'Deplorably readable' *Guardian*

'Well constructed, fast-paced, Jardine's narrative has many an ingenious twist and turn' *Observer*

'[Quintin Jardine] sells more crime fiction in Scotland than John Grisham and people queue around the block to buy his latest book' *The Australian*

'Perfect plotting and convincing characterisation . . . Jardine manages to combine the picturesque with the thrilling and the dream-like with the coldly rational' *The Times*

'There is a whole world here, the tense narratives all come to the boil at the same time in a spectacular climax' *Shots* magazine

'The perfect mix for a highly charged, fast-moving crime thriller' *Glasgow Herald*

'Remarkably assured . . . *a tour de force*' *New York Times*

'Engrossing, believable characters . . . captures Edinburgh beautifully . . . It all adds up to a very good read' *Edinburgh Evening News*

Also by Quintin Jardine and available from Headline

Bob Skinner series:
Skinner's Rules
Skinner's Festival
Skinner's Trail
Skinner's Round
Skinner's Ordeal
Skinner's Mission
Skinner's Ghosts
Murmuring the Judges
Gallery Whispers
Thursday Legends
Autographs in the Rain
Head Shot
Fallen Gods
Stay of Execution
Lethal Intent
Dead and Buried

Oz Blackstone series:
Blackstone's Pursuits
A Coffin for Two
Wearing Purple
Screen Savers
On Honeymoon with Death
Poisoned Cherries
Unnatural Justice
Alarm Call
For the Death of Me

DEATH'S DOOR

QUINTIN JARDINE

headline

First published in 2007
by HEADLINE PUBLISHING GROUP

First published in paperback in 2008
by HEADLINE PUBLISHING GROUP

1

Cataloguing in Publication Data is available from the British Library

ISBN 978 0 7553 2911 3

Typeset in Electra by Avon DataSet Ltd,
Bidford-on-Avon, Warwickshire

Printed and bound in Great Britain by
Mackays of Chatham plc, Chatham, Kent

HEADLINE PUBLISHING GROUP
An Hachette Livre UK Company
338 Euston Road
London NW1 3BH

www.headline.co.uk

Ten years ago, on a Saturday afternoon, May 3, the world became a smaller, lesser place, when Irene, my first wife, drew her last breath. Her special light wasn't extinguished, though. It will shine on, until the last person who ever knew her is gone, and beyond, I hope, through these words, on whatever library shelves they may come eventually to gather dust.

Acknowledgements

My thanks go to

The inestimable Mira Kolar Brown, for setting me on the road with a batch of names and with a piece of S-H slang.

Frank Mansfield and Jenny Pollock, my in-laws, for rebuilding their house so that it can no longer be mistaken for one in this book.

Martin Fletcher, Jo Matthews and Hazel Orme, for their invaluable roles in making sure that this work got from me to you.

One

'If there are such things as angels,' the big detective whispered, 'that's what they look like.'

Detective Inspector Stevie Steele said nothing. He was not given to pondering spiritual concepts, and especially not when he was standing at a crime scene.

He glanced at the head of CID: not so long ago, such a remark would have taken him by surprise, but over the past few months he had come to know Detective Chief Superintendent Mario McGuire much better, through close contact on the job, and through small things that his new wife, Maggie, had let slip about her first husband. It was his Italian blood, Steele supposed, from which the closet romantic within him flowed, just as the Irish strain that he had inherited from his father marked him out as uncompromising, and on occasion fearsome.

Steele looked at the girl. '*Girl?*' he pondered silently. '*Maybe that's all she is, maybe not. People always look younger when they're dead.*'

She lay on her back on the yellow sand, her face serene, framed by blonde hair, her pale lips set in what might almost have been a smile. She wore open-toed sandals, bare-legged; her arms were by her side, palms down and her long white dress was spread out, fan-like. Her eyes were open and gazed up at the clear blue afternoon sky. May was only just into its second week, but the weather was more than comfortably warm: summer often comes early in Scotland, although it can leave just as suddenly as it arrives.

'She looks almost transparent, doesn't she?' said McGuire, absent-mindedly, still musing somewhere.

'Has anyone touched her?' Steele asked.

'The local doctor's certified death, but that's all. The officers who were first on the scene had more sense than to disturb anything. They reported directly to Graham Leggatt, as the divisional CID commander, and he called me; all strictly by the book when it comes to a suspicious death. The locals' first thought was that it was an overdose, some poor sad kid finding a quiet spot to end it all. That's happened out here before and, of course, we've heard it elsewhere too. But when Graham described the scene, I thought I'd better take a look for myself, and that you should see it too. You agree with me, do you, that it's just like the other one?'

The detective inspector nodded. 'Absolutely. The way the body's arranged, the fact that it's a female, the age group, it all matches. She's dressed differently, and her hair colour is different, but otherwise it's identical.' He glanced around. 'Has the area been disturbed at all?'

'I'm assured that it hasn't; not since she was found, at any rate.'

'Well, that knocks the supposition of suicide on the head. There's no sort of paraphernalia around, no pill containers, no syringe, no booze bottles, no blades.'

'And no blood, just like the South Queensferry murder. It looks as if she died instantly.'

'You reckon she might have been killed somewhere else and brought here?' asked Steele.

'That's a possibility, I suppose, but look around you, look at the sand: it's unremarkably flat around the body. If she'd been dragged, it would show. If somebody had carried her here, surely his feet would have dug deep under the weight, and we'd still see the tracks. There's been no wind to smooth them over; at least, that's what the local officers told me. It just looks as if she was walking on the beach when someone came up behind her and . . . whap!'

'Yeah. That's what we reckon in the other one too, but we've never been able to say for sure.'

'No: because it's still unsolved.'

The inspector winced. 'We've done everything we can, boss. But every lead we've followed has wound up taking us precisely nowhere.'

'Hey, I'm not knocking your investigation, Stevie,' McGuire assured him, 'just stating a fact. You couldn't have been more thorough; whoever shot Stacey Gavin was either very clever, or very bloody lucky. Normally I would expect the latter, but if this is a repeat performance, Christ, it looks ominous.'

'Might it be a copycat?'

'How? You know as well as I do that all our press statements were cleared through Neil McIlhenney, and the crime scene was never described in any of them. No, we begin with the assumption that it's . . .'

The head of CID stopped in mid-sentence. 'No, we

don't. If our deputy chief constable was here he'd kick my arse . . . and an arse-kicking by Bob Skinner is something to be avoided. We begin by following proper procedure. Let's allow the doc in for a more thorough examination, and an estimate of time of death.' He turned and lifted the flap of the enclosing screen that had been erected all around the body, holding it up for his colleague as they stepped out on to the beach.

Aidan Brown, the pathologist, was waiting a few yards away, clad in the same crime-scene tunic as the detectives. He was a tall man, in his mid-thirties: he had been on the scene for a few years and was known to both of them. 'Sorry to keep you, Doc,' said McGuire, as he approached. 'I wanted to let DI Steele see things exactly as they were found. You can go in now and take a look at the body.'

'I suppose you want my thoughts on cause of death, as well as time?' His accent was light, Irish.

The head of CID nodded. 'I do, but I suggest that you begin by taking a look at the base of her skull.'

The medical examiner frowned. 'Have you . . .?'

'We didn't lay a finger on her. There's a tenner on it if you fancy a bet on the cause, though.'

Brown chuckled. 'That'll be the day. I'm a scientist, man: I don't indulge in such frivolities.'

'You mean you're a tight bastard.'

'It's in our Irish blood, Mario,' the pathologist shot back. 'You should know that.'

Steele glanced at them: McGuire had switched from tender to hard-boiled mode in a few minutes. Yet he knew that it was forced, the copper's defence mechanism against the realities of the job. Not for the first time, he found himself wondering about his unborn child, his and Maggie's: a daughter, as they knew already. How would her personality be moulded . . . blessed or cursed . . . with two police officers for parents?

'How's Mags?'

The question, thrown from out of nowhere as he watched Brown move off towards the tented area, took the inspector completely off-guard. 'She's fine,' he replied, a little abruptly. 'How's Paula?' At once he regretted his impetuosity. McGuire's new partner, Paula Viareggio, had been, briefly, a figure in his past, but that was not something the two men had ever discussed.

But the big man simply shrugged. 'She's good. Busy as ever; maybe busier, now that the family business is a public limited company. She's got more legal stuff to look after, and she spends more time talking to the accountants.'

Silence fell between them for a few seconds, until McGuire broke it awkwardly. 'I'm sorry, Stevie,' he said. 'Don't think I'm prying, please. But Maggie and I were . . . Shit, you know what I mean. Her being pregnant, it's so . . .'

'Unexpected?'

'Well, yeah. Tell me if I'm wrong, tell me the two of you planned it, but I'd guess it came as a hell of a surprise to you both. If that's so, it hasn't exactly happened at the best time for her career.'

Steele looked out to sea. They stood in the middle of a wide bay, bitten out of the coastline by nature and defined by a semicircle of sand dunes, which formed a natural bridge to the bents above. The tide was at its highest and the water was millpond-calm, so flat that the sound of the engines of a distant tanker carried all the way to shore. 'You're not wrong, Mario,' he replied. 'And I hear what you're saying about timing. But does she want a career any longer, assuming that everything goes all right with the baby? That's the question you really should be asking.'

'You're kidding me!' McGuire exclaimed. 'Maggie's thinking about packing the job in? She's one of the most career-minded people I've ever met.'

'She's mentioned the possibility; that's all I'll say for now. That's strictly between you and me, by the way. Understood?'

'Of course. So she hasn't discussed it with anyone else? The DCC, for example, or Brian Mackie, now that she reports to him?'

'She hasn't had the opportunity to discuss it with Mr Skinner, even if she was inclined to. Remember: he's been on sabbatical since the end of January. As for our new assistant chief constable, they may have known each other for a while, but she's not ready to discuss careers with him.'

'Why not?'

The inspector frowned. 'I'm not sure, but I don't think she trusts him enough.'

'Brian Mackie? Why wouldn't she trust him?'

'Because he's new in post: people change when they go into the Command Corridor. I reckon she has a concern . . . I'll put it no stronger . . . that if she went into a meeting with him to discuss career options, she might come out without any. No, let everyone assume what they will, I reckon she'll say nothing about her future until after the baby's born and maybe not till she's getting close to the end of her maternity leave.'

'When does she go off?'

'In three days. She finishes on Friday.'

'How long can she take?'

'A full year from then, if she wants; and just between you and me again, that's her present intention.'

'Jesus! She'll be bored stiff after a month.'

'Maybe, but a month after that she won't, not with the baby on her hands.'

'I suppose you'll be going off then too. Bloody paternity leave,' he grumbled. 'Losing Neil McIlhenney is something I did not need.'

'You're complaining about that?' Steele laughed. 'I thought you were going to be his new son's godfather.'

'Louis? That I am. I'm his big brother Spencer's too, but Neil didn't get swanning off for a fortnight when he was born.'

'Times change, sir.'

'I don't know what you're grinning about,' McGuire retorted. 'With Bandit Mackenzie off on extended sick leave, you're running your subdivision, and with Neil away . . .' He broke off, as Dr Brown re-emerged from the green enclosure. 'Well, Doc?'

'I'm glad I didn't take the bet.' The Irishman grimaced. 'It looks as if death was caused by a single gunshot fired directly into the brain, upwards through the second spinal vertebra. It wasn't a contact wound, but the muzzle was close enough to singe the surrounding hair. As you've seen, the bullet hasn't exited, which, given the range, would indicate something like a point two-two or nine-millimetre weapon. You'll know when we recover the thing, if it's not too misshapen from rattling about inside her skull. Time of death? Six to eight hours ago, I'd say.' He glanced at his watch. 'That would make it, neatly, between six and eight a.m.

'Obviously I can't carry out a complete examination here, but I could see no other signs of violence on the body, save one, and it hardly qualifies. There is very slight bruising on the left shoulder; it could be the print of a hand, possibly indicating that the woman was gripped from behind and shot. There's no indication of any resistance whatsoever, so chances are, she never knew a thing, just the lights going out.' He paused. 'Any of that significant?'

'All of it, worse luck,' McGuire growled. 'Thanks, Aidan. When can you do the post-mortem?'

'As soon as I can round up someone to assist, or find someone more eminent than me to take the lead.'

'I don't want to wait for the professor for this one: I'd like to get my hands on the bullet as soon as possible.'

The doctor's eyebrows rose slightly. 'For comparison with another case?'

McGuire winked at him. 'Come on now, Doc, you know we always run ballistic comparisons.'

'But maybe not as a matter of urgency.'

'Bugger off . . . with respect to your professional status, of course.'

Brown smiled. 'I'll take that as a yes. Get her to the city mortuary as soon as you can. I'll be ready, even if it means working this evening, so you'd better have your witnesses in place too. If I'm breaking my back over this I don't want you lot holding me up.'

As soon as the Irishman headed for his car, McGuire beckoned to a red-haired figure who stood waiting, amid a group of tunic-clad officers. 'DI Dorward,' he called out. 'Your team can get to work now.'

'Are we looking for anything in particular?' the man asked, as he approached.

'The day I tell you how to do your job, Arthur,' the head of CID replied, 'mine will really have gone to my head.'

'Come on, boss, give us a clue.'

'Well, first of all, we'd like to know who she is, so you should make identification a priority. Also, if you find a spent cartridge casing, that would be very nice.'

'That's assuming that the uniforms haven't ground it into the sand . . . or you, for that matter.'

'Give us credit for a wee bit of professionalism.'

'Not after being in this job for the time I have.' He glanced around. 'Will this be a media-free zone?'

'As free as we can make it. We can keep the beach clear, but anybody with the wit to hire a boat from North Berwick and run it along here will have a clear view.'

'And they'll do that too,' Dorward muttered. 'We'd better get cracking, in that case.' He turned, signalling to his team to join him on the beach.

'So where do we go from here, sir?' Steele asked; the question was loaded.

'I go back to Fettes,' the detective chief superintendent

replied, 'back to Headquarters. You take charge of this investigation.'

'It's outside my area,' the inspector pointed out. 'It's in East Lothian.'

McGuire sighed. 'How did I know you were going to say that? I don't care where the fuck it is. This murder is identical in every respect to the Stacey Gavin killing two months ago, and you're carrying the ball on that one. I'm not having two teams chasing the same person, you must realise that.'

'I do, but will DCI Leggatt understand? He's the divisional commander here.'

'Of course he will.'

'Are you sure, sir? He's relatively new in his position; put yourself in his place and you might fancy a nice high-profile murder, especially in a rural area. A quick result would make your name.'

McGuire glanced sideways at his colleague. 'Forgive me, Stevie, if I sound political, but this isn't any old rural area. We are just outside the village of Gullane. Who lives here?' He looked to the west. 'Not a mile away, as the fly crows, or whatever.'

'DCC Skinner.'

'Exactly. Big Bob may be in the middle of this study break of his, but he's still around. He's been damn good so far about keeping away from the office, and letting us get on with our jobs; better than I expected, to tell you the truth. But I'm not so naive that I wouldn't do him the courtesy of advising him of what's happened on his own doorstep.

'He might not interfere in the investigation, but as sure

as God made Motherwell supporters, he will want to be sure that it's being run to the best of our ability. That does not mean entrusting it to a new DCI whose biggest success to date, good collar though it was, is a white-collar scam involving a bogus property portfolio and some duped investors.

'Stevie, your first task will be to identify the victim. There's every chance she's local, and every possibility that the boss knows her. So don't you be too bothered about Graham Leggatt making his name; you concentrate on yours.'

Steele winced. 'Am I supposed to thank you for that?'

The head of CID smiled affably. 'No. Custom dictates that you say, "Yes, sir." Anyway, you know I'm right to keep the two investigations under one roof. Don't worry about DCI Leggatt: I'll explain my decision to him. And when I do, I'll bet he bloody thanks me.'

'Do I keep him in the loop?'

'If you want to do that as a courtesy, I've no objection, as long as you make it clear that it's in confidence. Otherwise, you report to Detective Superintendent McIlhenney, when he's back from changing nappies, and to me until then.'

'What about manpower?'

'Use the same core team that's on the Stacey Gavin investigation, but you can augment it out here with locals as you need them, for door-to-door enquiries and the like. I'll square that with Leggatt as well.'

'What about the mobile HQ unit?'

'There's no point in bringing the van down here, even if we could find somewhere flat to put it: this is too isolated.

You'll have the odd beach rambler, like the man who found the body, and a few family picnics at weekends, but nobody else will come by here. If we have to you can set up the mobile unit in the village, but maybe we can borrow a public building for the purpose. Whatever suits you best.'

Steele nodded back towards the bents. 'The road I drove down to get here: is that public? Is it a right of way?'

McGuire chuckled. 'To the likes of you and me, maybe, but even then only by invitation or under warrant. It runs across Muirfield golf course, and that's strictly private.'

'So,' the inspector scratched his chin, 'only golf-club members would know about it.'

'In the main, yes.'

'And there's no other vehicle access?'

'There might be one through the Archerfield estate, but you'd need a tractor to get across here.'

'So if we're wrong and the victim was brought here, not killed here . . .'

A broad, piratical grin spread across the head of CID's face. 'I see what you mean, Stevie. Your first port of call will be the golf club itself. In that case, take my advice: walk very carefully.'

Two

'I've just checked the weather forecast,' Neil McIlhenney murmured. 'It's set fair well into May. It looks as if I picked a good time to exercise my new politically correct rights.'

'Are you dropping a hint of cynicism about gender equality?' Paula Viareggio asked.

'Not me,' the new father replied. 'I am but a humble servant of the people. If it's their will . . . or at least the will of about a quarter of them, if you look at the percentage of the apathetic buggers who actually turned out to vote for the present government . . . that I should have two weeks' paid paternity leave, then who am I to say that they're wrong? Who am I to say that it's another burden upon hard-pressed employers struggling to keep their businesses afloat, or that it's another cost to be borne by the public purse?'

He held his three-week-old son to his barrel chest, and rubbed two fingers, very gently, between his shoulder-blades. 'Seriously, though, Paulie, I know that grumpy old bastard of yours thinks of it as an example of the nanny state at work, but seen through my eyes at this moment, it's a great innovation. My wife and I have two weeks in which we need do nothing but welcome wee Louis into the world.'

'And spoil the hell out of him,' came a retort from across the room.

'You can't spoil a baby, McGuire,' McIlhenney retorted. 'All you do is feed them when they yell, burp them . . .' he paused, 'right on cue, wee man, well done . . . and change them when they yell some more.'

'Aw, look,' exclaimed Paula, standing behind him, 'he's smiling at me.'

'They say,' Louise McIlhenney told her, 'that at his age, when he does that it's just wind. Don't you believe it: he smiles at us too, and at Lauren and Spence. He has done since the day he was born. Do you want to hold him?'

'If I do, will I get broody?'

'There's been no sign of it yet, has there?'

'I wouldn't know. I've never held one of those before.'

Even Mario looked surprised. 'What?' he gasped. 'You've never held a baby? What about your nephews, Ryan and David?' He glanced at McIlhenney. 'You'd never guess their dad was a Man U fan, would you?'

No,' Paula confessed. 'I never got to play with either of them. My sister hardly ever went out when they were very young, and when she did she always asked Mum to babysit. My nephews and I have never been close: no way was I getting stuck with the maiden-aunt tag.'

'Come on, then,' said Neil. 'Take a chance.'

'I'm not so sure about that,' McGuire muttered.

'Ah, you be quiet. You can have a turn too if you like.' The smiling father leaned over and placed the baby gently into Paula's arms, as she settled herself against the arm of a big, soft sofa, showing her how to hold him and how to support his head.

'God,' she whispered, as she looked at the tiny round face. 'God. Hello there, wee Louis. I'm your auntie Paula. Will you and I be friends?' The infant blinked up at her, and the corners of his mouth twitched, to form what might or might not have been a smile. 'Looks like it, eh?'

McIlhenney turned to his friend. 'Time for your feed as well?' He walked across to the bar, which stood in a corner of the living room.

'Well, if you've got something open . . .'

'Since it's you, I've got some nice Valpolicella here.'

'Perfect.' He watched as Neil poured two glasses, held one out towards him, then picked up the other. 'I thought you were off that stuff,' he said.

'Not completely. Lou isn't drinking alcohol while she's feeding the wee one, and Paula said she's driving. As for Lauren and Spence upstairs, we do give them a taste occasionally, but very little and never during the school week. So if I don't give you a hand you'll finish the bottle all on your own, and probably want to start another.'

'True,' Mario muttered. 'Fuckin' spoilsport, aren't you?'

The two men wandered through to the kitchen, where Neil had prepared a bowl of salad, ready to accompany four steaks, which he had seared earlier. He switched on the eye-level gas grill, and sipped his wine as he waited for it to heat. 'What was that on *Scotland Today*,' he asked, 'about a suspicious death in East Lothian?'

'We aren't allowed to talk shop,' Mario reminded him. 'I'd cross many people, but not your wife, not ever.'

'She can't hear us.'

'I'm not going to take that chance. You just concentrate on those fillets.'

The cook fell silent as he laid the four steaks on the grill tray, and slid it under the flame. 'Near Gullane, was it?' he ventured, at last.

McGuire gave up. 'Just by Muirfield; you know, the golf course where half the Supreme Court judges are members.'

'Mmm. On the golf course itself?'

'No, on the other side.'

'On the bents?'

'No.'

'On the beach, then.'

'That's right.'

'Mmm.' McIlhenney peered into the grill, concentrating on the steaks. 'Does Paula still like hers well done?' he asked.

'No, I'm trying to wean her off burned meat; she'll have it just shy of medium like the rest of us.'

'That's good. I can turn them all at the same time, then.' As he spoke, a pinging sound began and the microwave indicator display flashed. 'That's the spuds baked,' he said, as he switched it off. 'Sweet potatoes.'

'Yummy,' Mario murmured, deadpan.

Neil wore a concentrated frown as he flipped the four steaks over, then slid them back under the grill. 'Another few minutes and they'll be fine. I'll be doing six, before you know it: it can't be long before Lauren won't be put off with early supper and insist on joining us. And that'll mean Spence too.'

'You'll be doing seven soon.'

'What do you mean?'

'That wee boy through there, mate. He'll be your height before you know it.'

'Jesus, man, don't wish his childhood away.'

'Sorry. I'm not, really; as a caring godparent, if I could keep him in a time warp of innocence I bloody well would. But life ain't like that.' Mario's face grew dark. 'I saw an angel today, pal; cut off in her prime.'

'That's the job.'

'Sure. But she had a father too, just like wee Louis.' He shook his heavy shoulders. 'Don't mind me,' he said. 'You know it always affects me like this when I visit a murder scene.'

'Good. I'll start to worry about you the day it doesn't.'

'Yeah. Be sure to tell me, too.'

'In a loud voice.' Neil peered into the grill once more. 'Not long now.' He opened the microwave and used a glove to lift out the baked yams on the revolving glass tray. 'The dishes are warming in the oven. Do you want to get them out?' he asked rhetorically, as he carried them across to a work surface.

'Sure.'

When the plates were laid out, Neil laid a baked potato on each, slit it open and dropped in a spoonful of mustard mayonnaise, then returned to the grill and waited for the steaks to cook to his satisfaction.

'Did you brief the big man?' he murmured casually.

'Bob Skinner? Of course I did,' McGuire replied. 'I'm not daft. I looked in on him before I went back to Edinburgh.'

'How did he react?'

'He thanked me, and wished us well with the investigation.'

'Does he expect daily reports?'

'No. He never asked.'

'Jesus!' McIlhenney gasped. 'How is he?'

'Haven't you seen him?'

'Not since February. That's the last time he was at our Thursday-night football; I had to go straight home afterwards, so we didn't have time to talk. He visited Lou in the maternity, of course, the day after the baby was born; brought him a very generous present. But I was in the office so I missed him. How's he looking?'

McGuire's eyebrows rose. 'Fit as hell. To be honest, I haven't seen him looking better in years.'

'Did he say what he's been up to?'

'He said, and I quote, that he'd been farting about on some study projects he's been putting off for years. He was in Toronto during the Easter holidays while the kids were with their mother in Connecticut; he didn't go into detail, but I got the impression that it might have been job-related. I think he's been writing too.'

'So the marriage break-up with Sarah isn't getting to him?'

'Why do you ask? You're closer to him than I am.'

'Not so close that he pours out his soul to me.'

'As far as I can see, he's over it. Who knows? Maybe he's

well out of it. Maybe they both are. Besides, he's involved elsewhere, isn't he? The story's all over town.'

Neil turned off the grill. 'How do I put this? He's involved discreetly? No, that isn't the word: the deputy chief constable doesn't do discreet very well. Yes, he is, but he's trying his best to keep it low-key; that just about sums it up. I heard that one tabloid was going to run a feature on him and his new lady, until he phoned the editor and squashed it. Whether it was by threat or blackmail, I don't know, but neither would surprise me.'

He carried the steaks across and laid one on each plate. 'Graham Leggatt's going to have to be careful, I guess. Interviewing some of those Muirfield members will call for a bit of diplomacy.'

'Not from him. Stevie Steele's fronting the investigation.'

'Mmm.' No more than a whisper. 'I'll take the girls' steaks through to the dining room. You bring the salad.'

'That's all right.' Louise's voice came from the doorway: she was smiling as she stood there with the big glass bowl in her hands. 'I've got it. And what did I say about talking shop? It's like telling the sun not to set.'

Three

'Most times it's obvious, isn't it?' said Detective Sergeant Ray Wilding. His face was pale in the neon light of Edinburgh city mortuary's observation gallery.

'What?'

'Cause of death.'

'So?' Stevie Steele challenged.

'So it doesn't make any difference. They still go through the whole rigmarole, and it still takes a hell of a long time. I had a victim once; he was brought in here with a knife stuck in his chest, wedged right in his sternum like the sword in the fucking stone, and yet it was four hours before they were done with him. Look at this poor lass . . .'

'The pathologist's name wasn't Arthur, was it? Arthur King?'

Wilding stared at the inspector. 'No, it was Sarah Grace, the DCC's ex-wife. There isn't one called Arthur King, is . . .' He broke off, as the point struck home. 'Very funny. Anyway, as I was saying, look at this lass. She's got a bullet hole in her head, but you can bet they'll open her up, take all her bits out . . .'

'Enough, for Christ's sake!' Steele protested. 'I don't

need a commentary. However clear-cut it looks, it's all necessary. What if they go in there and find the bullet lodged in bone? What if it didn't kill her, and she died of something else? I read of a politician in Ireland, years ago, who was shot five times in the head and survived.'

'His brain must have been so small they couldn't hit it,' the sergeant growled. 'What odds are you offering against this girl having died of a gunshot wound?'

'That's not the point. The autopsy report goes beyond immediate cause of death because that's how the procurator fiscal wants it. The Crown has to build a complete case: by the time the thing comes to court there just can't be any questions that it can't answer. Look at it another way: it's an important part of our own investigation; a full examination can throw up all sorts of things that might help us.'

'Like what? She had sand under her fingernails?'

'A hell of a lot more than that, Ray, and you know it. Okay, her clothing was undisturbed and there was no sign of sexual assault when she was found, but the likelihood is her killer was known to her; that's true of most homicides. Maybe they had consensual sex, and maybe he left his DNA inside her.'

'I hope he did.' Wilding sighed. 'We've got no clue to her identity so far. She doesn't match any missing-persons' reports, and there've been no alarms raised in and around Gullane since the news broke.'

'Early days yet, Sergeant. What's got into you, anyway? It's not like you to be so bloody negative.'

'Don't mind me, gaffer. Autopsies always get to me.'

On the other side of the glass screen a door opened. Dr

Aidan Brown and a similarly gowned colleague stepped into the examination room, where the body of Mario McGuire's angel lay naked on a steel table.

Steele felt his forehead tighten. 'And me, Ray. And me.'

Four

Louise McIlhenney looked at Paula Viareggio across the dinner table. Only a few crumbs of cheese remained on the board, and the coffee jug was almost empty. The level of the second bottle of Valpolicella was below the top of the label. 'I've got to hand it to these guys,' she said. 'They can do it when they have to.'

Neil jerked his thumb in Mario's direction. 'What the hell did he do?'

'I brought the cheese!' McGuire protested.

'You were always at your best with takeaways.'

'That's what the bachelor life does for you.'

'Bachelor?' Neil laughed. 'Who are you two kidding?'

'Most of Edinburgh?' Paula ventured.

'You're not even kidding most of your respective streets. Either your car's parked at his place overnight or his is at yours.'

'Maybe we should use taxis, in that case.'

'Maybe you should just do the sensible thing, and have one home.'

'We're thinking about it,' Paula admitted. 'God, holding that wee one tonight . . . Suddenly I'm thinking about lots of things.'

A look of undiluted amazement spread across Mario's face. 'You what?'

She winked at him. 'Don't worry, love. It'll have worn off by morning.'

'Change the subject, quick,' Neil exclaimed.

'Okay,' said his wife, 'since supper's over, we'll relax the ban on talking shop. Why will Inspector Steele be interviewing Muirfield members?'

'We found a body on the beach down there this afternoon,' Mario told her. 'A young woman.'

'How dreadful!' Louise paused. 'You'd better tell Neil all about it, otherwise he'll be gnawing away at it all night.'

'He has done already,' McIlhenney said, 'whether he knows it or not.'

McGuire frowned. 'How come?'

'She looked angelic. She was found on a beach. You've just described Stacey Gavin. Stevie Steele's fronting up, rather than the local divisional commander. This isn't a new investigation: it's an extension of one that's already running.'

'What else did I tell you without knowing it?'

'Small-calibre gunshot to the head?'

McGuire nodded.

'No other sign of violence; no sexual assault?'

'No . . . not in the examination at the scene, at least.'

'Body arranged as if she'd been laid out?'

'Yes.'

'Victim as yet unknown?'

'So far. There were absolutely no personal effects on the

body, nothing to identify her. But how did you work that out?'

'If you knew who she was, you wouldn't be here. You'd either have worked out a connection between her and Stacey and you'd have pulled someone in already, or you'd be out there helping Steele to find a link. You said you briefed the boss. Did you let him see the body?'

'No. She was on her way to the morgue by the time I called on him. Why?'

'If she's local, there's just a chance he'd have known her.'

'True, although the beach walker, the guy who found her, he told us that he's lived in Gullane for nearly thirty years and he didn't recognise her.'

'So what's Stevie going to do?'

'He's got a techie working on a photograph of the body, trying to make her look as lifelike as he can. After the publicity, she might be reported missing overnight, but if not, then tomorrow his team will start knocking doors and showing it around. If we haven't identified her by late afternoon, he'll release it to the media and ask the TV stations to show it on the news.'

'That's horrible,' Paula exclaimed. 'A dead woman's photo on telly!'

'It won't be the first time,' McIlhenney told her.

'Excuse me,' Louise interrupted. 'I guess I haven't been taking enough interest in my husband's work. Who is Stacey Gavin?'

The two detectives looked at each other for a second or two, until McGuire nodded, as if in signal.

McIlhenney leaned his head back; suddenly it was as if

his eyes were fixed on something far away. 'Stacey Gavin,' he began. 'At five minutes past ten on the morning of March the thirteenth, she's lying on a quiet beach near South Queensferry, almost under the Forth railway bridge. She's on her back, looking up at the sky. Her arms are by her sides, palms down. It's a clear morning, but chilly, so she's wearing an Afghan coat, over a sweater, and a long dress that's spread out as though she arranged it that way when she lay down. She looks very peaceful, so peaceful that three people walk past her, before a fourth, a lady called Irene Chettle, says, "Good morning," but gets no response.

'Mrs Chettle thinks she's rude, and carries on with her constitutional. On the way back, she hails her again: no answer again, but she's a wee bit closer this time, and there's something, some indefinable thing about Stacey's stillness, that makes her stop and go over to her. She stands over her and says, "Hello, dear." Even then she thinks she's being ignored; she gets annoyed. "I'm sorry if I'm disturbing you," she says. She's decided that the girl's what she still thinks of as a hippie, and that she's playing some game. She's going to leave her to it when the sun comes out and washes across her face.

'Two things strike her: she's very pale, and her pupils don't react. She reaches down and touches her cheek. It's cold, even allowing for the weather. She shakes her, but there's no reaction. Finally Mrs Chettle, a recently retired civil servant who's never seen a cadaver in her entire life, realises that she's dead. She doesn't carry a mobile, so she legs it back up to the town and goes into the Hawes Inn, where she asks the receptionist to call the police.'

He paused, took a sip of wine, and refilled his glass. 'We attend, initially in the form of two uniforms from the Hopetoun Road office: they look at her and they think, "Junkie." A doctor arrives, closely followed by two detective constables, and they all think the same thing. The doc declares that to be the probable cause.

'To be fair that's not unreasonable, because there's nothing that screams "suspicious death": there are no signs of a struggle, and she's a strong-looking girl. So the alarm is not raised: death is pronounced and the wagon's called to take her away to the morgue, off the Cowgate.

'There's nothing in her pockets to identify her, no purse, driving licence, no mobile, no nothing, but by sheer chance, the driver of the ambulance is a South Queensferry lass and recognises her as a girl she knew at school: Stacey Gavin, number thirteen Wallace Court, age twenty-three. Chippy Grade, the inspector from the local office, goes to the house, with the female uniform who attended the scene. It turns out that Stacey lives with her parents, and her mum's at home. They break the news. Naturally the mother's stunned, too stunned to cry, like the bereaved can be until they've actually seen the body.'

Neil broke off and looked into his glass, as if it was a window into his past. 'People have an off switch, you know. There are things that . . . We react when we're told, but inwardly we refuse to countenance them until we've seen the truth, and know that it's real, that there isn't any way to avoid it any longer. Believe me when I tell you that.' He drew a deep breath, as Louise reached out and squeezed his hand.

'So there's Mrs Gavin,' he continued, 'staring at the wall, in her own corner of hell, and suddenly she says, "What about Rusty? Where's poor Rusty?' Inspector Grade, bless his wee silver epaulettes, thinks nothing of it. He assumes she's talking about her husband. His name's Russ and he's an engineer with a local firm, they've discovered, and so the inspector leaves the constable with the mother, and goes to see him, to break the news and to take him to the mortuary for the formal identification.'

'So who was Rusty?' asked Paula.

'Rusty was her dog, but I'll get to him later. The dad's shattered too, as you'd expect. On the way into the city, Grade asks him, as delicately as possible, he swore afterwards, about his daughter's drug habit. Mr Gavin blows up at him, but Grade thinks it's hysteria and calms him down. He makes the ID, and he's taken home to his wife. The pathologists are busy that day: there's been a multiple fatality on the city bypass. So the autopsy is set for ten next morning, Wednesday. But there's a delay: it doesn't begin until eleven fifteen, and that's when it hits the fan. That's when the hole in the back of her head is discovered, and that's the first time we realise that we have a homicide on our hands, a full day and more after the discovery of the body.'

'What happened next?' Louise leaned across the table, her face serious but her eyes bright with interest.

'The pathologist was working alone,' Neil told her. 'He stopped and called for a colleague as corroboration, and he phoned me. I called Stevie Steele and we sat in on the resumed examination: we were there when the bullet was recovered.'

'Why DI Steele? I thought Chief Inspector Mackenzie was in charge of that area.'

'The Bandit? No he's still on sick leave.'

'What's wrong with him?'

'They're calling it post-traumatic stress, after that big armed incident in St Andrews that we got drawn into. Within this room, he went on the piss in the wake of it, and it turned into a breakdown.' He glanced at his friend. 'That one there's muttering about a pitch for early retirement on health grounds, but I'm not going along with that.'

'You're too soft,' Mario grunted.

'No,' Neil retorted. 'The opposite: I'm probably too bloody hard. I was there and I saw the same bodies and blood that Bandit did. You think I didn't get the shakes after it? I got over them, that's all, just like I did when my best friend got himself shot a few years back. And as I remember it, you weren't all that fucking nonchalant, even after they'd patched you up.'

'Point taken,' said McGuire, quietly.

Louise brought the discussion back on track. 'So Inspector Steele headed the murder investigation?'

'Yes, reporting to me, but he was under a major disadvantage from the off, because he had no crime scene.'

'Why not?'

'More than twenty-four hours had gone by since the body was discovered. It was hopelessly compromised: any forensic evidence discovered there would have been absolutely useless in court. We didn't even have a reliable time of death, because the autopsy had been delayed so long.

'Steele began with the parents, looking to build up a list of Stacey's acquaintances, since nine times out of ten the victim knows the killer, but before that he spoke to Chippy Grade, who mentioned the Rusty remark. As I said, he was her dog, a Westie. She walked him every morning; her mother said that sometimes she stayed away for two or three hours looking at the seascape and such, stopping to sketch on occasion, and so there was nothing unusual about her not returning. She'd gone out around eight that day, so that gave us a firmer idea of the time of death. Or rather deaths: we found the poor wee mutt Rusty a couple of days later, washed up in Granton, with its lead still attached to its collar. It had been shot and, yes, we had a vet do an autopsy, and the bullets matched, so that's something else we're going to do this bastard for when we run him to ground.'

'Did Stevie make any progress?' asked Paula.

'He eliminated a lot of people. He and his officers created a pretty thorough model of Stacey's life. She was a full-time artist: she graduated last year from the art college up in Lauriston, and worked out of a studio in her folks' attic.'

'Did she sell much?'

'For a newcomer she was doing all right; she specialised in coastal views, not just scenery, though, impressionistic and very colourful. I saw some of her work in the Scottish Gallery; it's good, very good, and as far as I can tell, unique. It's going for about a grand on average, depending on the size; her records showed her gross income since last October as just under fourteen thousand, less commission.

The gallery people said that wasn't bad at all for a newcomer, that she'd found a niche for herself and could have looked forward to making a good living from prints as well as sales of original works.

'Apparently she was quite a talented portrait painter too. Stevie told me that he saw pictures of her mum and dad in the house. She didn't do much of that, though: one or two freebies for friends, but that was all. She was a very focused girl, and wanted to cement her reputation in what she did best, before branching out into less commercial work.'

'What about her social life? Boyfriends?'

'Not active. She had a circle of art-school friends, a mix of guys and gals. The team interviewed them all, and were pretty certain that there was nobody special. One bloke told us that he'd had a thing with her in their first year at college, but it ended when Stacey asked if they could just be friends. That's what they've been ever since, he said.

'Stevie dug as deep into her background as he could. He looked into her e-mails, her mobile records, calls to the family phone: nothing. He put out the usual request for information, but all he got were responses from the three people who'd walked past her on the path above the beach. Stacey wasn't the only one who walked her dog there in the morning. None of them were any bloody use at all, though: they all said they'd thought she was sleeping.'

'They would, wouldn't they?' Louise murmured. 'Those who behave like Levites rarely own up to the fact. So where does the investigation stand now?'

'Until this afternoon it was standing still. Now, it's got

some momentum again, and a new urgency. I'm pretty sure we have a double murderer on our patch. And the scary question is, if we don't catch him will he stop at two?'

Five

'When does a multiple murderer become a serial killer?' Margaret Rose Steele put the question to her husband as he dried his hair with a towel in their big kitchen watching her remove the stone from an avocado. It was his unshakeable practice to take a shower as soon as he returned home after witnessing an autopsy before doing anything else.

'You're a copper,' he retorted. 'You should know that.'

'Maybe, but I don't. "Serial killer" is one of those phrases the media loves to throw about, but I've never seen it defined.'

'What are we having for supper?'

'Just a couple of prawn thingies. It's nearly ten: we shouldn't eat too much. But don't change the subject. Come on, tell me. Or don't you know either?'

'As it happens, I do. We had a guest lecturer on a course I was on at the police college who specialised in the subject. He said that the FBI came up with the term thirty years ago.'

'So it's an American phenomenon?'

'Hell, no, it's as old as time. The definition we were given is that serial killers are people who commit three or more murders over a period with gaps between. Often they will appear quite normal, and their hobby goes unsuspected by their friends and neighbours. Usually, there's a sexual aspect to their crimes, but there doesn't have to be; there wasn't with Shipman, for example.'

Maggie shrugged. 'So they're just mass murderers.'

'No,' her husband contradicted her. 'That's different: mass murderers are defined as those who kill three or more people in a single event and at a single location. Suicide bombers are the classic modern example. And there's an accepted third category, spree killers, people who go on a rampage, popping victims off all over the place. They don't revert to normal behaviour between kills, though: they're driven by an overwhelming homicidal urge, and they carry on until they're caught or killed. It doesn't mean a lot to the public, though; whatever you call them, they're all seriously disturbed.'

'Crackers,' said Maggie, tersely.

'But not legally so; not in the case of serial killers, anyway. Most of them, when they're brought to trial, will try to plead not guilty on the ground of insanity, but very few of them succeed. The legal definition of who's nuts and who isn't is still based on the McNaughten rules. They date back to a case of that name in the nineteenth century, in England; it set the principle that a person is sane if he knew the difference between right and wrong at the time of each crime. The premeditation in serial cases, plus the murderer's clear success in avoiding detection for what can be long periods, makes an insanity defence very difficult to sustain.'

'So if you're right about these two killings being connected . . .'

'I am right. It's not just me, either: Mario's just as certain. Neither of us saw Stacey Gavin's body at the scene, but we did see the only two photos that were taken. The mere description of the second body made him drop everything, head out to East Lothian and call for me. But we'll know for sure when we get the result of the ballistics comparison between the two bullets.'

'So: what will you have?'

'We'll have a bad bastard.'

Maggie frowned, as she spooned cooked prawns from a sieve and arranged them over the halves of the avocado. 'That covers all of your definitions. Be specific, Inspector.'

'That may depend on who the second victim is. Does her circle of acquaintances overlap with Stacey's? I've already checked . . . or, rather, I had a detective constable, Tarvil Singh, check . . . all of the interviewees in the Gavin investigation. He got hold of them all, so she isn't one of them, but tomorrow we'll go round them all and show them a touched-up photo, see if we get any reactions.'

'I'll bet you do; just give their breakfast time to go down, that's all. But so what if the two are connected? Where does that take you?'

Stevie stared at her, as she finished preparing their light supper and carried two plates across to the refectory table in the corner of the kitchen. 'What's with you?' he asked. 'It's not so long since you were an ace detective yourself.'

'Maybe being back in uniform's made my brain go soft.'

'Well, let's toughen it up,' he retorted, as he uncapped a

bottle of sparkling water, and began to fill two glasses. 'You tell me what I'll have.'

She sat on a long bench on one side of the table. 'Hopefully, you'll have a prime suspect. A connection between them would rule out, almost certainly, unless it was a slight or accidental connection, the notion that they were random victims. If you find a link you'll see where it takes you, or rather, to whom it takes you. But if they are random . . .' She whistled. 'Nasty.'

'Very . . . and my arse will be on the line as senior investigating officer.'

'Now you're being over-dramatic,' she said. 'From what you've told me about the Gavin case, there's no evidence pointing you towards anyone. Maybe you'll get lucky: maybe the second victim will give you some. But if it doesn't, that won't mean that you've fallen down on the job. It'll simply mean that you're up against a very careful, methodical villain. You won't be condemned for that.'

'I'll be in the spotlight, though. Investigating a potential serial killer get you lots of attention, even if he is just starting out. I'll be under more pressure than I've ever known.'

'What if he isn't?'

A forkful of prawn in thousand-island dressing paused halfway to his mouth. 'Isn't what?'

'Starting out. What if Stacey wasn't his first victim?'

'Come on, love, give me some credit. We checked the markings on the first bullet through the national database. The weapon hasn't been used in any other crimes, solved or unsolved.'

'What if he has more than one gun?'

Stevie frowned.

'What if the two bullets don't match?' she continued. 'Will that put paid to the idea that it's the same killer?'

He shook his head slowly. 'Not as far as I'm concerned. I feel it in my gut that these crimes are related.' He glanced at her. 'Hey, Mags, promise me something, right now: promise me you'll still challenge me, won't you, even if you do leave the job?'

'You don't need me to do that. You always get there.'

'Maybe, but sometimes you help me get there faster. Like now: one of my priorities tomorrow will be to run both crime scenes, photos and descriptions, through the national computer to see whether we get any matches.'

'How far back will you go?'

'As far as I can. Now, please, let's talk about something else.'

'Such as?' She grinned.

'Anything,' Stevie pleaded. 'Your day, for a start.'

'Mine was pretty ordinary. Tomorrow I start the handover to my stand-in.'

'Ah, you've got one at last. Who is it?'

'Your old boss, Mary Chambers; for the moment at least. They'll review that when I tell them how long I'll be staying away, and I will not do that until the baby's safely delivered. I had a visit from the ACC today. I don't think he's too pleased with me over that, but he didn't say as much.'

'Brian Mackie knows you too well to do that. Anyway, I reckon you're wrong: I reckon the assistant chief constable would be just a wee bit relieved to see you go, if you did.

You're a better copper than he is, all round, and you're a better leader. The whole bloody force knows that, and so does he.'

'You're biased.'

'Sure,' he agreed, 'but that doesn't stop me from being right.'

'You're underestimating Brian. He's had "Command Corridor" written in his stars for years.'

'And so have you,' Stevie insisted. 'He beat you there on seniority, that's all, but he knows that if you're both in the game he won't beat you to the next level. It'll suit his long-term ambitions if you're not around.' He grinned. 'It's too bad that he'll be disappointed.'

'What do you mean?' She frowned across at him, and her tone was defensive, for all that she tried to disguise it.

'I mean, love of my life, that I don't buy into the notion of you putting motherhood before the career that's been the focal point of your adult life. Yes, you'll take your maternity leave, and you'll devote all that time to the baby. Then when it's up, we'll find a carer and you'll get back on the ladder. A year or two after that, you'll start looking for promotion opportunities . . . that's if they don't come looking for you first. The chief retires in less than a year, remember.'

'And I'll still be on leave.'

'That doesn't stop you being considered for the vacancy that'll arise when Bob Skinner steps up.'

'You're getting miles ahead of yourself there. Who says the DCC will take over as chief constable?'

'Who doesn't?'

'Maybe he doesn't,' she retorted. 'I was his executive officer for a while, remember. I know him, and I'm not sure he wants it. The job would frustrate him: he's a hands-on guy, always has been. Stevie, he could have been a chief five years ago; he would have been in with a shout for every vacancy that's arisen since that time, anywhere in the UK. There was even a rumour not so long ago that he'd been sounded out about the Met.'

'Maybe, but this is his patch. He loves Edinburgh; he's been happy as long as our present chief's been in post, but can you see him welcoming an outsider into Sir James Proud's office with open arms?'

'That might depend on who the outsider is. What if Andy Martin goes for it?'

Stevie's grin became a laugh. 'Andy Martin was his protégé until he moved to Dundee. The two of them are blood brothers. Do you really see Andy going for Proud Jimmy's job over the head of his best friend?'

'I do, if Mr Skinner tells him to.'

'Which he won't. Look, Mags, what's the big man doing now?'

'He's enjoying a well-earned sabbatical, after a most horrendous year.'

'Which he's using to prepare himself, so the story goes. Tarvil Singh's wife works at Heriot-Watt, in the Borders campus: according to her, he did a specially arranged six-week course during February and March, researching the management of stress in the workplace. Then, last month, he spent three weeks in Toronto, on secondment to the RCMP.'

'How do you know that?' She paused. 'Of course: your cousin Joey.'

'That's right, he's a Mountie sergeant in the Ontario division. I had an e-mail from him last month: he told me that our DCC had been on a tour of all their offices, spending time with each of the departments. It was all set up through their CO.'

'You never told me!' Maggie exclaimed.

'Okay, but there are things you don't tell me, operational stuff. I wouldn't expect you to. By the same token, I reckoned that if this wasn't on the bulletin board, maybe I wasn't meant to know about it.'

'Secretive bugger.' She sniffed. 'They should have given you the Special Branch job, rather than plucking Dottie Shannon out of her inspector's uniform.'

'Sorry.'

'You're forgiven. I still don't go with your theory, though. He's got to fill in his time somehow, and the whole point of sabbatical leave is that you use it for professional development.'

'So what are you going to do on your maternity leave? Just feed the baby and nothing else?'

'Maybe.'

'Indeed? In that case, what was that stuff about an Open University business management course that I found in the printer the other day?'

She glowered at him. 'Bloody detectives: you're never off duty.' She paused. 'Stevie, the truth is I don't bloody know what I want to do. But if I did an OU course, would it bother you?'

'My darling, nothing you do could bother me. If that's what you want, go for it. Just hold off till the baby's born and you've recovered, that's all.' He slapped himself on the side of the head. 'Ah, that reminds me: I checked the answerphone when I was in the bedroom. There's a message for you from the maternity unit at the Royal: they want you to call them.'

'Did they say about what?'

'No. All the guy said was that it was purely routine.'

Maggie laughed. 'Purely routine: even medics are using police-speak now. Next thing you know I'll be helping them with their enquiries.'

Six

'This is all right,' said Detective Constable Tarvil Singh, as he looked around the room, 'apart from the noise of the kids next door. What's this place called?'

'Gullane Village Hall,' DS Ray Wilding replied, 'simple as that. The playgroup doesn't last all day, and it was a lot easier to borrow this office than to bring a mobile unit down. And, by the way, it's a truly sad bastard who hardens his heart against the joyous sound of children at play.'

'Spoken like a single man. I'm well familiar with that sound, believe me. I get plenty of it at home.' A wooden seat gave an ominous creak as he settled his massive frame into it. 'Where do we start?' he asked.

'We've started,' said the sergeant. 'We've got uniformed officers down on the beach and in the car park behind it, interviewing people, looking to find those that go there every day, showing them the photo and asking if they know who she is. You and I are going to do the rounds of the pubs in Gullane, Aberlady, Dirleton and North Berwick to see if she's recognised in any of them.'

'What about the DI? Where's he?'

'He's down at the bents, briefing the uniforms and getting them under way.'

'What about the golf club? He doesn't really think there could be a link there, does he?'

'Of course not,' a voice from the doorway exclaimed. Stevie Steele stepped into the room. 'We had to check out the possibility that the victim might have been brought to the scene using the road that runs across the course, but that's been eliminated. I spoke to the secretary last night, and to the steward and the head greenkeeper. There's a gate at the top of the road, beside the clubhouse, and it's padlocked overnight. The greenkeeper's an early bird: he was there at seven, and he didn't unlock the gate till eight.'

'Could somebody have opened it before seven?' Wilding asked. 'Picked the padlock?'

'Then locked it again on his way out? Hardly, but if he'd tried, the steward would have seen or heard him: he was up early too. I showed all three of them the girl's picture, but none of them recognised her.' He looked at Singh. 'Tarvil, if we don't have her identified by this afternoon, I want you to have some posters done. We'll put them up in shops, hotels, banks, pubs, clubs and post offices in all the coastal towns.'

'Will do, boss. Pubs first, though, yes?'

'Absolutely. I want an identification this morning, if possible. This girl didn't parachute in here. Somebody saw her before she was killed.' Steele headed for the door once again. 'Come on, let's get to work.'

'Are you going to help us, sir?'

The DI grinned at Singh. 'You think I don't get my

hands dirty any more? You two split up: there's three hotels and one pub in Gullane, two coffee places, and other shops all along the main street, so do half each. I'll talk to the post office and the bank staff, after I've made my priority call on the local VIP.'

'Who's that? The wee actor chap?'

'No, Tarvil,' Steele chuckled, 'more important than him, as far as we're concerned. I'm going to see the DCC, as per the head of CID's order. He might not have asked to be kept informed, but we're going to do him that courtesy anyway . . . and show him the picture while we're at it.'

Seven

Alex Skinner was smiling as she replaced her phone in its cradle. Leaning across her desk in her small screened office space, she thought no one had noticed, but she was wrong.

'That's the weekend fixed up, is it?' asked Pippa Clifton, the secretary she shared with two other associates of Curle Anthony and Jarvis, Scotland's leading business-law firm.

'Mind your own, woman,' she replied cheerfully.

'Come on, spill it. That was him, wasn't it? Your new Mr Perfect.'

'I don't know what you're talking about.'

'You damn well do. You had your girlie face on, and these days that's a dead giveaway: it was him.'

'Pippa, we're too busy for this,' Alex protested.

'It's now or I'll hound you after work.'

She sighed. 'Okay, that was my next-door neighbour and friend, Detective Constable Griffin Montell. As it happens, he was apologising for breaking a date tonight as he's been roped into a big investigation.'

'But you were smiling.'

'Yes, because I didn't really want to go out tonight.'

'Ah!' Pippa's eyebrows arched. 'So he's coming to your place once he's finished.'

'No, he's not. How many times do I have to tell you? Griff's a friend, that's all. I like him, he makes me laugh, and that's fine, for there is no way on this earth that I'm ever getting seriously involved with another copper. I repeat, but for the last time, he's just a friend.'

'Mmm.' The secretary sniffed. 'There's nothing in my rule book that says a friend can't give me one on occasion without either of us assuming that we're engaged.'

Alex felt her cheeks flush and hoped that her tan disguised the fact: she kept her face straight.

'Your dad approves of your friend, doesn't he?' Pippa continued relentlessly, even as her boss picked a folder from one of her trays.

'I don't seek his approval, any more than he seeks mine.' She almost bit her tongue as she finished the sentence.

'Which reminds me. I meant to ask you: is it true about him and the new First Minister, Aileen de Marco? The word is out, you know.'

Alex glared across her desk, signalling a jibe too far, and with it, the end of the conversation. 'Pippa,' she snapped, 'there is office gossip, and then there is pushing your luck. Guess where you're at? Get to work, now.'

As her secretary beat a hasty retreat, the young lawyer focused on the work before her, a study for a retail client on the consequences of a potential acquisition. She sketched out her analysis and her recommendations, then dictated it in memo form into a handheld recorder for Pippa to type and pass to Mitchell Laidlaw, the practice chairman, for his approval. Next she turned to her notes of an early-morning meeting with Paula Viareggio, the chief executive of the company to which she was legal adviser. As she turned them into a formal report, with action points, she found herself thinking about Paula.

The two women had become good friends, although there was the best part of ten years between them in age. They were confidantes: where Alex would not have dreamed of discussing her sex life with Pippa or, for that matter, with anyone else in the office, she was able to be reasonably open about it with Paula, knowing that if she asked for it, she would receive very good and very direct advice.

She smiled as she recalled what her client had said about Griff Montell: in fact, she had expressed much the same view as Pippa. 'Okay, you like him,' she had said, 'but you don't love him. You don't want to marry him. You're not yearning to have his babies. Fine, now we've dealt with all that. Do you fancy fucking him? Yes? In that case, if the opportunity arises, so to speak, what the hell's stopping you? If I was in your shoes, or underwear, or whatever, I bloody know I would.'

In turn, Paula had felt able to discuss her relationship with Mario, confessing that, cousin or no cousin, she had been hopelessly in love with him since her mid-teens, and that she had never wavered in that, not even when he had married Maggie Rose. She had wished them no harm, but she had been sure from the start that they were wrong for each other, and had simply waited them out. Any relationships she had had herself before or during that time, including her brief fling with Stevie Steele, had been short-term affairs, safe and with no chance of permanency.

And yet, that morning, Alex had sensed a difference in her: she had not been the usual razor-sharp Paula, and once or twice, in mid-meeting, she had seemed to drift off somewhere else. It was as if there was something on her mind that she felt unable to discuss, even with a friend. There were no business worries, of that Alex was certain, and so her strange mood had been even more troubling.

Finally, she had asked her. 'Paula, is everything all right? You and Mario haven't had a row, have you?'

She had been quietly, and politely, brushed off. 'Mario and me? Row? No way: he wouldn't dare. We're fine, I'm fine. But how about you? What about Griff the friendly detective?' Subject closed, and not too subtly.

'Him?' she had lied. 'Let's just say I'm still thinking over your advice.'

'What's holding you back?'

'I don't want to spoil a nice friendship. You know the trouble with hunks: they have so much expectation to live up to, usually too much.'

Paula had smiled, normal service resumed. 'Usually, but not always. I used to have a simple philosophy with guys like that. I thought of them as very expensive sports cars, sitting on their lacquered tyres, gleaming in the showroom. You know what I mean: the running costs might be prohibitive but you can always take them for a test drive.'

'The Ferrari syndrome? Nice one, Ms Viareggio. I wonder if men think about women like that?'

'Are you kidding? They invented the game. But the great

thing is that nowadays, as often as not, the players are women like us. Role reversal at its finest.'

Alex smiled as she finished the report; she dictated it on to the same tape as the earlier document, filled in her time-sheet on her desktop computer, then took the micro-cassette along to the secretarial area. Pippa was absent; coffee break, she guessed. She checked her watch and decided that she too could afford five minutes for a break.

She walked along the corridor to the professional staff rest room, bought herself a diet drink from the dispenser, and picked up a copy of the first edition *Evening News* from the table, nodding to Grey Bauld, another associate who was the only other person in the room. He was sitting crouched over *The Times*, concentrating on a sudoku game.

The picture jumped out at her from the front page. There was something odd about it, something strange about the face, its lack of expression, perhaps. Yes, that was it: the eyes, they were vacant, emotionless. 'My God,' she whispered 'she's . . .'

She began to read the story below, to confirm her realisation. 'Police investigating the murder of a young woman,' she murmured aloud, 'whose body was found on an East Lothian beach yesterday afternoon, admitted today that they are no nearer identifying her. Releasing an artistically improved photograph of the victim, media spokesman Alan Royston said, "We are appealing for the public's help in identifying this unfortunate girl. Anyone who thinks they know her should . . ."

'Artistically improved.' Alex snorted. 'She's bloody dead.' Although the background was a hazy blue colour, giving nothing away, she would have bet that the shot had been taken on a mortuary table, and retouched later using computer software to make the subject look as lifelike as possible. But nothing can truly restore life, once its light has been extinguished.

She stared at the page, not realising that she was frowning, until Bauld, frustrated once again by his puzzle, called out to her, 'What's up? Did your team lose?'

'Don't be daft,' she replied. 'I don't have a team.' She held up the paper. 'It's this photograph; this murdered girl. I can't put my finger on it, but I have this weird feeling that I know her.'

Eight

'I'm very impressed,' said Louise McIlhenney.

'Oh, yeah?' said her husband, rising to the bait.

'Yes, it's Wednesday, you've been at home for three days, and not once have you picked up the phone to check on what's happening at work.'

'That's the deal. That's why they call it leave. You go away and you forget about it.'

'Fine. That's for normal people, but this is you. I'd expected you to be a fidgety bear by now, especially after that burst of shop last night with your pal Mario.'

Neil smiled at her. 'You want the truth?' he asked, looking down at her as she cradled Louis. 'What's happening in this house right now is the focal point of my life. It's more important than any crime, any investigation; at least it is for the next week and a half. He's just wonderful, you're just wonderful, and it's a huge privilege to be able to spend this time with you.'

She gazed up at him. 'You really mean that, don't you?'

'Every word of it.' He paused. 'Hey, what about Paula last night? Did she get misty-eyed or what when she was holding the wee chap? Amazing: she'd never held a baby before in her life.'

'Yes, I did notice how she was. I wonder if Mario did.'

'If I get your drift, it's academic,' said Neil. 'McGuire's tadpoles don't work. You know that.'

'I only know what you told me: that Mario had a test when he was married to Maggie, and they found that he had a low sperm count. That doesn't mean they don't work: it means that there aren't enough of them to give a realistic chance of one getting through to base camp . . . and that's all it takes, just one. Did he ever tell you if they suggested a cause of the problem?'

'No. We didn't discuss it at length, love. He told me, I said, "Tough luck, mate," and he shrugged his shoulders as if he wasn't all that bothered.'

'Did he ever have a follow-up test?'

'What would be the point? You either make enough or you don't.'

'I've heard that occasionally it can be a short-term thing, stress-related. I suppose being shot might do it. But even if it isn't, the sperm that are produced can be used in IVF.'

'How do you know all this?'

'My first husband,' she said. 'He had that problem . . . not that I encouraged him to look for a cure, mind you.'

'Ah.' Neil chuckled. 'So based on that, and based on Paula going all teary for a minute or so, you're packing the pair of them off to the test-tube doctors.'

'No, I'm just saying that if they wanted kids, they might be able to.'

'Maybe, but they'd both have to want them . . . Except,'

he scratched his chin, 'maybe not. The truth is that Mario would give Paula the Crown Jewels if she asked for them. If she really did want a baby, he'd probably go along with it, regardless.'

'That would be great.'

'Maybe yes, maybe no. McGuire's a great godfather, he takes it very seriously, but I'm not so sure that he's one of nature's dads. I could see him being too hard on a son of his own, demanding achievement beyond the kid's capabilities, yet going completely in the opposite direction with a daughter.'

'But Paula would be around to counter that; she'd probably behave in the opposite way, so there would be a balance between them.'

'My darling,' said Neil, 'I have news for you. Parenting does not work on the basis of good cop, bad cop. Done right, it's a partnership: you show a united front to your kids in every respect.'

'You mean that "Wait till your father gets home" is not the thing to say?'

'Exactly. Whether it's correction or encouragement, it has to be done at the appropriate moment, in a consistent way.'

Louise took his hand and kissed it. 'I bow to your experience.' She looked down at the sleeping baby in her arms. 'Although I can't imagine this little chap ever needing correction, can you?'

'Oh, he will, and much sooner than you think . . . that's if his brother was anything to go by.'

'Not his sister?'

'Lauren? From an early age she was correcting me; still is, as you'll have noticed.'

'There you are: you're doing just what you said Mario would, being hard on one and soft on the other.'

'Not true. I'm an equally soft touch for both of them, as you well know.'

'I had noticed that, I admit.' She moved in her chair. 'Take this one, will you? He should go into his cot for a while, till he needs his next feed.'

Gently, Neil took the baby from her and carried him upstairs to the nursery. When he returned, he found her in the kitchen, scooping coffee into the basin of a percolator. 'I wonder how Mario's doing with his murder inquiry?' she murmured absent-mindedly.

'You mean how Stevie's getting on? With a bit of luck, he'll have an identification of the second victim by now.'

'And if not?'

'He'll keep trying.'

'The first victim, Stacey, the girl we were talking about last night: would you think I was ghoulish if I told you I'd like to see her work?'

'No, I wouldn't, because having seen it myself, I know it's the kind of thing you like. She's dead, but her paintings aren't.'

'Would it be possible?'

'No, I'm afraid not; not for a while, at least. Her parents withdrew all her unsold stuff from the galleries a couple of days after her death. Russ, the dad, told me that they wanted to keep everything that was hers close to them, for a while at least. He said that at some point they might hold a memorial exhibition and auction some of them for charity, but that's in the future.'

'What about her pad? You said last night that when she walked her dog she was in the habit of stopping to sketch things. So when you found her, you must have found her pad. Maybe I could look at that . . . or did you give that back to the parents, too?'

She broke off as she realised that he was staring at her. 'You know, love,' he said slowly, 'sometimes I wonder how the hell I functioned as a detective before I met you.'

He picked up the phone, dialled the Leith divisional office and asked for CID. 'This is Superintendent McIlhenney,' she heard him say. 'I want you to get hold of DI Steele, wherever he is, and have him call me at my home right now.'

Nine

'I'm sorry, Sergeant,' said the proprietor of the Mallard Hotel, as he walked back into the bar, 'I've never seen her before, and neither has anyone else here.' He handed the photograph back to Ray Wilding. 'I've shown it to my family, and to all the staff on duty, but nobody recognises her.'

'What about the off-duty people?'

'There are a couple of them,' the man admitted, 'but they all tend to work alongside other people. It's unlikely that she'd have been seen by one of them and by nobody else.'

'Fair enough. Look, we may have some posters to distribute around the village. Would you display one for us?'

'Sure, if you think it'll help. One of my regulars might have seen her.'

'Thanks, Mr Law. I'll bring one down, if it comes to that.'

The detective left the hotel and turned into the first street on the right. He had almost reached the village hall when he saw Stevie Steele heading towards him. He waited until the inspector caught up with him, then led the way into the building. The pair drew stares from the playgroup children, and glances from one or two of their mothers.

'Any joy?' Steele asked, as he closed the door of their temporary office.

'Not in the slightest. I did the deli, the chemist, one coffee shop, the Co-op, the butcher's, the charity shop, the fruit shop, the Old Clubhouse and the Mallard Hotel. There was one old dear in the Co-op who gave me a moment of hope, until she decided that the girl just looked like her granddaughter.'

'Is her granddaughter dead?'

'I never asked. You had no luck either, then?'

'Nah. I called into the golf club, the pro shop, the bank and the post office, like I said. Not a flicker, anywhere.'

'And the DCC?'

'He asked me if he was a suspect.'

'But he didn't know her?'

'Of course he didn't bloody know her: if he had that's the first thing I'd have told you. Ray, if you don't mind me saying so, that was a fucking stupid question. I feel that we're off the ball here: let's get back on it again, sharpish.' He looked at the uniformed constable who was seated at a table by the far wall. 'Any reports back from the uniforms on the beach?'

'No, sir,' he replied. 'Nothing positive at any rate.'

'Maybe Tarvil will get a result,' Wilding suggested, in a slightly wounded tone.

'If he had, he'd have called it in . . . or he'd better have.'

'Excuse me, sir,' the PC interrupted. 'There are faxes for you, from the lab.'

'More than one?'

'Two.'

'Let's see them.'

He walked across and took them from the man as he held them out. He read through the first quickly. 'That's it, Ray,' he said. 'Confirmation: the bullet we took from Jane Smith matches the one that killed Stacey Gavin. We've got a double murderer on our hands.'

'Is that good news or bad news, boss?' Wilding asked. 'Or was that a stupid question too?'

Steele grinned. 'No, but that one was verging on the insubordinate. Sorry for snapping at you, mate. I guess being in the spotlight's getting to me. To answer you, it's got to be easier to catch one killer than two, so from that viewpoint, it's probably good. The bad news is that we don't have a single line of enquiry till we identify the victim, and even then, maybe not.'

He was in the act of laying the first report on the table when the phone rang. He waited as the constable answered. 'Gullane incident room.' Pause. 'Yes, he's here.' Pause. 'Yes, I'll tell him.' He hung up and looked at the detective. 'Message from Mr McIlhenney, sir. He asks if you'll call him at home straight away.'

'I wonder what he wants,' Steele mused. 'He told me that nothing was going to get in the way of his paternity leave.'

'Maybe he's been told it has to,' Wilding suggested.

'And who'd tell him that?'

'DCS McGuire?'

'No chance.'

'The chief?'

'Sir James never interferes with CID operations.'

'ACC Mackie?'

'That would be overruling Mario: Brian Mackie wouldn't do that. Let's find out what it is.' He took out his mobile, found McIlhenney's home number in the phone book, and called it.

Louise answered. 'Hold on, Mr Steele. He's in the kitchen.'

That's what I like to hear, the inspector thought.

'Stevie.' The familiar voice sounded in his ear. 'Thanks for calling: there's something I need to check, thanks to my wife's idle curiosity. When Stacey Gavin's body was found, did she have any possessions with her, any at all?'

'Some change, a couple of felt-tip pens, and a half-finished packet of white chocolate raisins; they were all taken with her to the mortuary. Then, when we found out what had happened to her, they were sent, with her clothing, to the lab for DNA and fingerprint sampling, in case the shooter had touched them by accident, then returned to us when that proved negative. They're still at my office in Leith.'

'There isn't a sketch pad?'

Steele frowned. 'No, there isn't; I've told you everything that's there.' He was silent for two or three seconds. 'And yet,' he went on slowly, 'her mother told us that she often stopped to draw on her walks with the dog.'

'Exactly. I'm sorry to cut into this new inquiry, but we'll need to check it out. Maybe she didn't take it that morning. Maybe she did and the officers at the scene missed it. Or maybe . . .'

'Maybe the killer took it as a souvenir. I'll get on to it

straight away. Griff Montell's minding the store at the office today. I'll send him out to talk to Mrs Gavin, and to the Chettle woman as well, if necessary.'

'Fine.'

'I'll keep you informed, yes?'

'I'm on leave, remember, Stevie: too many phone calls and Lou will kill me.' He chuckled, and his voice dropped to a murmur: 'The odd e-mail wouldn't be noticed, though.'

'Whenever I can. There's one thing, before I go: as we suspected, Gullane isn't a separate investigation.'

'After what Mario told me last night, that's no surprise. Good luck: you're going to need some, and soon.'

'Don't I know it,' Steele muttered, as he snapped his phone shut, ending the call. He turned to the second fax from the lab: as he had anticipated, it was a report on the analysis of samples taken from the unknown girl's body. He read through it slowly.

'All internal organs normal,' he said to Wilding, and to Tarvil Singh who had come into the office during his conversation with McIlhenney. 'Oh, yes! The vaginal swab showed traces of nonoxynol-nine.'

'What the fuck's that?' Singh exclaimed.

'A well-chosen phrase, for once, Constable: nonoxynol-nine is the active ingredient, it says here, in contraceptive creams and gels, and it's also used as a condom lubricant. The finding indicates that the victim had consensual sex in the period leading up to her death.'

'Does it tell us what sort of johnny we're looking for? Durex, Mates, Co-op own brand?'

'That's not as daft as it sounds: we might have to ask the

lab to check which brands use it. But it doesn't necessarily mean that a condom was used. It's sometimes used as back-up by women who have diaphragms.'

'Did the tests on Stacey Gavin show up the same stuff?' asked Wilding.

'No, but remember, that post-mortem was delayed for more than twenty-four hours. It might have dissipated in that time. That said, there was nothing, no information from her friends, to indicate that Stacey was sexually active in the time leading up to her death.' He looked at the report again. 'Hey, the swab showed something else: two grains of sand.'

'Does it say which beach they were from?'

'Tarvil, shut up.'

'Sorry, boss, but they are clever bastards at the lab. So the guy got his end away with the girl, and then he killed her.'

'Maybe, but we can't assume that: we have to find him, and then prove it.' He turned back to the report. 'Stomach contents . . . tell us nothing, other than that she died hungry. She hadn't eaten breakfast, and her previous meal had been absorbed . . . apart from . . . This is interesting. A piece of fibre found trapped between two of her back teeth turns out on analysis to be lemon grass.'

'Lemon grass?' Singh exclaimed. 'What's that?'

'You married guys should do your share in the kitchen,' said Wilding. 'Us single blokes don't have any option. It's a plant, a favourite ingredient in eastern food, especially in Thailand.'

'Do we go back round the restaurants, then?'

'Maybe,' said Steele, 'but let's not build our hopes up; it's in pretty common domestic use these days too. Still, we've got to start somewhere. There's a Thai in the main street, isn't there?'

The sergeant nodded. 'That's right, boss, but it doesn't open at lunchtime. I checked on my rounds, but there was nobody in.'

'Then find the owner or the manager and talk to him. Show him the photograph; it's a long shot but we have to take it. If we get lucky and he recognises her, find out if you can who else ate there.'

Ten

'I have to tell you, ma'am, that being back in uniform hasn't been on my agenda ever since I moved into CID, and certainly not in a position like this one . . . even if it is only temporary.'

Detective Superintendent Mary Chambers was normally a confident, assertive woman, and so the anxiety that was apparent on her face surprised Maggie Rose. 'For God's sake, don't call me "ma'am",' she replied. 'You're about to take over my post. I suppose I thought the same, but then I was offered promotion when Manny English retired, and I didn't hesitate for long. Don't worry about the uniform side of it, though; if you don't want to wear it about the office, don't bother.'

'Och, I know, the ACC told me that too, but that's not really what concerns me. Your job's high profile: you have to be seen out and about on big occasions. I've never been in the public eye before, not in the way I will be as acting divisional commander. Since I came through here from Strathclyde, I've only worked with a small circle of people, on the Drugs Squad and in this office. That's going to widen a hell of a lot.'

'So?'

'Maggie, you know what I'm working up to saying. A gay cop might be acceptable in the closed world of criminal investigation. But among the Charlie Johnstons of this world, it's going to attract attention and cause more than a little gossip.'

'Fine, but I think you'll find that for every old diehard like Charlie, there's a young copper like Sauce Haddock, who's more than ready to tell him that his head's up his arse. You live with another woman. So? What business is that of your junior officers, or seniors, for that matter? In the twenty-first century, what's wrong with it? When I was a kid I had a great-aunt. She was a district nurse and she lived with another district nurse. In those days they still called women like her spinsters; today they'd call them lesbians and no thinking person would have a problem with them being so.'

'They call us other things too.'

'Thinking people don't. Listen, Mary, do you think the foot-soldiers of our division have had no one to whisper about until now?' She laughed. 'There's me for a start. My first husband, a cop, left me and took up with his cousin. Then I moved in with another cop, a junior officer to boot, got myself pregnant and married him, all in that order. After me, honey, you'll be light relief. You can handle any of that crap. If I thought there was any chance of it hurting you, and I did consider it, I wouldn't have leaned on Brian Mackie to have you stand in for me.'

'I didn't think anyone could lean on him.'

'Okay, "given him strong advice", if you'd prefer that. He

might be an assistant chief now, but Brian and I go back a long way. If I give him a firm recommendation, I do not expect him to reject it.'

'Does he know about me?'

'He didn't, until I told him. When I did, he didn't bat an eyelid. He's like most senior officers in this force: he's of the Bob Skinner school. Unless your private life harms your job performance, and if it's legal, it has nothing to do with us: that's the DCC's rule.'

'And a good one it is,' said Chambers, smiling at last. 'Have we anything else to do here? Otherwise I need to get back to CID.'

'No, we're fine.'

As her successor left the room, Maggie leaned back in her chair, and as she did, without any warning, she felt her daughter kick inside her. In that instant, she saw her world from a completely different perspective, as she always did when she was reminded of the awesome thing that she and Stevie had achieved. In that instant, her accomplishments, her career, the route to command that she had carefully planned for herself, were as nothing alongside the vibrant life force that she could feel within her.

In that instant, Stevie's forecasts, and her own plans to use her maternity leave were swept aside, all replaced by an absolute certainty that when she left her job on the following Friday, she would never return.

She contemplated picking up the phone, calling Brian Mackie, and telling him of her decision, there and then. She might have done so, too: her hand was reaching out for it when it rang.

'Call for you, ma'am,' the telephonist said.

'Okay.' She waited.

'Mrs Steele?' The hospital: nobody in the job ever called her that.

'Yes.'

'This is Aldred Fine, your consultant. I left a message on your machine last night: I asked you to call me this morning.'

'My husband picked it up: he said it was routine. Mr Fine, I'm very busy here, I wasn't proposing to call you until next Monday, when I'll be on leave.'

'I'd like to see you before then, Mrs Steele.'

'When?'

'Today.'

She felt a strange fluttering in her stomach. 'But if it's routine . . .'

'I'm always circumspect when I leave a message on a machine. It's something that's arisen from the last routine scan we did, hence my use of the word. I need to discuss it with you.'

The butterfly that had been fluttering in her stomach turned into a dragon. 'I'll be there in half an hour,' she said.

Eleven

At first, Griff Montell was unsure whether he had entered a gallery, a studio or a shrine. After two minutes with Doreen Gavin, the mother of Stacey, he was in no doubt.

The murdered artist's work was everywhere in the spacious detached house, in the entrance hall, on the wall beside the staircase as it rose to the upper floor and in the drawing room into which he was shown. A portrait of her parents hung over the fireplace: there was a lighted candle on either side of the frame.

'There's more, you know,' the bereaved mother said. 'It's in Stacey's studio, up in the attic. I plan to rotate them so that they're all shown.'

'Your husband told my boss that in time you might auction them for charity,' Montell ventured.

'Never!' Mrs Gavin snapped: her close-cut, permed, blue-blonde hair seemed to bristle. 'I will never allow one of my daughter's paintings to leave this house, unless it's rolled up in my coffin. She put a little bit of herself into each one: she's alive, on these walls, and she'll stay there.'

'I understand,' the detective murmured, hoping that he

sounded sincere. In a way, he was. There was something about the desperate house that made him think of his sister, Spring, and of how he would react if anything ever happened to her. And then there was Alex Skinner . . . not, of course, that he thought of her in the same way as Spring, but nonetheless he cared about her, maybe more than he wanted her to know.

And then he remembered that if he had not been on hand a few months before, something would have happened to Alex, something terminal. He shuddered at the thought.

'About your daughter's sketch pad, Mrs Gavin,' he said, in an effort to banish the memory. 'As I said when I phoned you, we didn't find one among her effects, so we need to verify whether she took it with her that morning.'

'Stacey had dozens of sketch pads,' the mother replied. 'They're all up in the attic.'

'Do you know which one she was using when . . .' he broke off for a second '. . . two months ago?'

'No, but I can easily ascertain that. Everything she did was dated, with a note of the location. Let me go and check.' She turned and left the room.

'The studio must be the holy of holies,' Montell thought. *'No one else allowed.'*

He stood in the centre of the room, his eye resting in turn on each of the ten paintings shown there. He had never thought of himself as an art critic, but he knew that these were exceptional works. More than that, they reminded him of something: it gnawed at him, something he had seen, a link.

He was still contemplating when he heard the front door open, then close again.

'I'm home, dear,' Russ Gavin called out from the hall. 'Lunch ready?'

'I'm afraid not, sir,' the young detective told him, as he stepped into the living room. 'DC Montell, CID. Your wife's checking something for me.'

'Of course.' The man looked up at him; he was of medium height, and although the detective knew from the investigation files that he was forty-nine, and a year older than his wife, his sandy hair and firm jaw-line made him look at least five years younger. 'That's not an Edinburgh accent,' he remarked.

'South African; I transferred over here last year.'

'Ah, that explains it, then. What can we do for you, Mr Montell?'

'I'm trying to establish whether Stacey had a sketch pad with her when she left the house. Your wife's upstairs checking for me.'

'No need. I can tell you that. We both left the house at the same time, she with Rusty, me heading for work. I kissed her goodbye . . .' He fell silent for a few seconds, covering the awkwardness by glancing at the portrait over the fireplace. 'She had her pad with her. I remember, because it was awkward for her, stuffing it into the big pocket of that jacket of hers, while holding the dog's lead. Why do you need to know this?'

'Because we don't have it.'

'What does that mean?'

'Maybe nothing. It could have fallen out of her pocket

while she walked the dog, before she met the person who killed her. On the other hand, we might have screwed up.' He shrugged. 'To be honest, and I could get sent back to South Africa for saying this, we did. The officers who attended the scene jumped to the wrong conclusion, and the doctor who was there didn't conduct a thorough enough examination. Maybe when they gathered Stacey's possessions together the book was lying apart from the rest, and they missed it.'

'Could it have simply blown away?'

Montell looked at the man, surprised. Instantly, he had begun to regret his impulsive remarks, fearing that they might be seized upon as the basis of a complaint to the chief constable, and yet the victim's father was making nothing of it: indeed, he was holding out a straw for him to grasp. He was too honest to seize it. 'No, sir,' he said. 'That's not a possibility. If you recall, that morning was very still: there was no wind to speak of.'

Russ Gavin frowned. 'Yes, now that I think about it, you're right. But it's two months ago. What made you so sure?'

'I was on another inquiry that morning, in Granton. I remember looking at the river and noting that I'd never seen it so flat. There was barely a ripple on it.'

'I'm sorry, Mr Montell.' Doreen Gavin's voice came from the hall. 'I can't find it.'

'It's okay, dear,' her husband called to her. 'We've dealt with that.'

'Oh! Good. In that case, since you're back, I'd better get on with the lunch. Excuse me, Constable.'

'To come back to my original question,' Stacey's father said. 'Two months on and you're looking for my daughter's sketch pad. Why is it so important?'

Montell hesitated, until he had formed his reply in his mind. 'You don't have it, we don't have it. It didn't blow away; it might have been left on the beach, or dropped along the path. But there's a possibility that the murderer might have taken it.'

'As a trophy, you mean?'

'It happens. If that's part of his behaviour pattern, we need to know about it.'

'It isn't a coincidence, is it?' said Gavin, quietly.

'What, sir?'

'The girl in East Lothian: I read about her in *The Scotsman*. You think it might be the same man.'

'No, sir. We know it is. Same weapon, both cases: my inspector told me when he sent me to see you.'

'So your investigation will be moving forward again. That's wonderful.' He stopped, then gasped. 'Jesus Christ, what have I just said? Another girl's been murdered, two more parents are facing the loss we have, and I'm pleased. What sort of a bloody man am I?'

'A normal one, Mr Gavin, that's all. What you said is true; we were stalled, and now maybe we'll find some evidence that just wasn't there in Stacey's case. Don't feel guilty: that won't bring either of them back.'

Twelve

To Maggie Rose Steele, Mr Aldred Fine was a caricature, with his tall, cadaverous frame, his round spectacles, his pencil moustache and his slicked-back hair. But no run-of-the-mill caricature: she had spent weeks after their first meeting, early in her pregnancy, trying to work out which face from her past he called to mind.

It was halfway through their second and, up to that point, last consultation that she had realised that she was gazing at a double of Ron Mael, one half of the 1970s pop band Sparks. This had given her something of a start, since that visage, part scarecrow, part vampire, had scared the five-year-old Maggie witless, and sent her scurrying behind the sofa, every time he had appeared on *Top of the Pops*.

When she had told Stevie that evening, he had dredged from his encyclopedic knowledge of modern music the fact that the brothers were still out there, somewhere, little changed in the thirty years since their heyday. 'Are you trying to tell me,' she had chortled, 'that I might have had the real Ron Mael looking up me this afternoon?'

'I'd like to think not,' he had replied, 'but if there's one thing we learn on the job, it's that you never know.'

There was no laughter in her heart as she looked at her consultant, across the desk in his office in the Royal Infirmary, in Little France. It was said that the district had taken its name from the servants of Mary, Queen of Scots, located there on their mistress's return to claim her crown; Edinburgh being Edinburgh, there was a rival school of thought.

'What's so urgent, Mr Fine?' she demanded.

He removed the spectacles, and tucked them into a pocket of his lab coat. His hair was less well groomed than it had been at their earlier meetings and she was grateful for that also. *If he'd only shave off that fucking moustache*, she thought.

'There's something I have to talk to you about,' he began, 'something to do with your pregnancy.'

She felt all her strength and much of her self-control drain away. 'Is she dead? My baby? Is she dead? She can't be: she kicked me just this morning.'

'Calm yourself, Mrs Steele. Your baby isn't dead.'

'Is she deformed? Is it spina bifida? Down's syndrome? I know that can happen to first-time mothers my age.'

Aldred Fine swung round in his chair and leaned forward. His eyes held hers, and Ron Mael was gone, gone for good. His gaze was kind, comforting, reassuring, and although his face was still serious, she felt her panic subside, her breathing steady and her heartbeat slow to its normal steady rate.

'At this stage of the pregnancy, your baby couldn't be better,' the consultant said. 'She's not too big, but that's not a problem. No, my concern is with you.'

'Me?' Maggie laughed spontaneously. 'Mr Fine, I've never felt better in my life.'

'I don't doubt that for a moment. However, as I said, there is something that's arisen from your most recent scan. You'll recall my explaining that a second scan isn't usual but that we sometimes do it in the case of ladies who were once somewhat indelicately categorised by my profession as "elderly primagravida". "Special mums" is the currently fashionable term. When we did yours, I'm afraid that it revealed a shadow on your right ovary.'

The butterflies returned. 'What sort of a shadow?'

'That we do not know. Ultrasound only shows up abnormalities; it doesn't usually define them, not in the mother at any rate.'

'Did it show in my first scan?' Maggie asked.

'No, but that doesn't tell me categorically that it wasn't there.'

She steeled herself to ask the question. 'What could it be? Be straight with me, please.'

The consultant's eyes fixed on hers again. 'It could be, and I am sure that it is, an ovarian cyst; on the other hand, there is a chance that it could be something more problematical.'

She felt a cold wave break over her; she waited until it subsided. 'If it's not a cyst, then what? Do you mean cancer?'

'That's one possibility.'

'How can we find out?'

'The best way would be a CT scan, but we can't do that, since it uses X-rays and would be harmful for the baby. So I propose that we give you an MRI scan . . . That's an acronym for magnetic resonance imaging.'

'I know that,' she snapped. 'Sorry,' she added quickly. 'How does it work?'

'The process is much the same as a CT scan; different technology, that's all. We put you in a tunnel and take a cross-sectional picture of the abdominal area. Magnetic resonance should give us a decent image, and help us to make a diagnosis.'

'An unequivocal diagnosis?'

Fine shook his head. 'In your situation, probably not. It'll give us an indication, that's all. However, I should say that the ultrasound only showed an abnormality in that one ovary, nowhere else.'

'Where else might it have been?'

'In the other ovary, and in the uterus. Mind you, your womb has a tenant at the moment, and the ultrasound can't see behind her. Mrs Steele, can I ask, is there a history of ovarian cancer in your family?'

'No,' she replied. 'My mother died of breast cancer, and my sister's perfectly healthy, as far as I know. She's in Australia; I haven't seen her in years.'

'How about grandmothers, aunts?'

'My father's mother was Portuguese; I never met her and I've no idea what happened to her, but as far as I know, he was an only child. My other granny died when I was seven, and my aunt Fay, my mother's older sister, she died when I was fifteen, of stomach cancer, I believe.' She paused, then went on. 'The MRI scan: is there any danger for the baby in that procedure?'

'None at all.'

'When do you want to do it?'

'I've booked you in for tomorrow afternoon.'

She looked at him. 'You were sure of yourself.'

'Not really,' he told her. 'I was sure of you. I must stress that this is purely precautionary, so please don't go fearing the worst, but on the infrequent occasions that I have this type of conversation, I've never encountered a patient who didn't want to rush straight into the scanning tunnel afterwards.'

Thirteen

'Hey, before I forget,' Stevie Steele exclaimed, 'did you call that guy from the Royal?'

'Yes,' Maggie replied. 'It was a mistake: his secretary had mixed up my notes with someone else's. It wasn't me he wanted at all.'

'Jesus! Makes you think, doesn't it? People go on about the dangers of computerisation, but you can't beat good old-fashioned human error when it comes to fucking things up.'

'Indeed. Speaking of which, how's your investigation unfolding?'

'Thank you very much, my darling.' He chuckled. 'I love you too. We've established for sure that the same gun was used in both shootings: no surprise there. Thanks to Neil McIlhenney, or rather his wife, we've turned up the possibility that he might be a trophy-taker. But we still don't know who the second victim is. She isn't a local: I'm certain of that much.'

'If that's as far as you've got, Inspector, what the hell are you doing phoning me?'

'I'm keeping tabs on my wife, like I do every day. Where

are you, anyway? I can hear traffic noise. Are you out of the office?'

'The window's open,' she replied circumspectly, pushing the one-touch button on the driver's door to close it.

'Ah, okay. I really do have to go, love. Look after yourself, and I'll see you tonight.'

'Okay. Be lucky.'

'I need some. 'Bye.'

He flipped his mobile closed, and slipped it back into his pocket, then picked up the phone on the desk. He consulted a Post-it note, with a direct number he had used earlier, and dialled it again. 'Dorward,' a familiar voice announced in his ear.

'Arthur, this is Stevie. Any joy on that ballistic search of the PNC?'

He heard a sigh. 'Son, there's a queue, even for you. Computers are supposed to be instantaneous, but when you have human interface . . .'

'Funny,' said Steele. 'I've just had this conversation with my wife.'

'One day I'll have direct access, but until then, it can get frustrating.'

'Okay, I'm sorry I rattled your cage.'

'Apology accepted, but actually I was rattling yours. I've just had a call back: your gun's a virgin, at least it was when it killed the Gavin girl. There's no record of it being used in any other crime. I can tell you a couple of things about it, though. I had some very specific research done on it.'

'Such as?'

'It's a very special gun; a SIG Sauer automatic, popular with competition shooters. We ran the ballistic-test results past the manufacturers, and they confirmed it. The current model would cost you going on for two grand, if you could buy it in the shops, that is. It's a state-of-the-art nine-millimetre automatic, nineteen-shot magazine, single-action trigger, low-profile adjustable sight, eight point eight inches long, weight when fully loaded, just under three pounds. When you come across it, be very careful, especially if it's in the possession of its owner. Anyone who has a gun like this will know how to use it: he'll be able to take your eye out from fifty yards away, and do the other one before you hit the ground.'

'So far he's only used it close up. Maybe that's his limit.'

'No chance. This guy's a marksman: the gun says so. I'll bet my pension on it.'

'Who would have a weapon like that?'

'A criminal, maybe, Stevie?' Dorward grunted.

'Funny guy. If he was the sort of criminal you're talking about, he'd have left a trail behind him, surely. This is a guy stalking young women and killing them, point-blank. That doesn't make him an ace marksman.'

'You're forgetting the third victim.'

'What?'

'Rusty, Stacey Gavin's Westie: he hit that on the run.'

'How do you know?'

'From the doggie autopsy. The poor wee thing was shot more or less right up the arse and through the heart. The examining vet was thorough. He called in a human pathologist, and between them they traced the angle of the wound and worked out that Rusty had been at least thirty feet away from the shooter, maybe forty.'

'Do you have any conclusions about him?'

'He must have been a smart wee dog: he knew enough to leg it.'

'Arthur, for fuck's sake,' Steele exclaimed. 'The shooter. Any ideas?'

'Okay, I'll be serious. I'd be looking for someone with a military or law-enforcement background, maybe a gun-club member who keeps his hand in using air weapons. I'd suspect that he acquired the weapon abroad, because very few of these weapons are supplied in this country, absolutely none these days to private owners, and the theft of one of them from a police or military store would attract a hell of a lot of attention. Your man won't just be cuddling this weapon, he'll be practising with it, covertly. He uses a silencer: we know that from markings on the bullets we recovered. He could be shooting at targets in his garage, or in a cellar, or taking it out on wildlife in the country. If you want to try a long shot, so to speak, you might put the word out among rural officers to keep an eye out for birds, rabbits or foxes that are found blown to fuck. He uses soft-nosed bullets and they'd make a hell of a mess of an animal: Rusty's insides were all chewed up, apparently.'

'I'll do that.'

'Discreetly, mind: you don't want anything leaking out.'

'Teach me, DI Dorward.'

'Sorry, I get carried away sometimes. There's one other thing, though. When you find him, and you take the weapon from him, handle it very carefully, especially the silencer. We'll want to take a look at it: when these things are used at close range it's possible that they'll pick up minute tissue traces from the victim.'

'I'll remember that, when the time comes. Soon, I hope.'

Steele hung up, checked his watch, then looked across at Singh. 'Tarvil,' he said, 'get on to Sergeant McNee, from Haddington: he's in charge of the people down at the beach. Tell him to split his troops into two groups and send the first lot to the Mallard Hotel for lunch: it's soup, sandwiches and coffee in their function room.'

'Can I go too, boss?'

'No, you wait till later. There'll be no bloody sandwiches left for the rest if you're in the first batch. And ask the sergeant to come and see me when he's on his break. I need to talk to him about getting door-to-door interviews under way.'

The detective constable had barely picked up the phone before the door opened and Ray Wilding burst into the room. Steele looked up, and saw that he was smiling. 'Did you get a result at the Thai?' he asked.

'Indirectly. There's still work to do, though. When I contacted the owner, he told me that they close on Mondays, and that they were quiet the night before. Anyway, he'd seen the photo in the *News*, and he was sure he'd never seen the girl. But he told me that there's another Thai restaurant in North Berwick, that doubles as a coffee shop during the day. So I took myself along there, and got lucky. The victim ate there on Monday night.'

'On her own?'

'No, she was with a guy, but she paid: with a credit card.'

'Yes!' the inspector exclaimed.

'There's only one problem.'

'Ah, shit. There's always one problem. Spit it out.'

'The waitress in the restaurant couldn't remember which card slip was hers.' He tossed an A4 envelope on to the table. 'So we'll have to find out the hard way. These are all the slips they took on Monday evening.'

Steele emptied the envelope on to the desk: he counted twenty-seven slips. 'They were busy.'

'They do takeaways.'

'But our victim ate in?'

'Yes.'

'Did you get a description of the guy who was with her?'

'Of a sort: the woman said that he was in his early to mid-twenties, dark hair, a bit unruly, casually dressed, needed a shave.'

'That's a start, I suppose. We'll go back and ask her to do us an e-fit. Did you ask her about the woman?'

Wilding nodded. 'Yeah. She seemed to be a very lively, vivacious type. From what the waitress recalled, she did most of the talking; he mainly listened. She didn't detect any tension between them, though. I asked her that specifically, and she said that they seemed very happy. She also said that the guy, when he did speak, was very polite.'

'Accents?'

'She couldn't place them, but she was Thai, so it could have been difficult for her to distinguish. Not local: that was as far as she could go.'

'Better than nothing.'

'And there's something else: it looks like they caught the bus. They were quite late in, the last customers in fact, apart from a couple of takeaways. They finished about half ten, and the place closed then. But the staff cleared up so it was going on eleven before the waitress knocked off. She was going along the high street with the chef, who's the owner, when she saw the couple waiting at the bus stop in Church Street. The victim waved to her.'

'Score! Who's the bus operator?'

'Out here it's First Bus. I checked the timetable on the bus stop when I was in North Berwick. They leave at ten past the hour from there in the evenings: our two were waiting for the last one.'

Steele looked across at Singh, who was listening intently. 'Tarvil, get on to their operations centre, wherever it is; find out who the driver was, and get him interviewed.'

'Should I talk to him myself, boss?'

'Find out where he is first. If he's on duty, find out where his current run ends. If not, find out where he lives. Either way, if it's close to here you do it. If it's in Edinburgh, tell Montell to track him down. If it's outside our area, let me know and I'll brief the local CID. Whoever talks to him, we need to know if they both got on the bus, whether they got off together, and where.'

He turned back to Wilding, who was standing beside his desk, sorting through the card slips he had picked up from the restaurant. 'This is going to be easier than I thought,' the sergeant told him. 'This chip-and-pin technology's magic. The transaction records all show the name of the card-holder, and most of them have the gender as well, so I've knocked out all the ones that are "Mr" something. That leaves just five possibles.'

'Are they timed?' asked Steele.

Wilding picked up a slip and peered at it. 'Oh, Christ, yes. I never noticed that: timed and dated. This one says twenty forty-two, way too early.' Quickly he sorted through the other four. 'This has to be her,' he said, excited, waving another piece of paper in the air. 'It's the only one after ten.'

'Bag it, before you do anything else,' said the inspector. 'We'd better print it . . . if you and the shop people haven't destroyed any traces that were there.'

'She won't have touched this one,' the sergeant told him. 'This is the trader copy.'

'Okay, what does it tell us?'

'Her name's Z. Boras, Miss. It's a Visa card, expiry date next February.'

'Z. Boras?'

'That's what it says here.'

'What sort of a Christian name begins with a Z?'

'Who says she's Christian?' Wilding pointed out.

'True. What's the issuing bank?'

'It doesn't say on any of the slips.'

'The first four digits of the card number should tell us.'

'Four, three, one, nine.'

'How do we track it down?'

'There's a Visa centre in Fife. Get on the phone and see what help they can give you. Meanwhile I'll call DCS McGuire, to let him know we're making progress at last.'

Fourteen

Unusually, Griff Montell was mildly annoyed; his sister had a day off from her job in Harvey Nichols, and he had promised her that he would find time to go home for lunch. Instead he found himself standing in Torphichen Street, at Haymarket, waiting for a bus.

Not that he had any intention of boarding: he was waiting for the arrival of the service from Dunbar and Haddington, and for its driver, Josephina McTurk. The existence of female bus drivers in Scotland had come as news to him when Tarvil Singh had called him, passing on the DI's orders. He had assumed that the demise of conductors would have made the job men only, on security grounds if nothing else.

Mrs McTurk was a good timekeeper. Her single-deck vehicle drew up at its last stop almost exactly at quarter to two, disgorging its last three passengers. As the last one stepped on to the pavement, Montell boarded, to be faced by the driver's surprisingly small, upraised hand.

'You cannae get on here, sir: this is drop-off only. The return service leaves frae West Maitland Street.'

He took out his warrant card and held it up. 'CID,' he said.

'See you polis!' the driver exclaimed. 'Some of you think you're special, honest tae God. Get round the corner and wait wi' the rest of them.'

Montell grinned. 'I don't want to go to Dunbar, Mrs McTurk . . . not that I've got anything against the place, of course. I need a word with you.'

The woman stared at him: she was somewhere around thirty-five years old, fresh-faced, with a touch of the sun on her cheeks, and her naturally frizzy brown hair was pulled close to her head by a heavy band that held it in a ponytail. He had expected her to be bigger than she was, to be driving such a large vehicle: all in all, he reckoned that she was the most attractive bus driver he had ever seen. 'Me?' she exclaimed. 'What the hell have I done? Gone through a red light or something?' She stopped, frowning. 'It's no' my Dylan, is it? Has he been at it?'

'Not as far as I know, Mrs McTurk,' said the detective, 'although I can find out, if you like. No, I want to talk to you about Monday night, about two passengers you picked up on the last run out of North Berwick.'

'From Church Street?'

'That's right.'

'Blonde lass, dark-haired lad.'

'You've got a good memory.'

'At that time of night, wi' the pubs closing, you tend to take a good look at young people gettin' on your bus, even in North Berwick. Monday nights are the quietest, though. It was just them got on.'

He took out a copy of the retouched photograph of the dead girl. 'Is this her?'

Josephina McTurk took it from him and peered at it. 'Aye, that's her. She's a bit livelier than that in the flesh, though.'

Montell frowned. 'That wouldn't be hard. She was dead when that was taken.'

'My Goad,' the driver gasped, 'you're kiddin' me. You mean she's the lassie they're talkin' about in the papers this mornin'?'

'I'm afraid so. How did they seem when they got on your bus? How did they act?'

'Fine. They were a very nice young couple.'

'Was there any tension between them?'

'No; quite the opposite, in fact. They looked like they wanted tae eat each other.'

'Where did you take them?'

'Gullane. I dropped them at the bank, then picked up two lads for Longniddry.'

'This would be . . .?'

'Eleven twenty-four; bang on time.'

'Good for you.' Montell chuckled. 'Listen, you didn't happen to see where they were headed, did you?'

'As a matter of fact, I did. I looked in my side mirror before I took off and they were heading across the street, humphin' all their gear.'

'What do you mean?'

'They both had rucksacks. She was carryin' another bag too, and he had a tent on top of his.'

'A tent?'

'Aye, one of those micro things. My Dylan's got one: big enough for him and his dad tae go campin' in it, but it's amazin' how small it is when it's packed away.'

Fifteen

Mario McGuire was smiling when he picked up the phone. Although he had not been putting pressure on the men in the field in Operation Gabriel, as he had code-named it after the link between the South Queensferry and Gullane murders had been confirmed, he knew that in the absence of progress a time would come, and fairly soon at that, when he would have to lead from the front, whatever his remit from the deputy chief constable might have been.

When McGuire had been appointed head of CID, Bob Skinner had told him that his job was not that of a general leading his troops into battle, but that of a manager, ensuring that the force's criminal investigations, major and minor, were carried out efficiently and effectively. That meant motivating, enabling, supervising and encouraging, but not intimidating or interfering. Within the city of Edinburgh, day-to-day control was in the hands of Neil McIlhenney. He knew that one phone call to his friend would have him back in the office, but he had no intention of making it, for the same reason that he had no intention of interrupting Skinner's hard-earned sabbatical: to do so would seem to some like a lack of self-confidence and even, to a few, like weakness.

Stevie Steele's call, telling him that they had a positive ID on the second victim, and had begun to trace her movements on the night before her death, had come at just the right time. The investigation was regaining the momentum it had lost when the last potential lead to Stacey Gavin's murderer had proved to be yet another false hope.

McGuire rated Steele. They were personally linked through partners past and present, but that had nothing to do with it. He played no favourites, not even with McIlhenney: if he were to fail in his job, he would face the consequences like everyone else. No, he had given the young detective inspector command of Operation Gabriel because he believed that he had one of the best analytical minds in the force. As a crime-solver he placed him ahead of anyone he knew, save two men, Skinner and Andy Martin, a past holder of his own office, gone to become deputy chief in Tayside. '*Give Stevie a bone,*' he thought '*and he'll chew it up in no time flat.*'

'Mario,' he said, to the mouthpiece of his direct line. He used it more for outgoing than incoming calls, and not too many people had the number.

'Hello, love.' Paula's voice had a sigh in it: he picked up on it at once.

'What's up?'

'I want you awful bad. My head's fucked up.'

'Eh? What's the matter, honey?'

'Remember last night, when I said that the effect of holding wee Louis would wear off in the morning?'

'Yeah.'

'Well, it hasn't, and I've been thinking about it all day. I need you to tell me not to be so bloody silly, that the two of us have everything we ever wanted and that we're going to live happily ever after.'

'Consider it done, and get on with your day.'

'No, it's not as easy as that. When you say it, I need to be looking you in the eye.'

'Princess, nothing's as easy as that. Would you like to go out tonight? Somewhere nice and expensive?'

'I'd prefer somewhere nice and quiet, like your place.'

'Pasta supper?'

'If you cook it, that'll be nice. Bacon rolls for breakfast?'

Mario chuckled. 'You go for them, that'll be great. See you tonight.'

Sixteen

'Campers?' Ray Wilding's tone was almost scornful.

'That's what the bus driver said.'

'Montell, she must have been winding you up. There are no camp sites in Gullane.'

'This lady would not wind people up. She's a straight talker. What she told me was what she saw. They had rucksacks and the guy was carrying a tent; they crossed the road, for what that's worth.'

'That doesn't mean they were going to pitch it that night. Chances are they were heading for an address in the village. I suppose that now we know what side of the road they were on, that might give us a clue, unless, of course, they were going for a last drink in the Golf Inn.'

'Listen, Sarge,' said Montell; it was hard to irritate him, but not impossible. 'I've interviewed the bus driver, like I was asked to by Tarvil, and I'm making my report. That's what the witness told me and I have no reason to doubt her. What you guys do with the information, that's up to you.'

'Okay, thanks. When you get back to the office, do the usual: turn it into a formal note and send it to me through the Intranet so I can enter it in the investigation file.'

He hung up and glanced at Steele, seated at a desk close to the table, at the far end of the room. He too was finishing a phone conversation, on his mobile. 'Yes,' Wilding heard him say, 'do that, and get back to us.' The DI ended the call and swung round to face Wilding. 'She used a Barclays Visa debit card,' he said. 'The Z stands for Zrinka: that's our victim's name, Zrinka Boras.'

'There can't be too many of them to the pound. What is she? Asylum-seeker?'

'Don't know yet, but I wouldn't have thought so, not with a Visa card. I've got someone on to Barclays just now, to track down where she keeps her account and to get an address for her.'

'That might not be as easy as you think. My waitress in North Berwick forgot to mention something. Montell's bus driver says that she and her boyfriend were carrying rucksacks and a tent.'

'A tent. And it was a nice warm night, nearly a full moon too. Shit.' Steele glanced to his right at the uniformed officer, who sat at the table. 'PC Reid,' he said, 'you're a local guy. Is there a place in Gullane where you can camp if you want to, without being obvious?' There was an awkward silence. 'It is fucking obvious, though, isn't it?' the inspector added, as he answered his own question in his mind. 'Right down to the sand traces in her vaginal swab.'

'That's right, sir,' said the constable, carefully, 'there's the beach. We don't encourage it, but there's no by-law against it so it happens. We get youngsters camping out there sometimes. If you go into that buckthorn in the high dunes at the east end, there are wee clearings where you can pitch a tent. I don't mean local kids, like: their parents are too responsible to let them do that. If they get camping out, it'll be in the garden. My own have done that in their time. Naw, I'm talking about students and the like, going down there for a bit of, well, peace and quiet, and maybe to smoke a wee bit grass where they'll no' be bothered by us.'

'Or by anybody else?'

Reid frowned. 'No' necessarily, sir. That area's got a bit of a history.'

'And somebody might just have written a new chapter.' Steele pushed back his chair and stood up. 'I'm off to the Mallard. Sergeant McNee should still be there on his break. I want a search of that buckthorn.' He paused. 'Hold on a minute,' he said. 'There's an easier way than that. Ray, get on to the traffic boys. I want a helicopter to over-fly the area, as soon as possible. We can bet that Zrinka's boy-friend's long gone, but maybe he left his identity behind.'

Seventeen

'Who?' the belligerent telephone voice exclaimed.

This was not someone, she thought, who would ever hold down a job in a call centre. 'It's Maggie,' she repeated. 'Your partner's sister. Is Bet there?'

'Of course she's here.' Sarcasm took over. 'It's twenty before three in the bloody morning. Hold on: give her a second to come round.'

She waited; the man's voice became indistinct and then she heard a rustling noise as the phone was passed over. 'Margaret, it's you?'

'Yes, it's me. Hello, Sis, how are you doing?'

'I'm fine. I'm even awake now.'

'God, I'm sorry: I thought you were ten hours behind us, not ahead.'

'No, it's tomorrow where I am.'

'I'll call you again, tomorrow morning our time. How would that do?'

'Margaret, I'm awake now, so talk to me. Who's dead?'

'Nobody.'

'You're not calling to tell me that Dad's surfaced again,

are you?' Suddenly Bet's tone was fearful. 'You're not going to say he's in Australia, are you?'

'No,' said Maggie, hurriedly, 'you can relax on that score. Look, he is dead, for sure: he was shot . . .' she hesitated '. . . that's to say he shot himself, a couple of years ago.'

There was a long silence, until 'Our father died,' her sister repeated, 'and you didn't call or write to tell me?'

'I chose not to. Maybe I should have, but I didn't think you'd want your life tainted by him again; not after what he did to us when we were children.'

'No, when I think about it, you're right about that,' Bet conceded. 'It would have been good to know that they'd finally screwed the lid down on the bastard, though. I haven't forgotten, you know, any of it, even though I was younger than you when it all happened.'

'How could we forget? It's haunted me all my life; or at least it did, until recently.'

'And me. I went halfway round the world to get away.'

'You can't run away from memories, or bad dreams.'

'I know that. I ran as far as I could from the possibility that he might ever come back into my life.'

'I guessed as much, even though you never spelled it out at the time.' Maggie sighed. 'He's kept us apart, you know, as sisters.'

'At least he didn't prevent us making lives for ourselves.'

'No, he didn't do that. Who's the guy? Husband?'

Bet laughed; the sound seemed to disperse the dark cloud that had linked two continents. 'No, thank you very much. Boyfriend, that's all; he doesn't live here. In fact he's just gone stumbling off to dress and hit the road. How's the bloke you married? Do you still outrank him?'

'Not any more, but I'm not married to him any more either. We divorced last year; I'm on my second husband now, and you, sister, haven't even scored up one.'

'Is that why I haven't had a card from you, the last two Christmases? Or a birthday card?'

'Mainly. I was a bit screwed up for a while, and I didn't want to inflict it on you.'

'So you're giving me insomnia instead?'

'Sorry.'

'Just kidding. Tell me about the new man.'

'His name's Stevie, Stevie Steele; he's almost three years younger than me, very bright, very calm, dark hair, good-looking, just a lovely guy.'

'What does he do?'

'He's a detective inspector.'

An explosion of breath covered ten thousand miles in an instant. 'Bloody hell! Another copper? Don't you have any imagination?'

For the first time that afternoon, Maggie smiled. 'I did fuck an actuary once,' she said. 'That was enough to make me stick to my own kind. No, that's not strictly true. Actuaries don't fuck; like everything else, they do it by numbers. Actually, I shouldn't blame the poor sod. Until Stevie, nobody ever rang my bell, not even Mario . . . and he certainly has some clapper.'

'Confession time for both of us,' Bet murmured. 'I may live a free and single lifestyle, but I've always been pretty repressed too, in that respect. The difference is, I'm still looking for my Stevie. The guy in the bathroom? Nowhere near it.' She paused. 'You know, Margaret, this is the first sister-to-sister talk we've ever had, and it's taken us more than thirty years. Tell me something. Have you ever travelled in your life? I don't mean a fortnight in Shagaluf, I mean really travelled.'

'I haven't even been to Shagaluf. I went to Italy with Mario a couple of times, and once to Paris for a long weekend, but that's it.'

'In that case, why not come to Sydney?'

'I think I'd like that, Bet, but there's something getting in the way right now. I'm pregnant.'

'You?' Maggie's sister gasped. 'Oh, Christ, I'm sorry, I didn't mean for it to sound like that, but I can only take so many shocks at one sitting.'

'Don't worry about it; a year ago I'd have said exactly the same thing. But now it's happened, I don't know what to say, other than that it's magic.'

'How long do you have to go?'

'About ten weeks. According to the scan, it's a girl.'

'That's wonderful: I'm going to be Auntie Bet.' There was a sound in the background. 'Okay, Bradley, close the door hard behind you. Call me in a couple of days.' Pause. 'That's him gone, face tripping him.'

'Sorry again.'

'Cobblers, you've done me a favour. He's a sour-faced bugger in the morning.' Maggie stared at the closed door of her office. There was something about her sister's voice, its vivacity, that sent an enormous pang of regret running through her for all the years she had kept her at a distance; her eyes blurred.

'Now, come on,' Bet exclaimed. 'I'm going to take it for granted that you'd have called me once the baby was born to give me the good news. But it's five years since we've spoken . . . my fault as much as yours, I admit . . . so what's made you call me right now, in the middle of my night? My super-efficient sister doesn't get mixed up with time zones, unless there's something wrong.'

'It's nothing, Bet, just something I need to ask you.'

'Everything's nothing with you. Out with it.'

'There's something on my last scan: my consultant says it's probably an ovarian cyst, but he asked me about the family medical history. Have you ever had a problem like that?'

'I had a polyp in my womb three years ago. Had it removed and that was that. Nothing else, though.'

'Did Mum ever talk to you about Granny Kellock dying? I know we were only kids when she did; she never discussed it with me, but she never discussed anything with me. I think she blamed me for what happened with Dad.'

'Come on, Margaret,' Bet protested. 'I remember her battering you when you told her about it, but blaming you, that's daft. You were only a kid at the time: you hadn't even started your periods.'

'Nonetheless, that's how she felt. We never spoke much after that.'

'She only spoke to me about Granny once; I asked her when I was doing my nursing training before I turned to design. All she said was that it was a cancer "down there".

That was how she put it; to Mum, everything below the navel was just "down there".'

'What about Aunt Fay? Hers was in her stomach, as I remember.'

'Yes, but it was a secondary. It was discovered very late, and she was riddled with it by then. They never did know where the primary was. Margaret, this consultant of yours, he's not worried about you, is he?'

'No, no, not at all; just routine, he says. That's the exact word he used, routine.'

'Have you told your husband?'

'No, but I only just found out today. I don't see why I should, though; Stevie's like any other new father-to-be. He'd worry himself silly for no good reason.'

'Isn't he entitled to do that?'

'He's got enough on his plate. I've got a follow-up scan tomorrow; once I've had the result I'll probably tell him then. There'll be no reason not to.'

'And will you tell me too?'

'I will, Bet, I promise.'

'You'd bloody well better. And not in the middle of the night either.'

Eighteen

Stevie Steele happened to be glancing out of the window when he saw the Vauxhall pull up in the village-hall car park. 'Just what I need,' he muttered, as a tall, bald man stepped out, placing a heavily braided cap on his dome-like head. He walked to the door to greet the new arrival. 'Afternoon, sir,' he said, extending a hand. 'I wasn't expecting you.'

'Don't worry, Inspector,' said ACC Brian Mackie. 'I'm not here to crack the whip, but I thought that I should show my face. Moral support, nothing more: I even played it by the book and told DCS McGuire that I was coming.'

'I appreciate it, sir. So will the uniformed troops: they've been on a thankless task all day. Come on inside.' He ushered him into the headquarters of Operation Gabriel.

PC Reid was alone in the office; he stood to attention as they entered. 'Relax, Ian,' Mackie told him. 'You'll pull something, going all stiff like that. I know this old lag,' he explained to Steele, 'from when I was CID commander out here. I thought you'd have retired by now, Constable.'

'So did I, sir,' the PC replied mournfully.

'Hard slog, is it, Stevie?' the ACC asked.

'Yeah, but we're moving. We've got an identification from a woman in North Berwick, confirmed by a bus driver who picked her up, and a male companion, on Monday night. I've sent Ray Wilding and Tarvil Singh back along there to re-interview the witness, in the light of what DC Montell got from the driver. We know who she is; now we have to find out where she's from, and where the hell the boyfriend is.'

'He's your prime suspect, is he?'

'Not necessarily. My concern is that he might have got in the way. We believe that the two of them may have camped on the beach on Monday. I've got a chopper up there now, I hope, doing a scan of the area, looking for signs they may have left behind.'

'That'll be the one I saw when I was into the village.'

'Let's hope so.' As he spoke, the phone rang. 'Will you excuse me, sir? I'd better take this.'

'Of course.'

Steele snatched the handset from its cradle. 'Inquiry HQ, DI speaking.'

'It's me, sir,' Griff Montell said. 'I'm sorry it's taken so long but the woman I spoke to at Barclays decided that she had to clear the release of this information at the top of the tree. It turned out that nobody was nesting there until after four. There was a management meeting under way.'

'That's okay. I half expected them to ask us for a sheriff's warrant. You got it now, though?'

'Yes. Zrinka Boras has been a Barclays client for three years: she's twenty-four years old and the address they hold for her is High Laigh House, Wimbledon, London.

According to their information she's unmarried. She has an overdraft facility on the account, guaranteed by her father, Mr Davor Boras, also of High Laigh House.'

'What else would they tell you?'

'They have her listed as a student; they volunteered that. They won't give me any account details, but they did confirm that the most recent withdrawals were made by debit card, in Scotland, specifically Edinburgh and North Berwick. There have also been several deposits made to the account, all through their Edinburgh branch.'

'Cheques from Daddy, do you reckon?'

'I asked that question myself. No, they weren't: the bank lady was quite open about that, although she wasn't authorised to release names or amounts. There have been regular pay-ins over the last couple of years, most by cheque but some in cash.'

'So she's been economically active in Edinburgh, yet the bank doesn't have a local address for her.'

'She's an online customer, sir, like a lot of people are, these days, my sister and I included.'

'Me too,' Steele admitted, then stopped. 'Okay, Griff, you seem to be on a roll today, so I want you to keep playing. We've got two witnesses putting her in North Berwick, and that ties her to the bank slip. There's no doubt about her identity. It's time to get in touch with the father.'

'Mr Davor Boras,' said Montell, 'age fifty-five, born Sarajevo, Bosnia, then part of Yugoslavia. Built a successful engineering business in his twenties, before selling to a larger company and moving to London in 1989. Set up Bolec, a retail chain selling electronic and household goods, focusing on out-of-town locations, and grew it into one of the biggest in Europe. Sold out seven years ago for an estimated one point two billion. Two years later founded a computer business selling hardware, peripherals and supplies, exclusively online, throughout the European Union. Continental IT, the new company, thanks to spectacularly low overheads, is hugely profitable and is now bigger than the one he sold. Personal interests include the arts . . . he has galleries in London and in Sarajevo . . . and football; he's a significant shareholder in clubs in England, Bosnia and the USA. He and his wife, they were married in 1976, run the Davor and Sanda Boras charitable foundation, which has funded relief operations in Africa as well as post-war rebuilding projects in the Balkan states. He has two children, both born in the former Yugoslavia: there's Zrinka, and a son, Dražen, aged twenty-eight. Davor, his wife and the children became naturalised British citizens in 1992.'

'Are you trying to impress me, or maybe even the big chiefs?' asked Steele, slowly.

'I'm sorry, boss. It's an unusual name, so I ran it through Google and that's what I came up with. I found it on an Internet encyclopedia.'

'It's okay, Griff.' The DI chuckled. 'I'm not getting at you; that's good police work, no kidding. It lets us know who we're dealing with.'

'Kid gloves?'

'I reckon all bereaved parents should be treated the same, but the commissioner of the Met might not share my view. Leave it with me. The ACC's here just now. I'll talk to him about it.'

'What's that?' Mackie asked, as Steele hung up. The inspector had made notes during Montell's briefing: he referred to them as he relayed what the DC had learned from the bank, and what he had discovered on his own initiative about the dead girl's father.

'Montell,' the ACC said, when he had been brought up to speed. 'Is that Alex Skinner's boyfriend?'

The question took the inspector by surprise. 'It's news to me if he is.'

'And maybe news to Bob as well. That's just idle gossip, though: my wife's niece works at Curle Anthony and Jarvis.' He frowned. 'I agree with you about the father, Stevie. We do not send a couple of uniforms in a panda to this man's door.' He took out his mobile and dialled a number. 'Ruth,' the DI heard him say, and knew that he had called his secretary. 'ACC here. I want you to do something for me: find out which of the Metropolitan divisions Wimbledon's in . . . That's right, as in Roger Federer . . . then get in touch with its commander: from what I remember he or she is probably . . .' He paused as the landline rang and Steele picked it up once more. '. . . a chief super. Whatever, I need to speak to them at once, like ten minutes ago, on this number. Thanks . . . Yes, I'm still at Gullane. I don't see me being back this afternoon.'

'Yes?' Mackie heard the inspector exclaim, as he finished his call. 'That's excellent. I'll take it from here.'

'What now?'

'The chopper: it's got a result. They spotted a tent pitched in a clearing in the bushes, just where Reid said it might be. They've photographed it, and they have the technology to transfer an image straight into our system. I can pick it up here, from an e-mail, so that we know exactly where to go.'

'Good man. I'll come with you. You know,' Mackie said, 'I used to wonder about Bob Skinner and his insistence on being hands-on whenever he can. Now I think I understand him. I think maybe I should phone him, leave or not, and see if he wants to get in on the act.'

Nineteen

It was one of those embarrassing moments: Alex Skinner was in conference with the chairman of the firm when her mobile sounded. 'Sorry,' she said to Mitchell Laidlaw. 'I forgot to switch it to silent.'

'No problem,' he replied. 'It might be a client. Take it: we're done here anyway.'

'Thanks.' She picked up her papers in her left hand and the phone with her right, hitting the accept button as she stepped through the door, which the chairman held open for her. 'Alex,' she said. 'How can I help you?'

'You could cheer me up by coming out with me tonight,' Griff Montell exclaimed. 'I'm having a hell of a busy day and I need to relax.'

'What do you have in mind?'

'Movie?'

'I can't think of anything I fancy at the moment, truth be told. I was at the Ocean Terminal multiplex on Sunday with my dad and my young brothers. None of the trailers appealed to me. Let's just go and eat.'

'Sounds good. Anywhere in mind?'

'No,' she said, as she settled behind her desk. 'We'll take

a taxi up to George Street and pick somewhere; it's mid-week, so we'll have plenty of choice. Ring my doorbell at seven thirty: we'll have a drink first.'

'Okay.' Alex was about to hang up, but he continued. 'Speaking of your dad, how is he?'

'He's fine. I was worried about him a few months ago, but the time he's spent by himself seems to have done him good.'

'Why were you worried about him?'

'For a couple of reasons: he was involved in a very big incident towards the end of last year. You'll remember it: there were people killed. He's had a few very rough scrapes in his time, has my father, but I don't recall ever seeing him so badly affected as he was by that one. Then, just after it, he went off to London on some hush-hush inquiry. He didn't tell me anything about it, but I got the definite impression that it was fairly nasty too. On top of all that, he's had to deal with the break-up of his marriage.'

'Bad timing?'

'Not good, but it was more than that. Pops isn't used to failure in any aspect of his life: if he undertakes something, he has to succeed. He's bad enough when a four-foot putt lips out, so imagine what he was like when he had to admit that he and Sarah weren't going to make it work. He took it personally, carried all the blame on his shoulders.'

'Shouldn't he? Isn't he . . .' Montell started to venture.

She cut him off: 'I know what you're going to say; you've heard the gossip too. Well, it's wrong. Aileen de Marco wasn't a factor in the split. It wasn't all his fault, either: he and Sarah both made mistakes, and in the end there wasn't enough left to hold them together. But everything came to a head at once, her going, the horrors he was involved in.' She paused. 'Griff,' she asked, 'have you ever met my father?'

'Once,' he replied. 'After you had your own trouble, and I was on hand to sort it, he sent for me, called me up to his office, to thank me personally.'

'You never told me that. He wouldn't, but you might have.'

'I didn't like to. I don't know why, unless I was embarrassed at being thanked for just doing my job.'

She laughed. 'That's all I am, is it? Just another victim?'

'That's what I tried to tell him . . . although not quite in those words . . . but he wouldn't have it. He said he owed me one, as a man, not as the deputy chief, but if he could use his office to repay it, he would. So I asked him if I could carry on working with DI Steele and Tarvil; they're my kind of cops, see. He fixed it there and then.'

'Good for him. And at that time, how did he seem to you? What did you think of him?'

'Honestly? How do I describe him? It was like being in the same room as a volcano: the intensity of him. I've never met anyone like him.'

'You're not the first to say that. But honestly, he's not usually like that. He really was wired directly into the mains then. I'll tell you how bad he was. Last January he actually asked me to move back in with him for a while.'

'You refused him?'

'Obviously. I still live next door to you and your sister, do I not? I told him the truth: when daughters leave home they're gone for good.'

'After the day I've had,' Griff said, 'that's maybe the wrong thing to say. I've spoken to the parents of one daughter who sure is gone and I've tracked down the father of another.'

'The girl on the beach near Gullane? The photo on the front page of the *News* today? There's something about her that's been gnawing at me all day.'

'Yeah, we know who she is now: we . . .'

And then it came to her, as if an unseen hand had swept a curtain aside. In that instant she was somewhere else as a scene replayed itself in her mind. 'And so do I,' she exclaimed. 'I don't remember her name, but I've met her. I'm sure of it now: she was a very striking girl, blonde and really beautiful; not just on the outside either. She had a really bubbly personality.'

'When was this?' Montell exclaimed.

'About three months ago. I was with my dad and the kids one weekend; we went to a street market in Leith, fashion, CDs, arts and crafts, that sort of stuff. She had a stall, selling paintings, originals, all her own work. I stopped and looked at it, and I saw a couple that I was sure Pops would like. He was down at the time, still wounded by everything, so I bought him one, the biggest, as a cheer-up present.'

'How did you pay her?'

'It was a few hundred quid so I wrote her a cheque.'

'Payable to Zrinka Boras?'

'That's it! Ms Z. Boras: I asked her where her name came from. She laughed and said that it came from her dad and that he was from Bosnia-Herzegovina.'

'Jeez!' Griff whistled. 'Your old man must really have

been off the ball back then. Stevie Steele showed him that photograph this morning and he didn't recognise her. Maybe you should tell him, before your name shows up when we access her bank records.'

'That's a good point. I will, but don't be too hard on him,' Alex protested. 'The way he was back then, he could have met Charlize Theron and forgotten about it.'

Twenty

'You cut it fine,' the woman exclaimed. 'I was on my way to the door when the phone rang. If I had closed it behind me, I wouldn't have come back in to answer, you know.'

'I know, Sylvia, and I'm sorry,' said Maggie Rose, making herself sound contrite. 'I won't keep you long, honest.'

'Och, it's all right. I'm in no rush. And . . .' she drew a breath '. . . I like to keep in with the police.'

Rose had enjoyed a working relationship with Sylvia Thorpe for several years. She was an executive officer in the General Registers Office of Scotland, and she had been a useful contact on several occasions. 'That's what I like to hear. By the way, how's Jim Glossop, your old boss? Enjoying retirement?'

'You know Jim: he can't sit still. He was choked when he had to pack it in, so now he works for half a dozen charities for nothing. Not me, when I get to that age: I'll be off round the world. Now, what can I do for you, Maggie? Which villain's antecedents are you trying to trace this time?'

'Mine. This isn't an official request; I'm asking for a favour.'

Thorpe chuckled. 'A parking ticket's worth?'

'Ouch! I can't even make my own tickets disappear, Sylvia. Let's just say there's a drink in it.'

'And you know that on a big night out I might have one Bacardi Breezer.'

'I'll buy you a case.'

'God forbid! What do you want?'

'Stuff I can't get in the Scotland's People website, or I'd have logged on there. I'm looking for the death records of my grandmother and my aunt Fay.'

'Where and when?'

'I don't have exact dates, but my granny died thirty years ago, and Aunt Fay died eight years later, both in Edinburgh.'

'Ages?'

'My aunt was forty-two and my granny was sixty-one.'

'Full names?'

'My granny was Mrs Martha Kellock, maiden surname McKinstry, and my aunt was Miss Euphemia Kellock. No middle names: we don't go in for them in my family.'

'Your grandfather's full name?'

'Herbert Kellock.'

'Do you want his record as well?'

'No, just those two.'

'Okay,' Thorpe declared. 'I can find them from that information. How urgent is this?'

'Whenever you can?'

'Okay, I'll try to get it done tomorrow morning. Do you want me to post the extracts to your home address, since it's a personal enquiry?'

'No. Send them to the office, please; first class, so they get there on Friday. It's my last day before I go off. Give me a note of the cost of the extracts, and I'll send you a cheque.'

'Don't be daft. What do you mean, you're going off?'

'Maternity leave. Stevie and I are having a baby in a couple of months. Eleven weeks on Saturday, according to the timetable.'

'That's wonderful! Congratulations. It couldn't happen to a nicer couple.'

'Thanks.'

'Maggie,' suddenly Sylvia Thorpe sounded serious, 'why do you want this information? Are you growing a family tree?'

'God forbid. There'd be too much bitter fruit on it if I did. No, let's just say that I want my daughter to know what might be in store for her.'

'Ah.' Rose heard a sigh on the line. 'Look, I know you well enough to be blunt. We get quite a few requests for this, the bulk of them from women; you were a detective, so you can work out why. Have you got something to worry about?'

'Maybe, Sylvia, maybe. The women in my family have an unfortunate history: they tend to die young. At this moment I need to know a little more about it. But please, keep this between the two of us.'

'That's why you want the extracts sent to the office, isn't it? Maggie, whatever this is, doesn't Stevie have a right to know?'

'It's probably nothing, so he doesn't need to at this stage. If it is a problem . . . we'll deal with it together.'

Twenty-one

'We take a right turn here, sir,' said PC Reid, leading the way, trudging heavily through the sand. 'Then we follow the path that skirts the golf course. Round the first bend there should be a fork, where we'll go left.'

Mackie, perspiring in his uniform, Steele and Wilding, with their jackets slung over their shoulders, followed in his tracks as the rising trail crossed a small spring and became firmer underfoot. The warmth of the May evening had taken them by surprise. On the drive to the beach, they had seen that the public car park on the bents was busy, and Steele had spotted at least two vehicles with media logos emblazoned on the side.

'Follow me,' Reid called out. As they did so, they found themselves climbing, through a maze of head-high thorn bushes, thick with yellow flowers. The path turned into sand once more, until, without warning, it came to an end and they found themselves in a clearing in the middle of which a square tent, with an arched top and a small awning in front, was pitched. A rucksack lay at the closed entrance.

The area had been secured by two uniformed officers, both women: they had attached a circle of tape to the thick bushes. Slightly pointless, Steele thought, since there was only one way any human could approach, but he was not inclined to fault them for following procedure. Reid introduced the pair to Mackie. 'Sergeant Grey, sir, and PC McGregor, both from Haddington.'

'I know, Ian.' The ACC turned to the senior uniform. 'It's as you found it, Alison, yes?'

'Yes, sir. Neither of us have been into the tent.'

'Good. Stevie,' he said to Steele, 'this is your investigation, your call. Do you want to go inside?'

'Is the DCC coming?' the inspector asked.

Mackie grinned. 'No. He said he didn't want to stand on your toes.'

'Jesus,' Steele exclaimed. 'If you don't mind me saying so, sir, that's a first.'

'Tell me about it. What do you think?'

'I think I'm going to look inside.'

'Has it occurred to you that the victim's companion might still be in there?'

'And armed, Stevie,' Wilding added.

'It's occurred to me. But if he is still here, unless he's the stupidest murderer I've ever encountered, he's lying in that tent with a bullet in his head.'

'Unless he was afraid to make a break for it after he killed her.'

'Come on, Ray, is that likely?'

'Let's put it to the test.' Mackie stepped up to the tent, crouched in the small porch section, one knee on the ground sheet, and opened the flap that covered the doorway. 'Empty,' he announced.

'I thought you said it was my shout,' said Steele, quietly, as the ACC straightened up, easing the kink out of his back.

'Christ, I'm stiff these days,' he complained. 'It is, Inspector, but I'm the senior officer here, by quite a way. If you'd been wrong about the guy waiting in there with a gun, and I'd let you go in before me, I'd have carried that with me through whatever was left of my short and inglorious career. Would Bob Skinner have let you go in first, if he'd been here?'

The inspector was about to answer the question, although it was virtually rhetorical, when Mackie's mobile sounded. 'ACC,' he answered. 'You have? That's good, Superintendent; thank you very much . . . He's what? . . . Jesus, I wasn't expecting him till tomorrow. When's he due to take off? . . . Them? Has he thought that . . . Forget that, who thinks at a time like this? Okay, I'll handle this end. Thanks again.' He ended the call and pocketed the phone. 'Sorry, Stevie,' he said. 'You guys will have to find your own way back from here. The girl's parents are coming up to Edinburgh this evening. They have a private plane and it's taking off from Gatwick as soon as they can get fuel into it. I'll have to meet them at Turnhouse and take them to the mortuary.'

'You could always delegate it,' Steele suggested.

'Let me point something out to you,' said Mackie. 'The morgue is in which division?'

'Maggie's.'

'Exactly. If I delegate this, it has to be to the divisional commander.'

'Mmm. Forget I said that, will you, sir?'

'I've forgotten. You carry on here. I'll catch up with Mario tomorrow on what you find.' He turned and left the clearing, PC Reid at his heels.

'He's a cool one, isn't he?' said Wilding, once the assistant chief constable was out of earshot.

'That's an understatement. When he was making his way up through the ranks, there was a time when he was known as "Fridge". But that changed: later he was called "Dirty Harry". There's a story about him from years ago. Remember that time when there was trouble at the Festival? There was an armed incident and one of our guys was killed. Brian Mackie took down the gunman with a single shot from a Colt forty-five calibre pistol. The guy was on a motorbike, moving fast, and yet he hit him dead centre from seventy-five yards away. Maggie was there; she told me about it. It was an amazing shot, but the thing that everybody remembered was that afterwards he didn't bat a fucking eyelid. He went over, looked at the dead guy on the ground, nodded and walked away. He's the best shot on the force, no kidding.'

'I'll remember that if I ever have to ask him to sign an overtime chitty.'

'Do that. But first, I'm going to see what's inside this tent. I want the SOCOs in here, Ray. Dorward's been warned. He should be on his way down. Give him a call and see where he is.'

'You're not going into the thing, are you?' the detective sergeant asked. 'You're not suited up.'

'No, I'll just look from the doorway. I won't go any further in than the ACC did.'

Before he had even started to move, another mobile sounded: his. 'Fuck,' he whispered, impatiently. 'Steele,' he snapped.

'DC Montell, sir.'

'Griff, what is it? I'm busy here.'

'Sorry, boss, but I thought you'd want to know this: I'd have been on twenty minutes ago, but I've had trouble getting a connection. It's about the dead girl: Alex knows her.'

'Alex?'

'Alex Skinner. I've just been speaking to her. Well, when I say she knows her, she's met her. She knows who she was . . . and she knows what she was. Believe it or not, she's an artist, just like Stacey Gavin.'

'She's sure about this?' He was aware of Wilding and the two uniforms staring at him, caught by the sudden urgency in his tone.

'Certain. Alex bought one of her paintings for her father. Direct from the victim, off her market stall.'

'Lovely,' Steele murmured. 'Just fucking lovely. Griff, are we chasing an art critic, do you think?'

'If we are, it's a pity he doesn't specialise in rap music instead.'

'Don't put that in your note. Write one up all the same, and add it to the investigation file.'

'What's Montell been up to?' asked Wilding, a barb in his tone. From time to time, Steele thought he detected a touch of animosity in the sergeant towards their newest recruit, but there was no sign of it affecting the performance of their unit, and so he had decided that, for the time being, it was as well left to lie undisturbed.

'He's been up to getting a result, mate,' he replied, 'but I'll tell you about that later. Meantime . . .' He walked over to the tent, knelt under the small awning, as Mackie had done, taking care not to touch the rucksack, and opened the flap.

He tingled, as he felt her presence inside, almost tangibly: it was as if she was haunting the space in which she had spent her last night on earth. A sleeping bag lay on the ground sheet, unrolled but crumpled: it looked big enough for two. Items of clothing were strewn around, jeans, bra, knickers and a long-sleeved cotton shirt, bright orange in colour, matching the description that the Thai waitress in North Berwick had given to Wilding during his second interview. Two KitKat wrappers and a Tetrapak of Sainsbury's orange juice lay on the far side of the bag, alongside a used condom, knotted, and its torn foil capsule. 'I hope he was worthy of you, kid,' Steele whispered to the dead girl's spirit. There was an unlit Tilley lamp against the far wall of the tent, and a flashlight close to where he knelt. Beside it, taking up most of the rest of the floor space, he saw a big black bag, a metre square with a zipper running round three of its sides. It was undone and, from what he could see, it was empty.

He eased himself out of the space and returned to Wilding, at the entrance to the clearing. 'What's he left us?' the sergeant asked.

'Apart from a copious DNA sample, and almost certainly fingerprints, nothing that I can see. I'm not going to open it, that's for Arthur, but I'll bet you that rucksack over there is Zrinka's.'

'That's a move forward, though. He left us nothing at the last scene.'

'What makes you so sure that the boy's our killer?'

'Who else would it be, Stevie?'

'Maybe you're right; maybe it was him. But if it was, it's a hell of a change in his behaviour. Stacey Gavin was killed clean as a whistle; even allowing for the fuck-up at the crime scene we weren't left a single clue. Why would he advertise himself the way he has here?'

'Maybe he was just lucky the first time.'

Steele shook his head. 'I don't buy that, Ray. We're good at our job: we've worked the Gavin investigation for two months and don't even have any viable suspects, far less an arrest. You cannot get that lucky.'

'We'd better get a description out, then.'

'An e-fit if we can.'

Wilding whistled. 'I've been thinking about that, boss. I'm not sure that my Thai witness will be up to that.'

'Maybe not, but Montell's bus driver might be: she gave him a far better description than your waitress gave you. Get on to him: tell him to find her and get it under way.'

A small smile fleeted across the sergeant's face. 'With pleasure. I'll tell him we want it for release tonight.'

'Do that,' said Steele. 'I only hope we need it,' he added.

'What do you mean, sir?'

'Maybe we're meant to spend time and resources looking for Zrinka's boyfriend. Remember poor wee Rusty?'

'You're saying . . .?'

'Last time he didn't even leave a dog around as a witness.

He shot it as it was running away in terror. If the boy didn't do it, then . . .'

'. . . then there's every chance that the killer did the boy.'

'Exactly; then hid him, and all his kit.'

'Could he have chucked him in the sea, like he did to wee Rusty?'

Steele frowned. 'What do you think, Ray? He'd have had to drag him a good distance, through the bushes and across rocks. Even then the tide might not have been right; if it was still coming in, and from memory I reckon it would have been, it wouldn't have taken him offshore. Nah, that would have been too risky all round: if the lad's dead as well, he's not far from here.'

'Jesus,' Wilding whispered. 'We could be standing on him. It wouldn't take long to bury a body in the sand.'

'I reckon not,' Steele agreed. 'Let's cover all the options. You have Montell re-interview his bus driver, and ask her to do us a likeness. While he's doing that we'll clear this area, and hold back Dorward's team until we can get sniffer dogs in here.'

Twenty-two

Brian Mackie scanned the horizon to the south, looking across the Pentland Hills. From behind him came the roar of an easyJet flight taking off from the main runway, but he ignored it, scanning the skies for another aircraft, one that air-traffic control had assured him was on schedule.

Edinburgh's general aviation terminal was familiar territory for him; many VIP flights were routed there rather than to the principal airport, on grounds of privacy, security and ease of access. He had welcomed many official visitors, and in the process had come to regard himself as something of a connoisseur of private aircraft.

The Boras plane came in low; he failed to pick it up until it was in the final stages of its approach. 'Learjet,' he whispered, but as the craft grew closer he became less certain. Its engines were distinctly rear-mounted and its lines were sharp and sleek. He gave in. 'What is it?' he asked the facility manager.

'It's an Embraer Legacy 600,' she replied, 'small executive jet of choice of the super-rich. It may not be a jumbo, but that thing will get you to New York, no problem.'

He watched as the pilot made a faultless landing, then

followed the guide car, which led him across to the section of the taxiway where Mackie stood.

The assistant chief constable waited as the twin engines were cut and wound down, then as the aircraft door opened and its steps extended automatically. He was about to climb them when the doorway was filled by a stocky, heavy-shouldered man, who seemed at first glance to be almost as wide as he was tall. He was balding; the hair that remained was swept back from his forehead. His nose was the most prominent feature of his face, its size enhanced by two small, dark, piercing eyes, and by a tight-lipped mouth. If he had sported a small moustache, Mackie thought, he might have been taken for the television incarnation of Hercule Poirot.

That image vanished in the instant that his gaze fell on the police officer. There was none of David Suchet's charm and bonhomie, only a cold, hard stare, full of rage. He paused for a moment, then trotted down the stairway.

'From the look of your uniform,' he said, as he approached, 'I guess that you are the man in charge.' There was no offer of a handshake.

'That's right. Brian Mackie, assistant chief.'

'Don't we rate the chief himself?' The question, in flat, accent-free English, snapped out like a whip. For all that Davor Boras was a newly bereaved father, Mackie felt his hackles rise, but fought successfully to keep the fact from showing.

'Rating doesn't come into it, sir,' he replied. 'This has all happened very quickly. If I'd had time to brief Sir James Proud, I'm sure he would have come to meet you.'

'You're sure, are you?' The little eyes blazed. 'There is no doubt about this?' he asked. 'You are certain that this is my daughter? For let me promise you, if my wife and I have been put through this by mistake . . .'

'Mr Boras, if that turns out to be the case, I'll take whatever flak may come my way and I'll still be very happy for you. But, no, there is no doubt. Didn't the Met show you a photograph?'

'Yes,' the man admitted, 'but it had been altered. It might have been my Zrinka, it might not. I must see her for myself. Where is she?'

'The body's still in the city mortuary. I'll take you straight there if you wish.'

'In time.' Boras glanced around. 'Where are the cars?'

Mackie turned and pointed to two unmarked police vehicles, parked close by. 'I hope those will be enough. I assumed that your pilots would be staying in Edinburgh.'

'They are not my cars. I instructed my staff to have two limos waiting here for us to take us to the Caledonian Hotel. I must ensure that my wife is comfortable in her surroundings before I put her through this ordeal.'

'You're ahead of schedule,' the facility manager pointed out anxiously, 'and it can be difficult getting out of the city at this time of day. I'll check the car park if you like. They may be waiting there; we wouldn't allow them on the Tarmac, I'm afraid.'

'Fuck them,' Boras growled. 'They're not here, and that's all I care about. My wife and I will travel with you, sir; my personal assistant will come too, in your second car, if need be. The pilots and Sanda's secretary can come in one of the limos, if they ever arrive.'

'Of course.'

The dark man turned, jogged heavily up the stairs and back into the jet; after around a minute he reappeared, followed by a slim, blonde woman. If there had been the tiniest sliver of a doubt in Mackie's mind about the veracity of the identification of the body on the beach, it vanished as soon as he saw her.

A second man brought up the rear, ducking as he exited the aircraft. He was tall, dressed in a double-breasted suit that screamed Savile Row, with sandy-coloured hair so perfectly arranged that it might have been lacquered, and ginger eyebrows. The assistant chief constable had an excellent memory for faces, an attribute of most successful police officers, and he knew at once that this was one he had seen before.

'My wife, Sanda,' Boras said gruffly, in introduction. Close to, Mackie could see that the woman's eyes were puffy; she clutched a handkerchief and he guessed that she had cried all the way to Edinburgh. He nodded to her, a brief bow. 'And my personal assistant, Keith Barker.' With the name, the ACC's recollection was complete: formerly the business editor of ITN, Barker had gone, in the face of much criticism from his peers, from reporting on the Boras empire to representing it.

He and Mackie shook hands. 'Shall we be going?' he said. 'I'd like to get to the hotel as quickly and as quietly as possible. There are people who make a career out of following the movements of Mr Boras; we gave them the slip when we left Gatwick and I'm anxious that we retain that advantage.'

'Sure,' the assistant chief replied. 'Let's head off.'

'I'd like to travel with you, Mr Mackie, if I may,' said Barker.

'Yes,' Boras barked. 'That would be best.'

'If that's how you want it,' Mackie replied evenly, 'it's fine with me. I'll take the lead car with Mr Barker. You and your wife take the larger vehicle, please, Mr Boras. It's more comfortable.'

'No blue lights, I notice,' Barker murmured, as the police officer slid after him into the back seat of their Mondeo, tapping the driver on the shoulder as a signal to move off.

'No. There's no point in attracting attention to Mr Boras. His daughter's identity hasn't been picked up by the media yet, and I want to keep it that way until the formal identification's been made. As an ex-journalist you'll understand that, I'm sure. Once the news breaks the family will come under intense scrutiny.'

'Of course. But as I said earlier, Mr Boras himself is always under intense scrutiny. That's why this business needs to be very carefully managed. There could be significant financial implications.'

'In what way?'

'The City's a very sensitive animal, Mr Mackie. Although Continental IT has become a massive business, my employer remains extremely hands-on in its day-to-day management. I'm not saying that he is the company, you understand, but the financial markets recognise his importance to its well-being. Therefore anything that happens to distract him in his personal life will be seen to have a knock-on effect.'

'And the share price might suffer?'

'Exactly. This is why I wanted to travel with you, Mr Mackie: to make you understand the sensitivity of this situation, at all sorts of levels.'

'I think I do already, but carry on.'

He did. 'Make no mistake, Mr Mackie, Zrinka's death is a tragedy for the Boras family; I cannot tell you how badly it has affected Davor and Sanda. What we must do now is ensure that it does not become a tragedy for others. Continental IT employs thousands, indeed tens of thousands of people across Europe and at our call centre in Mumbai; a crisis of confidence among the institutional shareholders could put many of those jobs at risk. For that reason, I'd like to work with your media people in preparing any public statements about Zrinka, and I'd like her father to be involved in every press briefing, so that he can answer questions directly and send out the right business message: so that he can be seen to be in control.'

The assistant chief constable frowned. 'I hear what you're saying, Mr Barker, and I've got no problem with putting Mr Boras in front of the press. But I'd like to check our perspectives here. I suppose that Zrinka's death is a tragedy for you too . . .'

'Of course, of course,' Barker exclaimed, a little too quickly.

'. . . being so close to the family, so maybe your professional thinking is affected. As I understand it, Continental IT is a hugely successful company. Last year it returned profits of more than a half a billion euros. Or am I wrong?'

'No, that's correct.'

'In addition to that fifty-five per cent of the shares are held by an investment trust owned by the Boras family; so, although it's a public company, effective control still lies in their hands.'

The ginger eyebrows rose. 'You have been doing your homework. You're an unusual policeman, if I may say so.'

'I like to know who I'm dealing with. But I'm not so unusual: I had a good teacher. What I'm getting around to saying is that, from where I'm sat, you're anticipating a crisis that isn't going to happen. Okay, so some institutional shareholders get a bit twitchy, short term. That isn't going to affect the employees' interests at all, and long-term it isn't going to affect the company's stock-market value.'

The ex-journalist shifted in his seat, glancing out of the window at the Gyle shopping mall as the car cruised through the roundabout that led into it. 'Ah, but with respect,' he ventured, 'the issues are greater than you know.'

'So enlighten me.' Barker winced, slightly, and nodded in the direction of the driver. Mackie caught the implication. 'Don't worry about PC Cash,' he said. 'In this car he never hears what's said in the back seat. Isn't that right, Wattie?'

A voice came from the front. 'I beg your pardon, sir?'

Boras's assistant frowned. 'On that basis, then.' Nonetheless his voice dropped to little more than a whisper. 'At this moment,' he continued, 'Mr Boras is negotiating an agreed takeover of Continental IT by a very large American company. In these circumstances the share price is of paramount importance. Nothing can be allowed to destabilise it, even in the short term. That's why it has to be clear to everybody that it is business as usual for Davor Boras, in spite of his grief.' He sighed. 'This couldn't have happened at a worse moment.'

'Is there an ideal moment for a father to lose his daughter, Mr Barker?' asked Mackie, quietly.

'Of course not, but happening when it has, so close to the takeover, I'm tempted to wonder whether the two events might be connected.'

The police officer gasped. 'Are you suggesting that the Americans might have arranged a hit on Zrinka to devalue her father's business?'

'Dark things happen; you must know that.'

'Yes, but in this case that isn't one of them. Ms Boras's murder has got nothing to do with Continental IT. We may not know who killed her, not yet, but we know that much. Mr Barker, you can have everything you ask for in terms of the media. Our PR manager, Alan Royston, will clear our statement with you. When we brief the press, your boss can sit beside our head of CID. All that's fine.'

'Thank you very much.'

'In return . . .' he paused 'I . . . want Mr Boras, and his wife, if she's up to it, to be available for interview by our investigating officers tomorrow morning. We need to talk to them about their relationship with Zrinka.'

'They may not like that.'

Mackie made eye contact and held it. 'I may not give a fuck,' he said quietly. 'That's what's going to happen.'

Twenty-three

Mario was in the kitchen of his penthouse in Leith's gentrified quarter; 'Willow', from the first Café del Mar *Aria* album, was playing on his stereo system, yet he was aware nonetheless of the apartment's main door opening. He did not react; instead he carried on chopping a large red pepper until he felt two slender arms slip round his waist, two firm breasts press into his back, and a head settle on his shoulder.

'You're late,' he murmured, as he turned in her embrace to kiss her. 'It's quarter to seven.'

'Things to do,' Paula replied, after a while.

'Such as?'

She jerked a thumb over her shoulder and he followed its direction. A brown-paper bag lay on the work surface. 'Rolls,' she murmured, 'for the morning.'

'What about the bacon?'

'Don't kid me. You've always got bacon in the fridge.'

'I'm that predictable, eh?'

'Only in your shopping habits. The rest of the time you're as daft and impulsive as you ever were.'

He pressed her closer to him. 'Much like yourself, then.'

'Is that what you think? Is that what's wrong with me?'

'I don't see anything wrong with you. You wanted me to look you in the eye and tell you that, and here, I'm doing it.'

'I know, love.' She took a button of his open-necked shirt and twirled it in her fingers. 'And I love you for your faith in me; but that's not what we were talking about earlier. I was going on about last night, and the way I felt when I held the baby.'

'And I told you it would wear off.' He looked at her, suddenly serious. 'Hey, you're not working up to tell me that you want to try for a kid with someone else, are you?'

Her mouth fell open; and then she laughed. At that moment, it ranked among the most delicious sounds that Mario had ever heard. 'Daft,' she exclaimed, 'unpredictable, and at times plain bloody stupid. With or without a baby, I'm every bit as happy as Lou McIlhenney, and it's all because of you.'

She eased herself out of his grasp, walked to the wine cabinet and took out a bottle of Pinot Grigio. 'I'm not just unsettled because of last night,' she said, as she pulled the lever of the wall-mounted corkscrew. 'I've felt this way for a while, and it's only now that I've worked out in my head what it is.' She handed him a glass, as he looked at her quizzically. 'The way we live is great; let me say that straight off. It's easy, no commitment either way, both of us independent. But the thing is, love, I just feel it's time to become a proper couple.'

'You mean as in married?'

'I don't give a toss about being married. But I want to give you more, I want to make a commitment to you. The independence notion is nonsense; my happiness depends on you.'

He sipped his wine, its chill contrasting with the warm wave that he felt flow through him. 'And mine on you,' he told her, 'every bit as much. Whatever you want, it's yours.'

'You always say that. Sometimes I feel that I'm taking advantage of you.'

'No.' He grinned at her. 'Paula, let's stop faffing around. After tonight, I don't want you just to go home as usual. Neil and Lou are right, we're not fooling anyone. I'd like you to move in here. Or, if you prefer it, I'll move into your place. Or, if you want a third option, we could buy a house together. I've been up for this for a while; I felt it had to come from you, that's all.' He paused and the grin became a chuckle. 'Hey, do you think Nana Viareggio's ready for it?'

'Nana Viareggio's ready to see off Armageddon,' Paula retorted. 'She can handle the idea of two of her grand-children living together. I know this, because I've spoken to her about it. She told me that she's been waiting for it to happen for twenty years, and if it does, she'll die happy . . . although she did add that she doesn't plan to do that for a while. As for our mothers, they're used to the idea.'

'Okay,' he said. 'Now that's sorted, when do we make the move?'

She winked at him. 'I've got two suitcases in my car: that's the real reason I was late. But, Mario, there is some-thing else, and it does have to do with last night. For all your fertility situation, as long as we've been . . . together, I've been on the pill. Silly of me, maybe, but I've always been one for belt and braces, if you know what I mean.'

'And now you want to take your belt off?'

She nodded.

'To give an even break to the few miserable sperm that I might produce?'

She nodded.

He put down his glass and took her in his arms again. 'Then unbuckle the damn thing right now, although I warn you, we've got a better chance of winning the lottery than of you getting pregnant with me.'

'Hey, somebody wins that every week,' she pointed out. 'But I just want to buy a ticket, that's all.'

'You can have as many tickets as you like,' he lifted her off her feet and headed for the door, 'starting right now.'

He had almost reached the bedroom when the phone rang. He swore quietly. 'I've got to answer it,' he said, setting her down. 'You know that as long as I'm in this job, I'll always have to answer it?'

'I can live with that,' she replied. 'Go on.'

He took one pace towards the sideboard and snatched a cordless telephone from its cradle. 'McGuire,' she heard him bark testily, and felt a moment of sympathy for whoever was at the other end of the line.

'Yes, Stevie,' he continued. His forehead twisted into a heavy frown. 'Shit. It doesn't get any easier, does it? I'll be there inside half an hour.' He paused. 'Of course I've got something better to do,' he bellowed, 'but it's my fucking job to be there.'

He slammed the phone back into its cradle. 'Sorry, love.'

'It's all right,' she said. 'It is your fucking job, right enough. I'll come with you. I'll wait in the car while you do what you have to do. Once you're done, it'll cost you dinner somewhere fancy: sod the pasta for tonight.' She laid a hand on his cheek, and flashed him a smile that on anyone else might have seemed demure. 'Get used to it, love: this is how it's going to be.'

Twenty-four

'Maybe I've been at this game too long, boss,' said Ray Wilding, as he forced his way past the last thorn bush and back on to the sandy path. 'I can't remember the last time I chucked my load at a crime scene.' His tunic was splashed with the evidence of his weakness.

'Don't worry about it,' Steele reassured him. 'I can . . . and it wasn't that long ago either.'

'What do you think got him in such a state? He's only been there for a day and a half, yet the poor bastard's face is chewed off. Was it crows, or seagulls, do you think?'

'I doubt it,' PC Reid muttered. 'Normally you'd say so, but I doubt if birds that size could have got to him through the bushes. If they did they'd have been trapped there. No, I'd say it was foxes. There are plenty of them around here.'

Sniffer dogs had found the young man's body. There had been two false alarms, both due to the searchers happening upon the remains of cats in the undergrowth, but the third time had proved lucky, if not for the victim. He had been dragged, naked, for a hundred yards, before being left, jammed between two bushes, food for the scavengers. They had gnawed on more than his face, as the two detectives had discovered when they had forced their way through the tangle to reach him; his genitals were mangled, and blood-smeared bone was exposed in several places.

'That could not have been easy,' Steele murmured to his sergeant. 'This guy is strong; that's the one thing we do know about him. Him? Yes, almost certainly. I don't see a woman doing that. Strong and agile.'

'He'd have dragged him in a straight line from the clearing, I suppose, whereas we forced our way through from the nearest path. Maybe that was easier.'

'I don't see that: it's fucking jungle in there, all of it.'

'He must have picked up a few scratches doing it,' Wilding commented, licking blood from a tear on the back of his hand.

'Depends what he was wearing. Gloves, a heavy anorak: they'd protect him from the thorns.'

'True, but I bet you he didn't get out of there intact. What do you think he did with the boy's gear? He's moved his clothes and his rucksack.'

'The dogs are looking now,' Reid told the sergeant. 'If he's dumped them around here, they'll find them, now that they've got the lad's scent.'

'I can smell him from here,' said a voice from behind them, as Mario McGuire trudged along the path. He glanced at Wilding's tunic. 'Or is that you, Ray? Nasty, is it?'

Steele nodded, then described what they had found.

'I suppose I'd better take a look.' The head of CID sighed.

'I doubt if you could, sir. It was a tight squeeze for Ray and me, and you're bigger than either of us. Anyway, Arthur

Dorward's sent his smallest officer in to photograph the body *in situ* and to look for anything else that shouldn't be there, anything personal that the killer might have left behind.'

'If it's that tight, how are we going to get the body out?'

'Reid's fixed that: he's been on to a farmer he knows. Once Dorward's team have finished in there, he'll go in with a chainsaw and cut a pathway for the mortuary crew.'

'He knows what he'll see in there?'

'The body'll be covered up.'

'Fine. Why do you think the shooter hid the man,' McGuire asked suddenly, 'yet left the woman for all to see?'

'I reckon he's playing games, running blockers, trying to distract us, making us use up our resources doing all this stuff.'

'I think I agree with you. He's using up the first vital hours after the crime. He's smart and he knows his statistics. Most murders are solved within a couple of days; those that aren't might never be.'

'He may have picked the wrong force, though. How many unsolved homicides have we got on our books?'

'One or two,' the head of CID pointed out, 'including one in this very village. Twenty-five years on and we still haven't cleared it up.'

'In the DCC's home town?'

'Indeed. It was before his time here.'

'Still . . .'

'I know what you mean: he wouldn't let it lie. And he didn't. He reckons he's solved it. As for clearing it off our books, he says that God's done that already.'

'I could do with his help on this one, sir,' said Steele.

'God's or Bob Skinner's?' McGuire grunted. 'In the absence of either, you'd better carry on with the search of the area, and get the body out of here. I'll call Brian Mackie and let him know what's happened; right now he's giving the woman's dad the VIP treatment. Midday tomorrow, I'm taking a press briefing accompanied by Mr Davor Boras.'

He caught the inspector's surprised expression. 'ACC's decision,' he explained. 'Before that, though, you and I are going to interview Boras and his wife, in their suite at the Caledonian Hotel. Some time between now and then, I suggest that you get home to Maggie.'

Steele nodded. 'I called her a while back, as soon as the dogs found the body. She knows I'll be late. I'm sorry I had to break into your evening, though.'

'Don't worry about it. You had to, and that's that. There's one thing you could do for me, though.'

'What's that?'

'You could recommend somewhere to eat around here.'

'Bar meal okay?'

'No, no, Stevie.' The big detective beamed. 'This is Paula we're talking about.'

'Ah,' the inspector chuckled, 'you mean expensive.'

Twenty-five

'Why do I have to come here? Why is my daughter still in this place?'

'First and foremost,' Brian Mackie began, 'because she hasn't been formally identified. But once that is done, release of her body must be authorised by the fiscal's office.'

'Who?' Keith Barker exclaimed.

'The procurator fiscal; that's the Scottish legal title for the public prosecutor at local level. He's a part of the Crown Office, which is headed by the Lord Advocate . . . that's the Scottish equivalent of the Attorney General.

'I should explain that in criminal investigations the police act as agents of the fiscal, and report to his office. So Zrinka is in his care, not ours. I should warn you, though, that in homicide investigations it's quite common for the body to be retained for some time. Once an arrest's been made, there could be circumstances in which the defence requires a second autopsy.'

'This can't be!' Boras protested. 'I can't allow this.'

'Let's deal with that later,' said Mackie, firmly. 'First things first: let's get the formal identification over with.'

He opened the front passenger door of the car and

stepped out into the small courtyard in front of the square, grey single-storey building on the Cowgate, at its junction with Infirmary Street. He could understand the father's distress. The mortuary was an ugly building, bleak and forbidding. He hated having to take family members there to see the remains of their loved ones, but since the council's so-called refurbishment of the building there was usually no alternative.

He led his two companions to the door, opened it, and held it for them. Walton Blackwell, the mortuary superintendent, was waiting for them; he had been fully briefed about the visitors. 'Mr Mackie, gentlemen,' he said, 'we're ready for you. The viewing room is this way.'

Boras stepped forward; his personal assistant made to follow him, but his employer put a hand on his sleeve. 'No, Barker, this I do myself.'

'Mr Blackwell and I have to come with you,' Mackie explained gently. 'It's part of the formality: your identification has to be witnessed.'

'I understand that.'

The superintendent led the way into a small windowless chamber; there was an extractor fan set in the ceiling, whirring noisily. A trolley lay directly below it, and on it, a human figure, under a white sheet.

'Ready?' asked Blackwell. As Boras nodded assent, he drew back the cover, to reveal the dead face. 'Is this the body of your daughter, Zrinka?'

The question was unnecessary, they all knew why they were there, but Mackie had to put it. He gazed at the man, expecting him to crack, to break down, as most visitors did in there at such a time. But Davor Boras held himself upright, his face impassive and his broad shoulders square; he gazed at the pale, lifeless girl for several seconds, and then he said, 'Yes,' crisply, turned on his heel and marched out of the room.

The ACC followed, expecting him to stop in the reception area, but he did not. With a gesture of command to Barker, he strode into the courtyard, opened the car door and slid inside.

'I'll need you to sign a formal statement,' Mackie told him, when the three were together once more.

'Of course. Now take us back to the hotel, please. I must be with my wife.'

'Sure. Wattie, take us to the Caley.'

'You will speak to your fiscal, Mr Mackie,' Boras exclaimed. 'You will tell him that my daughter's body must be returned to her family. Her mother cannot see her in this place and, besides, we must take her home.' For the first time, a trace of an Eastern European accent sounded in his voice.

Assistant chief constables are unused to orders, especially from civilians, but Brian Mackie had sympathy with the man. 'I'll be happy to put your request to him,' he replied. 'In this case, I can see no good reason not to release her. There are no grounds for dispute that I can see: the cause of death is very clear and there were no other physical injuries. However, I have to repeat that it's his decision.'

'If he is difficult, then go to his boss, this Lord Advocate.'

'That I can't do.'

'Then I will. I am a man of influence, sir. I have friends in government.'

'But possibly not in the Scottish government. Look, sir, let's not go looking for problems before they happen. I know the fiscal well, he's a reasonable guy and he usually takes police advice. It'll be okay, I'm sure.'

'It had better be.' Boras frowned, then fixed his piercing eyes on the police officer. 'Tell me everything, sir. Tell me everything about how my daughter died. Don't soft-soap me; don't play things down. I want to know exactly what was done to her.'

'She was found yesterday morning, on a beach about twenty miles east of Edinburgh, near a village called Gullane.'

'That is where the golf courses are?'

Mackie was taken by surprise. 'Yes, do you know it?'

'Golf is my one form of relaxation, now that I am too old for more strenuous games. I am a member of the new Archerfield Club, and I have played all the other courses there.'

'When you played there, was your family with you?'

'Not every time, but the first time, yes. I played on Muirfield fifteen years ago and we took rooms in Greywalls Hotel.'

'Can you remember whether your wife took your children to the beach while you played?'

'Yes, she did. I recall that they crossed the course to get there. Is that significant?'

'It may explain why Zrinka chose to go there. She was last seen alive on Monday night in Gullane, getting off a bus she had caught in North Berwick, with a male companion. They camped overnight in the bushes, near the beach. We found their tent this afternoon.'

'This man; he killed her?'

'No.'

'What makes you so sure?'

'He's dead too. We found his body this evening, hidden in the bushes. We haven't had time to examine him, but I'm sure we'll find that he was shot too.'

'Shot?'

'Yes. Your daughter was killed by a single shot to the back of the head, Mr Boras, fired at close range. For what it's worth, the officers who attended the scene believe that she never knew a thing, and the autopsy bears that out. There are no marks on her body, nothing that would indicate a struggle.'

'Thank you, I will tell my wife that.'

'I hope it helps.'

'It will not, but I will tell her anyway. What progress have you made?'

'We're still trawling for witnesses, people who might have been on the beach yesterday, around the time of the murder. So far, we haven't found any.'

'Do you expect to?'

'To be honest? No, I don't. We believe that we're confronted by a very resourceful, efficient murderer, someone who takes great care to leave no trace of himself at the scene. That's not easy, these days, given our forensic resources, but so far he's succeeded.'

'Could this be a professional hit, Mr Mackie?' asked Barker.

'I thought we'd dealt with that earlier,' the ACC replied, uncharacteristically brusque. 'It isn't, at least not in the sense you mean. The person who shot Zrinka has killed at least one other woman that we know of.'

'When?' Boras snapped.

'Two months ago, on the other side of Edinburgh. Like your daughter, she was killed on the seashore early in the morning.'

'You're telling me that you had two months to catch this animal, but you failed. You allowed him to remain at liberty, you allowed him to kill my Zrinka.' His voice rose, climbing to reach a crescendo of rage.

'I can't deny any of that, sir,' Mackie admitted. 'Our priority now is to find him before he does it again.'

Twenty-six

'Seven thirty!' Alex exclaimed, as she opened the front door. 'Bloody cops: you're all the same.'

'Sorry,' said Griff Montell, hanging his head like a guilty dog. 'I did phone; you have to give me that.'

'Yes,' she retorted, 'and I told you that by eight thirty I'd be long gone from here. So what the hell are you doing ringing my doorbell?'

'Spring said that she hadn't heard you go out,' he told her bravely, if a little tentatively. 'So why the hell are you still here?'

'Why do you think? Because I'm not so bloody liberated that I like trawling bars and restaurants on my own.' Finally she relented and allowed him a small smile. 'Come on in.'

He stepped into the flat. 'Where do you want to go?'

'Nowhere.' She reached up and rubbed the back of her hand against his chin. 'Griff, you look knackered, plus you need a shave: I wouldn't be seen dead with you like that. I've cooked something for us . . . against my better judgement, mind you.'

'How did you know I'd ring your bell, me being so late and all?'

'I told your sister to send you in when you got back; from what you said she was subtle about it.' She frowned at him. 'Before you get any ideas about the two of us around the supper table, I asked her if she'd like to join us, but she'd already eaten.'

'What sort of ideas would I get?' he asked, affecting an innocent expression.

'None that are going to do you any good.'

'I could go next door and shave, if that would help.'

'Not in the tiniest,' she answered sincerely. 'We've had one fling, you and I, and it was very satisfactory, but we agreed afterwards that it was just between friends, and that we weren't going to let it become a habit. What you can do, though, is come into the kitchen and grab yourself a beer from the fridge, while I finish throwing the salad together.'

Griff winked at her as he followed her out of the living room. 'That sounds like a decent compromise,' he conceded. 'What are we having, apart from the salad? I'm not being presumptuous,' he added. 'You did say you'd been cooking.'

'It's a chicken casserole, Spanish style, a recipe I picked up from my dad.'

'He cooks too?'

'You better believe it; while I was growing up he didn't have the option. Now he's a one-parent family again, he has a live-in nanny to do that for the kids, but he still has to fend for himself, and cook for them all at weekends.'

'How long was he on his own after your mother died?'

'About fifteen years,' she told him, 'and he really was on his own too. If there were any women around, I never knew about them. I was so pleased for him when he took up with Sarah.'

'I suppose you must have been gutted when they split up.'

'Only for the three kids. The pair of them had grown well apart by then, so it was for the best. I'm glad that they came to an amicable agreement about parenting, even if it does put most of the responsibility on him.'

'What if she remarries and wants to change the deal?' he asked.

'Then she'll have to go to court in Scotland,' Alex replied, 'and take me on into the bargain. But that won't happen. Sarah left for her career. Truth is, she's doctor first, mother second. Damn!' she exclaimed suddenly, in the act of taking the lid off the casserole dish.

'What's up?'

'I left my apron in my bedroom. Be a honey and get it for me, will you? I've got my hands full here, and this may splash when I stir it.'

'Sure. I remember where your bedroom is . . . even if it is off limits now.' He laid his beer on the breakfast bar and headed off on his errand.

Alex replaced the lid and waited for him, easing off her oven glove so that she would be able to tie on the apron when it arrived. He was gone for longer than she expected. She assumed that he had gone into the bathroom en route, until she heard him call to her. 'Come through here, will you, please?'

'Griff,' she called back, 'what is it? If you're thinking of chancing your arm, you'll be wearing this bloody supper.'

'I'm serious. I need to talk to you.'

Puzzled by his sudden change of mood, she did as he asked. She found him standing at the foot of her bed, staring at a picture set on the wall above the headboard. 'Has that always been there?' he asked.

'It's been there since I got it. You've seen it before; it was there when we did our thing. Obviously you were too preoccupied to notice it at the time. Why? What's so special about it?'

'This morning I found myself looking at a houseful of work by the same artist. You know who did this?'

'I confess that I don't.'

'Stacey Gavin, the girl who was murdered in South Queensferry two months ago, killed we now know by the same man who shot Zrinka Boras. Where did you get it?'

'My dad gave it to me,' she replied. 'It was my Christmas present. He's a bit of a closet connoisseur, my old man. He said I should look after it, that it was an investment. He's got one himself, out in Gullane. The picture I bought him, by the poor Boras girl, was partly to thank him. God, that's weird, isn't it? My father has work by two murdered artists hanging on his walls.'

Twenty-seven

There had been a period in his career, when he had been Bob Skinner's executive officer, when Brian Mackie had been a regular visitor to the Edinburgh procurator fiscal's office. But times had changed, and the promotion ladder had taken him back into uniform, so he felt almost a stranger as he stepped into the Chambers Street building.

The fiscal had moved on too since those days, into a grand new home, cheek by jowl with that of the Lord Advocate, of whose department he was a functionary. The assistant chief constable looked around with a slightly cynical eye. He was not comfortable with opulence in government offices: having seen his mother die in a shabby, badly painted room in an outdated, overcrowded hospital, his preference was for more spartan conditions for civil servants . . . and he counted himself among their number . . . and maximum investment in areas of greatest need.

Inevitably some detectives are antipathetic towards fiscals, seeing them as nit-picking barriers to the clearing up of a crime, rather than as players on the same team, but in his CID days, Mackie had always done his best to understand their position and the needs of the court in terms of evidence. However, from time to time, he too had found himself frustrated.

Gregor Broughton had been no roadblock, though: he and the ACC had worked together on several occasions over the years and the police officer had always found him to be constructive and co-operative. 'Hello, Brian,' he said warmly, rising from his swivel chair as Mackie was shown into his office. 'It's good to see you again, even if it is a surprise. I can't remember the last time a cop in uniform walked through that door. I was quite taken aback when my secretary said you wanted to see me. Have a seat, man, have a seat. Would you like a coffee?'

Mackie shook his head. 'No thanks, Gregor. I ration those, and it's not that long since breakfast.'

'Welcome to the world of regular office hours.' The big lawyer chuckled. 'How's Sheila?'

'She's fine. How's Phyl? I'm presuming that we're still on first-name terms since her elevation to the bench.'

'I'm not even sure I can do that, mate. Lady Broughton is very well, thank you, although it can be a bit of a bugger when she's on circuit, sitting in the High Court in places like Airdrie, Inverness and, next week, bloody Wick.'

'All new Supreme Court judges have to go through that, though, don't they?'

'Yes, it's part of the breaking-in process. It doesn't matter that we have two sons at secondary school. Mind you, it's never mattered for her male colleagues, so why should it for her? It's a part of the changing world we live in. In the old days, in the unlikely event of a woman being appointed to the bench, she'd have been a grandparent by the time it happened. The judicial appointments board has swept all that away, for better or worse. Now, when a vacancy comes up, applications are invited, and recommendations are made to the First Minister on the basis of ability and experience; there are no barriers on grounds of age or gender.'

'Which do you think, better or worse?'

'Privately? A bit of both. The principle is okay, but the practice isn't. I don't know a single lawyer who agrees with the present make-up of the board, half lay members and half professional, with a lay chair having the casting vote. Lawyers will always know better than lay people who will make a good judge.' He paused and smiled. 'Of course, my disapproval is tempered by the fact that they chose to recommend my wife.'

'Of course,' said the ACC, with a smile. 'You must be very proud of her, Gregor.'

'Pleased as Punch, my friend, and so are the boys. The thing that gives us all the biggest kick, is that she chose to use her married name as her judicial title, could have called herself Lady Anything-she-bloody-liked-within-reason, or used her maiden name. Frankly that's what I expected, since she practised as Phyllis Davidson QC. I was delighted when she told me what she'd decided.'

'There won't be any conflict of interest, will there, with you being in criminal prosecution and her being a judge?'

'None that haven't been thought of; Phyl will never try a case where I've been involved, even if it's only in the earliest stages. I'm a district fiscal: my appearances are limited to the Sheriff Court, so there's no chance of me ever appearing before her as a prosecutor.'

'You have appeared in the same court, though, haven't you?'

Broughton laughed. 'You remember that, do you? Yes, once when I had a merchant banker in the dock pleading not guilty to his third drunk-driving offence. He'd retained senior counsel who came down with appendicitis on the eve of the trial, and the dean of the Faculty of Advocates, mischievous bugger that he was, parachuted Phyl in as a replacement. She gave me a hell of a time; Sheriff Boone was most amused, and let her get away with murder . . . not that her client got away with anything at the end of the day.' He slapped his desk. 'Now, Brian, to business, since we're both busy men: what can I do for you?'

'A favour. You've got the Boras investigation on your desk, haven't you?'

'Yes. I've just been looking at the post-mortem report, in fact. It doesn't make pretty reading, especially with the Gavin investigation still open. But that's not in your court any longer, is it? McGuire's overseeing that in Bob Skinner's absence, isn't he?'

'Yes, but . . . the victim's parents are in Edinburgh, and I've been looking after them.'

'Ahh. The very wealthy Mr Boras. Is he making waves?'

'Not so far, but I have a feeling that he could if he tried.'

'Would it cut any ice with you if he did?'

'Not a single cube. No, Gregor, that isn't why I'm here. The man wants to take his daughter's body with him when he goes back to London. You can authorise that.'

The fiscal frowned. 'Just forty-eight hours into the investigation?' he murmured. 'It would be unusual.'

'Sure, but not unprecedented.'

'What about the defence interests?'

'There's no guarantee of there being any defence . . . not in the near future at any rate. It's two months down the road in the Gavin inquiry and we don't have a single suspect.'

'No, but you'll be looking for cross-overs between the two, won't you?'

'Sure, but McGuire and Steele tell me that this isn't an ordinary criminal. His tracks may be well covered. But leaving all that aside, there are no unresolved issues relating to the cause of death in either case. You released Stacey Gavin's body after eight days.'

'True. When's the man going back?'

'He wants to leave today, after he's faced the press.'

Broughton looked surprised. 'You're putting him through that ordeal, are you?'

'He's insisting on it. He has his media guru with him. They have an eye on the London Stock Exchange.'

'Jesus,' the fiscal gasped, 'some people! You know, Brian, the longer I live the more cynical I get. Let me get this clear, you said you want me to do this as a favour.'

'Yes, but not for him: I'm asking for me and for the guys in the investigation. I don't want to give Boras any reason to hang around Edinburgh. I want him out of town as quickly and as neatly as can be managed.'

'In that case, I'll do it. But I'll release the body only for burial: no cremation certificate will be issued. I must keep my arse covered to some degree, lest at some time in the future it winds up being kicked by one of my dear wife's colleagues.'

Twenty-eight

In the twenty-first century the Caledonian Hotel may carry the name of an international chain, but to Edinburgh's citizens it is still known, with simple affection, as the Caley. For over a hundred years it has stood at the west end of Princes Street, glaring along its length at its rival, the Balmoral, formerly the North British, with its red sandstone seeming to blush against the greyness of the rest of the famous thoroughfare.

For all that, the majority of Edinburghers have never set foot in its foyer, or been escorted by an usher to the lifts that carry guests to the five-star accommodation of its upper floors.

'I thought the ACC would have come with us,' said Stevie Steele, as they stepped out into a long, carpeted corridor.

'No,' Mario McGuire replied, 'he reckoned that if he did it would look as if he was making sure we behaved ourselves. But reading between the lines, I suspect that he had enough last night of Mr Boras and his bag-carrier, Barker, to do him for a while.'

They counted off the numbers until they reached their destination. Steele checked his watch to make certain that it was exactly ten a.m., then rapped on the polished wood and waited.

A tall man, immaculately dressed and groomed, opened the door; both detectives knew at once that he was Keith Barker. Mackie's description had been perfect: '*So fucking smooth it's a wonder the clothes don't slide off him, and I'm sure he wears a touch of eyeliner.*'

'Gentlemen,' he said, extending a hand first to McGuire in the assumption that as the older of the two he was the senior officer, 'you will be the police officers.'

The head of CID resisted the urge to reply, 'No, we're the fucking chambermaids.' Instead he nodded, then introduced himself and his colleague. Barker stood aside and ushered them into the suite.

Davor and Sanda Boras were seated in armchairs, he with the air of a monarch, or perhaps a Mafia don, she with the slightly vacant gaze of one who has been heavily sedated. Neither rose as the aide presented the two detectives and offered them seats on a couch that faced the couple.

A woman in a dark grey suit, worn over a black blouse, hovered behind Sanda Boras. McGuire glanced at her and then at Barker, who read his silent question. 'This is Camilla Britto,' he said, 'Mrs Boras's secretary.'

'Okay,' said the chief superintendent. 'We had assumed that we would be conducting this interview in private. On balance, I think we'd prefer that.'

'And we would not,' Davor Boras snapped. 'Miss Britto will remain, to attend to my wife's needs as they arise. Mr Barker will remain to attend to mine.'

Steele glanced to his right, looking for the first signs of an eruption, but the head of CID simply shrugged. 'If that's how you wish it, sir,' he replied.

'I will start with a question,' the stocky millionaire announced. 'What are you doing here?'

'I beg your pardon?'

'What's not to understand? I'm asking what you are doing here, talking to my wife and me, when you should be out somewhere pursuing this man who has killed our daughter, and that other poor woman.'

McGuire drew a breath; he knew that command had brought with it an added need for patience and yet there were times when it ran up against his nature.

Steele read the moment. 'You are part of the investigation, sir,' he interjected. 'We need to know everything that you know about your daughter, her recent life, her movements, her associates, because in there may be one tiny piece of information that will lead us to this man. This may seem intrusive to you, and it may even seem like a waste of our time and yours, but it is necessary.' From a corner of his eye, he saw Barker look towards his employer and give a tiny nod.

'Very well. If you say so. But how long has your investigation into the first death been running?'

'Two months.'

'Were that girl's parents of any help to you?'

'Yes, and they still are. Questions arise all the time, and often they help to answer them.'

'Okay, okay.' Boras sighed. 'Go on, then.'

'Thanks,' said McGuire. 'When was the last time either of you saw Zrinka?'

'In February. She came home to see her mother.'

'You were away at the time?'

'No, I wasn't, but she didn't come to see me.'

'Are you saying that you and she weren't close?'

Boras's tiny eyes blazed. 'I am saying that I am an extremely busy man, sir. Often I work from the moment that I rise until the moment that I retire. Zrinka knew that, and she understood. She and I got on well enough; we didn't talk a lot, that was all.'

'How long had she been in Edinburgh?'

'For almost two years.'

'Where did she live? Did she flat-share? All the records we've accessed so far show her as residing with you.'

'She had a small flat off Princes Street,' said Sanda Boras, slowly. 'It has a view of the castle. She chose it and I bought it for her.' Her husband seemed to stiffen in his chair. He stared at her, in evident surprise.

Steele frowned. 'We checked the property register yesterday,' he murmured. 'We didn't find anything with your name.'

'We used my family name, Kolar,' the mother replied. 'So my husband wouldn't know. He is a kind man, you understand, but he believes that his children should either follow him into his business or make their own way in the world. Zrinka and her brother both chose to go their own way. I agree with him, you understand, but a little help doesn't do harm. It's a nice flat. She worked there.' She smiled. 'The place was a mess, always.'

'Did she live there alone?'

'Yes. Recently, that is. There was a man not long after she

moved to Edinburgh, who stayed with her for a few months, but he moved on.'

'Did they argue?' McGuire asked.

'Not that she told me. She said that it had run its course and that he had left. If she'd been upset about it, I'd have known.'

'Did she say whether he was upset, the man?'

'She told me they were agreed, that they apart as friends.'

'Parted,' Boras grunted.

'Pardon, dear?'

'You said "apart". That is wrong. "Parted" is what you should have said.'

'I'm sorry.' She looked back towards the chief superintendent. 'I've lived here for a long time, but my English, it is not yet perfect.'

'Nobody's is, Mrs Boras; especially not mine. My Italian's probably better.'

'Italian?'

'I got that from my mother and my grandparents. My dad was Irish, a lovely man, but one of few words . . . long ones at any rate.'

'My husband's grandmother was Italian too. That is something you have in common.'

The big detective glanced at Boras: he looked impatient and irascible. 'The only thing, I reckon,' he said gently. 'Can you tell me anything about Zrinka's boyfriend, this man?'

'I never met him. I never came to visit her in Edinburgh after we bought the flat. I spoke to him only once, when I called Zrinka's mobile and he answered.'

'How did he sound? Did he have an accent?'

Mrs Boras ran her right hand over her hair. Her reddened eyes creased slightly as she frowned, trying to summon up a memory. 'He spoke well, as if he was educated: like many of the people we know in London.'

'What was his name?'

'Dominic. Dominic Padstow. That's all I can tell you about him.'

'Not him, then,' Steele murmured.

'What do you mean?' Keith Barker interrupted.

'We believe we've identified Zrinka's companion in the tent,' the inspector replied. 'We found his belongings last night in the bushes, well away from where the body was hidden. They included a photographic driver's licence in the name of Harry Paul, of Aberfeldy.'

'That should be conclusive, shouldn't it?'

'No.' Steele stared at Boras's assistant, warning him not to take the matter further. 'It still has to be formalised.'

'Does that name mean anything to either you?' asked McGuire, moving on quickly.

Boras shook his head, but his wife nodded hers. 'Zrinka mentioned him last time we spoke. She described him as her boyfriend of the moment, and that there was a good chance he could turn into more than that. She said he was nice, and seemed safe. Safe,' she whispered. 'That's ironic, isn't it?'

'When was that, Mrs Boras? The last time you spoke?'

'Sunday evening: I called her to ask what she was doing this week.'

It occurred to the head of CID that the mother was

becoming stronger the longer the interview lasted, and less reliant on her medication, while, somehow, her husband, when facing personal issues, might be the weaker of the two. 'Can you remember what she said?'

'Yes, I remember very well. She told me that she has an appointment,' her husband twitched at her linguistic slip, but said nothing, 'in North Berwick the next evening, with a gallery-owner who was interested in putting some of her work on show. She was going to take ten pictures down there, and she hoped he would take them all. She was pleased because his commission on his sales was less than the Edinburgh galleries. Zrinka was annoyed by the amount some of them wanted to charge her.'

'She sold her work from a stall, I understand,' said Steele.

'That's right. She told me that suppose she sell only one picture a week, the rent of the stall was less than the commission she would have paid to a gallery. If she sell two . . .'

Davor Boras seemed to rally. 'She was my daughter, sir,' he barked. 'She knew that the fewer people between her and the buyer, the more she would make.'

'Was she happy?' McGuire asked the mother.

'Yes.'

'You never sensed anything troubling her, especially recently?'

'No. My daughter was always happy; she loved Edinburgh, she loved her work.'

'What was her ambition?'

'She wanted to be famous in her own right. She loved to

paint people caught off-guard in unusual situations. She had her own hero; she wanted to be another Jack Vettriano, with her work on posters all around the world. She signed everything "Zrinka", with a great flourish, but never with her full name.'

'Your family owns galleries. Isn't that right?'

'Yes,' said Boras, 'but the collections there are very serious. They are not places to indulge one's daughter. Zrinka understood that she could not be hung there until she had come to justify it.'

'But you have a passion for art, too?'

'Passion? No it's strictly business: art is a good investment. If one buys, and then puts the work on public display while it appreciates, that makes sense. My galleries do not offer free admission, and they do not run at a loss.'

'I think I understand that,' McGuire conceded. 'But, if you'll forgive me, I think you have a greater interest than you're letting on. No matter, though. We know from her bank records that Zrinka was doing fairly well. Did she have any well-known customers?'

Sanda Boras smiled for the first time since they had come into the room; for the first time, Steele guessed, since the chief super from the Met had driven up to her door. 'Not really,' she said. 'She sold a picture to a footballer once; she was very pleased about that, although none of his team-mates followed his example, as far as I know. The most excited I remember her was a few months ago, early this year. She said that a man and his family had come to the stall, and that one of them, a woman, the man's daughter, although the rest of them were children, had bought a picture for him, an expensive picture. She told me that she recognised him from his picture in the papers, and that he was a very important man in Edinburgh.'

'Can you remember his name?'

'No. I don't think she say his name. I had to go before she could.'

McGuire turned back to Boras. 'Your son, sir: does he know of his sister's death?'

'Not from me,' he replied. 'Dražen and I do not speak very often, either. I have not seen him in almost a year. Nor has his mother, I believe . . .' he paused '. . . although maybe I am wrong about that.'

'No,' said his wife, quietly, subdued once more.

'You didn't give him a little help?' the head of CID asked her.

'He wouldn't ask, or accept it.'

'My son has done well enough for himself,' Boras exclaimed curtly.

'Doing what, sir?'

'Trying to prove that he is a better man than his father. Three years ago, once I had seen him through LSE and Harvard Business School, he turned his back on Continental IT, which he would have been running before he was thirty, and set up on his own, in direct competition to me, only his company runs entirely through a website. I wouldn't have minded, but there was no original thinking in it at all. Everything he did, he copied from me. The last time we spoke I told him as much. He replied that I couldn't expect to have all the market, and I should be happy with what he had left me. Hah! A website!'

'What's it called? DraženBoras dot com?'

'My son doesn't use his family name any more. He anglicised it when he went to Harvard. Now he calls himself David Barnes. His company is called Fishheads dot Com. A nonsensical title.'

'I've heard of it,' McGuire admitted. 'Nonsense maybe, but it's not a name you'd forget. It supplies our family business with bulk stationery and consumables. Paula, my partner, swears by it.'

'Mr Boras is more inclined to swear at it,' said Barker. The beginnings of a smile at his small joke appeared on his face, but vanished under his employer's glare.

'It's doing well, then?' Boras said nothing. 'I'll take that as yes,' the head of CID continued. 'Don't you think you should contact your son, though? This is going to go public very shortly.'

'I told you. We have no contact with him. My son betrayed me; he is a stranger to me and to his mother, God damn him.'

'I've tried to reach him.' Camilla Britto's voice came across the room, from a chair beside the window. 'I have a home number for him. He called me one day, and gave it to me, for use only in case of extreme family crisis. I called it this morning, while Sanda was asleep, but it was on answer mode. I left a voice message, telling him where we are, and asking him to call his parents urgently.'

Boras twisted powerfully in his chair. 'Did you not hear

what I just said? You interfere in my family affairs, woman? As soon as we get back to London, you're fired.'

'No, she's not, Davor,' his wife told him calmly. 'Camilla works for me, not you. If there's any firing to be done I'll do it, and I wouldn't start with her. She's handled this exactly the right way, as you'll see when your anger lets you think logically again.'

Twenty-nine

Maggie Rose looked around her dingy office. When she had moved in there, into a senior command position, she had not given a second's thought to the end of her police career. If by some chance she had imagined that day, she would never have foreseen that it would have come there, or then.

She smiled at the prospect, simultaneously amused and amazed that she had reached her decision.

Overnight, she had managed to put her meeting with Aldred Fine into perspective. She had done some Internet research and had seen that there were many potential explanations for her ovarian shadow. The one that she favoured was that it was a simple mistake, a misleading shading caused by the technology that had spotted it. She was confident that everything would soon be clarified and the worry removed, without Stevie ever having to learn of it. She was pleased, oddly, that her decision to leave the force had not been influenced in any way by what might be or, much more likely, might not be wrong with her.

There was a soft knock on the door. She looked up and

called, 'Enter.' It opened and a young man stepped into the room, with a hesitancy that was unusual for him.

'Yes, Sauce,' Chief Superintendent Margaret Rose said cheerfully, on her last day in command. 'What can I do for you?'

Police Constable Harold Haddock stood stiffly before her. He had changed since the day she had appointed him as her unofficial leg-man, when first she had taken temporary command of the division. The gawky lad she had seen then had grown an inch or so and had filled out. From seeming to be composed almost entirely of elbows, he had become broad-shouldered and thick-chested, someone not to be messed with in a bundle, as he had proved on street patrol on more than one occasion. Maggie was not known to play favourites, but if she had been so inclined, young Sauce Haddock would have been one of them.

'Nothing, ma'am,' he replied. 'I'm sorry if I'm being presumptuous, but I'm going to do it anyway. I know we're having a goin'-away do for you tomorrow afternoon, and I'm coming in for it, but I'm off from lunchtime today. While I've the chance I'd like to thank you, just myself, for doing so much for me.'

She swallowed, completely taken aback and uncharacteristically touched. She looked at him, masking her feelings with a straight face. 'I haven't done anything for you, Constable. Everything you've achieved so far you've done on your own merits.'

'If that's so, ma'am,' he insisted, 'it's because of your encouragement. I just want to wish you luck, and I look forward to seeing you back here when you're ready.'

'That's very kind of you, Sauce, and I don't think it's presumptuous at all.' She smiled. 'What I just said about not doing anything for you: that's not quite true.'

'I ken, ma'am.'

'No, you don't get me. I was going to tell you this later, but I might as well spill it now. You know that our CID's been flying one short since my husband stole DC Montell? By the way, he swears he didn't but he's getting the blame. Well, I've had a word with my ex-husband and with Detective Superintendent Chambers, and they're both agreed. You are the replacement.'

The young constable's face widened. 'Are you serious, ma'am?' he exclaimed. 'I reckoned I wouldn't have a chance of CID for at least another couple of years.'

'Normally you wouldn't, but this force has a recent history of picking out people with potential and giving them a chance to fulfil it. Initially you'll be working with Detective Sergeant Regan; report to him on Monday morning. Make sure you learn as much as you can from him: he's a pretty good teacher.'

'I will do, ma'am. I can't thank you enough.'

'You'll have thanked me when you're sitting behind this desk or one like it.' Her phone rang. 'On you go now,' she said, as she picked it up. 'Rose,' she exclaimed, as the door closed behind him.

'Maggie,' a woman's voice replied, 'it's Sylvia Thorpe here. I've got some information for you. I'm putting it in the post as we agreed, but I thought I should give you a run-down.'

There was something in her tone that punctured Maggie's good humour. 'Go ahead then.'

'I've found both the registrations you were after. Your grandmother's cause of death is given as uterine cancer, that's all. Your aunt Euphemia's is more specific: she died of pneumonia.'

Maggie whistled. 'Terrible thing to say but that's a relief.'

'Maybe yes, maybe not: the underlying cause was ovarian and stomach cancer.'

The butterfly that she had fluttered the day before seemed to have evolved overnight into a rending carrion bird.

'I'm sorry, Maggie,' said Thorpe. 'But if I read the reason for your request correctly, you should share this information with your consultant.'

'I plan to do that.'

'And with your husband.'

'That I will not do, until it's absolutely necessary, or unavoidable.' She drew a breath. 'Sylvia, you wouldn't do anything silly, would you?'

'No, I wouldn't, I promise. But, please, think about talking to Stevie.'

'I'll think about it,' Maggie replied. 'Be sure I'll think about it. But that's not my priority: our child is. She's more important than anyone else.'

Thirty

'Is this going to be the norm?' Alan Royston whispered.

'Ours not to reason, mate,' Mario McGuire replied.

They were standing in the office of Chief Constable Sir James Proud, by a side door and far enough away not to be overheard as the head of the force extended welcoming hospitality to Davor Boras and Keith Barker. 'I do not like these affairs,' the media manager continued. 'Why did you agree to it? Having parents at our press conferences, getting emotional and so on; I always feel uncomfortable.'

'You're a control freak, Alan, that's your problem.'

'Too fucking right I am, especially when we're briefing on a very difficult homicide, with nothing positive to say.'

'Hey, come on. Stevie and I got new lines of enquiry from our interview with the parents, and I'm going to tell the media as much.'

'Why did the mother not come? Is she flaky, or half comatose with Valium?'

'No, she's together, but she's a background player in this family. He's the main man, or has to be seen to be at any rate.'

'Okay, but what's that smarmy bastard Barker doing

sticking his nose in? This is the first time I've ever had to clear a press release with someone outside the official circle.'

'The ACC says that's the way they wanted it, and that he saw no good reason to interfere. Did you moan to him about it?'

'No,' Royston confessed.

'Would you have moaned to big Bob if he was here, and had given it the okay?'

'No.'

'So why the fuck are you moaning to me?'

'Sorry, Mario. It strikes me as unprofessional, that's all. It has a showbiz feel about it.'

'Now you're getting to the heart of it. Brian Mackie didn't say as much, but Boras's presence isn't about the girl. It's about business. It's about the stock-market analysts, letting them see that whatever happens in his private life, he's still very much in control.'

'You're kidding!' Royston hissed. 'His daughter's been murdered and he's more concerned about his fucking company?'

'That's the way it looks to me.'

'I've seen it all now.'

'I used to think that too, but I know I never will.' McGuire checked his watch. 'That's it. Twelve on the dot. Time to go downstairs and get the event under way.'

Barker caught the gesture, rose from his seat and crossed the room towards them. 'You're clear about how this is going to run?' he murmured to Royston. 'You introduce Mr McGuire, he reads the announcement for the camera, then

I introduce Mr Boras and he makes a personal statement.'

'No,' said the head of CID, firmly. 'It'll just be me and your boss at the top table.'

'But your assistant chief promised me . . .'

'I doubt that he was that precise and, anyway, he's far too shrewd to be here. I'm running this thing, and I'm telling you how it will be.'

Barker's sandy hair seemed to quiver. 'I'll ask Sir James to override you,' he hissed.

The big detective smiled at him. 'You try that and two things will happen: one, the chief will tell you very politely to fuck off; and two, I'll take it personally. Trust me, both of those events would be unfortunate for you.' He patted the aide on the shoulder, as if in consolation. 'Mr Boras,' he called out, 'if you're ready . . .'

'Yes.' The man stood, and shook hands with the chief constable, who wished him luck, then followed McGuire out into the command corridor. An unfeasibly tall figure waited outside the door, Detective Sergeant Jack McGurk, Bob Skinner's executive assistant. 'I've just had word from Dr Brown at the mortuary, boss,' he said. 'We've confirmed the identification of Harry Paul. It seems he had a steel plate put in his right leg after a motorbike accident when he was eighteen. They took an X-ray of the body, and found it.'

'Okay.' He looked up. 'You ready for Monday?'

'Yes, sir.'

'What about Monday?' asked Royston, as the party moved on.

'I'm sending Jack to CID at Torphichen Place, working under George Regan as acting DI. Mary Chambers needs reinforcements while she's covering for Maggie. I did think about sending my guy, Sammy Pye, but my needs are greater than the DCC's at this moment.'

The quartet walked downstairs and took a left turn along another corridor, which led them directly into the briefing room. 'Mr Boras,' said McGuire, 'if you'll accompany me, we'll begin.'

Barker gave his employer a look that was more of a plea than anything else; it was ignored.

Seated behind a table, and before a backboard carrying the force logo, the detective chief superintendent looked around the room. He saw five television cameras, but did not bother to try to count the number of reporters gazing back at him.

'Good afternoon,' he began. 'I'm Mario McGuire, head of CID. You have our press release, but for the record I'll state that we are now in a position to name the woman found shot dead on a beach near Gullane on Tuesday. She was Miss Zrinka Boras, aged twenty-four, a full-time artist, the only daughter of the businessman Mr Davor Boras and Mrs Sanda Boras. Miss Boras had lived in Edinburgh for around two years prior to her death. She spent Monday night camping above Gullane beach, with a male companion. That young man was also found dead near the scene, yesterday evening, and a postmortem examination has confirmed that he was shot with the same gun that killed Miss Boras.' He paused, for only a second, but time enough for a chorus of questions to be fired at him.

He held up a hand and waited for quiet. 'Now for what isn't in the press release. As of two minutes ago, I'm in a position to name him as Mr Harry Paul, aged twenty-three, a musician, of Aberfeldy, Perthshire, the son of Travers and Marietta Paul. I'm also prepared to tell you that these murders are linked beyond doubt to that of Stacey Gavin, of South Queensferry, who was found dead two months ago, on the shore near her home. Stacey was also an artist.' He gazed out at his audience.

'I know that's going to lead to many columns and broadcast hours of media speculation. That's up to you: I understand it, but we're not going to comment on it in any way. We'll be too busy looking at the links between these brutal killings, the obvious and the less obvious, until we find the thread that will lead us to the person who carried them out. I'm not going to set specific times for future briefings. When we have something to tell you, we'll call you, be sure of that.

'Now, before you all start shouting at me again, I want to introduce the gentleman on my left. As I'm sure many of you are aware, he is Zrinka's father, Mr Davor Boras, and he has a statement that he would like to make.'

This time, as McGuire stopped speaking, the room remained absolutely silent. Boras straightened in his chair, flexed his shoulders and gazed, coldly and deliberately, into each television camera, one after another. Finally, he let his eyes rest on the journalists in the front rank. Most were strangers to Edinburgh, and McGuire realised that the man knew some of them. He understood, without asking, that they had been summoned there by Barker, who had taken a seat at the end of the row.

'I am a strong man,' Boras began. He carried no notes,

and spoke either spontaneously or from a memorised speech. 'I am a successful man. I am a rich man. Yet the strongest, most successful and the richest man can be brought down by a tragedy such as my wife, my son Dražen and I have suffered. I am here today to tell you that I will not be brought down.

'I am also a determined man,' he continued, 'and I find myself made even more determined by my daughter's death. You will know that in my business career I have created not one but two globally successful companies. I pledge to you that the same energy which enabled me to do that will be placed behind the search for my Zrinka's murderer, and I pledge to you that it will succeed.

'I stand four-square behind the police investigation and, although the murder of poor Miss Gavin remains unsolved, I have every confidence in them. Nevertheless, I appreciate that their resources are not infinite. I am a man of enormous personal wealth, and I am prepared to devote it to this manhunt. I will begin by announcing a reward of one million pounds . . .' The silence was broken by a collective gasp as the day's principal headline was determined. '. . . for information leading to the elimination of this beast. I make you this final promise.' As he stared again along the line of cameras, his little eyes became dazzling, mesmeric. 'I will ensure suitable justice for my daughter's death, as sure as my name is Davor Boras. Thank you.'

He rose from the table without a glance at his companion, beckoned to Barker, and strode from the room with his aide following at his heels.

McGuire looked at the media assembly, still stunned into a silence that was, in his experience, unique. Finally the arthritic hand of John Hunter, unofficial dean of the Edinburgh press cadre, rose into the air. The head of CID nodded. 'Yes, John.'

'Tell me if I'm right, Mario,' the old man asked, in his deceptively strong voice. 'Did he just promise, on national television, to kill a man?'

Thirty-one

'You could be forgiven for thinking that.' Stevie Steele answered the question as he, Griff Montell and Tarvil Singh stared at the live Sky News broadcast in the Leith CID office. He pointed his remote at the wall-mounted television and switched it off. 'But he chose his words very carefully.'

'Do you think he told anyone in advance that he was going to offer a reward?' asked Montell.

'No chance, or he'd never have been allowed to do it. I'm sure he told nobody on our side, that is. I'll bet you that creep Barker knew, though. Did you see Mario glare at him when Boras came out with it? I thought he was going to reach across and throttle him.'

'What's so bad about it?' Singh grumbled. 'The guy's mega-minted. If somebody killed my kid I'd want to tear him apart. I'd put up a reward if I had the money.'

'The principle's fine,' Steele replied. 'It's the practice that's difficult for us. We need a clear path on this investigation: we need precise and useful information. Thanks to Boras, we're going to have dickheads from all over bombarding us with useless witness claims, yet we'll have to check them all out. Congratulations, big man: with Ray Wilding still out at Gullane co-ordinating interviews you've just talked yourself into that job.'

'What's he going to get at Gullane, sir?' the South African enquired. 'The trail's pretty cold now.'

The inspector frowned at him. 'As far as the girl and young Paul are concerned, maybe, but what about the killer? He arrived there some time, he stalked them and he left. How did he get there, how did he leave? I want to track as many vehicle movements in and out of Gullane as I can. If it was an urban area we might have had the possibility of CCTV film, but out there we have to do it the hard way. We need to talk to as many people as we can find who drove out of the village on Tuesday morning, to see if any of them saw anything unusual, somebody in an exceptional hurry, for example.'

'Maybe he never left Gullane,' the South African murmured. 'Maybe he's local.'

'What makes you say that?'

'I'm just following the only link we have so far between the two girls.'

'We have one, apart from their occupations?'

'Yes.' Montell's face split into a wicked grin. 'DCC Skinner owns work by them both. Alex told me.'

Steele threw him a dark look. 'I think we'll just leave that one on the back burner, Constable, shall we? Look, you want to be a real detective, stop fucking me about and check out some leads. We know that Zrinka went to North Berwick to drop off some work for sale in a gallery. I want you to find out where that was, and how many they took.

Her art bag was empty when we found it, and we think that the killer took a souvenir from Stacey Gavin, so maybe . . .'

'The DCC's expanding his collection?'

The inspector's look turned the deepest black. 'Shut the fuck up, Griff, or I'll pass your thoughts on to him or, better still, to Alex. She'd have your nuts in a vice if she heard you joke about her old man like that.'

Montell frowned defensively. 'Why should it be a joke? You can't deny it's a link. Why shouldn't we follow it up?'

'Because some of us value our careers. Now go and do what you're fucking told.'

His gaze switched to Singh. 'Tarvil, while you're waiting for the crank calls to start, I want you to track down a man called Dominic Padstow, Zrinka's old boyfriend. That's all I know about him; just the name. Then get in touch with Stacey Gavin's parents. There was no sign in the initial investigation that she and Zrinka knew each other, but double-check it. Run the guy Padstow's name past Stacey's folks too, and see if it means anything to them.'

He looked at Montell. 'Griff, once you've made those calls to North Berwick, I want you to take Zrinka's PDA, and go through her contacts file. See if any names there appear in Stacey Gavin's circle of friends as well.'

He stood, ushering them towards the door. 'While you're doing that, I've got a job of my own to handle. Dražen Boras hasn't surfaced yet, according to his mother and her secretary. There's something worrying about that; I reckon it's time we tracked him down.'

Thirty-two

'It's just as well we had that slap-up meal in La Potinière last night,' said Paula Viareggio, 'and the bacon rolls for breakfast, for the way you looked on telly an hour ago, you were ready to eat somebody.'

'I was,' Mario replied wryly, 'but the dish of the day slipped out of the kitchen before I could ram a skewer through him.'

'You'll see him again, though?'

'Barker? No, he's going back to London with his boss. Brian Mackie talked the fiscal into authorising the release of Zrinka's body this morning. It was picked up from the morgue by an undertaker, and it'll be on board their aircraft when they fly out of Turnhouse in an hour.'

'Just as well for him, by the sound of it.'

'If you think I looked angry, you should have seen Alan Royston afterwards. I've never thought of him as an emotional bloke, but he was spitting feathers. He started with "unprofessional", "discourteous" and went on until he was using adjectives I hadn't heard in years.'

'Huh! That's saying something,' she grunted. 'What about the million? Is that going to make problems for you?'

'It'll be a nuisance for Stevie and the team,' he admitted, 'but nothing they can't handle. Anyway, that's pure bloody window-dressing. I'm more worried about Boras's attitude.'

'You mean the barely veiled threat he made?'

'Nah, I don't read too much into that: he's lost his daughter, he's bursting with rage. No, I'm concerned because although he said publicly that he's right behind us, I'm not sure that's true in private. He has political clout, and if we don't get a result soon, we may find it aimed at us.'

'Don't you have political clout too?'

'What do you mean?'

'Come on, I've heard the stories about Bob Skinner and the new First Minister.'

'Boras's influence is in London, and probably heavyweight. His foundation donates to both Labour and the Tories. But maybe I'm misjudging the guy. Maybe I'm misjudging my own troops as well. We might have an arrest by the weekend, and all my concerns will be academic. But that's not what my gut tells me: it says it's not going to be as easy as that. So we can't allow ourselves to be distracted by Boras: we have to concentrate on the job in hand.'

'Good for you. Where are you now? I can hear traffic noise.'

'I'm on my way up to Perthshire, to see the parents of the victim Paul.'

'Alone?'

'For now. It's in the Tayside area, so I had to clear it with Rod Greatorix, my opposite number up there. He told Andy Martin and Andy's decided to sit in on it with me.'

'That's good,' Paula declared. 'You'll have a familiar face

alongside you when you see them. It sounds like an unpleasant task.'

'Telling a couple their son was half eaten by foxes? "Unpleasant" could be an understatement.'

Thirty-three

'Dominic Padstow,' Tarvil Singh growled. 'Just who the hell are you?'

'You not having any luck?' asked Griff Montell.

'Not so far. There are no Padstows in the phone book for Edinburgh. There are none of them on the electoral roll, or on the valuation roll. This guy might have been in the city once, but he's no' here now.'

'Not necessarily: he could be registered to vote somewhere else, he could be living in digs, and he could have a mobile rather than a landline. How about criminal convictions? Does he have any of them?'

'Where d'you think I checked first?' the big Sikh snapped.

'Sorry. How about the Passport Office?'

'Done that too, but the Data Protection Act restricts the information they can give us. The guy isn't a suspect; and so he has rights to privacy.'

'Where do you go next? Inland Revenue?'

'I'd run up against the same problems there. No, I'll try the Gavin parents, like the DI said.'

'Good luck, mate!' Montell exclaimed, with feeling.

Singh picked up his phone, checked a number scrawled on a pad on his desk, and dialled. He hoped that his sigh of relief did not show, when Russ Gavin, home from work for lunch as usual, answered the call. Mrs Gavin was a nice woman, totally overwhelmed by a loss that no mother ever deserved, and she had the sympathy of all the detectives who had come in contact with her. However, they were all agreed that she was, as Ray Wilding had put it, 'as much use as a chocolate teapot'.

'DC Singh,' said Stacey's father, 'what can I do for you? Two calls in two days, first Mr Montell, now you: the investigation seems to be picking up pace again. It's tragic that it's taken two more deaths to do it, though.'

'I couldn't agree more, sir.'

'Hey,' he exclaimed, 'don't take that as a criticism. I'm not getting at you, honest, or at Mr Montell. The only guy I've got a down on was that clown in uniform who accused Stacey of being a junkie. I appreciate that you and all the rest of the CID team are doing your best.'

'No problem, sir. We're our own worst critics, I promise you. I want to ask you about the second victim, Miss Boras. She and your daughter were both young full-time artists working in Edinburgh. We're looking for any links between them, and we need to start by establishing whether they ever met, whether they knew each other.'

'Not to my knowledge,' the man replied. 'Hold on, though, my wife's here. I'll ask her. Doreen, the police need to know if Stacey was acquainted with the second girl who's just been murdered.' Singh heard an indistinct mumble in the background. 'Boras,' said Gavin, across his living room.

'Zrinka Boras.' The detective waited, but the answer came quickly. 'She's shaking her head. No, it doesn't mean anything to her either. I don't think it's a name we would have forgotten if Stacey had ever mentioned it.'

'No, sir, I don't imagine so.'

'What was she like?' asked Gavin, quietly.

Singh thought he heard his voice falter slightly. 'She seems to have been a very nice woman,' he told him. 'Just like your Stacey,' he added. 'Killed for no reason that we've yet been able to establish. She came from a wealthy background; her dad's a famous man but she wouldn't use his name to get on. She wanted to make her own way in the world, with little or no help from her parents, and like your Stacey, she was succeeding.'

'God, it's tragic, isn't it?' Gavin sighed. 'Can you imagine the mind of a man who would do something like that? Oops, sorry, I should have said "person". I'm jumping to gender conclusions.'

'No, you're all right there, sir,' the detective reassured him. 'We're more or less certain that we're looking for a man. The way the third victim's . . . the boy's . . . body was concealed would have taken a lot of strength. But, no, I can't imagine his mind. That's one of the reasons he's been difficult to catch so far: we've got no idea what his motive is.'

'He's an art critic.' Singh could almost hear Gavin wince as soon as the sentence had escaped from his lips. 'Jesus, that sounds terrible coming from me. You don't want to see the way my wife's looking at me.'

'That's been said already, sir, among our lot, and it'll be

said again too, so don't give yourself a kicking over it. Anyhow, it's right, in a way: the link between the victims' occupations gives us a line of enquiry. For now, though, we're concentrating on finding personal links between them, mutual acquaintances, and so on. I'd like to put a name to you, to see if it means anything.'

'Fire away.'

'Dominic Padstow.'

'Dominic Padstow?' Russ Gavin repeated. 'Dominic Padstow.' The detective constable sat patiently through a long silence. 'There was a Dominic, once, a year or so back, when Stacey was still at art college, but I don't remember his surname . . . if, indeed, I ever knew it.'

'He was a boyfriend?'

'I suppose so. She was living in a student flat in town at that point, so Doreen and I weren't really up to speed with her, er, romantic life. She did bring him to the house once, though.'

'You met him?'

'Yes, it was at the weekend. They arrived out of the blue, she introduced him as her friend Dominic, then whisked him up to her studio in the attic.'

'Can you describe him?'

'Roughly, I suppose. As I recall, he was a bit older than Stacey; yes, I recall mentioning that to Doreen at the time. I said that he was getting on a bit to be a student . . . although to be fair to the chap she didn't introduce him as such.'

'How much older?'

'He'd be about thirty.'

'Did he look like a student? Was he dressed like one?'

'A bit smarter than that, I suppose. He wore denims and a check shirt.' There was a sound in the background. 'What's that, dear? You sure? Okay. Doreen says that the shirt was Paul Smith. She noticed the label; she says they're pricey.'

'I'm an M & S man myself, sir,' Singh volunteered. 'Can you give me a physical description?'

'He was around the same height as me, I'd say, five ten, well built, but not fat, strong-looking, well groomed . . . By that I mean he was clean-shaven and his hair was longish, but properly cut. Now that I think about it, he didn't really look like a student. He had a more affluent air than that.'

'She never mentioned a surname? You're sure?'

'Certain. She only ever called him Dominic, or Dom.'

'How long did they see each other?'

'A few months.'

'Might it have carried on up to the time of her death?'

'No,' Gavin replied firmly. 'When Stacey graduated and moved back in with us to save money while she built up her reputation, and established regular sales, I asked her about him, "How's Dom?" just casually. She just smiled and said, "He's off down the road," her way of saying that it was all over. She wasn't upset, though,'

'Mmm.' Singh paused. 'I don't suppose you found a photo of him, sir, among your daughter's personal stuff? Maybe something taken *in* a group?'

The father chuckled. 'No, but I can do better than that.'

'What do you mean?'

'His portrait's upstairs. Stacey painted him. That's what

they were doing up in the attic: he was sitting for her. That's how I know he's well built: it's a nude.'

'She kept it?'

'Yes. I was up in the studio one day and she showed me it. She said that she'd have given it to him, but that he didn't stick around long enough.'

'Is it . . . how do I put this, sir? Is it a good likeness of him?'

'I can only speak for the part above the neck, Mr Singh, but if the rest of him is as near lifelike as that, he's an impressive bloke.'

In other circumstances Singh might have laughed, but his mind was focused. 'Would you mind if I borrowed it, sir? If it's that good I'd like to copy it. We may need to find this man.'

Gavin's tone became serious once more. 'Sure. Come on out; I'll look it out and bubble-wrap it for you. Handle it carefully, though.'

'Be sure of that, sir. It'll be as precious to me as it is to you and Mrs Gavin.'

Thirty-four

'You know, Andy,' said Mario McGuire, 'if I ever aspire to chief officer rank, which I won't, by the way, I'd like it to be in a place like this.'

'There's worse,' Deputy Chief Constable Andrew Martin conceded, as the two men stared along the length of Loch Tay. 'But you have scenery as nice as this in the patch you're in just now. There are some lovely spots in East Lothian and down in the borders.'

'True, but the incidence of crime in those spots is remarkably low, and crime is what I do, remember.'

'And out here . . . In fact, the incidence of anything is bloody rare out here. Why do you think I grabbed the chance to chum you on this interview?'

'Do I detect that you've had enough of the silvery Tay?' McGuire quizzed.

'Let's just say that I don't plan to spend the rest of my life here.'

'And Proud Jimmy goes next year.'

'And Bob's in line to succeed him,' said Martin, quickly. 'There are other jobs; there's Aberdeen, for example, then there's Glasgow. They'll be looking for a deputy in the

Strathclyde force next year. But who says I'm stuck in Scotland? The chief in Northumbria has only two years to go, and there's the Thames Valley area.'

'You're a jock copper, Andy; you wouldn't go south. Plus, I seem to remember that you never sold Karen's flat in Edinburgh after the two of you got married, so you're still on the property ladder there.'

Martin laughed. 'Stop being a bloody detective, man. Let's get serious and go and see these people.'

They climbed back into the deputy chief's car. They had met up at the tourist office at Aberfeldy, but the Paul family lived not in the town itself but a short distance away. The stop-off in the tiny village of Kenmore, where the River Tay flows into the loch that bears its name, had been made simply to allow them to catch up with each other's news.

'Do you know anything about the couple?' McGuire asked, as they drove off.

'Why should I?' the DCC replied. 'This is your interview; I'm just the legal necessity here.'

'Because old detectives never die, and they never talk to people on a business basis without knowing as much as they can in advance.'

'Okay, I admit it, I ran a check. Colonel Travers Paul is fifty-six, and he's retired. He was educated at Strathallan School, went to Sandhurst and served in the army for twelve years, until he was invalided out post-Falklands. From there, he joined a big tobacco company, and was a senior executive, working in Africa and latterly in the US, until he chucked it four years ago. He still has a consultancy role with the firm, but he spends most of his time in voluntary work. He's chair of the community council, and he and his wife have owned their present home for seventeen years. His interests include fishing . . . he's a supporter of the Atlantic Salmon Trust . . . and he's a regular at Pitlochry Festival Theatre. He and his wife Marietta have been married for twenty-eight years and Harry was their only son. I got all that from his official biog on the council website. They're members of the Church of Scotland, and regular attenders at the parish church in Aberfeldy. She's active in the care group, and in the guild. I got that from the minister. Harry, on the other hand, hasn't been seen in the place since he chucked the local youth group when he was seventeen, after what was described as an "incident" at a dance where his band was playing. According to the long-serving local constable, it involved his being caught by one of the supervising adults, horizontal jogging behind the kirk during a break, with a girl from Pitlochry. There was a row, the bloke said something crude about the lass, young Harry chinned him, and his band never finished the gig.'

'Pitlochry's beyond the pale around here, is it?' McGuire chuckled. Then he frowned. 'Poor lad. Shagging never did him a lot of good, did it? First it got him kicked out of the church and then it got him shot in the head.'

'Let's not put that thought to the parents,' Martin murmured. He drew to a halt as he saw a police vehicle parked by the roadside, then got out and walked towards the uniformed officers who were standing beside it. They saluted as he approached. 'Any press turned up?' he asked the older of the two, a sergeant.

'Quite a few, sir,' the heavily built man replied. 'We've had a couple of television crews, some photographers, and a freelance scribbler who covers the area around here, all more or less at the same time. We told them that the Pauls aren't seeing anybody, and most of them understood that. The local guy knows the colonel; he told me he'd spoken to him on the phone already, but he wasn't letting on to the rest. One of the television reporters got a bit stroppy, but she realised it wasn't getting her anywhere so she shut up. They all took some shots of the house and the loch, hung about for a while, then pissed off.'

'Fine. That's probably all you'll have, but stay here for another two hours, just in case. We'll go on up to the house.'

He returned to his car, drove past the patrol vehicle and turned off the loch-side road into a long drive that led up to an impressive stone villa. The roadway was covered by a heavy layer of red gravel chips, which crunched under the tyres, giving an audible warning of their approach.

As they drew up at the front-door steps, a tall man walked round from the side of the house. He wore a green sweater over a white shirt, and his dark trousers were tucked into an outsized pair of old-fashioned wellington boots. His complexion was ruddy, and crinkly grey hair was swept back from his forehead.

'You'll be the police,' he exclaimed, in a crusty accent that sounded only faintly Scottish. He focused on the fair-haired ACC. 'And you'll be Mr Martin,' he added. 'I recognise you from your picture in the last community newsletter.'

'That's right, Colonel Paul, and this is DCS McGuire from Edinburgh.'

'Colonel, eh?' Travis Paul retorted. 'You've been doing your homework. My military handle's only used in official publications these days; my company's annual report, that sort of stuff. You'll be getting used to this, Mr McGuire,' he said to the detective grimly. 'I suppose you'll have had a similar meeting with the Boras girl's parents.'

'There are some things that you never get used to, sir.'

'I suppose not.' He sighed; his face bore the lines of one who had missed a night's sleep. 'I had that duty myself, in the army, a long time ago. I lost a few men in Ireland, and more in the Falklands. I appreciate the guard you've given us,' he said to Martin. 'I'd have been rather abrupt if I'd had the press knocking on the door today, I'm afraid. Come into the house: my wife's waiting for us there. I've been killing time, and weeds, in the garden.'

He led them up the steps, pausing to remove a little mud from his boots on a black iron scraper by the door. The entrance hall was wide and imposing, panelled from floor to ceiling in oak that the police officers guessed had been there since the house was built. Paul pointed to the right. 'In there.'

As they entered, Marietta Paul rose from a big wicker-framed armchair that looked entirely out of place in a Scottish drawing room. As he introduced her to the visitors, her husband caught Martin's quick glance. 'I'm a collector,' he explained. 'I brought that chair back from Savannah, Georgia.' He pointed to a massive display case against the back wall. 'That thing came from Nairobi. If you look inside it you'll see various bits of metal that came from the Falklands. They were dug out of me, after one of my guys stepped on a land-mine. He was killed, I was torn up by sharpnel.' He looked directly at McGuire. 'I suppose you're going to ask me to look at Harry in much the same condition.'

'No, sir, I'm not. We've got a positive identification on your son's body from his medical records.'

'The plate in his leg?'

'That's right.'

'But we want to see him,' the ghost-faced mother protested.

'There's no need,' McGuire told her.

'But it's our right.'

'It is,' he agreed, 'but maybe you'd better not.'

'Exit wound?' Paul asked quietly, looking away from his wife, so that she could not hear the question.

The big detective shook his head, moving closer to him. 'No, sir, but Harry's body was hidden for over twenty-four hours, and exposed to scavengers.'

'I understand.' He turned back to Mrs Paul. 'We'll take the officer's advice, dear. It's in our interests. Now, Mr Martin, Mr McGuire, please sit and let's get down to business. What happened to our son?'

'He was shot twice in the head from a range of about four feet. We believe that the murderer had been stalking them since the previous night, and that he must have followed them to North Berwick, where they went to sell some of Zrinka's pictures. They caught the bus to Gullane; we guess that he followed them in a car, from a distance. We know that he wasn't a passenger himself. We're not sure about what happened next, but we reckon that he trailed them all the way down to the beach, where they pitched their tent.'

'Why there? Why did they go there?'

'We know that Zrinka visited the vicinity with her parents, when she was nine years old. It's our guess that camping there was her idea. They may have been there before, for all we know, but last Monday was probably the first night of the year that's been warm enough.'

'And he killed them there?'

'We believe that he watched them all night, from somewhere very close by. Zrinka was found on the beach. Harry was killed in the tent; we know that for sure, thanks to our lab people. Our supposition is that she decided to go for a walk, and that Harry stayed in the tent. When she had gone, the murderer emerged from his hiding place and shot your son. He then followed Zrinka and killed her, probably at the spot where she was found.

'Finally, he went back to the tent and hid Harry's body, clothes and rucksack, while leaving her things for us to find. He was probably hoping that we'd assume that Harry was the killer and that we'd waste time starting a search for him.' McGuire paused. 'But our people at the scene didn't fall for that one.'

'I see.' Colonel Paul sighed. 'What can we do?' he asked. 'How can we help you catch this murdering bastard?'

'We need to know everything you can tell us about Zrinka Boras,' the chief superintendent answered, 'anything that Harry might have told you about her.'

'Are you looking for a jilted lover?' Marietta Paul asked.

'It's too early to say that, although we are trying to find any connections between Zrinka and Stacey Gavin, a girl who was killed two months ago, and a man remains a possibility. At the moment our thinking is that Zrinka was the target, not Harry; he may have been killed just because he was unlucky enough to have been there.'

'Stacey Gavin?' the woman repeated.

'Yes. Harry didn't know her too, did he?'

'Not that I know of.' She looked at her husband. 'Did he ever mention her to you, Trav?'

'He did, actually, but only in the context of a television report of her murder that we were both watching. It was mid-week, but Harry used to come up then, since most of his band engagements were at weekends. They showed a picture of her, and he said, "Poor kid, she looks really nice. I hope they catch the . . ." I won't repeat the word he used, dear.'

'What about Zrinka?' McGuire continued. 'Were you aware of their relationship?'

'Oh, yes,' Marietta replied. 'Harry brought her up here. She was a lovely girl.' Her voice faltered for a moment, as she fought to keep a sob at bay. 'It's just devastating that this should happen to two young people; young, so young. How could it? How could it?' As the two police officers looked on, embarrassed and sympathetic, she broke down.

'Do you mind if we continue this without my wife?' asked Paul.

'For the moment, not at all, sir,' Martin told him.

'In that case, let me take her upstairs. I'll rejoin you in a moment.'

'Sure.'

'So Harry was still well in the bosom of the family,' McGuire murmured, as the couple left the room.

'Going back to what you were saying earlier,' his colleague said, 'would you cut yourself off from a place like this? Look at that view.'

They stood and gazed in silence through a big picture window that offered a panoramic vista from the hillside across the shining waters of Loch Tay and down its length. The day was calm and one or two boats were out, anglers with rods in the water. 'I take your point,' the Edinburgh policeman conceded eventually. 'Even for a boy with dreams of making it big as a musician, this is fucking paradise. Not a lot to do, I guess, but a hell of a place to practise.'

'I'm sorry,' said Travers Paul from the doorway, as he rejoined them. 'We've both been devastated since we heard the news. It took a big effort on Marietta's part to meet you at all; she really isn't up to it, you know. Not for now, at any rate.'

'Sure,' said McGuire, as they returned to their seats. 'We both understand that, so don't worry about it.'

'Thanks. You were asking about Zrinka, before.'

'Yes. What did you know of her?'

'Very little; Harry only brought her here twice. I knew that she was British, because the first time I asked her what her nationality was. She laughed and said that sometimes she wondered herself, given her Balkan ancestry, but that she was born in Yugoslavia, that her parents had migrated to the UK and that she had become a naturalised British subject at the same time as them. She had a very slight accent, assimilated from her home surroundings, I suppose, just as Harry's accent had a touch of American in it from the time we spent in Georgia. I knew what she did, of course; she was a very talented young artist. The second time she came, about three weeks ago, she gave us a picture. It's over there, in fact.' He pointed towards the wall, beside the door, at a watercolour that hung there. It was bright and vivid and showed the scene that the two police officers had been admiring a few minutes before.

McGuire rose from his chair, walked round, and examined it closely. 'That's the first time I've seen Zrinka's work,' he said, as he returned. 'I've a bit of a personal interest,' he explained. 'My mother paints, now that she's retired to Italy. You're right: the poor kid was damn good. My boss has one of her pictures, as a matter of fact.'

Martin glanced at him. 'Bob? Is that right?'

'Yes. Stevie Steele told me.'

'How did he find that out?'

'One of his DCs lives next door to Alex. She told him, and he told Stevie. Bizarrely enough he has one of Stacey's too.'

'Bob always was a bit of a closet art lover. He gave Karen and me a picture as a wedding present. It's by a Catalan artist he discovered in L'Escala, called Nada Sebastian. You should check her out; she has a website. Her name, that's all it is.' The deputy chief constable looked back at Paul. 'I'm sorry, sir, we're sidetracking here.'

'That's all right, Mr Martin, I started it off.'

'Did you know anything else about her parents, other than that they were originally from Bosnia?'

'I didn't even know that. She used the term Yugoslavia

when she spoke about it, as it would have been when they left, I suppose.'

'How long had Zrinka's relationship with Harry been going on?' McGuire asked.

'Not long. About three months, as far as I can recall. He told us not to read anything into it, that they were friends as much as anything else, but they were very relaxed in each other's company, very affectionate, and they had that way of looking at each other that suggested it might be more serious than either of them was letting on, or even appreciated. Zrinka talked to Marietta about it, though. She told her that she liked Harry very much, but that she was careful, and was taking her time, because of family circumstances, she said, but most of all because she had been badly let down by someone in the past.'

'Did she mention a name?'

'No, she didn't. Although Marietta said that she was very frank about it. She told her that meeting us had confirmed her good feelings about Harry. She said that he was helping her get over her earlier experience.'

'How did she and Harry meet?'

'In a bar, where his band was playing. You'll know that he was a full-time musician; I told the officer who called to ask me about him for your press conference. That's happened now, I suppose, from the evidence of the reptiles turning up to gawp and film the house.'

'You didn't watch it on television?' said Martin.

'No, we couldn't bring ourselves to. I gather that Zrinka's father was there. At least, that's what your colleague told me.'

'Oh, yes,' McGuire grunted. 'He was there all right. He's offered a reward for information leading to the arrest of the killer.'

'Good for him. I might just pitch in myself. How much has he put up?'

'A million.'

'A mi—! Good heavens! Out of my league, I'm afraid. I'll contribute if he asks, of course, but . . .'

'He won't. He was making a point to the murderer.'

'The point being?'

'The same one I made to him: that he has nowhere to hide that'll keep us away from him for long. Davor Boras made it more dramatically, that's all.'

'Davor Boras? Ah, but I've heard of him. What *Financial Times* reader hasn't? He's Zrinka's father, is he? Maybe I should have guessed, but I never made the connection. All she said about him was that he owned a couple of galleries. I assumed he was a shopkeeper. As, indeed, I suppose he is, on a very large scale.'

'You could say that. But let's go back to Harry, sir. He and Zrinka met in a bar, you said.'

'It was more of a dancehall, from the way he described it. He was playing and she was there for a drink, with a friend.'

'I don't suppose you know the friend's name?'

'Zrinka called her Amy, but that's all.'

'That's fine; we should be able to find her. Harry's band: they're full-time?'

'More or less. They're called Upload, a three-piece, but he was very much the leader. He was the lead guitarist, and singer, and composer, and arranger, and programmer of their various machines. He was beginning to get excited about them. They've made one album, so far, on their own initiative, but their manager told them she'd arranged a distribution deal with a major record company. They were going back into the studio next week, to re-record one of the tracks as a single, to break them into the national market.'

Paul looked at the police officers. 'Are you surprised that I'm up with the technology?' he asked sheepishly. 'I suppose it's a case of once a businessman always a businessman. It was the career my son wanted and so I took an interest in it, and had him explain to me what it was all about. Harry wasn't just a dreamer, you know. He graduated from Heriot-Watt University last year with a first in computer science, and did some lecturing there, part-time, to supplement his band earnings. He was a very bright young man, and music was a legitimate way of putting his skills to work.'

'Who managed them?'

'An agency called High-end Talent, but from what Harry said that was just a trading name for a woman called Hope Dell.'

'Where's she based?'

'Edinburgh. She has an office on King George IV Bridge. I've been there; went with Harry and his chums when they were thinking of signing on with her. He asked me to sit in on their meeting, to see if it felt right.'

'Obviously it did.'

Paul nodded. 'Yes. I was very impressed by her. She interviewed them rather than the other way around. She told them about all the pitfalls, and she left them in no doubt, to borrow a phrase she used on the day, that for every Oasis there are thousands of mirages with the metaphorical bones of the deluded scattered all around. When she was finished, Harry and the boys looked at me, I nodded and they shook hands on it.'

'The other band members?' McGuire asked. 'What are their names and where can we find them?'

'Buddy and A-Frame; that's all I ever knew them as. You'll be able to contact them through Hope. They won't be suspects, I'm sure. All their dreams of riches have gone up in smoke.'

'A-Frame?' Martin exclaimed. 'As in initial and surname?'

Colonel Travers Paul smiled, sadly. 'No, as in a fat boy with sloping shoulders and a pointy head; that's what Harry christened him. Among his other fine qualities, my son had quite a sense of humour.'

Thirty-five

'This comes out of a throwaway remark made during our conversation with Harry Paul's dad,' said Mario McGuire, 'but let's check it out anyway. I seem to remember from the file that Stacey Gavin had a website. Right?'

'Right.'

'Then let's check out whether Zrinka had as well.'

'Will do,' Stevie Steele replied. 'I take it your thinking is that maybe the killer sourced them as targets at random, through a search engine.'

'Something along those lines, yes.'

'If she had one, that would be a possibility. It might even throw up a few more potential targets in this area. We'll be better able to get on to it when we get into Zrinka's flat. At the moment the crime-scene technicians are giving it a thorough going-over.'

'What progress have you made since the press briefing?'

'We've established one thing that might be significant. Three of Zrinka's pictures are missing; we know that she took twelve pieces out to North Berwick on Monday, to an art gallery called the Westgate. The owner bought one for his private collection and took eight for stock, as many as he thought he could handle at one time, especially since they were unframed. Zrinka told him that she rarely sold work framed. She believed that it was better that the buyer decided how a work should be displayed, and that most artists did themselves no favours by using cheap or inappropriate framing.'

'Maybe she left the other three somewhere else.'

'No. We've established that. She went straight from the shop to the restaurant and straight from there to the bus. Her art bag was empty when we found it yesterday. The killer's taken them as trophies, just as he probably took Stacey's sketch pad.'

'I'll go with that. Anything else?'

Steele chuckled. 'Oh, yes, and with respect, sir, it's of a lot more immediate use than websites: we can put a face to Dominic Padstow. Stacey knew him, all right, and intimately too. He must have moved on to her from Zrinka. Tarvil's just back from South Queensferry with a near life-size nude portrait of him that she painted. Russ Gavin's met him and he reckons it's just about as good as a photograph, so I'm going to have the face scanned and printed out. If we haven't turned up an address for him soon, I'm going to be looking for the okay to release it to the media. Meantime, I'm going to ask Gregor Broughton, the fiscal, to declare him a potential suspect, so that we can set aside the Data Protection Act and pull his details from public agency sources.'

'You know this picture is Padstow? For sure?'

'Yes. Mr Gavin had the presence of mind to show Tarvil his daughter's catalogue. She listed every work she ever did, by subject name and number. That includes the portraits that she did occasionally for family and friends. He appears there, by name, in the entry for portrait number nine.'

McGuire whistled down the phone. 'You're sending a happy man back to Edinburgh, Stevie,' he declared. 'So Padstow didn't just know both women, he was intimate with them both. Finally we've got ourselves a prime suspect.'

'A suspect, yes, but that's all he is for now. We need more on him, from both victims' friends. Griff's been through Zrinka's palmtop and found some names there. Not many, though: she wasn't part of a student crowd, like Stacey.'

'Is there an Amy among them?'

'Yes, Amy Noone, seven Blinkbonny Vennel, Comely Bank.'

'I suggest you start with her. She was there the night Zrinka met Harry, so she may have known Padstow too.'

'I'll do that.'

'You'll look up Hope Dell too, for contact details for the other band members?'

'I will, but she'll have to wait till tomorrow.'

'Sure,' McGuire agreed. 'You're running things on the ground; you set your own priorities.'

Steele was about to hang up, when he spoke again: 'Hey, Andy tells me that he's got a DI vacancy in this division, and no obvious candidates. It has to be one of the great numbers of all time. If I didn't need you myself I'd have put your name in for it. Too bad: it's fucking beautiful up here; Maggie would just love it.'

Thirty-six

Maggie Rose had been conscientious throughout her police career. She had never taken time off duty without reporting the fact to a supervisor, and so it was second nature to her to pick up the phone at three o'clock and call Brian Mackie.

'Hi, Mags,' he said, as he answered, with warmth in his voice, 'how's your day going? Is Mary Chambers up to speed on everything that's coming up in the division?'

'It's fine,' she replied. 'To tell you the truth, I'm surprised by the way that people have been coming up to me privately and wishing me good luck. I never knew they felt that way about me. It's really touching. As for Mary, she'll be fine; you won't regret accepting my recommendation, I promise you.

'Actually, it's a good time for her to be taking over: the next couple of months will be as quiet as it ever gets. The football season's over, so she won't have the fortnightly turn-out at Tynecastle to police. That's the most consistently stressful part of the job, especially when the big teams visit, and Hibs.'

'I agree with that, for sure. But don't you go off worrying about Mary either. She will have my full and active support,

I promise you, until the moment she gets fed up with me hanging around and asks me respectfully to go away. Even then, she'll have it, if from a greater distance.' He paused. 'You don't have any plans to bugger off sharp tomorrow, I hope. You're not leaving without ceremony, I promise you that . . . even if it is only a temporary absence.'

'No,' she conceded. 'I'll be a good girl. I hope nobody's expecting a riotous assembly, though. Willie Haggerty's leaving do may have turned into a right session, but in my condition that would not be appropriate.'

'No, no.' Mackie laughed reassuringly. 'It won't be ambulances at midnight, I promise. Besides, you'll have Stevie there to look out for you.'

'If his investigation allows, I will. I wonder how it's going. I haven't spoken to him since breakfast.'

'Positively, from what I hear. I've just had a call from Mario, on the road back from Perthshire. They've got a suspect, a guy who seems to have been involved with both of the victims.'

'An ex-boyfriend? That's a break. It'll surprise Stevie too: he's convinced that these killings are ritual, that the women were selected more or less at random and that there's something behind them, a sort of purpose.'

'Is he indeed? Stevie's a damn good analyst. Still, he could be right in part: ritualistic killings but with sexual jealousy as the motive.'

'He won't be worried about his theory being right or wrong as long as he gets a result. Nor will my ex; even less so, I reckon. Have they traced this man, this lover they had in common?'

'Not yet, but they've got a scent and they're after it.'

'In that case I may be eating alone again tonight.' Suddenly she realised how hungry she was, having missed lunch at Aldred Fine's request. 'Brian,' she said, 'I didn't just call you up to pass the time of day but to check out of the office for a while. I have a hospital appointment in half an hour.'

'That's very formal and proper of you,' he replied. 'You'll never bloody learn, will you? Divisional commanders are their own bosses in these things. Anyway, your kid's a hell of a lot more important than the job. I'll see you tomorrow; get on your way.'

Maggie hung up, picked up her bag, took her coat from its hook and left her office. She looked in briefly on Mary Chambers, then headed for the car park.

The mid-afternoon traffic was relatively light, and so she arrived at the Royal Infirmary five minutes early for her three-thirty appointment. When she entered the MRI scan reception area, she was surprised to find Aldred Fine waiting there.

'I didn't expect you to be here,' she told him.

'All part of the service,' he replied, as jocularly as his appearance allowed.

As she looked at him, all the experience that she had amassed during her years in the police service told her, beyond reasonable doubt, that he was lying.

Thirty-seven

Stevie Steele looked out of the window. 'Mrs Boras wasn't kidding,' he said. 'It is a nice view.'

He was standing in the living room of Zrinka Boras's apartment in Castle Street, looking out of the window across Princes Street and its gardens. The great grey castle, on its rock, was bathed in the light of late afternoon as the sun made its way west.

'Must be worth a fortune too,' Griff Montell murmured. 'A duplex in the heart of this city is a rich girl's home.'

'Yes, but we knew that already.' He looked across the room to the desk at which the South African was sitting. Like the rest of the house it was tidy, with pens and paper-clips all in their proper containers, with a pile of grey business cards placed in front of the flat-screen monitor, and with a phone to the right corner, within easy reach. 'Are you into her files yet?' he asked.

'Sure, boss, no problem. She'd never heard of computer security, or so it seems. I can answer your website question: she had one. There's a folder here.'

'I have the answer already.' Steele showed him a business card that he had picked up. 'It's there,' he said.

'Want me to look at it?'

'Not right now.'

'I can access her e-mail if you like; the password's memorised to let me in with one click.'

'Do that later too. First I want you to look for a list of contacts. We didn't find anything for Dominic Padstow on her PDA, but maybe she kept an entry on him here.'

'She kept fuck all on her PDA, apart from a few notes of sales made, and a couple of phone numbers, for example Harry Paul's and Amy Noone's. I suspect that it was a Christmas gift she never really got round to using. Give me a minute and we'll see what's here.'

Steele stood back and watched as the detective constable opened the program menu, found an office package and opened it. 'Nothing here,' he declared, after a minute spent searching. 'There is a calendar, though, and she has appointments on it.'

'How far back does it go?'

'Let me see.' He began to click on an arrow, moving the display back month by month. 'A couple of years,' he announced eventually. 'This computer's newer than that, I'd say, so I guess she transferred files from an earlier model. There are regular entries, and quite a few of them involve the letter D, as in our man.' He chose one at random and clicked on it, watching as it opened into an extended note. 'Right; this one's for November the second, the year before last, and it says, "Four p.m., Dom, Harry Potter and the Giblet of Fire". I guess they went to the movies.'

'You mean "goblet",' said the inspector. 'As in "and the Goblet of Fire".'

'No, I don't; that's what's here. Either Zrinka couldn't type or she had a wry sense of humour.'

'Can you check every entry and print them out?'

'Sure, but I'd rather do it back at the office.' He produced a small blue plastic object from his pocket. 'I could copy all the files I need on to my flash drive.'

'If that's the easiest way, fair enough. Too bad about the lack of an address book, though. There's no trace of anything anywhere. For an outgoing girl, as she'd been described, she seems to have had hardly any friends.'

'I'm not done yet, though,' said Montell. 'She didn't have to use a specialist program. Many people don't; they just make an ordinary list.' He opened the computer's search facility, entered 'address', and waited. 'There you are,' he said triumphantly, as a single entry appeared in a window. 'Zrinka's documents, in a folder called "House", a document called "Addresses". And if we open that . . .' he clicked on the link and watched as the screen changed '. . . we have a list. There you are, boss: names, addresses and phone numbers, in alphabetical order.'

Steele slapped him on the shoulder as he leaned over to look at the monitor screen. 'Good lad, Griff. Scroll down and let's take a look at the P entries.' He watched as the DC spun the wheel on the mouse, pulling down pages of the file, slowing down as he reached O and coming to a halt as he arrived at the first P listings.

'HP,' Montell murmured, to himself. 'That's Harry's address and number in Edinburgh. The next one's Paul, T and M, his mum and dad, up in Aberfeldy. But no more Ps; the next entry's RG, with a mobile number, no address.'

'Maybe that's out of place.'

'No, the one after that's an S. Bloody hell! "Skinner, Alex", and with her office address and phone number. What's she doing there?'

'She bought one of Zrinka's pictures for her father,' Steele reminded him. 'I guess she kept details of her buyers wherever she could. These aren't just personal numbers: she's built herself a mailing list. That's why there are so many of them, compared to the very few numbers in her PDA.'

'But no Dominic Padstow, even though he's mentioned in her appointments calendar.'

'If he lived with her . . .'

'. . . she wouldn't need his bloody number. True, or maybe she just washed him right out of her hair when he moved on.' Montell's finger twitched on the wheel and more entries appeared. 'Hey, look at this,' he exclaimed. 'There's one for Stacey!'

Steele peered at the screen. 'All it says is "S" and a mobile number. How do you know it's her?'

'I recognise the number; it's noted in the case file. I'm dead certain, but we can call Tarvil in the office and have him check, if you like.'

'I'll trust your memory, Griff. That means the two victims did know each other.'

'Is that significant?'

'Who can say at this stage? All we're doing is establishing a series of points of overlap between their lives. Until now, that's been limited to the fact that they were both artists, and to them both having relationships with the man Dominic

Padstow. But now we discover that they were acquainted. How did they meet? What brought them together? How close were they? We need to talk to Amy Noone, urgently, and we need to re-interview Stacey's friends.'

'And we sure as hell need to find Padstow.'

'At the moment that's our only objective, but let's do it methodically. I want you to look at every file on that computer, and I want you to use that engagement diary to build me as complete a picture as possible of this woman's life, as far back as it will take you. I don't really care whether you do it here or whether you take the box back to the office, but the search needs to be complete. Copying selected items on to a flash drive isn't going to be enough.'

'No, I guess not,' Montell conceded. 'I'll take it down to Leith in that case, but first, do you want to check Zrinka's e-mails?'

'Yes, go on.'

'She has direct broadband access; the computer logs on automatically, so if I just click here . . .' He did as he said and watched as the dead woman's mailbox opened. 'Nothing,' he growled, as he scanned the list that appeared, 'other than bloody on-line newspapers. I'd have expected an artist to be a *Guardian* reader, but Zrinka went for the *Telegraph* and *The Scotsman*. Let's see what she's had recently.' He clicked on a box marked 'old e-mails'. A longer list appeared; he and Steele scanned down it, neither of them quite sure what they hoped to find. 'I'll go through these one by one at the office, boss,' said Montell.

'You'll still be able to access through our systems?'

'No problem: I won't change her set-up.'

'Right, close up and let's go.' Steele straightened up, and moved towards the door.

'Okay. Hey, wait a minute,' the detective constable exclaimed. 'She's got Messenger: it's signed on automatically. That means she has a secondary address, and I should,' he clicked the icon, 'be able to open it.' The program took longer to display on screen than its predecessor, but as it did, a grin spread across the South African's face. 'She's got mail!' he called out. 'And from her brother at that.'

'God,' the inspector sighed, 'I've been trying to trace that man since we left his parents this morning, and drawing blanks everywhere. I sourced his office number and called that, but his secretary told me that he was away on a business trip and out of touch.'

'Doesn't he have a mobile?'

'She said that he doesn't. Hard to believe in this day and age, but I don't think she was lying to me. She said that Mr Barnes was away sourcing suppliers and that he keeps trips like that absolutely secret, so that his competitors don't find out who he's dealing with. All I could do was ask her to ask him to make contact with us whenever he next got in touch. His mother's secretary gave me a home phone number for him in London. I rang that too, but all I got was the same answer-machine that she had earlier. Now the bugger pops up here out of the blue. Open it, and let's see what he's telling her.'

Montell double-clicked the sender name and waited for the seconds the message took to open. 'The title is "Keeping in touch", ' he began 'and it reads,

'Hi Sis
I'm on the move, so this will have to be a quick message. I hope you're well and selling your pictures like crazy. It was good, what you told me about the man being in touch about one of your pictures. You make a friend like him and word will spread around town. Just don't let him get too friendly! I can't tell you often enough, you can't trust men, but you know that from your own experience. I'm glad it seems to be working out for you with your new boyfriend. He has a good background. After you told me about him I checked out his father, and he seems like quite a man. He was very successful in business and before that he was a war hero. I wish our own dad was more like him. We know what he did when he saw war on the horizon.

I'm out of the country just now, finishing up a piece of business. I expect it to be taken care of in the next couple of days. Once it is, maybe I'll come to Edinburgh to see you and your little friend, and meet Harry.
Love, Dražen.'

'Looks like his secretary was telling the truth, boss.'

'I never doubted her. Is the message dated?'

'According to the heading it was sent today, at twelve fifty GMT.'

'That's well after the press conference. Griff, I want you to send a reply. Tell him it's from me, give him our office address, phone number and e-mail, and tell him that when he picks it up, he should get in touch with us as soon as possible.'

Montell's fingers were flashing on the keyboard even before he had finished speaking. 'I'm ahead of you, boss. I wonder who the man was that Dražen mentioned,' he added idly, as he worked.

'Maybe Zrinka's old e-mails will tell us. Finish up and let's get back to the office, so you can start to work on them, and on any other surprises that might be in there.'

Thirty-eight

There was nothing about the process of the MRI scan that was frightening, in itself, to a mature, sensible woman. She lay undressed, but under a sheet, on a movable bed, as it passed slowly through a giant, circular magnet. She kept absolutely still, as she had been told was necessary. The supervisor had offered her a mild sedative to help her, but she had declined. She felt no discomfort, no pain, as it progressed, and she was sure that her child was equally unaffected, since she felt no kicking or undue movement within her. She willed herself to concentrate on the scan itself, and to think of nothing else; she might have dropped off to sleep had it not been for the loud repetitive clicking that signalled each successive stage. Finally it was over. She would have guessed that she had been under the magnet's beam for less than half an hour, and yet a check of the clock on the wall, as she slipped on the hospital-issue dressing-gown, told her that fifty minutes had elapsed.

But, still, Maggie Rose was apprehensive, as she had been from the moment that she had seen Fine waiting for her in the reception area. She was strong-willed and had been able, if not to banish her fears, then at least to pack them away in a box at the back of her mind, but his presence . . . not routine, whatever he said . . . coupled with the disturbing family history that Sylvia Thorpe's research had uncovered, had unlocked it and set them free to push everything else aside.

She frowned as she dressed, rubbing her hand idly over her bump as she fastened the elasticated uniform trousers that had been made specially for her. She was still frowning as she returned to the waiting area. A nurse offered her a cup of tea and a biscuit, and she accepted, then left them untouched on the table beside her. She was so preoccupied that she failed to see Mr Fine until he was standing in front of her, hair slicked back, pencil moustache as neat as ever, round spectacles perched on the bridge of his nose.

'Would you like to come with me, please, Mrs Steele?' he said, in a voice that sounded reassuring, but was in total contrast to the signals that all his years of professional practice could not prevent from showing in his eyes. She followed him without a word, along the corridor and into a small narrow room with a curtained window, an examination table, a backlit display screen and three chairs, one of which was behind a desk.

Several transparencies were attached to the board, brightly coloured cross-sections of a human body that she knew to be hers. She stared at them, almost slipping as she lowered herself on to one of the two patient chairs. Fine put out a hand to steady her, then took the other himself, beside the board.

He pointed at the images. 'I could spend a while going through these in detail with you, Mrs Steele, as I've just done with my colleague Dr Goyle, our most senior consultant radiologist. I could point out to you what we've found, but it wouldn't mean anything to you, since it takes a couple of years' training and then several more years' experience to be able to interpret these pictures. So I'll just tell you what the position is.'

Maggie's heart was hammering. She hugged her abdomen, as if she was protecting her child, as, subconsciously, she was.

The consultant read her mind; he waited, giving her time to control herself, then caught her eyes, holding her attention. 'The scan,' he continued slowly, 'has detected abnormalities in both of your ovaries, and in your Fallopian tubes. There is also a shadow on your uterus. For one hundred per cent certainty we'd need to do a biopsy, but neither Dr Goyle nor I are in any real doubt. We believe that you are suffering from what is called an epithelial ovarian carcinoma. I'm very sorry, Mrs Steele, but that's the long way of saying that you have ovarian cancer.'

Maggie felt all of the colour drain from her face. 'Jesus,' she whispered. She had known fear throughout her life, and violence on more than one occasion, as an adult and as a child, but she realised that before it had always been mixed with anger, and that until that moment she had never felt true terror.

'Yes,' said Fine.

'The baby?' Her voice trembled.

'Your child is unaffected.'

Her breath exploded from her in a huge sigh, and she felt herself relax, a little. 'Oh, thank you for that,' she gasped.

Fine gazed at her kindly. 'It's not a matter for thanks.'

'I wasn't talking to you,' she told him, with a very faint smile: it showed for only a second or two, before her frown returned. 'That's my diagnosis, but what's my prognosis?'

'It's much more positive than it might have been,' he replied. 'Your condition has been detected fairly early, which isn't usually the case with this type of disease. With immediate intervention and a subsequent course of treatment, still to be determined, you have an excellent chance of recovery.'

'What do you mean by intervention?'

'We'll have to end your pregnancy now, and operate to remove your ovaries, tubes, womb and any other troublesome tissue that might have been hidden from the scan.'

'Terminate my pregnancy?' Maggie exclaimed. 'But I have eleven weeks to go.'

'Nonetheless, Mrs Steele, we have to act immediately.'

'By killing my child?'

'Your child has a fair chance of survival, even with such an early delivery.'

'But you've just told me she's small.'

'Yes, but she's viable.'

'What does she weigh, right now?'

'Maybe two and a half pounds . . .' he paused '. . . but babies of that size regularly survive nowadays.'

'Maybe, you're saying to me. As in "maybe but she could be less", right?'

'True,' Fine admitted. 'She could weigh less than a kilo just now.'

'And then what would her chances of survival be?'

'To be honest, they'd be poor.'

'And if I carry her full term?'

'She would be six pounds at birth, possibly as much as seven; most of a baby's weight is gained in the final stages. However, that could be affected by the development of your condition: she might grow more slowly than normal.'

'Could my disease spread to her?'

'Technically, yes.'

She stared at Fine. 'And practically?'

'Practically, the chances of that happening are minimal. Such an occurrence would be so rare that it would make the medical journals.'

'Could you give me chemotherapy, or radiotherapy, without harming her?'

'Absolutely not, I'm afraid.'

'Yet we're agreed that there is a far greater risk to my baby's life by curtailing my pregnancy than by continuing it?'

'That is true. But, Mrs Steele, the same applies to you in reverse. I've been comparing your ultrasounds, and while they're not definitive, they do indicate that your cancer is developing swiftly, as I'd expect it to. The growths in your Fallopian tubes are metastases, secondary tumours. That's not a good sign, but it's manageable. However, if there is a spread beyond the pelvic region, that will not be.'

'Manageable? Let's be more specific than that. Given my present condition, what are my five-year survival chances? Quote me figures; I can look them up on the Internet, I'm sure.'

For the first time, Fine looked down, away from her. 'Overall,' he replied, 'studies show less than fifty per cent. That's allowing for all age groups, all stages of detection.'

'In my case, if I follow your advice, what will the odds be?'

'I'd love to say better than even, but I can't.'

'So what it comes down to is this. If I risk my daughter's life, and somehow she overcomes the odds against her, survives and grows into a healthy child, I'm unlikely to be around to see her start primary school. Or, to put it another way, if I do what you say, the balance of probability is that my husband will lose both his wife and child.'

'Maybe, but, Mrs Steele . . .'

'Forget the bloody maybes. Yes or no?'

'Yes, but every case is different. These are statistics. Individual cases often throw up surprising outcomes.'

It was Maggie's turn to draw his eyes back to hers. 'With respect,' she said, not unkindly, 'you're asking me to gamble my child's life, and I will not, I cannot do that. I will carry her either full term or until you can put your hand on your heart and tell me that she can be delivered without risk above the norm. After that you can hollow me out, throw all the shit you like at me, and I will fight this disease with everything I have.'

'If that's your decision,' the consultant replied, 'I have to respect it.'

'I know, but thanks for saying so. In the meantime, is there anything I can do to slow this thing down?'

'Rest; that's all. Do you have domestic help?'

'No.'

'Then my advice is that you get a cleaner in, do your food shopping online, and generally avoid physical activity.'

'Including . . .?'

'Yes, I'm afraid so, that too.' He looked at her earnestly. 'Mrs Steele, Margaret: it might be a good idea if you asked your husband to come and see me, to let me explain what's happening.'

Her eyes flashed, and narrowed. 'No!' she snapped. 'Absolutely not. My husband is out there right now trying to catch a man who has murdered, so far, three people, and who may well be planning to kill even more. He needs to focus on that, not to be watching me every day for signs of deterioration. I love Stevie, I know the man he is, and I believe that if I put my decision to him, he'd back me up. He'll find out when he has to. In the meantime I forbid you to contact him, or to discuss my condition with him. If you do that behind my back, you'll find out why I made chief superintendent at my age. Is that clear?'

Fine smiled. 'As clear as day.' He rose to his feet. 'Come on with me and I'll make you a series of appointments. Come by taxi; it'll be cheaper than parking in this bloody place. If nothing else, I'm going to watch you and your child like a hawk in these coming weeks.'

Thirty-nine

'I wasn't surprised when you rang me. I've been expecting you since lunchtime.' Amy Noone's wide eyes and pale face were witnesses to her claim. As she perched on the edge of her couch, she clutched a can of Irn-Bru, white-knuckled.

'How did you find out?' Steele asked her.

'I was in the middle of shampooing a customer,' she told him, 'and STV was on the television like always. The news was on, then the woman said they were switching to Edinburgh, and two men walked in front of a camera. I wasn't really listening until I saw that one of them was Zrinka's dad. I knew him right away, from a photo she has in her flat. And then the other one, the big guy with the nice black curly hair, said that Zrinka was the girl that was murdered on the beach. I just screamed.' She pressed the cold can to her forehead. 'God knows what would have happened if I'd been cutting the woman's hair at the time, instead of just washing it. Mervyn, the boss, was at the other end of the salon; he came rushing up thinking I'd scalded her or something, then the man said something else about Zrinka being shot and he screamed too. Then Harry's name was mentioned, and the pair of us were in floods of tears.

Mervyn told me I should go home; gay blokes are kind that way. He said he'd finish off my customer, and cancel as many of the afternoon appointments as he could.'

'He knew them too?'

'Of course he did. Zrinka was a customer. That's how she and I met; she came into the salon a year and a half ago, no, maybe a bit more, and Mervyn gave her to me. She said that she wanted a makeover to surprise her boyfriend. I told her that if he didn't appreciate her as she was, he needed a mental makeover, or maybe changing altogether. She laughed at that, and we just got on from there.'

'Can you tell us anything about the boyfriend?' Tarvil Singh asked her.

'Dominic?' Amy frowned. 'I never liked him. I never trusted him either.'

'Why? Did he come on to you?'

She snorted. 'In his dreams! Nah, he just didnae seem right for her. He was older than her for a start. Zrinka was just twenty-two then, and he must have been into his thirties. She liked a laugh, and he was a dour bastard, unless he was making an effort, and he never did, unless she was looking at him.'

'Do you know why they broke up?'

'No, Zrinka never let on, not even when I asked her. All that I know is that she chucked him out, no week's notice, nothing. One day I went to see her and he was there. Next day he was gone.'

'Her mother told us that they broke up on good terms,' said Steele.

'That's what Zrinka wanted her to think. Wasnae true,

though. My theory is . . .' she looked at the detectives across her coffee table '. . . that he was a gold-digger.'

'That's a good old-fashioned term.'

'It fitted him, though. I reckon he was after her because her old man's filthy rich, and that Zrinka finally figured it out and bounced him. I suggested as much once, and she just said that if that was what I wanted to think it was all right by her.'

'What about Harry?'

Amy's face seemed to light up. 'Aw, Harry was different. He was such a nice guy; one for the women, right enough, but once he met Zrinka, that was that. It was me that introduced them.'

'How did you come to meet Harry?'

'Through A-Frame . . . Sorry, Lionel; Harry gave him that name and it stuck. He's my boyfriend. I took Zrinka along to hear the band one night . . . You know Harry had a band?' Singh nodded. 'I never thought she'd fancy getting off with him, but she did. Shagged him that very night, so she told me afterwards. I thought it would be a one-nighter, but that's not how it turned out: they were pretty much inseparable from then on. She even took an interest in Upload. Not that long ago she brought the three of them into the salon. She said that if they were going to cultivate a scruffy image, then at least it should be well-groomed scruffy. That was pure Zrinka.'

'Have you spoken to A-Frame this afternoon?'

Amy nodded, wiping a tear from a corner of her right eye. 'He was the first person I called. He hadn't heard. He was workin' when I rang him. He's still got a day job . . . just as well, now this has happened. He stacks shelves at Scotmid in Leith. He didn't believe me at first, until I told him to tune in to the Radio Forth news at one. I'm meeting him tonight, him and Benjy . . . that's the other lad in the band. We're going to have a wake for Harry and Zrinka up in the Pear Tree. They'd a record deal, too. That'll be well stuffed with Harry dead. He was the musician, you see, and the programmer. A-Frame does the drums, and Benjy does the keyboards, or so they say, but really they're just machine operators.'

'What's Lionel's surname?' Singh asked.

'Broad. Benjy's is Malcolm; Benjamin Malcolm.'

'Thanks,' said Steele. 'Did Zrinka ever mention a woman called Stacey Gavin?'

The girl squeezed her can even tighter as she nodded. 'She was that other girl that got shot, right?'

'Yes.'

'She knew her,' she told them, 'and so did I. That makes it all even scarier, I suppose.

'Up at the art college in Lauriston, the final-year students have a show, where you can buy their work. Zrinka took me up there last summer, on a Saturday, just to have a look. "Let's suss out the potential competition," was how she put it, but she was laughing when she said it. Stacey was there, showing quite a lot of her work. It was really, really good, as good as Zrinka's. It's funny, I never really knew anything about art until I met those two. Now I'm quite keen on it. Zrinka persuaded me that what I do is art as well, in its own way.

'Stacey had sold just about all of her stuff when we got to

her. In fact, yes, that was what happened, she sold her last piece when we were talking to her. A man bought it; he said it would do nicely for his daughter's new flat when she moved in. He was a nice guy; middle-aged, but he looked tough as fuck. He and Stacey did the deal, he took the picture away, and she said that was her done. So we went to the Pear Tree for a pint.'

'Did you see anything of her after that?'

'Zrinka did, more than me. She let her sell stuff off her stall last summer, until she had her own sales system lined up.

'The two of them fell out, though. I think it must have been over that bastard Dominic. Zrinka found out that Stacey was going out with him. She warned her that he was a no-user, and Stacey didn't like it. They had this discussion one lunch-time, when the three of us were in Bert's Bar, along from the salon. It started off about Dominic; it wasn't an argument or anything, Zrinka just said she was worried for Stacey. Stacey told her that her problem was that she never trusted any men, and Zrinka replied, "No, and you of all people shouldn't either." Then she stopped, but Stacey asked her what she meant.'

'What did she mean?'

'I dunno. I had to go back to work then. But Stacey and Zrinka never seemed to see each other after that.'

'Stacey and Dominic,' asked the inspector, 'do you know what happened there in the end?'

'She binned him. Stacey still came into the salon after the thing in Bert's, not very often, but every time she did I told Mervyn he should be paying me commission. The last time I saw her I asked her about him. She said that Zrinka had been right, and that she'd chucked him.'

Steele looked at Singh, eyebrows raised slightly.

'What about Zrinka's folks?' the big Sikh asked. 'She seemed to have cut herself off from them, from her father at any rate.'

'No, you're dead wrong there. Zrinka loved her dad. He understood when she said that she was moving up here to make her name as an artist, where she wouldn't be connected with him, and where she could be sure that people were buying her stuff because it was good, not because of who she was. Officially she was independent of him and her mum, but she bought her flat, and he slipped her cash every so often: I'm not talking about the odd tenner either. It was funny: neither of them knew the other was helping her. It was supposed to be a secret, but she told me.' Amy smiled. 'And then there was her brother.'

'Dražen?'

'Yeah. He calls himself David, though, David Barnes. Now he does have a problem with his old man.'

'You've met him?'

'Yeah. He came up here to visit Zrinka once. He took the pair of us out to dinner at Cosmo's, just along the road from her place. He was really nice, really, really nice.' For the first time since the detectives had arrived at her Comely Bank studio flat, Amy's face showed a touch of colour. 'In fact . . .' she continued, then stopped. 'A-Frame doesn't know about that. Anyway, he and I hadn't been going out very long then.

'Poor David.' She sighed. 'I think that Zrinka was the most important person in his world.'

Forty

If he had known that Gregor Broughton lived in Elie, Mario McGuire might have delegated thc visit to a junior officer. The Fife coastal village held mixed memories for him; some years before, when he and Maggie Rose had both been junior CID officers, they had been on a stake-out there and had wound up sharing the last hotel room in town. Their lives had been conjoined from that time, as they drifted into an ill-judged and ultimately ill-fated marriage, which had ended in relatively harmonious divorce. Many times he had wondered what would have happened to them both if, that night, there had been one more room at the inn.

He had avoided the place since then, but by the time the late-duty man in the Crown Office had called him back with Broughton's home address, there had been little or no option but to go himself. He had called Paula to tell her that he would be late; she had told him cheerfully that she was in the course of reorganising the kitchen, and that he could be as late as he liked.

The drive from the centre of Edinburgh took almost exactly an hour. As he drove down the broad avenue that led into Elie, his navigation system told him to turn right at the first junction. He followed its orders, noting, as he drove past it, that the big grey-stone hotel in which he and Maggie had got together had closed for business and had been converted into flats. 'I wonder where the weary travellers lay their heads in Elie now,' he mused aloud, 'and randy young coppers get laid?'

Broughton's house was a modern structure, half bungalow, half chalet, with a walled garden and a gate that led down to the beach. Forewarned of his visit, the fiscal greeted him warmly: he was pleased to have company, McGuire guessed, since Lady Broughton was on High Court business in Glasgow, and would be staying over.

'Have you eaten, Mario?' he asked.

'No. I came as soon as I had everything put together, the picture, the latest witness statements and the press release.'

'I thought not, so I've knocked us up some sandwiches. That okay?'

'Sure, thanks. That's much appreciated.'

Broughton led the way through to a garden conservatory: the sun was going down, but McGuire could still make out the grey sea, and the East Lothian coast beyond. *Okay*, he thought, *but not a patch on Loch Tay*.

The two men made small talk as they ate, of rugby, restaurants, wives and partners. They left the business until they had finished. Once they were ready, the detective gave the prosecutor a run-down of the investigation, and of the steps that had led them to Dominic Padstow.

'Is Steele confident about the Noone girl's memory?' he asked, as the chief superintendent finished. 'It's one thing being sure of yourself in a police interview, but I don't have to tell you that if she turns out to be a key witness she'll have to be more than that. The last thing we want is for her to become hesitant and evasive under defence cross-examination.'

'Stevie's my best officer,' McGuire told him, 'although I won't appreciate it if you pass that opinion on to anyone else. He'll have given her a quiet grilling himself, with that very thought in mind; if he's satisfied, so am I.'

'And you're satisfied, beyond any doubt, that Dominic Padstow is an alias?'

'We've searched every likely database in the UK and we've come up with nothing. He doesn't have a national-insurance number or an NHS number. There is no passport issued under that name.'

'Okay, I get the picture.'

'Good. Now can everyone else get it? Can I phone Alan Royston and let him issue it, and the press release to the media?'

Broughton picked up the draft release from the table in front of him and read through it. 'Should be considered dangerous?' he exclaimed. 'The public should not approach him? That's prejudicial. We could get stuffed by the defence on that.'

'They might try it. Now tell me honestly, if they did put up a defence that our warning, given in good faith in the interests of public safety, denied him a fair trial, and your wife was the judge, how far would she chuck it?'

'As far as she could; right out of court for sure. But that doesn't mean to say another judge would.'

'Name one who'd be likely to. Lord Nelson?'

'No, not even him, I'll grant you. Okay, you can have it.'

'And the picture?'

'There's hardly any point to the press release without the likeness, is there?' He picked it up. 'You're calling it an artist's impression?'

'Absolutely. There couldn't be a more apt description.'

'I know nothing about painting,' said Broughton, 'but this has to be a unique work. It could become priceless. Imagine, an artist using her brush to identify the man who killed her.'

Forty-one

'Just one more day,' he said, 'and Chief Superintendent Margaret Rose becomes Mrs Margaret Steele, full-time. Does the prospect scare you?' He tipped his glass of red wine in her direction as he sank back into his soft armchair.

'Not a bit,' she replied, stretched out on the couch with a tumbler of sparkling water resting on her mid-section. 'I've got other things on my mind.'

Since leaving the hospital, as the fearful reality of her diagnosis had set in, there had been moments when her resolve had weakened, when a voice inside her had said, '*Go back there, see Fine, tell him to operate, let the baby take her chances in an incubator for a few weeks and give yourself the hope of a cure, of a lifetime with Stevie, and with her if that's how it works out.*'

She had been tempted, once so strongly that she had been standing at the door, with her car keys in her hand. And then her baby had kicked inside her, and her strength of will had returned.

She had never seen the child, having refused to look at the ultrasound images of her, and yet in her mind she had a face, not newly born but a couple of years old, with reddish hair like hers, and Stevie's eyes and smile. She had a name, too, one that Maggie was keeping to herself, for good luck, until after she had given birth.

But even with her determination renewed in her mind, she had wondered whether she was right to keep her husband in the dark. She was afraid that she was thinking like a senior police officer, keeping him out of the decision-making process because, strictly speaking, he did not need to know. Over supper, delayed until he had come home from work after nine o'clock, she had almost blurted it out. Indeed she would have, had she not realised how tired he looked, and that although his body was with her, his mind was totally preoccupied by his manhunt.

And so, instead, she had let him eat, and unwind; she had topped up his glass before it was empty, and she had waited until he was hers again. By that time she knew that her weaknesses were selfish, and that she had to keep her secret, if for no other reason than that she would not have been able to bear the look on his face had she revealed it.

'I can see that.' He grinned at her. 'I tell you, tomorrow's been a long time coming for me. I know you delayed your departure to give yourself as much time off as possible after the birth, but I wish you'd gone a month ago. You've been growing a child inside you and running a city-centre police division at one and the same time. Even for you, love, that's a big ask.'

'Well, now you can be happy, okay?'

'Now I can start to be; but just stopping work isn't going to be enough. I know you: you'll find substitutes for the office. I'll come in at night and find that you've spent the bloody day at Sainsbury's in Cameron Toll, or that you've been rearranging the furniture, or that you've painted the downstairs toilet.'

He pointed a finger at her. 'Well, none of that's going to happen. This is DI Steele, Stevie boy, talking to you, and he's telling you that, for the first time in your adult life, you are going to have a proper rest for the next eleven weeks, or at least until that wee one decides to put in an appearance.'

'Oh, yeah?' she drawled, hiding her astonishment that he seemed to be beating her to the punch. 'And how's that going to happen?'

'We're getting a domestic,' he announced. 'Ray Wilding has a cousin. He's in the navy, and he's going on a six-month tour of duty in the Indian Ocean. His wife worked on the assembly line in a factory in Livingston until a month ago when she was made redundant. She's looking for a part-time job, at least for as long as her man's away, and she doesn't mind what it is. Where she worked, she was in a sterile area, and Ray says that their house is like that too. He says it's so clean he feels guilty even having a pee in their toilet. She's coming to see us on Saturday morning.'

'She is, is she?'

'Yes, and no arguments.'

Maggie propped herself up on an elbow. 'DI Steele,' she said, 'Stevie boy: my long-term mission in life is to make you happy. If that will do the job, I will see this woman, however grudgingly. If I like her, she's on, until her sailor gets home from the sea. What's her name?'

'Margot; Margot Wilding. Mrs Ray says you and she will get on fine.'

'We'll see. Want another refill?' She made to get up, but he told her not to be so bloody silly and fetched the bottle himself from the sideboard. 'Are you ready to talk about it now?' she asked, as he laid his replenished glass on a side table and slumped back into his chair.

'Just about,' he answered. 'What a day we've had. That man Boras! The word "sinister" could have been invented for him. No wonder Brian Mackie arm-twisted the fiscal to release his daughter's body so we could get him out of town. Trouble comes off the man in waves, and with that fucking city slicker of a PR man behind him, there's no telling what bother he might have caused in the media.'

'A million, eh? I'll bet your phones were busy.'

'Oh, they were, but it could have been worse. At least big Tarvil got a laugh out of it. He had a call from a psychic in London who claimed that she'd induced a vision by placing her hands on the telly during the press conference. She told him that we were looking for a criminal so clever, so devious and so influential that she makes Jack the Ripper seem like a shoplifter.'

'She?'

'That was what was wrong with her picture. We're looking for a man. When Tarvil told her that, she said that sometimes the visions aren't entirely clear and could he put her name in for the reward anyway?'

Maggie was surprised to find that she was still capable of spontaneous laughter. 'Priceless,' she chortled. 'Did he ask her whether she reads crime books or writes them?'

'No, he hung up. She won't be in the big prize draw. Nor will anyone else the way it's looking: we have a suspect.'

'I know, Brian Mackie told me. That's great.'

'It is and it isn't,' said Stevie, hesitantly. 'We've made a lot of progress today, but we're still short of a clear-up. Thanks to a nice girl called Amy, we know for sure that the two female victims were acquainted. More than that, we know that they had a boyfriend in common, a man who lived with Zrinka in Edinburgh for a while, and then after she broke up with him, moved on to Stacey Gavin, until she also showed him the way down the road. That's where we're focused: on him.'

'Well? That is great, isn't it?'

'On the surface, it seems that way. It's not what I expected, that's all. I was sure we really did have a serial murderer on our hands. That's why I feel just a bit uncomfortable. Still, my discomfort may well be irrelevant. So, the killer seems to have had a thing about art, and about female artists. So what? I'm forced to ask myself. The shootings, those of the women that is, look ritualistic, and maybe they were.

'Yet that doesn't mean to say that there wasn't a very simple motive behind them, one of the oldest in the book, namely, the hellacious fury of a cast-off lover. Both women had affairs with this man, both dumped him. The likeliest scenario facing us at this moment, indeed the only scenario, is that he took his revenge by stalking them and killing them, with Harry Paul, Zrinka's new man, thrown in as a bonus.'

Maggie frowned. 'He hid the boy's body, didn't he?'

'Yes; in the bushes.'

'Why would he do that?'

'To keep us confused, maybe; to buy himself extra getaway time, maybe. We'll ask him when we find him.'

'Do that, but as one detective to another, think about this: what if both girls dumped him because they found out something about him?'

Stevie looked thoughtful as he picked up his glass and took a sip. 'Then we'll have to look into that too. But if that was the case, why kill Harry?'

'Because he was there? Or was he afraid that the boy knew whatever it was too? Do you have a name for this suspect?'

'We do. He's called Dominic Padstow: only he isn't, and that's why he really has become our top target.

'That's the name Zrinka and Stacey knew him by. We've run every conceivable check on him. With Gregor Broughton's authority, we've consulted the Department of Work and Pensions, the passport service and every public body and agency where he should be listed. But he isn't. There is no Dominic Padstow anywhere. He doesn't exist.'

'Maybe he's a foreign national.'

'Amy says no. She's met him, and she says that he was British; she was at Zrinka's once, just after she and Padstow had got back from a weekend trip to Amsterdam. When she got there, they were still unpacking and some of their stuff was lying on Zrinka's desk. She remembers quite clearly, she says, seeing two UK passports there.'

'So what do you do next?'

'That depends on Gregor Broughton. We have a likeness of him, a scan taken from a portrait painted by Stacey, that her dad says is absolutely spot on. We'll need Crown Office authority to release it, but if the fiscal gives us the go-ahead, that's what we're going to do. Mario's gone across to see him in Fife tonight; he lives in Elie, apparently.'

'Does he indeed?' Maggie murmured.

'Yes. Rather him than me: it's a ghost town these days. Anyway, as soon as he gives us the nod, and clears the press release that Alan Royston's drafted, we're ready to go. Let's hope it flushes the guy out: otherwise we're at a dead end.'

Forty-two

Paula had been in the last stage of her major kitchen reorganisation when Mario had finally made it back from Fife, twenty minutes after ten.

'You don't mind, do you?' she had asked.

'Hell, no! It implies that you're going to do most of the cooking in this household and that's fine by me.'

They had watched the late-night news on the ITN satellite channel, sharing a bottle of Morellino di Scansano, a strong cherry-scented wine from southern Tuscany that Paula had begun to import on Mario's mother's recommendation, and so it had been well after midnight before they had begun to sleep off the day's exertions, after adding a few more.

The head of CID was still bleary-eyed, and ten minutes past his usual starting time of eight thirty, as he settled in behind his desk. He glanced up as his aide's head appeared round the door.

'Morning, boss,' said Detective Sergeant Sammy Pye. 'Want a coffee?'

'Christ, do I look that bad?'

'Put it this way, the staff are saying they've seen you

looking better. In fact they're even saying they've seen Dan Pringle looking better.' McGuire's predecessor had been a notoriously slow starter. 'Alan Royston's outside,' Pye continued. 'He wants to run through the media coverage with you.'

'Aye, okay, tell him to come in. Hold the coffee, though: I've just left breakfast, and I've still got Paul Newman's Colombian Especial coming out my fucking ears.'

'Could be worse. It could be Kopi Luwak.'

'What the hell is Kopi Luwak? Should the Viareggio delis be stocking it?'

'I doubt it. It's a very rare Sumatran product, made from beans found in the shit of a small jungle animal, the civet cat, after it's eaten them. True.'

'Jesus! I won't ask what it does with the local tea leaves. Now please, Sammy, fuck off.'

The sergeant left with a grin on his face, and moments later Royston walked briskly into the room. 'How have we done?' McGuire asked him.

'Very well. Yesterday was a slow news day, so the investigation is all over the front pages of all the Scottish papers. The early editions all led with Boras's "million-pound bounty", as the *Sun* called it, but later they all switched to the picture of Padstow, and to our release. The pattern was much the same with television.'

'Yes, I know. I caught some when I got in last night, and again this morning. Good. That was well done, Alan, to get it round everybody so late on.'

'Modern systems make that easy,' the media manager replied.

McGuire grinned. 'Shut up and take the credit.'

'Fair enough. I've had requests for follow-up interviews with you from STV, Sky and Forth News; I'll take the credit for them too.'

'No, you can take the media flak for turning them down. I've got nothing to add to what's in the release. Every word of that was cleared with the Crown Office, and I'm not going to risk compromising it by having others put into my mouth. I want you to pass that message down the line to Stevie and his team, just in case an enterprising reporter tries to doorstep them.'

'I've done that already. I've told them that anything relating to Padstow must come out of my office or yours.'

'Good.' He paused as the phone rang, then picked it up. 'Sammy, what is it?'

'I've got Mr Keith Barker on the line, Mr Boras's assistant. He'd like a word with you.'

'And I'd like a few with him.' He looked at Royston. 'Barker,' he said. 'This had better be private, Alan.'

'Pity, but I understand.' He picked up his papers and left.

'Okay, Sam,' McGuire grunted, as the door closed. 'You can put him through, and don't listen in.' He waited.

'Chief Superintendent.' A smooth, well-lubricated voice sounded in his ear. 'Good morning to you.'

'That remains to be seen,' the detective snapped. 'You've got some fucking nerve calling me after that stunt you and your boss pulled yesterday.'

There was a silence. 'Mr McGuire,' Barker protested, eventually, 'I'm not used to being addressed in that way. When you speak to me you are effectively speaking to Mr Boras.'

'Fine, for he was fucking lucky that he left this building yesterday before I could get my hands on him. You can feel free to pass anything I say on to him. I can understand a man with his wealth and in his situation wanting to do what he did. I can't understand, and I can't accept, his pulling it out of the hat like a white fucking rabbit, without prior warning or consultation! You're his adviser in this area: you must have known that.'

'Mr Boras is a man of independent mind: he can be impulsive.'

'And so can I, mate; another reason why you were lucky to get away unscathed. You're supposed to be a professional, yet I've just had to send Alan Royston, your opposite number in my camp, out of the room so I could speak to you without him trying to grab the phone out of my hand to tell you what he thinks of you for letting your boss do that.' He drew breath, to let his message sink in.

'Now shut up and listen,' he went on. 'The money is stupid, because it won't get you a result, and because it's a distraction to my officers. It's declared an open season for cranks. We've already had one medium on the line with the solution, only she doesn't quite know who the murderer is. But what I'm really concerned about is the rest of what Boras said. I want to lay this out for you. I've reviewed the tape and I consider that there is a clear implication that he plans to interfere in our investigation. If he does, I don't care who or what he is, I'll charge him.'

'You're imagining things,' Barker protested.

'Let's hope so, but if I'm not, be warned, on his behalf. Now, why are you calling me?'

'I'm following Mr Boras's instructions. He would like daily reports on the progress of the investigation.'

With difficulty, McGuire suppressed an explosion of spontaneous laughter. 'He'd what?' he said. 'Hey, how about this? Would you like me to give you a desk in the inquiry headquarters? Then you can sit in, and see for yourself?'

'Well,' the aide replied, 'not personally, but I could send a staff member.'

'Aw, Jesus, man,' the head of CID sighed, 'I'm kidding. Listen to me: I have respect for Mr and Mrs Boras and their bereavement, just as I have for Mr and Mrs Gavin and for Colonel and Mrs Paul. I'll give all of them any information I believe to be appropriate, whenever I can: I'll give it to them, understand me, not to you. But there are legal constraints on what I can divulge, even to victims' families. Right now, I suggest that you show your boss the latest press cuttings, for they reflect all that we know. Goodbye, and do not call me again.'

Forty-three

'How are the phones going, Tarvil?' asked Stevie Steele, as he hung his jacket over his desk in thc main CID room. He only used the detective chief inspector's empty office when there was a need for privacy or, as Ray Wilding put it, 'a bollocking to be administered', although only the sergeant himself had ever been in there for that purpose.

'They're quiet, boss. I had that psychic woman on again, though.'

'Who did it this time? The ghost of Harold Shipman?'

'She didn't mention him. But she did say that Padstow's too young, and that we should be looking for an older man, and fiendishly clever too. She's gone off the idea of a woman, but she's sticking to the Professor Moriarty theory.'

'Since you told her we were looking for a man.'

'True.'

'Did you hang up on her again?'

'No, I thanked her very much and said that I'd pass her information on to my inspector, and that maybe he'd arrange for the picture of Padstow to be made to look a bit more mature. Then I hung up.'

'Poor woman.' Steele chuckled. 'Next time, take her name and phone number, just to make her feel valued.'

Singh stared at him. 'You don't go for any of that stuff, do you, sir? Mediums and that?'

'Absolutely not. Yet I'm a wee bit on her side. Okay, everything's pointing us to Padstow; normally that would make it easy. But just because he's left a trail and given us a break, I don't think we should underestimate him. We don't know who he really is, he's still out there, and he's bloody dangerous. That's more or less what your lady caller was telling you, isn't it?'

'I suppose so. Okay, boss, next time she calls, I'll treat her like my auntie.'

'You do that, but don't hang around waiting for her. Ray's back here today. When he gets in, I've got a job for the two of you. I want you to interview a woman called Hope Dell, and a business called High-end Talent, up King George IV Bridge; source the number yourself. She's Harry Paul's agent; she's probably not going to be able to tell you much, but you never know, if he was a target . . . We have to talk to her, and that's all there is to it. Show her the Padstow picture; maybe it'll ring a bell.'

He turned and walked towards Montell's work-station. 'Griff, you wanted to talk to me.' The big South African nodded. He looked in need of a shave, and Steele realised that he was still wearing the same shirt as the day before. 'Have you been here all night?'

'Yes,' he admitted. 'I was working on this computer till late, so I crashed out in the rest room. I'm fine, though. I had a wash and I've been out for breakfast.'

'I didn't mean you to do that, man. It's above and beyond the call.'

Montell raised an eyebrow. 'Are you going to accuse me of sucking up to the bosses again? I know Wilding doesn't like me, but I hope you'll be fair.'

'Don't be so fucking prickly. For a start, it's Detective Sergeant Wilding to you. As for me, I respect commitment, and I won't make fun of it. How much progress have you made with the computer?'

'There are a couple of things on it that I need to talk to you about,' he nodded towards the unoccupied office, 'and it had better be in there.'

'Come on, then,' said Steele, and led the way into the glass-walled sanctuary. 'Okay,' he asked, as Montell closed the door, 'what's the big mystery?'

'I'll get to that, sir, but first, remember that phone number that we saw on Zrinka's contact list? It was listed under the initials RG?'

'Yes.'

'It's a pay-as-you-go number, non-contract, the kind you top up, but I've managed to trace the owner. It's an O_2 number, one of a batch allocated to the Carphone Warehouse and sold through their outlet at the Gyle shopping centre six months ago. I managed to contact them last night, and they found the transaction and the buyer's name. They know it wasn't an alias since it was paid for with a credit card. The phone belongs to Russ Gavin, Stacey's dad.'

'Russ? Why the hell would Zrinka have his private mobile number?'

'Good question, sir, but there's more to come. Just on a hunch, I asked the company if they have any other listings for that family. They have: the Gavins have a family contract under which Russ, Doreen and Stacey all had phones. We know that Stacey's was stolen by her killer, but the other two are still active. So why did he need another?'

'I guess you and I are going to have to ask him that, Griff. But first we should have another talk with Amy Noone, to see if she knows anything.'

'Yeah, I reckon.'

'And we will,' Steele went on, 'but there was nothing there that you couldn't have said in front of Tarvil. So what else have you found?'

Montell winced. 'This is where it gets tricky, very tricky. Remember Dražen's e-mail and the reference to a man, an important man by the sound of it, contacting her about one of her pictures?'

'Yes; he said good for her, but don't get too friendly.'

'That's right. Well, boss, when I checked her e-mails I found one from someone saying that he owned one of her works, and he'd like to buy another, or even commission one, as a birthday present for his daughter. The incoming e-mail address was robertmorgan, at downline dot co dot UK. He told her that his address wouldn't accept replies from people outside a very tight circle, so he asked her to call him, and left a mobile number. I tried to trace that, and ran up against a brick wall. Nobody would talk to me. So I tried to trace the e-mail subscriber through the ISP. Same result.'

'Why didn't you just call the number?'

'I was about to when DI Shannon from Special Branch

came storming in here. She threatened to rip my fucking balls off, told me to make no further enquiries and ordered me, as she put it, to make fucking sure that you went up to see her at Fettes as soon as you got in this morning.'

Steele's eyes blazed with sudden anger, in a way that Montell had never seen before. 'Hey, boss, I'm only repeating what she said,' he protested.

'Don't worry,' the inspector told him, 'I'm not swinging an axe at your neck. Dottie Shannon's got my home number: if she's got a gripe with a member of my team she should use it. She wants to see me and she will, but she isn't going to enjoy the experience; that I promise you.'

'What do you think it is? Have I stumbled on somebody under surveillance, or on witness protection?'

'Dunno. I'll find out when I get to Fettes. Meantime, Amy Noone's on hold, Griff. We'll go to her salon, once I've dealt with Dottie. I'll drop you at your place on the way there and pick you up again when I'm done. No offence, old son, but you really could do with a shower and a change of kit.'

Forty-four

They found a small enamelled plate set in a wall, beside a tenement doorway a few yards south of the city's Central Library, opposite the Soviet-style monolith that houses Scotland's National Library, and many of its greatest treasures.

'High-end Talent,' Ray Wilding read. 'Top floor. Funny, big man, isn't it?' he mused, to Tarvil Singh. 'There's an unwritten rule that says that whenever we visit a building like this, the office we want is always on the top fucking floor. Stevie Steele tells a story about being out with Dan Pringle once, and they had a climb like this. They get to the top and Dan gasps, with the breath he's got left, "After this, a refreshment will be in order." Any excuse for him, though.'

'And you,' Singh grunted. 'You used to work for him, remember.'

Wilding grinned. 'We'll see. Let's go.'

They stepped through the door, into a narrow corridor, and began the climb up a stone staircase. 'Talking about bevvy,' said the detective constable, as they passed the first landing, 'do you think it's true, about that being the real reason why DCI Mackenzie's off sick?'

'That's what the gossip mill says, after he was seen coming out of a clinic. But I don't know, any more than you do. All I do know is that the division's run better with Stevie in charge. My worry is that if Mackenzie does come back, the place won't be big enough for the two of them. He might sort out that boy Montell, though.'

'You want some advice, Sarge,' Singh grunted, beginning to pant as he heaved his bulk up the stairway.

'Go on, then.'

'You lay off Griff.'

'Why?'

'Because you're doing yourself no favours; worse, you're making a fool of yourself. The guy was a sergeant in South Africa, and he's got "flyer" written all over him. You're coming across as plain jealous.'

'You left out the bit about him knocking off Alex Skinner.'

'I also left out the bit about him being hard enough to crack you like a walnut if he heard you saying that. Just think about what I'm telling you, that's all.'

Wilding frowned. 'Jealous?' he murmured.

'That's how it looks.'

'Okay, I'll think about it,' he said, as they reached the attic floor.

There was a door at the end of the landing, with a glazed panel bearing the logo that they had seen on the plate at street level. Wilding rapped on the frame, then led the way into an office space that seemed to cover the full width of the building. It was open plan, apart from a glass office in the far corner where a woman sat behind a desk. The area was flooded with light from Velux windows. The sergeant glanced around expecting to find the walls filled with posters and pictures of the agency's clients but, to his surprise, they were bare.

'Yes, gentlemen?' a young man greeted them brightly. A big, broad lad, in jeans and a Coldplay T-shirt, he was well spoken and looked to be still in his teens; he was the only other person in the room, and judging by its furnishing, High-end Talent's only other employee.

'Police,' said Singh, only a little winded by the climb. 'We're here to see Hope Dell.'

'Do you have an appointment?'

The big detective constable sighed, then smiled. 'You didn't hear me, son. We're the polis; we don't do appointments. We want to talk to her about Harry Paul.'

The boy flushed slightly. 'Of course. Sorry, gentlemen. Just hold on a minute, please.'

The woman had looked up; as he walked towards her cubicle, she rose from behind her desk. 'Mum, it's the police,' they heard him say, as he opened the door. She nodded, and beckoned to them, an invitation to join her. She was dark-haired, of medium height, and wore a pale blue suit over a matching polo-neck that had the smoothness of cashmere. Singh's parents were in the rag trade; he knew quality when he saw it.

'Put the coffee on, Jacky,' she told her son, as the two men approached. 'Come in, take a seat.' She directed them to three designer chairs, grouped round a coffee table.

Wilding thanked her, then introduced himself and the detective constable. 'We've come about Harry Paul,' he told her.

'Yes, poor lad, it's appalling. Tragic for him and for his friends; the door had just opened for them, and they were about to make themselves some serious money.'

'There's one possible connection,' the sergeant told her, 'between Harry and the man who's our chief suspect at the moment. We're trying to establish whether there were any others.' He took the likeness of Padstow from his pocket and handed it to her. 'Is this person familiar to you?' he asked.

She took it from him and peered at it. 'I saw this in today's *Herald*,' she murmured. 'I don't know who he is, but I can tell you who the artist was. It was Stacey Gavin, wasn't it?'

Wilding stared at her. 'Yes, but how did you . . .?'

'Stacey was a client of mine. When you arrived, I didn't think you'd just come to talk just about Harry; I thought you'd be asking about all three.'

'Zrinka Boras was a client as well?'

'Yes.' She paused as the young man brought in a tray, holding a jug of filter coffee, milk, a plate of biscuits and three mugs, and laid it on the table. 'Stay with us, Jacky,' she told him, then turned back to the detectives. 'Clearly you don't know a lot about my agency. High-end Talent has only branched into music fairly recently, since my son left school, and decided that he wanted to work with me and study part-time, rather than go to college. Before that I represented writers and artists exclusively.'

'Isn't that an unusual spread?' asked Singh.

'Not really. Multi-talent agencies are quite common, although a business my size tends to concentrate on one discipline. I started my working life as an editor with a Scottish publishing house. I put my career on hold when I had Jacky here, and his sister, but when I was ready to restart I found that the industry was contracting and that there were no openings, not here at any rate. It had occurred to me as an editor that virtually all of the writers whose work was pitched to me were represented by agencies outside Scotland, and when I did some research I discovered that there were few here, worth the name at any rate. So I set myself up, working from home, focusing on general and children's fiction, and before too long I had a respectable client list.'

'When did art come into it?'

'After I lost my husband. He was killed in a car crash four years ago, and I was left with two kids to raise and a limited income. I had to make the agency grow, but it wasn't just a matter of taking on more authors: this business is driven by talent, not volume, so growth is dependent on finding the right clients, and you can't plan for that. Diversifying into art was my brother-in-law's idea: he has a passionate interest in it, and he knew that my core degree was in art history. He pointed out that there are many artists who could do much better for themselves if they had commercial representation. I did some more research, and I found that he was right. So I began by running a little strategically placed advertising. Then I produced a leaflet and I circulated it around the Scottish art schools, and the new division began to grow. I don't sell their work direct to customers, not as a rule, or through galleries, for there would be hardly any money left for the client if I did that. I maintain a database that's available to interior designers and architects, and to a few private buyers who are registered with me, and I look to develop new markets for them. Currently I'm opening up a website, where people will be able to buy signed and numbered prints on line.'

'I see,' said Wilding. 'So how did you meet Stacey and Zrinka?'

'Zrinka approached me a couple of years ago, more or less as soon as she moved here. She was young, but she had a very sharp business brain, inherited, no doubt.'

'You knew her background?'

'She told me. She never tried to hide it; she simply refused to trade on it. She was only ever known as Zrinka on my database. When we met, we had a two-way chat, but nothing was resolved. I'm sure she had me checked out, for it was a few days before she came back and said that she'd like me to represent her.'

'Has she been successful?'

'Oh, yes. If you look into her affairs, you'll find that she set up a limited company to handle the work she put through me.'

'But she was selling directly as well, from a stall.'

'She was, but that was part of our agreement, and I was happy, as long as she didn't undervalue her work.'

'And Stacey?'

'Zrinka brought her to me last year, after she had graduated from college, and introduced her. It was a very generous thing for her to do, but she was that sort of woman. Stacey was very talented too, maybe even more than Zrinka.' She held the print up. 'I could have landed her some pretty serious portrait commissions, you know, but she insisted that she wasn't ready for that. Too bad. I hope her parents have an idea of the long-term value of the work they're holding.'

'What about Harry, and Upload?' Singh asked her. 'Why did you go into music?'

'For Jacky.' She smiled at her son. 'He wanted to come into the business, and he persuaded me that music would fit naturally into a creative agency. He has a good ear for that sort of stuff. It's all beyond me, but he got it right with Harry and the boys, when Zrinka brought them along to see us. The contract they had . . . I can't bear to think of the money we'd all have made.'

'And still can, Mum,' Jacky told her. 'Harry can be replaced in the band. He's dead, but his compositions aren't.'

Hope Dell looked at him, surprised. 'Do you mean that?'

'Of course I do.' Suddenly, the boy was no longer an awkward teenager. Before the detectives' eyes, he turned into a sharp, fast-talking businessman. 'We've got a guy on our books, Craigie Speirs. Compared to Upload, he's been doing fuck-all . . . sorry, Mum . . . because it's a lot harder to push solo acts, but he would slot right in there. If A-Frame and Benjy are up for it, I'm going to talk to him about it.'

'Zrinka introduced Upload too?' said Wilding, bringing the discussion back on line.

'Zrinka did everything,' Jacky told him. 'Zrinka was pure gold.'

The sergeant showed him the print of Padstow. 'Do you recognise this man?' he asked.

'No,' the boy replied grimly, 'but if he did what you think he did, I know a lot of people who'd like to meet him, me included.'

Forty-five

Stevie Steele nodded his way past the officers on duty at the public entrance to the Fettes police headquarters, and headed straight for the Special Branch suite. Once he had entertained hopes that he might succeed Neil McIlhenney in that office, but the job had gone to Inspector Dorothy Shannon.

His brief disappointment had been ended by his wife, who had persuaded him that he was too gregarious to spend his working life in a regime that was of necessity secretive, and that he would be much happier in mainstream CID, where the breadth of his thinking and his innate popularity with colleagues would be an asset.

He had wondered for a while whether he might not have been considered tough enough for the job, but Maggie had disabused him of that notion very quickly. 'They might like you within the ranks, my love,' she had told him, 'but they know you're up there with Mario and Neil as someone not to be messed with.'

As he headed for Shannon's office, he had an inkling of why people might feel that way about him.

He opened the door of the SB suite and marched in.

Alice Cowan, the inspector's sidekick and general watch-dog, was at her post as usual. 'Is she in?' he asked, nodding towards the inner office door and barely breaking his stride.

'Yes,' Cowan replied, 'but you . . .' He ignored her, thrusting open the inner office door and stepping inside.

Dottie Shannon was standing beside a corner table, scanning that morning's *Times*. 'Alice, why don't you ever . . .?' She looked round impatiently as she spoke, her admonitory question ending abruptly. 'Oh, DI Steele,' she said. 'It's you, is it?'

'Reporting as ordered, Detective Inspector Shannon.'

'Now, Stevie . . .'

He stared back at her, his eyes like ice. 'Don't Stevie me,' he growled. 'What the fuck do you think you were up to barging into my office in the middle of the bloody night and haranguing one of my officers? That was out of order of itself, but to instruct him to have me come to see you . . . Inspector, you have let your new job go to your head.'

'And so have you, by the sound of things, Acting DCI. Or are you still holding a grudge?'

Steele gasped, then laughed out loud. 'Don't be bloody stupid, Dottie; I washed you out of my hair the day I chucked you. I never had a grudge to hold. If you remember, you and I had a thing that I thought was serious; then I found out you were banging George Regan on the side. So I pulled the plug on you.'

'Very sensitive, weren't you?' she retorted. 'We were both free and single.'

'Which is more than George was. Apart from being my mate, he's married, and I like Jen very much.'

'So much that you threatened to tell her about George and me.'

'Wrong. I'd never hurt her like that. All I did was tell George that you were a slag and, if he hadn't noticed, a mediocre lay, and that if he didn't straighten his act up he was in danger of losing both his wife and his pal.'

'Jesus, you really aren't Sir Galahad, are you?'

'I can put the boot in when I have to.'

'I'll remember that.' Her squared shoulders relaxed, just a little. 'Look, Stevie, that's all in the past.'

'You were the one who brought it up.'

'I know and I shouldn't have. I'm sorry I tore up your DC last night. By the book I should have called you, but I live just round the corner from your office, plus I didn't fancy waking up a pregnant chief superintendent as well as you, so I went round and dealt with it myself. If I laid into the guy more than I should it was because I don't appreciate being yelled at myself by my higher-ups.'

'Who yelled at you? Mario McGuire? Brian Mackie? The chief?'

'No, the higher-ups in Special Branch, specifically the security service. Some of them don't love me, I have to tell you, for reasons of their own.'

'I see,' Steele murmured. 'But where exactly do MI5 get off, interfering in a multiple-murder investigation?'

'They go off the deep end when you start making blanket enquiries about someone who, as they put it to me in a loud voice, couldn't have had anything to do with the situation and who is security cleared right up to God.'

'Did they give you the name?'

'Are you kidding? They gave me five minutes to shut your guy down or they'd ask Bob Skinner to do it.'

'Okay. I can see that you were under pressure; I'll explain that to Montell and give him your apologies.'

She glowered at him, then her eyes softened. 'All right, you can tell him I'm sorry. But explain to him that sometimes enquiries about specific people get them nervous. They didn't just want me to stop Montell, they wanted me to check that it was really him looking for the information.'

'Fair enough. We've done what they want, now let's see if they'll do us a favour in return.'

Shannon snorted. 'MI5 aren't famous for doing favours for local cops.'

'They've got a serious-crime function, haven't they?'

'Yes.'

'Three shootings is pretty serious in my book.' He took a computer disk from his pocket and handed it to her. 'That holds an image of the man we know as Dominic Padstow. We've drawn a total blank on him. I'd like you to send it down to them to see if it matches anyone on their files. If they're iffy about it, you can remind them that we know Bob Skinner too, and a lot better than they do.'

'All right, I'll ask them. I'll get back to you as soon as I can, one way or another.'

'Thanks.' He turned to leave, then paused. 'Hey,' he asked, 'does the name Robert Morgan mean anything to you?'

She shook her head.

He was about to open the door when she called after him. 'Stevie!' He glanced back at her. 'A mediocre lay?'

'I had to get through to George somehow.'

'Slag?'

'You decide.'

'Maybe,' she admitted. 'I knew he was married. How are you doing these days anyway?'

'Happy. You? Are you in a relationship?'

'In this job?' she replied. 'You have to be kidding.'

Forty-six

Mario McGuire was beginning to feel more human, although he still looked with a degree of suspicion at the coffee that, eventually, he had allowed Pye to bring him. He was looking through reports on outstanding investigations from the divisional CID commanders when there was a quiet knock on his door and Brian Mackie stepped into the room.

'Have you heard anything from Stevie Steele this morning?' the ACC asked.

'No,' the head of CID replied bluntly, 'and I don't expect to until he's found this man Padstow.'

'Has Dottie Shannon spoken to you?'

'No, but she wouldn't: she reports direct to the DCC, remember. In his absence she'd go straight to you.'

'Okay,' said Mackie. 'I was just wondering, that's all.'

McGuire leaned back in his chair. 'Come on, Brian, out with it.'

'I've just been in to see the chief. He's just had a call from Amanda Dennis, the acting director general of MI5, telling him that her duty officer had occasion to phone Shannon late last night to complain about one of our people, not in

Special Branch, making enquiries about an e-mail address and a mobile number that are on a sensitive list.'

'Do we know what she did about it?'

'Not from her, but Mrs Dennis told Jimmy that she called back shortly afterwards to say that it had been taken care of.'

'I can see why you're asking about Steele. His investigation is the only thing we've got live at the moment that would trigger that sort of incident. So why did Dennis call the chief?'

'I think she just wanted to make sure that it had been put to bed, because of the individual involved, the person whose identity MI5 were protecting. She told the chief, and this mustn't leave this room, that it was Bob Skinner.'

'Fuckin' hell!' the head of CID exploded. 'It must have been Montell doing the digging,' he continued. 'Stevie told me that he was going through Zrinka Boras's computer records to see if they threw up any recent contacts. I'd guess he was checking her incoming e-mails, and found one from him.'

'What are we going to do about it?'

The chief superintendent chuckled. 'Hey, Brian, you're the man from the Command Corridor. You tell me.'

Mackie ran his hand over his bald dome in a trademark gesture. 'No, I'm not going to do that. I'm not going to order you to do anything. This is a major investigation, and if you think this information will have any bearing on it, you're at liberty to advise Steele, and have him show you the content of the e-mail. If the pair of you feel it necessary, you're authorised to visit Bob, to tell him about it.'

'You mean interview him, as in eliminate him from our enquiries? Thanks, pal, for dropping this one in my lap.'

'What's your thinking?'

McGuire gazed at him, hard. 'My thinking, Brian, sir, is that I can spot the buck being passed a mile off, especially when it's aimed at me. Well, I'm not catching it. I'm saying fuck-all to Steele, and I'm going to pretend that you haven't been here. Can you imagine, for one second, what would happen if we did what you're hinting at? No, if we even discussed it, and one hint of that conversation found its way to the media?'

'Yes, but . . .'

'Brian, do some joined-up thinking here. Why do you think that the security service keeps an eye on big Bob's private e-mail and mobile numbers? I know he's a heavy and everything else, and that he's been well involved with them over the years, but it's more than that. You and I both know that he's not just the DCC any more, he's the partner of Aileen de Marco, this country's First Minister.'

Forty-seven

When Steele collected him from his apartment building DC Griff Montell looked a different man from the one he had encountered on his arrival at the office. He was clean-shaven and well scrubbed. He had changed from the previous day's clothes into black cords and leather jacket, worn over a white shirt that looked as if it might have been taken from the packet in which it had left Marks & Spencer. Only his brown-tinted sunglasses offered any hint that he might be feeling less than fresh as a daisy.

'Do we know where Amy's salon is?' he asked, as he slid into the passenger seat beside the detective inspector.

'Yes, it's along Raeburn Place, just before you get to Edinburgh Accies' rugby ground. There's a big clue. It's got "Mervyn" over the door.'

Steele found a parking place in the side-street beside the sports ground. As he had said, the hair salon was only a few yards away. As they entered they saw a girl's back, as she bent over a customer, rubbing so vigorously at her head that Montell winced. At first he thought that she was Amy, until she stood straight and he realised that she was older and taller.

As they stood in the doorway a man came towards them, tall, slim, in his thirties and wearing a violet smock that almost reached the ground. 'Good morning, officers,' he said. 'I'm Mervyn. What can I do for you?'

Steele smiled. 'It's that obvious, eh?'

Mervyn eyed Montell up and down. 'You don't look like the public-health department, that's for sure.'

'We'd like to see Amy Noone, please.'

'So would I. I've got four clients in already, and she hasn't turned up. I know she was upset yesterday, but I really need her.'

'Has she called in sick?'

'No, and that's the bugger of it. She doesn't seem to be at home. I called her half an hour ago, but got no answer. Her big fat boyfriend doesn't know where she is either; I rang him too. He told me that they had a drink last night, and that it seemed to cheer her up a bit.'

'Indeed? Well, thanks, er, Mervyn. We'll go and check her place anyway, just in case she was in the toilet when you rang her. When we find her we'll give her a lecture about responsibility, and advise her to get along here, pronto.'

'Don't be hard on her,' said the hairdresser. 'She's never let me down before, and she really was in a state when she heard about Zrinka and Harry.'

'We'll be gentle as piglets,' Steele promised him.

Amy Noone's tiny apartment was in a cul-de-sac off a side-street from Comely Bank Avenue. Once it had been a garage, or even a stable, but in common with most of the buildings of its type in Edinburgh, it had been converted for human habitation. It was one floor up, but the entrance was at ground level, with a buzzer and intercom. Montell leaned on the button for a few seconds. They waited, but no sound came from the speaker grille.

'No luck,' the DC exclaimed. 'Maybe she's gone home to her mum for a day or two. Come on, Amy,' he called out, 'you're holding up our investigation.' He thumped the black door with the side of his right fist. It swung open.

'Jesus, Griff,' said Steele, 'you haven't broken the bloody lock, have you?'

Montell peered at the door frame. 'No, boss, I haven't; it must have been on the latch.'

'Careless,' the inspector murmured, 'or . . . Let's take a look.'

A short narrow staircase, with rails on either side, rose up to the little flat. Steele led the way, opened the door to the living area, stepped inside and stopped in his tracks. 'Aw, fuck!' he moaned.

Amy Noone was lying on her back in the centre of the room, facing the morning sun and bathed in its light as it streamed through a big dormer window. She was naked, and her face was peaceful, as if she was in a dreamless sleep. Her dark hair, which had been in a ponytail when they had visited her the day before, was loose and neatly arranged, allowing them to see that it was streaked with honey-blonde highlights. Her arms were stretched out by her sides, palms down.

'The bastard,' Montell hissed. 'This is just too much.'

Steele saw that behind the glasses his eyes were squeezed tight shut. 'Hey,' he said gently. 'Hold it together.'

The DC nodded. 'I will, boss, don't worry. But you and

Tarvil were talking to this kid only yesterday, and now look at her. Why the hell did he need to kill Amy? She wasn't an artist.'

'Neither was Harry.'

'His body was hidden. Amy's is laid out just like the other two.'

'Yes. Now let's stop making assumptions and get back to being professional about this. Don't move; stay exactly where you are and look around. What do you see?'

Montell did as he had been ordered: slowly, carefully, he gazed round the room, doing his best to take in every detail. 'I see a pink towelling dressing-gown, thrown over one of the dining chairs. There's a T-shirt on top of it, and a pair of pants on the floor beside the gate-leg.'

'Yes, go on.'

'I see two mugs on the work surface, next to the sink beside the kettle, and a jar of coffee with the lid off. And a spoon. There are coffee granules spilled on the work surface.'

'What don't you see?'

The detective looked around the room for a second time, and then a third. 'A bed,' he replied eventually. 'This is a studio apartment, she was in her night clothes at one point before she took them off, but I don't see her bed.'

'No,' said Steele, 'because it folds up into the wall, there, between those two cupboard doors. See? The legs are hinged and they tuck away too, but you can see four marks on the carpet where they stand when it's down. She didn't undress for this guy, Griff; probably the opposite. She dressed to let him in, and he stripped her again, after she was dead.'

'How did he get in?'

'He talked himself in.'

'Or she knew him.'

'Maybe,' Steele conceded, 'but if she knew him, would she have bothered to put her bed away? Take a good look at her hair; the ends are still wet. Go into the bathroom; touch nothing, but go and look.'

Montell stepped over to the studio's only other door and opened it, then looked inside. 'The shower's been used today,' he called out. 'There's a damp towel on the floor, and a plastic cap.'

'Yes, now go and take a look at her T-shirt. I would, but I want to keep movement in here to a minimum: it's a confined space.'

'Okay.' Steele waited. 'There are damp patches on it.'

'I thought there would be. Are you getting the same picture as me? Amy's just got up. She's had a shower, being careful to keep her hair as dry as she can. She's a stylist: she won't do her own hair; she and her colleagues will go to work on each other's after the salon closes. Trust me on this: I've been out with a couple of hairdressers in my time, and both of them asked where my shower cap was.

'She's almost finished drying herself,' the DI continued, 'when the buzzer goes. She answers it, and the killer's there. She lets him in, but not before she's put on the T-shirt, her knickers and the dressing-gown, and pushed the bed back into its alcove. He talks to her for a bit. She's just up and hasn't had breakfast, so she asks him if he'd like a coffee. He says, "yes, please," so she goes over to the sink, fills the kettle, and she's spooning coffee into the two mugs when he shoots her in the back of the head. He strips her, lays her out like this and then leaves.'

'God,' Montell whispered, 'it's like we were in the room when it happened, watching it.'

'I wish we had been,' Steele murmured. 'Then we could have stopped the fucker.'

'Why's she naked? Neither Stacey nor Zrinka were.'

'He did them in public places. He didn't have time.'

'And Padstow had already seen them naked.'

Steele scratched his chin. 'I was at both post-mortems. Stacey Gavin was a pretty girl, but her body wasn't especially attractive. She had a thick waist and a big brown mole on her side, below her left breast. Zrinka had a figure like a model, but it was disfigured by a vivid appendectomy scar. On the other hand, Army's flawless; she's unmarked, and her skin's like fine china. Maybe he has a thing about perfection. Or maybe the sod just wanted to see Army naked, to humiliate her for her open dislike of him.'

'Wouldn't he have been taking a hell of a risk, calling at that time of the morning? A lot of people must have been going to work. There's a big chance he'll have been spotted.'

'Not as big as you think. The salon doesn't open till ten, remember, and it's just round the corner. He could have sat here, waited till it was quiet and then made his move.'

'Would she have let Padstow in? She didn't like him.'

'That's what she said, but you never know, that may have been loyalty to her friends.'

'Let's go back to the why, sir. Why kill Amy? What reason could there have been?'

'The most obvious one is that she would have been a key

witness in any trial. She was the only person who could have stood in the witness box, pointed to Padstow and identified him as the guy who was chucked by both of the female victims, then followed into Zrinka's affections, and bed, by Harry Paul.'

'In that case, is there anyone else who could identify him? Zrinka's mother, for example?'

'She never met him. They only spoke on the phone. But Russ and Doreen Gavin did. Griff, let's back out of here, get uniforms to seal the place off, and call in Arthur Dorward and his fine-tooth combers. Once that's under way, we need to get to South Queensferry, not just to talk to Russ Gavin but to make sure he and his wife are still in one piece. I'm going to send a car there right away, but meantime, without alarming her if I can avoid it, give her a call.'

Forty-eight

'Maybe it's Tuesday.'

'What?' Tarvil Singh exclaimed, gazing bewildered at Ray Wilding, leaning back in his chair with his feet on the desk as he gazed at the chart on the wall.

'I've just noticed. Both murders were on Tuesday: the first Tuesday in March and the first Tuesday in May. Maybe that's the real link between them and we've been missing it all along.'

'In that case we've got a bit less than two months to catch this guy before he does it again.'

'Bags of time.' Wilding sighed. 'Where does all that take us?' he asked.

'What?' Singh grunted.

'The information we got from Mrs Dell and her boy.'

'Nowhere forward that I can see. Okay, there's a new connection between all three victims, in that they all had the same agent, but we knew they were linked before we went up there. Okay, if you look at the three of them, Zrinka was very much the focal point, but we knew that too. For what it's worth, I'm still looking at Padstow and, right now, I don't think the DI will be handing out prizes for heading off in any other direction . . . like your Tuesday theory, for example.'

'No, he won't. You're spot on there; that's one I will definitely leave on the back burner. What have you got on your desk?'

'Calls while we were out. Two alleged sightings of the subject, and one . . . Hey, this is interesting: one from the woman I spoke to yesterday at the passport agency.'

'Why does everything have to be an agency these days?' Wilding mused, idly.

'So that the government can kid people on that the public sector is smaller than it really is.'

'That's a very profound analysis from a big lummox of a detective constable.'

'And that's more than a shade sarky from an idle dick of a detective sergeant. Actually, I'm quoting my old man; he's so far to the right politically that he'd join the British National Party, if they allowed guys with turbans to be members.'

'In that case he wouldn't approve of public money being wasted in meaningless chatter. Are you going to answer those phone calls or not?'

'If you'll shut up and let me.' Singh picked up his phone and dialled the passport service direct line number that had been left for him. He swore. 'Got it wrong. Your fault for sidetracking me.' He redialled and this time heard the ringing tone.

'Roberta Savage,' said a voice at the other end of the line, in an accent with West Indian overtones.

'Hello, it's Tarvil Singh here, up in Edinburgh. You rang

when I was out. What is it? Have you found Dominic Padstow after all?'

She laughed. 'No, don't build your hopes up. Our database never lies, and it's impossible to hide in it. No, something happened today that I thought you'd be interested in. Somebody else has been asking after the same non-existent person.' She leaned on the second syllable of the last word. 'He's a popular chap, this Mr Padstow of yours.'

'Let's just say he's much sought after. Who was it that rang you?'

'He didn't ring me. It was one of my team who took the call; I just happened to be close by and heard the name being mentioned. I waited until he was finished and then I quizzed him. The call came from a man called Dailey, Patrick Dailey, from the Home Office.'

'You mean the security service?'

'No, I don't. This chap's in the immigration division.'

'How did your colleague deal with it?'

Roberta Savage laughed. 'By the book. He told him that we were established as an agency to protect people from intrusion like this, and that he should go away and get legal authority.'

'And did he?'

'Actually he didn't need to do that: my colleague hadn't seen a newspaper this morning, so he had no idea that Padstow is a suspect in your investigation. But it seems that Dailey didn't know that either: he tried to bully my man, "I'm from your Head Office" sort of thing, but when he found that he couldn't, he gave up.

'I was suspicious about the approach, and so I called him

back myself, to verify that he was who he said he was. I asked him the reason for his enquiry. He got evasive, and told me he wasn't at liberty to say, but that it didn't really matter. In return, I told him to go away and read the Data Protection Act.'

'Nice one.' Singh chuckled. He imagined that crossing Ms Savage might be a mistake. In the background he heard another phone ring, but paid no attention.

'Do you have any idea what this might have been about?' she asked him. 'Yours is clearly a Scottish investigation; it has nothing to do with the Home Office. I know this, for I worked there myself before transferring here.'

'I have no idea, but I'm pretty sure that my boss is going to want me to find out. You didn't run across this man in your time there, did you?'

'No. He's new. I checked with a chum: he moved there last year, on a sideways transfer from the DTI.'

'Okay. Thanks for the information, Roberta. I'll see how my DI wants me to play it.'

'Keep my name out of it, please.'

'Absolutely, Roger. That'll be no problem.' She laughed again, and hung up.

Singh did the same, then entered her number into his personal contact book. When he was finished, he turned to Wilding. 'That was interesting, we've got competition from the Home Office. They're asking about Padstow too. When's the DI back?'

The sergeant was sitting upright, feet no longer on his desk, his face serious and more than a little anxious. 'No time soon,' he replied. 'That was him. There's been another death.'

Forty-nine

Happily, Doreen Gavin was alive, well and, as usual, generally bewildered when Steele and Montell arrived at the bungalow in South Queensferry.

'Why is that car outside, Inspector?' she asked, as she led them into her living room.

'It's nothing to panic about, Mrs Gavin,' Steele told her. 'Your husband isn't home yet, is he?'

'It's Friday,' she replied. 'Russ doesn't come home for lunch on Fridays. He's always away then, out of town on business trips; most weekends he doesn't get home till Saturday afternoon. In fact, there have been one or two times lately when he's been away until Sunday. They work him far too hard at that factory, you know.'

Standing behind her, Griff Montell rolled his eyes. 'He'll be home today, Mrs G.,' he said. 'We managed to catch him at the factory before he left, and told him we'd like to see him here.'

'But what is it? Have you found Dominic? Has he come forward to help you with your investigation? I'm sure he will when he hears that you're looking for him.'

'Let's hope so.' As Steele spoke he heard the sound of tyres on the driveway. He waited, silent, as Russ Gavin made his way in to join them.

'Hello, dear,' his wife greeted him brightly. 'Isn't this a strange to-do? And isn't it lucky that Mr Steele managed to catch you before you left on your trip.'

'Yes, Doreen, yes,' he agreed. 'It is. I was just about to leave when he called. What can we do for you, Stevie?'

The inspector felt a twitch in his eye at the familiarity, but decided to go along with it. 'You'll have noticed the police car outside, Russ,' he began.

'What police car?' Gavin looked out of the window to the street, where the patrol car sat. 'Ah, yes! You know, I came in so fast I didn't even notice it. Why is it there?'

'A young woman called Amy Noone was murdered this morning.'

For the merest fraction of a second, something that might have been fear, or panic, showed in Gavin's face, but then it was gone, to be replaced by an expression of deep concern. 'Oh, my,' he exclaimed. 'I know that name. I'm sure that Stacey mentioned her on occasion. What happened?'

'She was shot dead in her home, in exactly the same way that Stacey and Zrinka Boras were killed.'

'My God, why?'

'We can only guess at that for the moment, but one thing we know for sure is that she would have been able to give evidence that put Dominic Padstow together both with your daughter and Zrinka Boras, and she would have been able to identify him. I want to be clear about this. You told my officer that you met this man: I gather that Doreen did too. Is that correct?'

Gavin looked at his wife. 'Yes. That's right.'

'Yes,' she murmured, almost as if she was a spectator at the meeting. 'I certainly did, whenever Stacey brought him here.'

'Whenever?' Steele asked. 'He was here more than once?'

'Oh, yes. Stacey brought him out on several occasions, but usually on Fridays, when Russ was away. He stayed the night,' she glanced at her husband, 'and I'm afraid I let them sleep in the same room. I suppose that's why she only brought him on Fridays.'

Gavin shrugged his shoulders. 'She was a grown woman, Doreen.'

'Perhaps, but if you'd been here to back me up I would have objected. When you were away Stacey used to bully me.'

'Oh, come on, love.'

'Well, maybe not bully me, but she was firm with me, and always had her own way.'

'Doreen,' Steele said gently, 'we're not interested in Stacey's bedtime habits. We're here about your safety. One person who knew Padstow has just been killed. You and Russ are the only people left who can give hard evidence against him, even if you can't link him directly to Zrinka. With your permission, I propose to put you under police guard, twenty-four hours a day. You've got an alarm system and that's good. Russ,' he asked, 'does it have a night setting?'

'Yes. While we're asleep there are sensors active in all the rest of the house.'

'Fine. Obviously, Russ, you have to go to work, but we can look after you there. Doreen, during the day you don't leave the house without a plain-clothes escort. For night cover, we'll install video cameras front and back, and we'll have armed officers monitoring them in a van parked just up the street.' He paused. 'I don't really believe that Padstow would try anything here, but if he does, he won't get in, and he won't get away either. Are you both okay with that?'

'One hundred per cent,' said Gavin, anxiously.

'Good. We'll get it done, then.' He put a hand on the man's shoulder. 'Russ, I think you should cancel your business trip this weekend, don't you?'

'Yes, Stevie, absolutely.'

'Fine.' He lowered his voice. 'Now, Griff and I would like a word with you in private.'

'Sure. Hold on.' Gavin smiled at his wife. 'Doreen, since I'm home I might as well stay for lunch.'

'Of course,' she replied. 'I'll rustle something up. Gentlemen, would you care to join us?'

'That's very kind of you, Doreen,' said Steele, 'but we'll need to get back.'

As she left the room, the two detectives turned back to her husband. 'What is it?' he asked. 'Is the risk greater than you've been letting on?'

'No, that's as we set it out for you; it's there, but we have it under control.'

'Do you think this man will try to attack us?'

'It would be out of character. He'll probably assume that, after Amy's death, we'll be protecting you. This guy's very careful: he doesn't do suicide missions.'

'Stevie, didn't you anticipate that something like this might happen?'

The question riled Steele. 'Mr Gavin, if I had,' he said testily, 'the kid would still be alive. We didn't know she existed until yesterday, and there was nothing about her that marked her out as a potential target. All that she could have done was identify Padstow as Zrinka's boyfriend, and later Stacey's. That alone wouldn't have convicted him. Taking her out was . . . well, overkill is the best word I can think of. Literally true.' He glanced at Montell. 'But that's not what we want to talk to you about.'

'No, then what?'

'Mr Gavin,' the South African asked,' 'what was your relationship with Zrinka Boras?'

Another flash of consternation showed in the man's eyes, and he seemed to pale just a little, before recovering his composure. 'I never knew Zrinka Boras,' he replied. 'My daughter might have, but I didn't.'

'Oh, Stacey knew her all right; that's been established by Amy Noone, by other friends of hers, and by a barman at the Pear Tree pub, where they used to go. Have you ever been to the Pear Tree, Mr Gavin?'

'God knows. I've been to a few pubs in my time.'

'It's near Bristo Square, beside the mosque.'

'That still doesn't mean anything. There are so many bloody monuments in Edinburgh you ignore them after a while.'

'The barman I spoke about has a very good memory for faces. He told one of my colleagues that, as well as seeing Zrinka with Stacey and Amy Noone, he saw her there on a few occasions, last summer, with a man; an older man.'

'So?'

'So let's stop fucking about,' Steele hissed. 'We're doing you a favour here, Mr Gavin. We could be having this conversation with your wife in the room, and we will if you don't stop lying to us.

'For a period last year, beginning in July and stretching through to October, Zrinka's engagement diary, the one she kept on her computer, shows regular meetings with a man referred to as RG. Interestingly, these nearly all took place on Fridays and Saturdays. Most of them have venues attached, like the Pear Tree, on several occasions, the Bar Roma, the Edinburgh Rendezvous, and often just "here". Since her computer wasn't a laptop, I take that to mean that they met at her place.'

'The telephone directory's full of men with those initials.'

'Yes, but only one of them has a certain mobile number, one we found listed on Zrinka's palmtop. We've traced it, Mr Gavin. It's yours. It's the mobile your wife doesn't know you have, the one you use to call your girlfriends, to set up your Friday "business trips". If I really wanted, I could go to the mobile network and get a list of every call made from that phone, and then go and interview the recipients. At the moment my thinking is to do just that, unless you give me a bloody good reason not to.'

Gavin glared at him. 'You would too, wouldn't you? Okay, you win. I did know Zrinka. I met her last year, one Saturday when Stacey was selling work from her market stall down in Leith, and I went along to see how she was doing. We got talking; I liked her. She was one of those people who brighten up your day. Know what I mean?'

'Sure,' said Steele, 'I'm married to one of them. And if you took a really close look, instead of putting her down and treating her like a skivvy, you might find that you are too.'

'Are you a fucking marriage-guidance counsellor as well as a cop, Stevie?'

'No, and if that's your attitude, let's stick to "Detective Inspector Steele". Go on.'

'If you insist. I took one of her business cards; it had her website, her e-mail address, and her mobile number on it. I had a look at the website, and I sent her an e-mail congratulating her on it, and suggesting that she might help Stacey set one up. I got a reply saying, "Thanks. If she wants I'll do that." A couple of days later I called her and said that I'd like to thank her by taking her for dinner.'

'Did you call her on your mobile?'

'No, that time I called her from work.'

'What age are you, Mr Gavin?' asked Montell.

'Forty-nine. Why?'

'No comment; carry on. Where did you go?'

'The first time, to the Rendezvous; her choice, she liked Chinese.'

'Then back to her place?' asked Steele. 'It isn't far.'

'Not that time; it was just a friendly dinner. A week later we met for a pint after the stall closed . . . yes, at the Pear Tree . . . then went to a movie. I took her home and she kissed me. She kissed me, mind. We made a date for the next Friday, and that time I stayed over.'

'You spun her a story, yes? You told her your marriage was cold and loveless.'

'Which it is.'

'Whose fault is that?'

'Listen, I'm not going to discuss personal stuff between me and my wife.'

'Fair enough: we don't have time anyway. Go on. You were telling us how you wound up sleeping with your daughter's friend.'

'I know, it sounds callous. But we didn't have sex, not at first; it was just touching, know what I mean? Zrinka said she wasn't in love with me or anything, she just liked me. But eventually we did. The first time, when it was over, she just lay there, stroking my hair and looking sad. Looking back, I think she probably felt sorry for me; she was that sort of girl.'

'Who ended it?'

'She did. It went on for a couple of months more, until one night she told me that it was over. She said that she felt guilty, about Doreen, and about keeping what she called her dark secret from Stacey and Amy. To be brutally honest, as she always was, it was more than that; she said that I couldn't make her come, and she saw that as a sign that it was wrong. She said what she thought, did Zrinka; she told me that she had this feeling that I was just masturbating inside her. That was a new one on me, I'll tell you.'

'How did you feel about it?'

'I was sorry, and my ego was bruised by what she said, but she was being frank rather than unkind. If you really want to know, I've learned from her. Can you imagine that, a middle-aged man learning about love-making from a girl? When it came to the end, I respected her choice. I knew that I wasn't going to leave Doreen for her, even if she'd suggested that.'

'No?' Steele murmured.

'No! And I never will. She might be pretty much sexless, and a scatterbrain, but she's my scatterbrain. I might cheat on her, but I'll never leave her.'

'You're a noble guy at heart, aren't you?'

'Fuck off . . . Detective Inspector.'

Steele laughed bitterly. 'No, no. We're not done yet. When you were with Zrinka, did she ever mention Dominic Padstow?'

Gavin started to reply, then stopped short, as if he was searching his memory. 'Not by name,' he said at last. 'Early on, the first time we went out together, in fact, she told me that her last boyfriend had let her down, and that she was still badly affected by the experience. On the rare occasion she mentioned him after that, she called him "that so-and-so", bad language by her standards, but she never used his name. When we finished, she thanked me for giving her back some of her self-confidence. I was pleased by that. It's funny, I almost wound up thanking her for chucking me.'

'Almost, but not quite. Stacey never knew about you and Zrinka, you said?'

'That's right.'

'Are you quite sure about that?'

'Yes!'

Steele gazed at him. 'The two of them had some sort of fall-out, you know. Amy Noone was there when it happened. They were discussing Padstow initially, but it broadened out into men who couldn't be trusted. You know what I'm wondering, Mr Gavin? Whether Zrinka asked her how she could trust Padstow when she couldn't even trust her own dad. She told Stacey, eventually, didn't she? That's why they stopped seeing each other, isn't it?'

'Prove it!' Gavin snapped.

'That's a hell of an odd reaction to a straight question, if you don't mind me saying so.'

'I'm sorry.'

'Fine, but it is nonetheless. It's got me looking at another scenario.' He glanced at Montell. 'Are you thinking the same as me, Griff? What if Stacey did know, and it chewed away at her, until eventually she faced him with it, and threatened to tell Doreen?'

'That's how my mind's working, boss.'

'How about it, Russ? Just among us, did she, and did you stop her?'

Gavin's face twisted. 'She was my daughter, for Christ's sake,' he protested.

'Most murders are domestic. The way the body was laid out, it was almost reverential; it would fit. Then, having silenced Stacey, did you start to worry about Zrinka, more and more, until finally you decided she had to go too? Did you stalk her, and kill her, then leave her body neat and calm like Stacey's? And did you kill Harry too, not because you were jealous of him but just because he was there?'

'You're crackers.'

'Somebody is, crazy enough to kill four people. What about Amy Noone? When her name was mentioned as a witness, did you get nervous about her? Stacey's dad could have talked his way into her place this morning, I'm sure.'

Gavin looked at Montell, as if for support. 'You don't believe all this, do you, Griff?' he pleaded.

'It fits,' the detective constable replied. 'Where were you on Monday night, Russ, then on Tuesday morning?'

The man's face fell. 'I was away,' he murmured, 'on a business trip. But look, I don't own a gun. I've never fired a gun.'

'You were in the Territorial Army for eight years,' Steele retorted. 'Catering Corps?'

Gavin's legs seemed to give under him; he slumped into an armchair. 'I didn't kill my daughter. You must believe that.'

'I'd like to,' said Steele. 'Make me.'

'My business trip, on Monday night. She'll back me up.'

'Will she? Does she have a partner to protect?'

'No. She's a widow.'

'What's her name?'

'Hope. Hope Dell. She was Stacey's agent.'

Fifty

'Don't you think you should have waited till your DI got back, Sergeant, and discussed this with him?'

'I have thought about it,' said Ray Wilding, 'and decided that this can't wait any longer. The last time I spoke to Stevie he was at a crime scene, where he and Griff Montell had just tripped over our third murder victim in four days. He told me that once that was secure he was heading out to South Queensferry to make sure there wouldn't be any more. This thing's come up since then, and it needs looking into. When he does get back, he's going to want to hear the answer, not the question.'

'I suppose so,' Dottie Shannon conceded. 'But do you know what you're asking me to do here?'

'Yes, I'm asking you to use your channels to find out why some guy from the Home Office is second-guessing our investigation.'

'What makes you think I've got contacts who can do that?'

'If you don't, you'll know someone who has.'

'You CID guys have inflated ideas about the importance of Special Branch. But leave it with me and I'll try. What was the man's name, the guy who's been making these enquiries?'

'Patrick Dailey. He's in the immigration section.'

'He's way off his territory, in that case. I'll get back to you or Stevie. Let him know about this when you do hear from him.'

'Of course. I don't know where this might lead, Inspector. I just know that it needs to be looked at, ASAP.'

'You lot are like buses, aren't you?' Shannon hung up on a puzzled detective sergeant.

In fact, she did have contacts who could get things done. Chief among them was Bob Skinner, but he was on leave. When Steele had asked for her help earlier, she had almost interrupted his sabbatical, but had decided against it. Instead, she had considered playing it by the book and going to Brian Mackie, but that might have led to a discussion about her late-night confrontation with Montell, something she did not want to get into with the new ACC, a man she barely knew, for all her years of service.

Eventually she had decided to strike out on her own. When she thought about it, she was certain of what Skinner would have told her to do; and so she had called the person she had met with him, on their secret secondment to London almost half a year earlier, even though it did mean going to the top of the tree.

She had feared that she might have difficulty getting through, and so she was surprised when her call was accepted almost immediately.

'Hello, Dottie.' To her relief, Amanda Dennis's tone had been friendly. 'I've been hearing things about you.'

This time, after the conversation with Wilding had ended, she hesitated for a while. 'You're pushing your luck, Shannon,' she murmured. But finally she snatched up the phone and called the security service number once more.

This time she had to wait a little longer before being connected; when she was put through, the acting director general of MI5 sounded a little less patient. 'Has nobody been back to you yet, Dottie?' she said. 'I've put your request in motion, but finding a match on our database for a painting rather than a photograph might take a little time, if we can do it at all, that is.'

'I appreciate that, Mrs Dennis,' she replied, 'but that's not why I'm calling. As I've just said to someone, my requests from my colleagues are like buses: none for ages, then two at a time.

'The man you're trying to match for us was the subject of a fruitless search by the Passport Service yesterday, as I've told you. Today someone from the Home Office immigration section has been on to them making exactly the same request.'

'Oh?' Shannon could almost see Dennis sitting more stiffly in her chair. 'On what grounds?'

'He didn't have any. When the passport-service person challenged him he tried a bit of bluster, then backed off. Are we overreacting here? Could the Home Office have had a legitimate reason for following up on Padstow, just on the basis of the press reports of our announcement and the release of the image?'

'Hardly. If they had an interest in him, I'd have expected them either to contact you direct, and pool resources, or if there were security implications, to come to us, as you did earlier. What's his name?'

'Patrick Dailey. Apparently he's ex-DTI, and hasn't been there long.'

'Nor will he be much longer, unless he has a very good story to tell. Thanks, Dottie; you were right to bring this to me. I'll deal with this myself. The Home Office immigration section is unbelievably sensitive. We can't afford to have anyone there who's out of line.'

'Will you let me know the outcome?'

'Only if it's necessary. You've seen how we can operate. You might be better not to know.'

Fifty-one

'Are you absolutely certain that Russ Gavin isn't a suspect?' asked Mario McGuire. 'You're not protecting him from himself, are you?'

'No,' Stevie Steele replied. 'I never really thought he was in the first place, and now I'm entirely convinced that he's innocent. I didn't go easy on him: I made him give us his jacket and shirt for gunshot-residue testing, and I dropped them off at the lab on the way back into town.'

'What about testing him?'

'I thought about that too, but that would have been unnecessarily high-profile. His wife might have made a fuss, the thing could have gone public and got very messy. It would have been a waste of time too. Do you think he'd have been dumb enough not to wash his hands?'

'Or change his clothes?'

'No opportunity. If he did shoot Amy, we're more likely to find evidence on his garments than on him.'

'He's an engineer, isn't he?' McGuire asked.

'Yes, and I know what you're going to say next. In any trial, the defence would be bound to say that mineral traces could have been acquired in a variety of ways. It won't come to that, though, because before I came to see you Griff and I paid a call on Mrs Dell. She wasn't too pleased to see us, having been interviewed by Ray and Tarvil this morning, but I got her attention pretty quickly.'

'That must have been nice for her.'

'Actually she wasn't bothered. I told her that as a matter of routine we were checking the whereabouts on Monday night and Tuesday morning of every male remotely connected with the three victims. She told us straight away that on Monday evening she and Gavin were at a show in the Playhouse, that afterwards they had a late supper and went back to her place, where he stayed the night. He left for work from there next morning just after eight. No way he did it.'

'Could she have been lying to protect him?'

'No,' said the inspector, emphatically. 'Her son, Jacky, confirmed what she said. He works with her and still lives at home. He said that he gave Gavin his muesli and coffee.'

'Very domestic. And the Dell woman wasn't embarrassed by all this coming out?'

'Not a bit. She takes the view that if he's not happy at home, then Doreen has only herself to blame if he has a bit on the side. The arrangement suits her, she said, her kids don't mind, and that's all she cares about.'

'Why has it taken us all this time to find out that Stacey had an agent?'

'Because she doesn't mention the fact on her website, and because her father didn't volunteer the information.'

'And I can see why not. Did the boy give the impression that he didn't mind about the two of them?'

'Not a bit. He was cut up when he heard that Amy Noone was dead. He knew her, since she was going with one of the lads in Harry Paul's band. But he didn't seem perturbed by Gavin giving his mum a seeing-to, not a bit. Jacky's an ambitious boy, with other things on his mind. He reckons that Upload . . . that's the band . . . could be the start of a big-time career for him in music management, and he's concentrating on keeping them going without Harry.'

'Good luck to him. I think Harry's folks would like that. They'd see it as a memorial to their son. His dad certainly would: he was totally behind the boy's career.'

'I know. Jacky said that he's been in touch with him, to get his permission to bring someone else in to replace Harry in the band.'

'Jesus, that's a bit fucking callous. It's less than two days since the colonel found out his kid was dead.'

'I agree, but according to Jacky, he gave him his blessing straight away.'

The head of CID shuddered slightly. 'I never cease to be amazed by the different ways people react to grief. The mother could barely speak to us; I don't think she'll ever be the same. With the colonel, it's as if . . . I don't know.'

'Denial?' Steele suggested.

'Maybe. Maybe his enthusiasm for the band is his way of keeping the truth at bay. Some people are still adamant that Elvis is alive.'

'Yes, and that the lining of his coffin is all scratched to hell. Well, I know that Harry isn't. I saw the pathologist open him up yesterday morning, straight after breakfast.'

'Thanks for sharing that . . .' McGuire paused '. . . and, incidentally, for taking the time to come and see me. I appreciate it, for I was going to come looking for you.

'This is not good, Stevie. If we didn't have a public panic before, the Amy Noone killing's going to start one. Word's leaked out already, and the media have made the connection. A neighbour told them her name, and sent them to her work. A near-hysterical hair stylist told them all the rest. Have you contacted her parents?'

'Singh has. They divorced six years ago. The mother remarried and now lives in Gateshead. She and her husband will be on the way up by now. Dad was a drunk, who left them; he's currently in prison in England for credit-card fraud.'

'Okay. I can't wait till she gets here before I speak to the media. Royston's called them back in here for four o'clock.'

'I'll sit in with you, sir.'

McGuire frowned. 'In other circumstances, I'd be saying, "Too bloody right you will," but you actually found the body, so you and Montell are major first-hand witnesses. The press know that already, again from the neighbours; Alan Royston's been asked to confirm it.'

'Did he?'

'He said that the body was discovered by police officers, unnamed, who called at the address in the course of enquiries into the three earlier deaths. There was no point in being evasive about something we all know to be true.'

'No, I suppose not.'

'Since then, I've spoken to Gregor Broughton, and he agrees that you should stay out of it. Otherwise you'll spend the whole briefing saying, "No comment," to some very specific questions. So you brief me instead. Is there anything about the investigation that I'm not aware of? For example, your run-in with Dottie Shannon?'

Steele raised an eyebrow. 'How did you find out about that?'

'You were seen heading for her office this morning with what was described as "a face full of hell". I should tell you, Stevie, that nothing happens in this building that doesn't feed back to me, either through Sammy Pye or Jack McGurk.'

'I'll bear that in mind, not that I was planning to keep it from you. It was something I had to sort out with Dottie, that's all. She jumped on one of my guys and I wasn't having it.'

'It's all sorted, is it?'

'Yes.'

McGuire looked across his desk at the inspector. 'That's good. You see, I know that you have a history with her, and I wouldn't want it getting in the way of anything important.'

'It won't, but how the fuck did Pye find that out? It was a while ago, and it didn't cut across the job in any way.'

'He didn't find out, I did. She's Special Branch, so she was vetted, thoroughly, by Neil McIlhenney. Your name came up, so I got told. You used to be a legend for the women, Stevie, till you settled down: a pure legend.'

Steele ignored the jibe; his brow furrowed. 'Did . . .' he began.

'Yes,' said the head of CID, anticipating the question. 'George's name did come up, but I had it removed from the file.'

'That was good of you: you didn't need to do that.'

'I have my moments. So why did Shannon dig up Montell?'

'How did you know it was Montell?' Steele shot back.

McGuire sighed. 'Stevie.'

The DI grinned. 'Okay, you have your sources,' he said. 'He was checking the e-mails on Zrinka's computer. When he tried to run down one particular address it got referred all the way back to Thames House, and Dottie had a midnight phone call. I took exception to the way she reacted, so she and I had a wee discussion this morning.'

'And that's it?'

'Yes. I knew whose address it was anyway: it was the DDC's.'

McGuire's eyes widened, and his manner changed. 'How did you find that out?' he asked sharply.

Steele smiled. 'Thanks,' he said. 'Actually I was only ninety per cent certain, but you've just confirmed it. The e-mail screen-name was "robertmorgan", all one word. When the big man was awarded the Queen's Police Medal, his name was published in full in the citation: Robert Morgan Skinner.'

'You sneaky bastard; you set me up there.'

'I'm learning from my senior officers. And you can talk, sir. You knew exactly why I went to see Dottie. You were trying to find out how much I knew, that's all.'

'So you caught me. You've kept that information to yourself, yes?'

'Too fucking right I have.'

'Good man.'

'I wasn't too surprised, though: the boss has one of Zrinka's pictures, and one of Stacey's.'

'Come again?'

'It's a fact: Montell told me. He's pally with Alex, but you probably know that too. She has a Stacey Gavin original in her flat, a present from her dad. She told Griff that he has one himself, and that she bought him a Zrinka from off her stall. The e-mail was him asking Zrinka about buying a piece for Alex's next birthday.'

'Did she reply?'

'She couldn't, by e-mail. She could have phoned him, but we wouldn't know that without checking her phone records, and I don't plan to do that.'

'You sure don't,' McGuire confirmed. 'Has Montell figured out who the e-mail's from?'

'I don't think so. If he has he'll keep well quiet about it, unless he wants Alex to terminate their friendship on the spot.'

'Good. We're agreed, are we, Stevie, that we keep this entirely to ourselves as well?'

'Who else knows about the e-mail check and the run-in with MI5?'

'The chief and Brian Mackie, that's all, and they're both looking very hard in the other direction.'

'What e-mail?' said Steele.

'Fine. So, when I face the media to confirm the Noone girl's murder, what do I say?'

'That we're in no doubt about a link to the other two, and that we're in pursuit of the man known as Padstow, who is at this moment our only suspect. You could also say that we don't believe that there is a general risk to the public, as long as nobody does anything silly if they think they spot him. If you want to be controversial, you might add that Boras's million would be no fucking good to anyone if they were dead.'

'I might just do that. But what if I'm pressed on Padstow?'

'Tell them that we hope to identify him very soon.'

'Is that true, though? I'm telling them no porkies.'

'Yes, but I'll need to go back and see Dottie to chase it up.'

'Then what are you waiting for? Get along there.'

'I will, but there's something else you should know, something I heard from Ray Wilding before I came in here. Somebody else has been trying to trace Padstow through the passport service, a guy from the Home Office.'

'Why? Do we know?'

'My best guess is that he's in the pay of a newspaper, but hopefully Dottie will be able to shed some light on that too.'

McGuire pushed himself out of his chair. 'Then find out, preferably before that newspaper asks me questions at four o'clock.'

Steele nodded. He walked out of the head of CID's room, with a nod to Sammy Pye in the outer office, and headed for the Special Branch suite.

'She's on the phone, sir,' said Alice Cowan, as he entered.

'This time I'll wait,' he told her, with a smile, but as he did, the young officer glanced at an indicator on her desk.

'It's okay, that's her finished: but I'll let her know you're here.'

He allowed Cowan to observe proper practice and waited until she nodded for him to go on.

This time, Dottie Shannon was ready for him. 'Stevie, good; saves me looking for you. I've got some feedback from down south.'

'On Padstow?'

'No, not yet. They're making progress on that front, they've got a few possibilities, and they're looking into them before they give us the final verdict. But I have had a response to Wilding's request. Has he told you about it yet?'

'Yes. Thc Home Office guy: what's his story? Is he on a bung from someone in the media?'

'He's on a bung, but not from that source. MI5 reported him to the Home Office security people, and they pulled him in for interview, there and then. He spat it out straight away, looking to save his job, no doubt.

'When he was at the DTI, he was suborned by a man to provide what he described as "business intelligence", on a regular basis. He began to get nervous about it, but he found that he was in over his head, and that the only way he could extricate himself was by moving out of the department altogether.

'That's why he applied for a transfer to the Home Office. He thought he was free and clear, so it came as a hell of a shock to him when he was contacted late yesterday afternoon by his old benefactor and asked to get information on Dominic Padstow.'

'Yesterday afternoon?' Steele exclaimed. 'Before we went public with Padstow's name?'

'That struck me as peculiar too.'

'Did he give them a name?'

'Oh, yes, he gave them everything, all the detail, what he did, how much he was paid, and by whom. His paymaster was a man called Keith Barker.'

A broad grin spread across Steele's face. 'Mario McGuire will love that.' He chuckled. 'As far as he's concerned nothing that happens to that man will be too bad. He's Davor Boras's fixer.'

'Boras?' Shannon repeated. 'The dead girl's father? The millionaire?'

'The one and only. Not that he'll get sucked into this. Unless I'm very wrong about him, Barker will be deniable; there will be no paper that links him to his boss. What's going to happen about him?'

'To him, you mean: when it comes to corrupting the civil service, there's zero tolerance. The man Dailey has agreed to be a Crown witness, not to protect himself from prosecution, because they will do him, but to keep himself out of jail, and to hang on to his pension rights.'

'Will that be enough to charge Barker?'

'They think so: most of the payments are in cash, but they think they'll be able to establish a link between the two men through phone calls. They also hope to recover photocopied documents from Barker's office.'

'Unless he has time to destroy them.'

'He won't. Very soon, if it hasn't happened already, he'll be arrested by Met detectives and held in custody while his office and home are searched under warrant.'

'Is this likely to go public?'

'Do we want it to?'

'If charges are laid, we won't have a say, but right now? To be selfish, the headlines about this investigation are about to get bigger than ever. If something that might or might not relate to the case happened to divert some of them, I wouldn't mind a bit.'

Fifty-two

'You've had three murders in four days,' said a woman in the second row, 'and you're telling the public not to panic.' She was new to Fettes briefings, a London journalist parachuted into Edinburgh in the wake of the sensation caused by Zrinka Boras's murder and her father's million-pound reward.

The chief superintendent looked at her as if he was trying to decide whether she deserved scorn or pity. 'Would you like me to?' he retorted, stone-faced. 'Would your readers prefer me to declare a state of emergency and to advise people not to go out unless they have to?'

She shrugged, a gesture that annoyed the detective even more. 'I'm only asking a question. That is what we're here for, isn't it?'

'Actually, love,' he replied (he knew that Paula would kill him for using the term, if she saw the exchange on television, but he could not have stopped himself, even if he had tried), 'you didn't ask a question, you made a statement, designed no doubt to fit somewhere into a knocking piece you're planning to write. I'm not going to play your game.

'For the benefit of the serious people here, I'll repeat for the avoidance of doubt that, on the basis of what we know at this moment, we do not believe that any of these three killings, or the earlier, related, murder of Stacey Gavin, took place at random. All four victims knew each other; that's fact. Obviously they each had a wider circle of friends and family. I don't believe the threat extends to them, but they've all been given advice on personal security, and offered police surveillance if they want it.'

'Is anybody under police protection?' asked John Hunter, from his usual front-row seat.

The question did not surprise McGuire; he and Alan Royston had agreed that it might be asked, and had agreed that there was no point in deflecting it. 'Yes,' he told the old reporter, 'but purely as a precaution . . . and don't bother asking me who it is.'

'Chief Superintendent,' came a voice from the back row. It belonged to Grace Pretty, a *Scotsman* reporter with whom Royston was on particularly good terms. 'I've just been advised by my London office,' McGuire glanced at the media manager, seated by his side, and saw him wince slightly at the lie, 'that Keith Barker, who sat in on yesterday's press briefing with Mr Davor Boras, has been arrested by the Metropolitan Police. Are you aware of that?'

The head of CID held on to his deadpan expression. 'Yes.'

'Can you tell us whether it has anything at all to do with this investigation?'

He looked at her over the heads of the people between them. 'Grace, you know me, and you know that I like to give straight answers whenever I can.'

'Yes.'

'No comment.'

He waited until the buzz subsided.

'You're not saying that Keith Barker is a suspect, are you?' the woman in the front row demanded.

'Is there anything about "no comment" that you find hard to understand?' he replied. 'Any other questions?' As he spoke, he saw that Alice Cowan was approaching his table; he paused as she slid a note in front of him, then scanned it quickly. 'Thanks,' he said, as she left, looking up once more at his audience. 'Yes?'

'Dominic Padstow,' a television reporter intoned, 'the man we're all assuming is your prime suspect. Have you made any progress towards tracing him since you issued his image to the media last night?'

'As a matter of fact,' McGuire answered, pocketing the note and beginning to rise, 'as of this minute, we may know who he is. That's all, folks.'

Fifty-three

'He's a journalist?' Stevie Steele exclaimed.

'That's what MI5 believe,' said Shannon. 'They've e-mailed me a photograph and if he's not the man in the painting, he's his twin. I've forwarded it on to you, along with his file. Show it to your surviving witnesses and see what they say.'

'What's his name?'

'Daniel Ballester.'

'Unusual.'

'His grandfather was on the wrong side in the Spanish civil war; he dodged the firing squad and escaped to Britain. It's all in the file. It should be in your mailbox by now, so you can see for yourself.'

'Why does MI5 have a folder on him?'

'For the not uncommon reason that he's a pain in the arse. He's a freelance whose speciality is upsetting the government, enough for somebody to have ordered that tabs be kept on him.'

'Thanks, Dottie, I'll read it right now.'

'Five aren't done with this, Stevie,' Shannon told him. 'They have access where we don't; they're going to do what they can to trace his movements. In the meantime they've raised the alert at all points of exit from the country.'

'You must have a good contact there.'

'As good as they get. I'll be back if and when I hear anything more.'

Steele hung up, switched on his computer terminal and waited while it booted up. As soon as the cursor switched from hourglass to simple arrow, he clicked the internal mail icon and watched the screen. True to her word, Dottie Shannon's message was there; he opened it and clicked on the attachments, first to download, and then to display the photograph.

He called to Wilding and waved to him to join him. 'What do you think of this?' he asked, holding a print of the face from Stacey Gavin's portrait beside the monitor.

'That's the boy,' said the sergeant, at once. 'Mrs Dell was right: Stacey really could paint. He's a good-looking bastard, isn't he? What do we know about him?'

'Let's have a look.' Steele opened the other file, and read aloud, '*Daniel Ballester, aged thirty-two, white British subject, heterosexual, unmarried. Son of Archimedes Ballester, stockbroker, and Hilda Roberts, formerly of Hounslow, now retired and residing in Scottsdale, Arizona. No other known relatives*. That's fucking magic; sounds like a dead end already. *Graduated with honours in media and politics; vice-president of student union in his final year and a member of the executive of the National Union of Students*.'

'They probably started watching him then,' Wilding muttered.

'Could be. What's next? Hey, he has two criminal

convictions, one for being part of a disorderly crowd during his university days, but . . . get this . . . another for causing actual bodily harm to a girlfriend when he was twenty. He was given a jail sentence of one year, suspended. Jesus, Ray, if Zrinka had only known . . .'

'If wishes were horses, gaffer, we'd all get a ride. What about his career?'

'It says here that he joined the staff of Sky News as a researcher, straight from Keele, then moved on after a year to the *Guardian* features department. He made his name there with several exposés of politicians on the take from business, which led to a government front-bencher being thrown out of Parliament, and subsequently jailed . . . I remember that one. He was forced to resign from the *Guardian* just over two years ago after doing a piece for a left-wing magazine, alleging the assassination of Princess Diana.'

'What self-respecting radical journalist hasn't written one of those?'

'Ah, but this one was subsequently discredited and condemned by both the British and French governments, and the editor of the magazine was forced to issue a retraction and an apology. According to this, Ballester was fed false information by an unknown contact who posed as a dissident member of the French Sûreté, and showed him a fake document, purporting to have been signed by the French justice minister, approving the plot, and giving the go-ahead.'

'Don't piss off the government, eh?'

'So it seems. Since then he's been operating as a

freelance, doing the same type of stuff for whoever will pay him. He's been involved in a couple of stings on closet gay pop stars, on a kiddies' TV presenter with a drug habit and on a footballer's wife who was shagging his manager when he was away on international duty.

'He lives in London, but . . . and this is when it gets interesting . . . periodically drops off the radar. His "periods of inactivity", as they're called here . . . an excuse for sloppy surveillance if you ask me . . . appear to coincide with the times he was living with Zrinka and then going out with Stacey. His whereabouts are currently unknown; he was last observed in London in February.'

'That fits,' said Wilding. 'But what does it tell us, Stevie?'

'Nothing of itself, but it poses some interesting questions. Why Zrinka? Why does this guy, with his track record, suddenly pop up in Edinburgh and latch himself on to the artist daughter of one of the richest men in Britain?'

'Maybe he'd had enough of scratching around. Maybe he wanted to marry money.'

'So he targets a girl who's determined not to live off her father? No, that's not the reason. I reckon he was on a fucking story, that's why. He was out to dig up something on Boras. Think about it, Ray: Ballester made his name doing stories about business corruption, and what finer target than him? We know he's dodgy, that he's used Keith Barker to bribe a DTI official for useful inside information. Maybe that was the story Ballester was after, or maybe it was something else, but I'll bet you one thing. Eventually Zrinka found out who or what he was, and that was why she gave him the bum's rush.'

'What about Stacey? Why would he move on to her?'

'Because he didn't want to give up on his story. Remember, she and Zrinka didn't become friendly till after he was gone. He couldn't get to Boras's daughter any more, so he got to someone close to her. We know from Amy that she wouldn't have given him the time of day, but Stacey didn't know his history.'

'So why did he kill them?'

'A combination of rage over rejection, jealousy, and maybe frustration that his story was blown; that serious-assault conviction in his background suggests that he's capable.'

'It does. So where do we go now? We might know what his real name is, but he's still disappeared.'

Steele leaned back, gazing up at the ceiling. 'How did Zrinka find out?' he asked himself aloud. 'If I'm right, if he was researching a story on Davor Boras . . .'

He sat upright and looked at Wilding. 'I want to interview Barker,' he said. 'No, I'm going to bloody interview him. Ray, we're going to London. Maybe we could . . .'

He stopped short and looked at his watch. 'Shit!' he shouted. 'Maggie's leaving do starts in ten minutes.' He stood up and grabbed his jacket. 'We're going tomorrow. You make the arrangements: book us on an early flight, then tell the Met that we're coming and that we want to see Barker, wherever they're holding him.'

'What if he's on bail?'

'They'll still have him; tell them not to give him fucking bail. If you have a problem with them, go to DCS McGuire. Meantime, I'm off to join my wife.'

Fifty-four

'I can't tell you how pleased I am that you came, sir,' said Rose, to the tall, tanned man who stood by the window of the conference room in the Torphichen Place police office. He looked slimmer in the waist than at their last encounter, although the tightness of his jacket at the shoulders suggested this might be due to exercise rather than dieting. His steel-grey hair was cut much shorter than she had ever seen it, and seemed to shine, picking up highlights from the evening sun.

'Mags,' his sigh had a laugh in it, 'for once in your life, will you please call me Bob?' He glanced at his watch, awkwardly, since he was holding a glass in his left hand and a plate, laden with sandwiches, in his right. 'It's past five o'clock so you're a civilian, for a while at least. To tell you the truth, I thought about not coming. A lot of people here haven't seen me for a while, and might want to bend my ear about things. You're the centre of attraction here and I didn't want to take away from that.'

'I'm glad you changed your mind.'

'Thank my daughter. She told me that I'd an inflated idea of my own importance and that staying at home wasn't an option. She'd have come with me, by the way, only she's in Manchester today, on business. Bloody jet-setter; she's flying higher by the month, that one.'

'I know. Mario told me how highly Paula rates her, in what she's doing for the business; he says that Viareggio PLC, as it is now, was very much her creation.'

'Speaking of Mario, I don't see him, or your new husband for that matter.'

'Stevie will be here; he's on a three-liner. As for my ex, he's expected, but . . . they're both under a hell of a lot of pressure just now.'

'I can imagine. I feel a bit guilty about that too, Maggie. I did think about making my presence felt, and giving Stevie and the team my support, but the other lady in my life persuaded me that if DCC Skinner broke off a well-publicised sabbatical to take personal charge of the investigation, it would be seen by our enemies in the media as a vote of no confidence in them. That's why I've stayed out of it.'

'I guessed as much, and so did they.' She smiled up at him. 'Now if you hadn't turned up today, that would have been a cause for guilt.'

'You're looking great, you know,' he told her. 'Don't take this the wrong way, but I'm just gobsmacked by the turn your life has taken.'

'So am I, Bob; so am I. This time last year, if anyone had told me that . . . Jesus!'

Skinner thought he detected an edge in her voice. 'You've no regrets, have you?'

'Absolutely not. I have never in my life felt more

fulfilled. I am totally focused on delivering this child safely into the world, and I can think of nothing beyond that.'

'Having fathered some in my time, I know the feeling.'

'Thanks. Actually you're not looking too bad yourself, considering what you've been through.'

'And thank you,' he said. 'I'm fine now. I'm over the divorce and I'm content with the arrangements that Sarah and I have made for the kids, especially now that I've seen how it's working out. They had a great time in Connecticut at Easter and they're looking forward to the summer holidays already.

'Sarah's happy too: she loves being a proper doctor again, rather than a pathologist, working, as she puts it, with people who ain't dead yet, and trying to keep them that way.'

'You've seen her there?'

'I flew across with the nanny and the kids, hired a car and drove them up to her place. Then I headed north to Canada.'

'Now I did know that. Stevie's cousin's with the force there, and he told him. It's a tiny world.'

Skinner chuckled. 'You can't do a bloody thing, can you? The fact is, a sabbatical isn't a holiday, it's a working break. Since I've been away from Fettes, apart from my visit to the RCMP, I've spent some time with the Mossos d'Esquadra, the Catalan police force, and I've lectured at the FBI Academy in Virginia.

'There was a purpose to the visits to Toronto and Barcelona. Ontario and Catalunya have what are effectively unitary police forces covering those entire regions. I've been studying how they work; my findings will be contained in a paper I'm writing.'

'A thesis? For a doctorate?'

'No, that would just be another ego trip. It's for Aileen; she asked me to do it.'

'You mean the executive's looking at setting up a national force for Scotland?'

'Not officially; at this stage it's private enterprise on our part. If it floats, she might give it to a policy unit for a view to launching it. Why not? The population of Ontario is twelve million, and Catalunya has eight million. We have five. Mind you, Maggie, this is between you and me. The chief knows what I'm doing, so does Alex, and so does Andy Martin, but that's it.'

She gazed up at him thoughtfully. 'I'm more than a bit honoured that you've chosen to tell me.'

'Don't be; you're one of the best officers I've ever worked with, and you're a friend. I value your opinions and I'd like to talk my thoughts through with you before I finish my report. Can I do that?'

'Of course,' Rose replied. 'I'll have plenty of time on my hands over the next few weeks.'

'You sure will,' said Stevie, approaching from behind just in time to hear her last few words. He kissed her on the cheek. 'Sorry I'm late, love, but things have been moving fast. You're going to have to see Ray's cousin on your own tomorrow, I'm afraid. Ray and I are off to London to interview Keith Barker, that character I told you about.' He looked at Skinner, extending his hand. 'Hello, sir, good to see you. I'm chuffed you would make it.'

'I wouldn't have been anywhere else.' He glanced across the room and saw that McGuire had arrived also. 'Maggie,' he said, 'you should circulate. I want a word with your old man and your ex.'

As Rose headed off in the direction of the chief constable, Skinner caught the eye of the head of CID, who read the summons, and made his way through the assembly. 'Afternoon, boss,' he greeted the DCC.

'And to you. How are you guys getting on? I've been following with interest, don't worry.'

'We've identified Padstow,' Steele replied. 'He's really an investigative reporter called Daniel Ballester. We don't know where he is, but we do know that we're not the only people who have been after him; hence my trip to London tomorrow, to question Barker.' He glanced at McGuire. 'That's all happened since we spoke last,' he said.

'I know,' the head of CID told him. 'Shannon kept me in the loop.'

'The only family lead is to his parents, retired and living in Arizona. They need to be interviewed.'

'Give me the details,' said Skinner, 'and I'll use my FBI contacts. I'll make a call tonight; if his folks know where he is, you'll know by tomorrow.'

'What if they won't say?'

'They will: retired British subjects in the US need to be good citizens if they want to stay there.'

'Maybe he's on his way out there already.'

'Have you put out an all-ports-and-airports warning on this man?'

'That's in place; Dottie Shannon arranged it.'

'In that case, it's less than twelve hours since the Noone girl was killed. If he's your man and he has made it out of the country, his name will be on a flight passenger list somewhere. If he's landed, we have a hot trail. If he's still up in the air, when he gets down he'll wish he'd stayed there. Now, what the hell is this about Barker?'

Stevie chuckled. 'He came in handy,' he said to Skinner. 'The media are going crazy trying to find out why he's been lifted.'

'Why has he been?' asked the DCC.

'For bribing a guy in the Home Office.'

'Christ! That'll keep him out of circulation for a while. Have the Met tied it to his boss?'

'Not as far as I know.'

'See if you can help them. I took a big dislike to that man when I saw him on telly; it was plain as the scar on my forehead that when he sat in on your briefing he was looking right through the cameras at the stock market. Now,' he continued, 'about your inquiry; there's something I need to tell you. I've put you in an embarrassing position, and I apologise.

'I know what happened with young Griff; I got feedback from Five as well, and from Amanda Dennis herself, not from the duty officer. He called Shannon without reference to her, and he's still aching because of it.' He smiled, his eyes distant for a second.

'You guys are bound to be wondering why I didn't react when I saw the photo of Zrinka Boras. The answer is that I've never met her, as such. When Alex bought me that picture from her stall at the market, I was busy elsewhere.

In fact, I was trying to free my younger daughter from a faceful of candy floss, a job and a half, if you've never had to do it. When I opened the parcel at home, I found that Zrinka had put one of her business cards in with it. That's how I came to have her e-mail address.'

'I'd worked that out, sir,' said Steele. 'I took a couple of those cards from her flat.'

'Maybe so, Stevie, but you should have bloody asked me about it, for the book.'

'Sorry, boss.'

'Forgiven. Now, what else should you have asked me?'

'Whether you knew Stacey Gavin as well, since you and Alex each have one of her paintings.'

'Exactly. For the moment, we'll leave the question of how Montell came to recognise a picture hanging in my daughter's bedroom, then shoot his mouth off about it in the office. That's for me to raise with him on another occasion,' his eyes gleamed, 'although you can feel free to tell him that I plan to do just that.

'The fact is, I didn't know Stacey, nor did I make the connection until Alex told me about the good detective constable spotting it. I bought both of those works from a gallery; the signature she used was "Gavin"; that was all. The day that she was murdered, I flew out of Edinburgh for the start of a ten-day trip to Barcelona so I missed the press coverage. I saw references to the investigation in the papers after I got back, but by that time all the detail about her had been worked through.

'That's it; that's all I know. Now, what you must do is get that into the record and make fucking sure that the fiscal is aware of it. You're doing a first-class professional job, Inspector, but there must be nothing swept under the carpet in this investigation, or laughed off as ridiculous. Be absolutely clear about that.'

'Don't be hard on Stevie, boss,' said McGuire. 'He knew damn fine that if you had anything to add to the pool of knowledge you'd have got in touch with us. He's running this show in the absence of Mackenzie and Neil.'

'True,' Skinner conceded. 'I didn't take that into account. Plus he's got his pregnant wife to worry about, who is, let's not forget, the reason why we're all here. Okay, Inspector, I'll stop blaming you for my own sins of omission. Speaking of the centre of attraction, Brian Mackie's throwing us meaningful looks. I think he wants to get on with the formalities.'

They joined the crowd of officers of all ranks gathered in the centre of the room, where Maggie, looking a little nervous, stood beside Sir James Proud. The chief constable made a short speech, one of good luck, rather than goodbye. There was no presentation, since Maggie had expressly forbidden a collection within the office.

When Sir James yielded the floor, she gazed around her audience slowly. 'Chief, ladies and gentlemen, thank you,' she began, 'for coming along to wave me off on the road to maternity. If some of you are surprised by this development, I promise you that you ain't half as bloody astonished as Stevie and I were when we found out what we had done.' She paused until the laughter quietened.

'God willing, next time I see many of you, I'll be bringing our baby daughter into the office for inspection and approval, and for the pleasure of seeing hard-bitten . . . and in some extreme cases, like Charlie Johnston over there, thoroughly chewed . . . police officers acting like big soft nellies. But when I do, it'll be for old times' sake.' She paused again, taking in the puzzled expressions on several faces, particularly those of Stevie, Mario and Bob Skinner.

'Until this very moment,' she continued, 'and this is the truth, I had no intention of saying what I'm about to say today, in this room, but standing among my friends and colleagues I can see very clearly that, knowing what I do, it would be unfair and probably just a bit immoral if I didn't. I'm not going to do a Bilbo Baggins, put on a magic ring and vanish in a puff of smoke but, friends, this is the last day of my police career.

'Chief, Bob, Brian, but most of all Stevie, I'm not going to hang around on cushy leave for a year before giving you the news; I'm telling you now what I've decided already. My firm intention from now on is to pursue a career as a full-time wife and mother.'

Fifty-five

'I hope that my wife is getting on all right with your cousin's wife,' said Stevie Steele, as he and Ray Wilding stepped off the Heathrow Express at Paddington Station and headed for the taxi rank.

'I've told you, it isn't possible not to get on with Margot: she doesn't allow it.' The sergeant shook his head. 'I still can't get over Maggie's bombshell.' He laughed. 'The faces in that room must have been a picture.'

'They were, and I suspect that my jaw dropped furthest of all when she came out with it.'

'You had no idea?'

'Not that she was going to announce it there and then, I hadn't. I knew that she had it in mind, but I thought she was still thinking it over, and that she was going to wait till the baby was safely delivered to make a decision.'

'How long will it take you to stop thinking of her as a chief superintendent?'

'God,' Steele exclaimed, in disbelief. 'You're some machine. Do you see me as a common man version of Prince Philip, walking three paces behind his wife? Maggie stopped being a senior officer as soon as she walked in the front door. I haven't thought of her that way from the day we started living together . . . and since before that, if you really want to know.' He flagged down a taxi. 'Charing Cross police station,' he told the driver.

'It'll take me a while,' Wilding continued. 'I've known her for a while too, and I've never been able to imagine her as anything other than a police officer. It's one thing talking idly about giving up; I can imagine her doing that, in her condition. But for her actually to go through with it, to me that's incredible.'

Steele sat silent for a while, as the black cab pulled out into the Saturday-morning traffic. 'When I think about it, Ray, I have to confess that I find it remarkable too. Not that long ago we were talking about when the time would be right for her to move up to assistant chief, and whether she should move force to achieve it. Then all of a sudden there's this sea change in her, leading up to her announcement last night.

'I thought I knew her, better than I've ever known anyone in my whole life. I thought she'd never be able to surprise me again, and then she went and proved me wrong. I told her as much last night. She was sorry, you know, guilty that she hadn't told me what she'd decided in advance, but when she said that she did what she did on the spur of the moment, she wasn't kidding.'

'Did anybody try to talk her out of it afterwards?'

'Brian Mackie did. He pleaded with her to take longer to think about it, and not hand in her resignation straight away. He told her that replacing her permanently would be a big problem for him, one that he'd rather put off for the moment. He even said he'd been thinking about letting

Neil McIlhenney gain a year's seniority, but the DCC told him to forget that, pronto. He said that he wasn't pulling Neil out of CID.'

'The DCC,' Wilding exclaimed. 'Was he there?'

'Of course. Mags used to be his exec, remember.'

'How did he take it?'

'He was great. He was the only one of us that didn't bat an eyelid. He told her that she hadn't made a wrong move in all the time he'd known her, and that if that was what she'd decided, she'd leave with his blessing. They've always been close, those two.'

'You don't mean . . .'

'Don't be stupid; of course I don't. They've seen a lot of action together. It's the same with her and Mario, and big Neil too. There's some serious history there, and I'm not just talking about her first marriage. I don't think I know all of it, but if she doesn't choose to tell me, that's fine.'

'So who is going to take her place?'

'I reckon that Mary Chambers will carry on, for a while at least; they might bring Alastair Grant up from CID in the Borders, or they might even look outside our force. Time will tell. The only thing that's certain is that it won't be you or me.'

'Maybe it'll be Griff Montell,' Wilding muttered.

Steele smiled. 'Somehow, I don't think so.'

'Why do you say that? Is he in bother over that run-in with Special Branch?'

'Not at all. Forget it, Ray, I didn't mean anything by that. Griff's okay; he just needs a crash course in tact and diplomacy, and I think he has one coming.'

The two officers sat back in the spacious cab, enjoying the view as the driver took them on a tourist route that led round Marble Arch and down Park Lane, past Buckingham Palace, then up the Mall towards Trafalgar Square. Their destination was Agar Street, just off the Strand. When they arrived they were both taken by surprise: Charing Cross police station was a fine white building with a pillared entrance.

'Holy shit!' Wilding exclaimed, as Steele paid the driver. 'This isn't like any nick I've ever seen. It looks more like a fucking bank.'

However, inside it was very much a working police office. They stepped through the high double doors into a public reception hall. The inspector walked up to a divider behind which a sergeant and a constable were on duty. 'Morning, sir,' the senior officer, a black woman, greeted him. 'How can I help you?'

'DI Steele and DS Wilding, from Edinburgh,' he glanced at the name-tag on her tunic, 'Sergeant Baptiste. We're here to interview a prisoner.'

'Yessir,' she replied smartly. 'I was told to expect you. Hold on and I'll buzz DI Stallings.' She walked back to her desk, picked up an intercom and spoke into it. 'She'll be right down,' she called out.

Steele thanked her. They glanced around the entrance space as they waited. 'Probably goes all the way back to Sherlock Holmes,' Wilding murmured. 'Maybe even before him.'

'I don't recall Sherlock being a serving officer,' the inspector commented quietly.

As he spoke a door opened: a dark-suited, dark-haired woman appeared and headed in their direction. She looked at the visitors appraisingly, until her eye settled on Steele. 'Inspector,' she guessed correctly, offering a handshake. 'Becky Stallings; good to meet you.' She nodded to Wilding. 'You too, Sergeant. Welcome to Charing Cross. Come on, our guest will soon be ready for you.'

There was a stairway behind the door; Wilding took in his surroundings as they climbed. 'This beats Queen Charlotte Street,' he said, as they reached the top. 'Must be a cushy number being posted here.'

'Come and join us,' said Stallings, 'when there's a big demo in Trafalgar Square, and the place is full of anarchists, or even when there's a celebration there and we get more pickpockets than we can process.'

'I'll do that,' the sergeant replied, 'if you come and join us when Rangers play at Easter Road.'

She smiled at his comeback as she opened a door and showed them into her office. 'We're going to have to wait for a bit,' she told them. 'Barker wants his lawyer present when you see him, and he's not here yet. Saturday morning, too: he'll be pissed off.'

'We'll be sure to apologise,' said Wilding, cheerfully. As he spoke, he glanced casually at Stallings's hands and saw no jewellery. 'You must be pissed off too, Becky,' he continued. 'It's Saturday for you as well.'

She shot him a severe look. 'Yes, it's ruined my whole weekend,' she said drily.

'Maybe we could all go and grab some lunch when we're done here.'

'Yes, Sergeant,' she said, 'and then we could go shopping in the West End. You could buy a present for your wife.'

His expression turned mournful. 'I don't have one. I used to, but she left me for some bastard of a car salesman. She said she couldn't stand my working hours, but he works every bloody Saturday.'

'Ah, that's too bad,' said the Londoner; she seemed to loosen up slightly. 'It's not just the lawyer,' she said. 'Home Office security division want to sit in too.'

'Why?' asked Steele.

'Because of the civil-service involvement, or so they say. So far, Barker hasn't named anyone else he might have corrupted, but they want to be around if he does.'

'I don't actually give a damn about civil-service corruption,' the Scot confessed. 'We're after a multiple murderer, and so, it seems, is Barker. Has he said anything so far?'

'No. Hamilton, his lawyer, won't let him. He's waiting to see how much of a supporting case we can compile, to back up Dailey's confession.'

'How are you doing on that front?'

'Not too bad. We found some photocopies of DTI documents in Barker's office at Continental IT: they definitely should not have been there. We also found details at his home of a bank account in the name of Jack Frost. The balance is very healthy . . . it's several grand in credit . . . and there's a record of cash withdrawals. Some of the dates match up roughly with the DTI papers that we found. There was three grand withdrawn on Thursday; we found that in an envelope in Barker's desk. We're sure that it was destined for Dailey, only he didn't deliver the goods.

'The account was set up by Barker, not long after he left ITN to work for Davor Boras. The initial deposit was made by a cheque for twenty thousand pounds drawn on Barker's personal account. That received a cash injection for the same amount the day before. Since then it's been topped up a couple of times, in the same way.'

'Have you put this to Barker yet?' asked Steele. 'Have you pressed him about the money?'

'No, but when we do, you know what he'll say.'

'Sure. He'll tell us that he's a gambler and that sometimes he wins big. At least, that's what they all tell us at first.'

'You think you can crack him?'

'I've met the man; I think I can. I've been taught by experts . . . my wife among them.'

Out of the blue, Wilding chuckled. 'That's pretty good.'

Stallings stared at him. 'What is?'

'The bank account. Somebody's got a sense of humour. Jack Frost . . . It's a slush fund, isn't it?'

For the second time she smiled at him. 'Ray, you might not be as dumb as you look. Maybe we will go for lunch after all.' Before the sergeant could reply, her phone rang. She picked it up. 'Thanks,' she said, nodding across her desk. 'We're on.'

She led the way along the corridor and round a corner to a room that Steele judged, even before he was ushered inside, had to be at the back of the building, but there was nothing to confirm this, since its two windows were shuttered.

Barker was waiting for them, immaculate in a pale blue open-necked shirt and tan slacks. As before, his hair was perfectly groomed. He looked like a man who had spent the night in a five-star hotel room, rather than in a police holding cell. He was flanked by a fat man in a business suit.

There were four seats on the other side of the long table at which they sat. One of them was occupied by a woman who rose as they entered. She was small and very slim, bespectacled, and with hair so red that at once Steele pictured Maggie standing in her place. 'This is Rhonda Weiss,' Stallings announced, 'from the Home Office. Mr Barker, you know; the other gentleman is Lancelot Hamilton, his legal adviser.' She introduced the two officers.

'I'll be sitting in,' said Weiss. 'I reserve the right to ask questions as I see fit.'

The Scottish inspector looked at her; she returned his gaze, unsmiling. 'Can I see your warrant card?' he asked politely.

'I beg your pardon?'

'You heard me.'

'You mean do I have identification?' she spluttered. 'This is ridiculous.'

'No. I asked if I might see your warrant card. In other words, I'm asking if you're a police officer.'

'Of course not. I'm a civil servant.'

'Then you have no locus,' Steele told her. 'This is a serious interview, part of a murder investigation. You can stay, but you will not utter a word unless invited by me, and you'll sit at the end of the table, so that you cannot make eye contact with the prisoner. Are you carrying any form of recording device?'

'Yes, but . . .'

Steele held out his hand. 'Give it to me, please. I'll return it when we're finished here.'

'I will not!'

'Then leave.'

'I'm here with the approval of the Metropolitan Police.'

'Which can be withdrawn.'

'Not by you.'

'Trust me, it can.' He turned to Stallings. 'Becky, I don't want to put you on the spot, but . . .'

'No problem,' she told him. 'If you'll come with me, Ms Weiss.'

'Okay!' The woman took a small personal-memo device from her bag and handed it to Steele.

'Thanks,' he said. 'Now, if you'll take your place along there, we can begin.' He took a seat, with Stallings on his left and Wilding on his right, and smiled across the table. 'Good morning, Mr Barker,' he began, once Stallings had activated a twin-tape recorder. 'We'll just go through the introductions again for the record.' He recited the time, location, and list of those present, then continued: 'I'm sorry about that piece of housekeeping, and that we're meeting again in these surroundings. It might be palatial as police stations go, but it's a hell of a change from the Caley, you'll agree.'

'Yes indeed,' Barker murmured coldly. 'It's outrageous that I've been held here overnight, Inspector. Did you have something to do with that?'

'I think that bribing a civil servant to provide sensitive information had a lot to do with that, Keith.'

Lancelot Hamilton leaned forward. 'At the moment, Inspector,' he pointed out, 'no charges of that nature have been brought against my client.'

'No, but if you weren't damn sure that the Met have grounds to lay them whenever they think fit, you'd have screamed bloody murder to have your client released last night. However, Mr Hamilton, that's not why DS Wilding and I are here. We want to talk to your client about four murders that have been committed in Scotland over the last two months.'

'My client had nothing to do with any of those terrible crimes. He knows nothing about them.'

'That's what we're here to find out.' Steele leaned forward slightly and gazed at the lawyer. 'Look, sir, I don't want to be rude, but we'll be done a lot quicker here if you let me get on with my job with as few interruptions as possible. In the process you might save your client a few quid in solicitor's fees.' He suppressed a smile, as Hamilton reddened.

'That is a very well-made point,' said Barker, grimly.

'Of course, you won't be picking up your legal tab, will you?' said Steele, lightly. 'Davor Boras will do that, won't he?'

'What makes you think that?'

'Come on, when you leaned on Dailey, you weren't acting on your own behalf.'

'Who is Dailey?'

'He's a guy with your cellphone number on the SIM card memory of his, but let's not get tangled up in that stuff.

I'm interested in why, not who. Why should you try to track down Dominic Padstow through the passport agency?'

'Good question, why should I?'

'You're using the royal "I" there, Keith. You really mean "we" and when you do you're talking about you and your puppet-master, Boras. We're after Padstow. Your boss offered a million quid to anyone who finds the man and puts him away. So why should he use a bent contact in the Home Office to try to track him down? Does he think that if he does the job himself, he'll save a million?'

'Hardly. A million is nothing to that man.'

'Hey, that's a sea change,' Steele exclaimed. 'A couple of days ago you were kissing his arse. Today, he's "that man". He's denied you, hasn't he?' He glanced at Stallings. 'That's right, Becky, isn't it? You interviewed Boras and he told you that if Barker had bribed anyone he had done it on his own initiative, and expressly against his orders.'

'No,' she replied. 'We haven't. I was going to, but I had orders to leave him alone.'

'Orders? From whom?'

'Upstairs; to be exact, from Deputy Assistant Commissioner Davies, the director of operations in the Specialist Crime directorate. He's overseeing this operation and he set the parameters. He told me that Boras was off limits.'

'Jesus!' Steele was incredulous. 'You're saying that he's behind the bribing of a public official and you can't touch him? I know he's a business leader and all that but . . .' His eyes flashed along the table and locked on to Rhonda Weiss. 'Your lot are pulling the strings here, aren't they? That's why you're here. You're not interested in some middle-ranking twerp who sold information for money. It goes deeper than that.'

'I can't comment on that,' the woman replied, quietly.

'Well, I can.' Keith Barker's voice was laden with bitterness. 'Through his company, Davor Boras is a major supporter of the Labour Party. Through his charitable foundation, he backs the Tories. He helps both of them, plays one off against the other. Some of the things he's asked me to do, people he's asked me to check up on, had nothing to do with business.'

'And yet you've been fired, Keith, for doing his dirty work. You might as well tell me: we could find a journalist in around two seconds who'd call the Continental IT press office and confirm it.'

'Yes,' said Lancelot Hamilton. 'Formal notice of dismissal was delivered to my client's home late last night.'

'On what grounds?'

'Redundancy, I believe.'

'That was quick off the mark, considering your client hasn't been charged yet.'

'What were the severance terms?' Ray Wilding asked quietly.

'That information's privileged.'

The sergeant glared at the lawyer. 'Do you think I'm an idiot? It's fuck-all privileged. You've just said that it was delivered from Boras to your client's home, not to your office, and not through you. The Met have already searched the place; they have an existing warrant so they can go back any time and pick the document up.'

'Two years' salary, in lieu of notice,' Hamilton muttered.

'Louder, please, for the tape.'

He repeated the terms of Barker's sacking.

'What's your annual salary, Keith?' asked Steele.

'My business.'

'Who paid you? Boras personally, or Continental IT? If it's the latter we can find out easily.'

'Okay! Two hundred and fifty thousand.'

The inspector whistled. 'So you've pocketed half a million. And I bet a good chunk of it goes into your pension fund to minimise tax. If that's the going rate for gross misconduct, I'm strongly tempted . . .' He grinned and broke off. 'No, I'd better not say that with the tape running.'

Barker shot him a half-smile. 'Perhaps not.'

'Where does that take us?' Steele went on. 'You've been bought off. Clearly, you can't work for Boras any longer, not after this. You might even have to do a year or so inside, unless the Home Office leans on the Crown Prosecution Service too, but it'll be worth it to you, won't it? I can fire questions at you all day and you'll keep your mouth shut.'

'That's the way it is,' the man said cheerfully. 'And it serves you bastards right, for implying to the press that I'm somehow mixed up in these murders.'

'Hey, Mr McGuire implied no such thing. All he said was "no comment". He let you off lightly. Of course your arrest was linked to our investigation. You were trying to trace our prime suspect, on behalf of your boss . . .' Barker made to interrupt, but Steele cut him off. 'Save it, we'll just take that as read. The follow-up question is, what would have happened if you'd found him? After Boras's statement at our press briefing on Thursday, we have grounds for thinking that his life would have been in danger.'

'Why were you trying to trace him?' Ray Wilding asked. His intervention seemed spur-of-the-moment, but he and Steele had conducted many interviews together.

'You're wasting your time too.' Barker looked back at the inspector. 'Look, can we please wrap this up? Mr Hamilton has secured an agreement that I be bailed after this interview and I really would like to catch some of the play at Lord's.'

'Yes,' said Steele, pleasantly. 'I can imagine; it's a nice day for it. I have to get back to my wife too, Becky and Ray are going for lunch and I'm sure that Rhonda has to fit in Sainsbury's before she reports back to her bosses that you haven't said anything that would land any of them in trouble.'

He started to rise, then seemed to change his mind. 'But, Keith,' he murmured, 'while you're in the Tavern stand watching Middlesex whack it around, there's something you might want to think about. That funny Jack Frost bank account of yours, the one the Met uncovered when they searched your place . . .'

'Winnings on the horses, old boy.'

Steele looked at Stallings and laughed out loud. 'Of course. And I'm sure you've still got the betting slips. You'd better have them.' He paused, for long enough to allow the first crack to appear in Barker's mask of control. 'You've moved a total of ninety thousand pounds through your personal account into old Jack Frost over the last three years. I'm a betting man too, Keith, and I'll wager that you haven't paid a penny in tax on any of it.

'So, while you're slurping your Greene King, or whatever

it is you drink out in St John's Wood, think of the line that the Inland Revenue takes with people who evade thirty-six grand's worth of tax, and the national insurance as well. I'm afraid that, unless you can account for all that cash, the tax man will nail you, and there will be nothing that Boras's friends in dark places will be able to do about it. There'll be personal humiliation and jail time, there'll be a huge fine, and there will be the back tax due, all liable to interest at a rate that will make you cry.

'But how will the taxman find out about it, you ask me? How? Because we will fucking tell him, that's how. Becky and I will dump your bank statements right down his insatiable, rapacious maw.' He grinned and rose quickly to his feet. 'Enjoy the cricket, pal. I hope you haven't bought any Test-match tickets for the next few years, though. I don't imagine they have satellite television in the nick either. Personally, I think it's a disgrace that cricket was taken off the terrestrial channels.' Steele reached across and switched off the recorder. 'Interview terminated,' he said.

He was less than halfway to the door when Barker called after him: 'You've made your point, Mr Steele. Please come back.'

The smile had gone from the inspector's face by the time he turned around. 'Will it be worth my while?' he asked.

'I'll answer your questions, if that's what you mean.' He looked along the table. 'But I would feel more comfortable if it was just you and me.'

Steele shook his head. 'I can't do that, Keith, I'm afraid; this has to be formal. But I can ask Ms Weiss to leave if that would make you feel better.'

'It would.'

'I'm not going anywhere,' the Home Office woman protested.

'You're going out of this room, now,' said Becky Stallings, firmly. 'Your presence here is no longer in the best interests of the Scottish investigation.'

'I'll call my section head.'

'You can call the Home Secretary, as far as I'm concerned, but from outside this building.' She looked at Wilding. 'Ray, would you do me a favour and take Ms Weiss downstairs to the front office? Tell the staff there to make sure that she leaves.'

'My pleasure, Becky.' He beckoned to the woman. 'Come on, Miss, do as she says.'

'I want my memo stick,' she snapped. Steele took the device from his pocket and handed it to his sergeant. He and Stallings watched as the pair left the room.

'I'd like to reach an understanding,' Lancelot Hamilton announced, 'that the interview that is about to take place will deal purely with the matters under investigation in Edinburgh.'

'That doesn't work either,' Steele told him. 'We've got your client, sir; he knows it and you do too. If we throw him to the Revenue it'll all get very sticky for him. My only interest is in the murders, and the recording of this discussion will be going back north with me. If anything comes up that crosses over into the other matter, it's for Inspector Stallings to handle that as she thinks fit.'

'That's all right, Lance,' Barker told the solicitor. 'Let's proceed.'

'If you're ready,' said Steele. He switched on the recorder once more and repeated the location and list of participants. 'Interview resuming with DI Steele questioning Mr Barker. Sir, did you cause enquiries to be made of the passport service, seeking information about a man named Dominic Padstow?'

'Yes, I did.'

'On whose instructions?'

'Those of my employer, Mr Davor Boras.'

'How were those instructions conveyed?'

'In a conversation in Mr Boras's suite in the Caledonian Hotel, Edinburgh.'

'Was anyone else present?'

'No. Mrs Boras and Miss Britto, her secretary, had gone to the funeral director's office to make arrangements for Zrinka.'

'Arrangements?'

'To choose a coffin and make sure that she was properly . . .'

'I understand.'

'When did you receive your instructions from Mr Boras?'

'On Thursday afternoon, at approximately four p.m. That was not long before Mrs Boras and Miss Britto returned, and shortly before we left for the airport to return to London.'

'You're sure about that timing?' asked Steele, as Wilding re-entered the room and took his seat at the table

'Certain.'

'Are you aware that Mr Padstow's name and image were not released to the press until late on Thursday evening?'

'I am now.'

'You were also present at a discussion in the same place that morning, when Detective Chief Superintendent Mario McGuire and I interviewed Mr and Mrs Boras.'

'Yes, I was.'

'Do you recall Mr Padstow's name being mentioned at that time?'

'Yes, I do, by Mrs Boras. She said that was the name of a man who had lived with Zrinka for a while, in Edinburgh.'

'Had you ever heard the name before?'

'No.'

'To the best of your knowledge, had Mr Boras?'

'No, I don't believe he had. When we returned to the hotel, after the press briefing with Mr McGuire, he asked me if I had any idea about this man before, and if I knew anything about him. I told him that I hadn't, and that I didn't. He looked puzzled, concerned.'

'When he gave you your orders, did Mr Boras tell you why he wanted to trace Mr Padstow?'

'No, all he told me was that I should trace him as quickly as possible and obtain a photograph of him.'

'Did he tell you how to go about this?'

'Yes he did. He told me to contact Patrick Dailey, in the Home Office, and ask him to use his influence to obtain the necessary information and photograph from the passport agency.'

'For the record,' said Steele, 'Mr Dailey tried to comply with this request, but was apprehended. Those circumstances are under investigation elsewhere and are not directly relevant to our enquiries. So, Mr Barker, you obeyed your boss's instructions, without asking questions.'

'You don't question Davor Boras. You may advise him professionally, but ultimately, if you work for him, you do what he tells you, and that's an end of it.'

'Did you ask yourself any questions? Did you wonder why he might want to trace this man?'

'I did.'

'What was your conclusion?'

'The obvious one: that Mr Boras wanted to find out for himself whether Padstow knew anything about Zrinka's death.'

'With respect, Keith, that isn't obvious to me. My first assumption would have been that he intended to use his contacts to help the police investigation.'

'Then you didn't know Boras. He is not a sharing type. Why do you think his son left him to set up his own business, in competition with his father, and why are they now bitterly estranged? I'll tell you, because that much I do know. Davor simply assumed that his son would join him in Continental IT, and for a while that might have happened. Only Dražen asked his father to draw him a career path, putting a rough date on when he would retire and hand over control of the business. Davor told him that would never happen until God made it so. In other words, as long as he was alive, Dražen would always be subordinate to him.'

'How do you come to know this?'

'Because Dražen told me. I met him once after he struck out on his own, and I asked him why he had done it. He came right out with it, chapter and verse.'

'Did it surprise you, what he told you?'

'Not when I thought about it. Dražen and Zrinka were very much alike, from what I knew of them. Neither was prepared to stand in anyone's shadow for ever. He had plans for Zrinka too: he wanted her to run both of his art galleries; her brother told me that as well. She managed to deflect him, though. She persuaded him that nobody in the art world would respect her until she had established herself. She was supposed to settle in Edinburgh not just to paint but to find work in a national gallery, and gain experience there. Once she got up there, she forgot about that side of it, conveniently.'

'So back to Padstow: you're saying that Boras wanted to get to him himself, to get information out of him. How would he have done that?'

'I do not know, and I do not care to speculate.'

'Would he have used physical persuasion?'

'I don't know.'

'Do you believe him capable of it?'

Barker glanced at the recorder, then back at Steele. 'I believe that if he has succeeded in finding Padstow before you, and if he is convinced, as you seem to be, that he murdered Zrinka, then you have a better chance of finding Lord Lucan than of catching up with the bastard. Boras won't leave a single trace of him.'

'Just as well that the Home Office woman didn't hear that,' Stallings murmured.

'Maybe she should have,' Steele replied quietly, his head turned away from the recorder. 'Maybe she knows things about him that could point us in the right direction.'

'Want me to go and get her back?' Wilding whispered.

'Except,' said Barker, startling them all, 'that there's a hell of a lot more to it than that.' They turned back towards him. 'Now I've seen Padstow's image, I know why Boras wanted me to find him. I should have worked it out for myself straight away, but I didn't.'

'Go on,' said Steele.

'Almost three years ago now,' said the prisoner, 'not all that long after I went to work for Boras, I became aware that someone was asking questions about us, about the business, about Boras himself, about me and what I had been recruited to do for him. Word filtered back to me, from employees, from suppliers and from former associates of mine.

'I had no idea who the man was, but I knew that he was hostile, as such people almost invariably are. I made that assumption because no approaches were ever made to me, to any of my subordinates in the press office or in the consultancies that we use. At that point in time, I didn't want to go to Boras, as I knew him well enough by that time to understand that you didn't bring him suspicions, you brought him facts. So I began to seek the man actively, and to build up a dossier on what he was up to. I intended to trace him myself, but I never did. He was too good, too thorough. Finally, I decided that he was probably an industrial spy, hired by one of our smaller European rivals or, more likely, by an American outfit. That I had to take to the boss.'

'How did he react, when you didn't bring him hard facts?'

'To my surprise, he was fine. He thanked me and he told me to leave it with him. A week later, he called me into his office. I should tell you that he never discusses anything sensitive outside his room at Continental; he has the place swept every day for listening devices. He showed me a folder and said, "That's our man." It contained photographs and a complete biography of a man called Daniel Ballester. He was a journalist, that sort of spy.'

'Where did the information come from?'

'He told me he'd hired a private security firm: its name was Aeron, according to the heading on the report I saw.'

'Did he say whether he had acted on it?'

'I asked him if he wanted me to do that, but he told me that the Aeron people had been instructed to talk to him, tell him that we knew who he was and to stop being bloody silly. That alarmed me a little; I asked if they would do anything physical, but Boras just laughed, a rarity for him, and said that he wasn't worth it.'

'Did you believe him?'

'Yes, I did. As it happened, Ballester was all over the press himself just a little later, after coming spectacularly unstuck by doing a piece on Diana, on the basis of bogus evidence that he fell for.'

'Then three years on, you find out he had moved on from that setback to get onside with Zrinka.'

Barker nodded. 'As soon as I saw the image you released, I knew who he was.'

'When did you see it?'

'In *The Times*, yesterday morning.'

'What did you do?'

'The obvious. I took the newspaper straight into Boras's office, but he'd already seen it. I said to him, "You know who this is, don't you?" and he nodded. I said that Aeron obviously hadn't been persuasive enough. He replied, "Maybe they'll be more efficient this time." I warned him not to cross the police, but he told me not to worry. Then he took out the folder he'd shown me three years ago and shredded it before my eyes.'

'Did he say any more than that?'

'Yes, he did. Frankly, I was shitting myself by this time. I asked him point-blank what orders he had given the people at Aeron. He promised me that they had instructions to trace Ballester and report back to him, no more than that. When they did, he would hand everything over to you.'

'Did you believe him?'

'I honestly can't say. But if Aeron are the sort of people who are prepared to go all the way, my guess is that either the man will disappear and they'll report failure or that he'll have some sort of an accident.'

'How did your discussion end?'

'Effectively, Davor fired me. He said that he felt I was becoming too anxious about events to continue to perform on his behalf in the City, and that he needed to make a change. He told me what my severance terms would be and promised me another half-million in an offshore account in two years if I stuck to the confidentiality agreement that he would ask me to sign. I accepted dismissal, since that was in my financial interest, and we agreed that I would leave that afternoon.' He smiled weakly at the three detectives. 'I had my fucking jacket on when Inspector Stallings arrived to arrest me.'

Steele leaned back in his chair. 'That's the whole story?'

'The part that concerns me.'

'Okay, Keith.' He glanced at his watch. 'Interview terminated at twelve fifty-seven.' He switched off the recorder, removed the disks, pocketed one and handed the other to Hamilton. 'You can negotiate the terms of your client's bail now,' he told the lawyer.

'I'm not sure I want to be bailed,' Barker murmured.

'Don't worry,' Stallings told him. 'We'll look after you. If Boras does something silly, Scotland may need you as a witness.'

'Shit!'

'Hopefully, we'll put a lid on it before then,' said Steele. 'Our next port of call has to be Aeron Security. It's time they were told that they ain't a private police force.'

Fifty-six

'There's them and us, you know, Griff,' said Tarvil Singh. 'There's the DI and Ray off swanning in London, and you and me holding the fort here, sifting bloody interviews and chasing up sightings of Padstow all over bloody Scotland.'

'Yes, but on overtime, remember, unlimited on this job.'

'Maybe we should take our time catching him, then.'

'Don't let the bosses hear you saying that, pal. Anyway, if you weren't here, what would you be doing this afternoon?'

'Shoving a trolley round Safeway,' Singh admitted.

'Where?'

'Sa . . . Ah, sorry, I forgot you're new in Scotland. Round Morrison's, I should have said. The name changed a few years back. The trolleys are still the same, though. What about you, what would you be up to? Battering some poor sod around a rugby field, I suppose.'

'Nah, the season's over. I'd probably have bumped my trolley into yours.'

'And who are you shopping with these days?'

'My sister,' Montell replied, 'so don't get any funny ideas. By the way, I don't think London will be a swan for those two. Interviewing somebody else's prisoner is never easy, especially when two investigations run across each other.'

'You sound like you've had experience.'

'I have, back home in the South African Police Service.'

'What did you do there?'

'Detective service; serious crime division, including organised crime.'

'Heavy?'

'Believe it. Wilding would not be so laid-back there, I'll tell you.'

'Ray would be laid-back anywhere. He and the DI flew down together, but they're on open tickets. I will bet you a nice chicken Balti that he winds up persuading the boss to let him stay over in London till tomorrow.'

'Deal. If you're right, bring your wife and we'll make it a foursome.'

'With you and your sister?'

'Maybe.' As he spoke, the phone rang. 'Thank Christ,' he said, 'I was beginning to think that Padstow had been caught and nobody'd told us.' He snatched the phone from its cradle. 'Montell.'

'Griff,' came a tired voice, 'it's Willie at the front desk. I've got a guy here wants to talk to the DI or whoever's in charge in CID in his absence. Do you and the big fella want to toss for it?'

'What does he have for us?'

'He won't say. He just wants to talk to somebody, and he doesnae look like he's going to take no for an answer.'

'How would he feel about "fuck off"?' The South African chuckled. 'I'm kidding, Willie. What's his name?'

'David Barnes.'

'Barnes, you say. What's his connection?'

'Hey,' Singh called to him. 'First name David?' Montell nodded. 'He's Zrinka's brother; that's the name he took after he set up his own business.'

'In that case he's responding to an e-mail the DI had me send to him. Willie, show Mr Barnes into a vacant interview room, give him a cup of coffee and tell him we'll join him in a couple of minutes.'

'Will do, Griff.'

The detective constable hung up. 'We see him together, Tarvil, okay?'

'Shouldn't we get somebody senior in?'

'Like who?'

'DCS McGuire? He lives not far from here.'

'And he's probably on the golf course, or whatever he does at the weekend. Do you ever want to make sergeant? You don't do it by shirking responsibility. We'll call McGuire if it becomes necessary, but only then. Look, I'll see him on my own, if you don't want to come.'

'No, I'll chum you. Why go downstairs, though? Why not just bring him upstairs?'

'With photographs of his dead sister and her boyfriend pinned to the whiteboard, and him half-eaten by foxes?'

'True,' Singh conceded grimly. 'I'll put the phones on divert to Willie. Let's go.'

The two detectives jogged downstairs to the public entrance. 'Room two,' said the desk sergeant. Montell nodded and led the way along a short corridor to a white-painted door; he knocked, and swung it open.

The man who waited there turned to face them as they

entered. He was smaller than either of them, but still stood around six feet. He was casually dressed, in blue denims, jeans and jacket, with a white T-shirt with a garish design on the front, tight-fitting and tapering into a narrow waist. On his head sat a baseball cap embroidered with parrots, and a slogan, 'Margaritaville'.

'Mr Barnes.'

He looked back at the South African, his ice-blue eyes made all the more vivid by a deep tan. 'Yes,' he replied quietly. 'And you are?'

'Detective Constables Montell and Singh.' Griff smiled. 'Guess which is which. Our senior officers are out of town on the investigation, I'm afraid.'

'The investigation: does that mean that you know who I am?'

'Yes, we do. You only call yourself Dražen when you're with your sister, isn't that right?'

'How did you know that?'

'I saw the last e-mail you sent her. I typed the reply, on my boss's instructions.'

'In that case, I appreciate the way you used the present tense just now, but it was unnecessary. I know that Zrinka is dead, and how.'

'I'm sorry you had to find out through the press.'

'What makes you think I did?' David Barnes asked him. 'I flew into Gatwick from JFK early this morning. After I'd picked up my luggage, I switched on my lap-top at a Wi-fi hot spot, to check my e-mails. I found a shedload of messages including a triple urgent one from my secretary.

'I called my mother straight away and she told me what

had happened. I couldn't believe it; I just couldn't believe it. I jumped in a taxi, and went straight to their place. We spent some time together. Then I read the rest of my mails; I saw yours, and decided that I should come up to Edinburgh straight away.'

'You didn't have to do that,' said Montell. 'A call would have been enough.'

'No, I wanted to see you; I want to find out about the investigation. My father told me that his man Barker has embarrassed everyone, and got himself into trouble. My father and I have been estranged for some time, but he felt that I could do some good by coming to Edinburgh. He feels that Barker's stupidity may have compromised him in some way. Is that so?'

'That's why DI Steele isn't here,' Singh told him. 'He's in London, putting the thumbscrews on the guy.'

'I shouldn't say so,' said Barnes, 'but I'm glad to hear it. I never liked that man, although in truth I didn't mind my father employing him. My dad and I are business rivals, as you probably know by now, and I've always thought that Barker was more of a hindrance to him than a help.'

'Look,' Montell said suddenly, 'this isn't going to be a formal interview and this is a fucking awful place to be stuck on a nice day. If you'd like, we can go somewhere more pleasant to chat.'

'I'd appreciate that. I've never been in a police office before and, no offence, but if this one is typical, I don't want to be in any others.'

'Come on, then; we'll go to the Waterfront. Tarvil doesn't drink, so he can drive us.'

'Thank you, sir,' the big Sikh grumbled, but he fished his car keys from his pocket and waved them towards the door.

Singh had what he sometimes called copper's luck. There was an empty parking space fifty yards from the Waterfront wine bar, and a spare table in a quiet corner of the conservatory area when they went inside.

'This is much better,' said David Barnes, as he chose a seat with a view across the waters of Leith Docks, their surroundings much changed by the construction of upmarket new flats. As he hung his jacket over the chair, the detectives caught a glimpse of vivid embroidery on the back.

'Yes,' Montell agreed. 'Way back, this place was a waiting room for passengers on the Leith to Aberdeen steamship route.'

'I never knew that,' Singh exclaimed.

'It's true, Alex told me.'

'It'll be gospel, in that case,' said a voice, from behind him.

The South African turned, and looked up at Mario McGuire. 'Boss, I never saw you when we came in.'

'That should go without saying: ignoring me would not be good. I'm at a table just round the corner, with Paula.' He paused, unsmiling. 'I thought you guys were on duty.'

'We are, sir, but we felt these surroundings were more appropriate.'

'In the circumstances I agree.' He leaned across and offered a handshake to Barnes. 'My condolences for your loss,' he said.

'You know who I am?'

'The name's McGuire; I'm the head of CID here. I've forgotten more things than these guys know, but they still can't catch me out. I recognise you from a photograph on our investigation file: it's very thorough.' He looked at Montell. 'Have you ordered yet?'

'Not yet, sir.'

'In that case I'll send you over a bottle of something. It'll save you the embarrassment of asking Stevie to sign your expenses. There's a South African riesling on the list; that okay?'

'Excellent, thanks. And a fresh orange and soda for Tarvil, if you don't mind.'

'Your wish is my command.' His gaze switched back to Barnes and became serious once more. 'I don't want to crowd you, so I'll leave you with the lads. Once you've spoken to them, if there's anything you'd like to take up with me, I'm not far away.' He turned and walked away, around the corner and back to his table; in the window opposite, Montell saw Paula Viareggio, reflected.

'He's very impressive,' David Barnes murmured. 'He must have scared the crap out of a few villains in his time.'

'He has,' Singh told him, 'not to mention a few police officers, like us two, right now. But if you really want scary, you want to meet his boss. Isn't that right, Griff?' Montell's reply was no more than a grunt. 'My colleague,' Singh explained, 'is walking a tightrope across the chasm of insanity by going out with the deputy chief constable's daughter.'

Barnes smiled, as a waiter arrived bearing a tray with two glasses, a bottle in an ice bucket and Singh's soft drink. 'I want to thank you lads for this,' he said, as the wine was poured. 'I've been screaming inside since I spoke to Mum this morning. You're being a great help to me.'

'Think nothing of it,' said Montell. 'We feel for you. You should realise, David, that people like us, doing what we do, become very familiar with murder victims, even if they're dead. We're their advocates. We pursue justice on their behalf, and although we shouldn't, often we become attached to them. We feel as if we knew Zrinka, and what we've learned about her has made us very fond of her. The same's true of Stacey Gavin, and young Harry Paul.'

'As for Amy,' Singh added, 'I really did know her. DI Steele and I went to see her the day before she was killed.'

'In that case, you may know that she and I . . .'

'She told us that you'd met and . . .' He stopped. 'She was really fond of you.'

'It's good to hear that. She was a nice kid.'

'Which makes us all the more determined to catch the man who killed her,' Montell told him. 'We have open minds, David; you must appreciate that. At the same time we are determined to find this guy Padstow. He ties all of them together.'

'How are you doing?'

'We know who he is now.' He raised an eyebrow at Singh, who nodded. 'I reckon we can tell you. His real name is Daniel Ballester; he's a journalist, of questionable reputation.'

'I knew that,' said Barnes.

'You did?'

'Yes. My sister told me, after they broke up. She said that

he told her he was a lecturer in politics, doing some post-graduate study in Edinburgh. She believed it, and so did I when I met him, the first time I came up to visit her. I was just a little wary of him, given that he had popped up out of the blue and was living with Zrinka, our family being very wealthy and all, but his act was really good, and so was his cover story. I bought it too.'

'How did Zrinka discover the truth about him?'

'He slipped up: he left his passport on the table, she mistook it for hers and opened it.'

Singh leaned forwards. 'Amy told us that they went to Amsterdam together. He couldn't have flown as Padstow.'

'He didn't want to go. He kept making excuses, pleading poverty, but Zrinka was dead set on seeing the galleries there. He gave in eventually, but said that he'd handle all the arrangements, which he did, through a travel agent. He got away with it all the way through the trip, and for a little while after they got back. He was glib, and for maybe the only time in her life, she was gullible. Christ,' Barnes muttered, 'I can talk. He fooled me.'

'After Zrinka saw the passport, what did she do? Come to you?'

'She didn't need to. She just entered the name into a search engine; she built a whole file on the guy, pictures, everything.'

'And confronted him?'

'No, she didn't. She felt hurt by him, she felt betrayed, but she didn't want a big scene. She simply told him that she didn't love him, and that their relationship had run its course. She didn't tell him that she knew who he was. She didn't tell anyone except me, and eventually Stacey Gavin, when she discovered that Ballester had moved on to her.'

'That explains a lot. It ties in exactly with what your mother told DCS McGuire and DI Steele.'

'No doubt, but Mum never met the guy.'

'And your father?'

'He never even knew about the relationship. Our father is old-fashioned. He may have cut and run from Yugoslavia when he saw what was going to happen there, but he retains the strict Orthodox values with which he was raised, and they definitely do not allow for his daughter living with a man to whom she is not married. No, my father never knew about it, or he would have put his foot down.'

'Could it be, David,' Montell asked gently, 'that your father did know but chose to do nothing to avoid provoking a split with his daughter? As you've told us, you and he are estranged. Is it possible he couldn't face being at odds with both his children, so he turned a blind eye?'

'Not in the slightest, I promise you. Davor Boras sees everything.'

Fifty-seven

'Mags, love, I'm really sorry that this should happen, today of all bloody days, but the situation down here has developed in a way I didn't anticipate. I'm waiting for some intelligence reports and then if I can find him there may be a man we need to call on. If I can, I'll catch the last shuttle.'

'Do you want me to pick you and Ray up?'

'Hell, no, I'll take a taxi. If I do make it I'll be on my own. That smooth bastard Wilding's made alternative arrangements, and as far as I can see they're looking better by the minute. I promise, I'll do my best to get home.'

'Fine, just let me know; I'll be in. As it happens I'm expecting a visitor in a couple of hours.'

'Who?'

'Bob Skinner. He called and asked me if he could visit to follow up something we spoke about yesterday. I'll tell you what I can when you get back.'

'What you can? What does that mean?'

'You know the DCC, he also moves in mysterious ways. Love you.'

'Me too. So long.'

Steele flipped his Motorola shut to end the call, then

opened it again and dialled his office, only to be surprised when the desk sergeant answered the call. 'Where are my troops?' he asked.

'On enquiries, you might say, sir. They'd a visitor, a guy called Barnes, and they went out with him.'

The inspector smiled. 'Any excuse,' he said, although he understood why the two constables would want to take Zrinka's brother out of the depressing drabness of the office. He found the South African's cellphone number in his directory and called it. 'Are you still with Boras?' he asked.

'David? No, sir. Tarvil's taking him up to the George Hotel and I'm walking back to the nick.'

'He got our e-mail?'

'Yes, boss; this morning, as soon as he got back from America. He got on the shuttle and came straight up.'

'How was he?'

'Cut up about his sister as you'd expect, but helpful. He's dead certain that his father had no idea about her and Padstow living together.'

'That more or less confirms Barker's story.'

'David knew about it, though, and he knew who he was. Zrinka discovered his real identity, and told David, but she persuaded him to keep it from her parents. She didn't want them upset.'

'No, she wouldn't. She might not have wanted her father to do anything drastic, either.'

'Did you get something out of Barker, then?'

'Oh, yes,' Steele murmured. 'We hold the mortgage on his soul. We're just about to follow up his information.'

'Good luck.' Montell paused. 'Just out of interest, sir, can you tell me if DS Wilding's staying in London tonight?'

'Yes, he is. Why?'

'Bastard! I owe Tarvil and his wife a curry, thanks to him.'

'I won't tell Ray, or he'll want the fucking poppadoms. Cheers.'

'What was that about poppadoms?' the sergeant asked.

'An "in" joke,' Steele told him. 'Doesn't matter. Dražen Boras turned up in Edinburgh this afternoon; the lads have been babysitting him.'

'Damn!' said Becky Stallings. 'I was hoping he'd come looking for you here. I've seen his picture in *Hello!* magazine; he's a looker, and eligible, too.'

'Detective inspectors don't read *Hello!* do they?' asked Wilding, with a hint of scorn.

'Detective inspectors go to the dentist like everyone else,' she replied, then looked towards her office door as it opened, and a black man in shirtsleeves handed her a folder.

'Sorry about the delay, ma'am,' he said. 'We'd to dig out the SIA duty officer to get this, but it's finally come through.'

'SIA?'

'Security Industry Authority; they're phasing in the licensing of security firms, and Aeron comes under their umbrella. That's what they hold on them.'

'I see; thanks, Wayne.'

She opened the slim folder as he left, and scanned through the file within, reading as she went. 'Aeron Security plc. Michael Spicer, aged fifty-two, chairman and CEO. Founded 1995, registered office and trading address seventeen Aeron Passage, NW1. A total of twenty employees, five administrative and clerical and the rest all holders of the appropriate SIA licences. No member of staff has a criminal record of any sort. Firm was among the first to seek licensing and met all criteria at the first time of asking. No complaints against Aeron have ever been registered with the SIA, and they are regarded as maintaining high professional standards.'

'What about Spicer himself?' Steele asked her.

'According to this he has a military background. Good: Wayne's found his private address and telephone number.'

'Where does he live?'

'Van Dyke Terrace, Blackheath. Posh.'

'Is it far away?'

'We should do it in half an hour. Do you want to call first, to make sure he's there?'

'Wait a minute,' Wilding interjected. 'We're assuming that he's at home. Aeron's a security business: its office is probably manned at weekends.'

'Let's find out.' The two Scots watched as she picked up her phone and dialled, then they listened. 'Aeron Security? . . . Ah, good, you do have somebody on duty. This is Detective Inspector Stallings, Metropolitan Police; something's come up relating to a security issue we believe you were involved in. We've come into possession of some information, and want to cross-check it with you . . . No, I'm afraid I can't do that: this is too sensitive to discuss over the phone. Who's your managing director? . . . Pardon, I didn't catch that . . . Mr Spicer, you say. I really think I have to speak to him . . . Yes, I'll hold on.'

Stallings put her hand over the mouthpiece. 'We may be in luck.' She removed it again; her face fell slightly. 'He isn't? Who's in charge? . . . You're the general manager, did you say, Mr Lemmon? In that case, we'll speak to you, in Mr Spicer's absence. We'll be there inside twenty minutes, if the traffic permits . . . Okay, that's excellent. I appreciate that.'

She grinned at her visitor colleagues. 'How about that, then? Come on, let's commander a patrol car and turn up there like the Sweeney, with lights and sirens blazing. My job's usually boring, dealing with white-collar crime; I miss the excitement.'

The sergeant looked at her, pure admiration in his eyes. 'You really are nuts, Becky, aren't you?'

She smiled back at him, and nodded. 'Just a little.'

Aeron Passage was hard to find, a side-street off a side-street, behind Euston railway station. The sirens were entirely unnecessary there, but Becky Stallings had them sound until the car drew up outside number seventeen, an ugly modern four-storey building. The company's offices were on the first floor and so the three detectives used the stairs, rather than the lift.

A middle-aged man was waiting in the reception area as they stepped inside. He was small and lean, with bags under his eyes. 'What the hell was the noise about?' he asked abruptly. His accent was strange, a little guttural.

'It helps to clear traffic,' Stallings replied cheerfully. 'Are you Mr Walker Lemmon?'

'Yes.'

She introduced the two Scots. 'It's really them who need to talk to you,' she added. 'I'm just the facilitator here.'

Lemmon frowned. 'Okay, but I don't have a lot of time:

Saturday's a busy day for us. Come through to my office.' He led the way into a small room at the back of the building. The window was open, but it still reeked of cigar smoke. Wilding sniffed theatrically; the man ignored him. 'What is it you want?' he asked.

'We're involved in a multiple murder investigation in Scotland,' said Steele. 'You've probably heard about it. One of the victims was the daughter of a client of yours.'

'We don't discuss our clients . . . Inspector, was it?'

'Detective Inspector, yes, and I'm not here to discuss anything. I'm here to ask you some specific questions and to obtain any information you might have that will assist my sergeant and me with our enquiries. We've been told that about three years ago you investigated a man who had become a nuisance to your client Mr Davor Boras, of Continental IT. You identified him as Daniel Ballester, a journalist, and delivered a dossier on him to Mr Boras.'

'I don't know anything about that.'

'Wait till I'm finished, please,' Steele told him curtly. 'We're not clear on the instructions which Mr Boras gave your firm after that. However, it's been suggested that you were told to persuade him to desist from making a nuisance of himself, but that when you went to do that, he'd disappeared.

'Yesterday, Ballester was identified as the prime suspect in our enquiries, a man we were seeking under the assumed name of Dominic Padstow. We believe that before that you received further instructions from Mr Boras to trace Ballester. We need your co-operation, Mr Lemmon. We need all the information you have on this man.'

'This is all conjecture,' the general manager protested. 'Why are you so sure this dossier exists?'

'Our informant saw it.'

'And you believe him?'

'He has every reason to tell us the truth.'

'Then get the dossier from Boras.'

Steele shook his head. 'That would be very difficult. He shredded his copy yesterday afternoon.'

'Why would he do that?' Lemmon asked.

'This really is conjecture on our part,' Wilding told him, with a casual smile, 'but we reckon he was taking no chances of being accused of withholding information from the police investigating his daughter's murder. Now we could, if we were so inclined, put a hundred officers on to searching through the Continental IT rubbish bins, and piecing together all the shredded paper, but actually, pal, we don't need to, because we know that folder existed, we know what was in it, and we know your company provided it. What we want from you is quite simple: any new information you or your people might have dug up on where Ballester might be hiding.'

Lemmon's mouth twisted. 'You have to understand this, Sergeant. This business delivers confidential services to its clients; that's our stock-in-trade. Any information we possess belongs to the client, because he's paid for it. A court can require us to disclose, so maybe you should go and get an order.'

'Naw, that's not how it works,' Wilding retorted. 'You have to understand this, pal. While you're standing there spouting shite about clients and ethics in an industry that basically involves renting out muscle, a man we want for four murders is at liberty. If you make us go to court then we'll do it.' Lemmon's eyes went to the impassive Steele.

'Look at me when I'm talking to you!' the sergeant barked, startling him and securing his renewed attention. 'We'll do it,' he repeated, 'but while we're hauling a bad-tempered judge off the golf course, we'll hold you in custody and we'll fill this place with uniforms to make fucking sure . . . pardon my Scottish, Becky . . . that no information is destroyed or leaves this building. We might not be able to touch Boras, but we can fucking well touch you. If that's what you want, that's what you'll get.'

'Give me time to think about it,' the man muttered.

'You've got three seconds,' Steele told him. 'One, two, three. Right, Becky, who's the nastiest judge you know?'

'Okay!' Lemmon shouted angrily. 'I'll co-operate.'

'Then talk.'

'I don't know anything about this.'

Steele glared down at the man; he stiffened, and seemed to become an inch or so taller, and, suddenly, menacing. 'Now listen, chum . . .'

'I don't, honestly, not the detail. Mr Spicer always deals with Mr Boras personally. All I know is that he was contacted by him yesterday and after that he was very busy. Then, in the evening, he called him back. Today, just before midday, he had another call from Boras. When it was finished, he and Ivor, his personal assistant, left in a hurry.'

'Did he say where he was going?'

'No. All he said was that they'd be gone for the rest of the day.'

'Is he contactable?'

'Yes, if his phone's switched on.'

'Then call him,' Steele ordered.

The three officers watched as he took out a mobile and selected a number. 'Mike,' they heard him say, 'it's Walker. Something alarming has happened. The police are here, asking questions about Mr Boras.'

'Let me speak to him,' the Scot demanded. Tamely, Lemmon handed him the phone.

'Mr Spicer,' he began, 'my name's Steele; I'm a detective inspector from Edinburgh. I've just interviewed a well-placed informant, who has given me chapter and verse on your dealings with Davor Boras in respect of a man named Daniel Ballester, a suspect in an investigation on which I'm engaged. I require you to tell me where you are, where you're headed, and what your instructions are.'

'I'm not obliged to do any of that,' said a terse voice, slightly distorted by the connection. Steele listened for background noise, but heard nothing he could identify.

'I think you'll find that you are. This is a homicide investigation, and I believe you have information I need. You either answer me or your colleague will give me the number of your vehicle, and within five minutes every police force in Britain will be on the lookout for you. Please don't make the mistake of thinking, for a single moment, that I'm not serious about this.'

'No,' said Spicer. 'I can tell that you are.'

'Good. Now pull over so we can talk.'

'I don't have to; my colleague and I have just arrived at our destination.'

'And where is that?'

'We're in Northumberland, in a village called Wooler. We've discovered a possible location for Ballester. Last year his grandmother died, and left him her house; we're just outside it. He's been living here on and off, or somebody has; the telephone is still in his grandmother's name, E. Maybole, and it's been used recently.'

'How do you know that?'

'Don't ask, please.'

'Okay, I'll allow you that much. What's the address?'

'Hathaway House, Gallow Law.'

'And you reported this to Boras?'

'Yes. Yesterday evening.'

'What instructions did he give you when he called you today?'

'He told me to get up here and apprehend the man, if he's here.'

'Apprehend?'

'Yes. He said that he wanted to hand him over to you personally.'

'He instructed you to kidnap this man?' Steele exclaimed.

'To make a citizen's arrest.'

'There's a fine line between the two, but we'll discuss that later. Where are you right now?

'We're overlooking Hathaway House.'

'What can you see?'

'Not much. There's no sign of movement. However, there is smoke coming out of one of the chimneys.'

'Describe the place, please.'

'It's more of a cottage than a house, built in a dip in the land. You can barely see it from the road. There's a car in the driveway, a blue Suzuki saloon. I've used a contact to check the number. It's registered to Ballester's grandmother, but I reckon it's been used recently because it's splattered with mud. What do you want us to do?'

'Nothing. Keep the house under observation until police officers arrive. If Ballester leaves before, then do not let him see you, and do not confront him, repeat do not confront him: assume he is armed. If you have an opportunity, do your best to trail him, but from a distance, and call in his position and direction of travel to Northumbria police as soon as you can. Got that?'

'Yes, I understand.'

Steele handed the phone back to Lemmon, and turned to Stallings. 'Becky, could your air support unit get me up there?'

'I'm sure they could, but it'll take a formal request from further up the line than us.'

Steele took out his own mobile and called Mario McGuire. 'I need your muscle, sir,' he told the head of CID, as he answered. Quickly he explained the situation.

'Okay,' the chief superintendent responded. 'I'll get you airborne. I'll also alert Northumbria and get an armed-response team on station; you take command on arrival and run the operation. It's your bus, Stevie, you drive it. While all that's happening I'll advise the fiscal that we might be on the edge of something. Who are you with down there?'

'DI Becky Stallings, Charing Cross station.'

'I'll ask air support to liaise with her. I'll tell them to get you up in the air as quickly as they can.'

'Thanks.' He ended the call and nodded to Stallings and Wilding. 'Mario will make it work. We need to get somewhere that a chopper can land to pick us up.'

All at once, the sergeant's face fell. 'Stevie,' he said slowly, 'I've been in a helicopter before. The noise, the smell of the engine . . . I can't find the words to tell you how sick I was.'

The inspector looked at him, and took a decision. 'Okay.' He chuckled. 'You can stay here as planned, and come up tomorrow. I'll have more than enough back-up in Wooler. I'll call you to let you know how it goes.'

'Thanks, pal.' Wilding sighed.

Stallings reached out and punched him lightly on the arm. 'Hey, Ray,' she said, 'if that's how you react to choppers, how would you feel about the view from the London Eye?'

Fifty-eight

W*hy do I feel happy?* Maggie Steele asked herself. She sat in what she and Stevie called their 'playroom'. *I've been diagnosed with a cancer. I'm carrying a child and I may not live to see her first birthday, I've given up a job I've loved for nearly twenty years, yet I've never felt so fulfilled in my life.*

She was still pondering the mystery when the doorbell chimed. She checked her watch. It showed six on the dot; the big man was always punctual.

He was standing on the top step when she opened the door, dressed in a dark suit, immaculately pressed, worn over a pale blue shirt and tie that looked newly unwrapped. He was carrying a black leather document case. 'Very smart,' she said. 'Is this normal for a Saturday evening?'

Bob Skinner grinned. 'No way: Aileen's holding a formal dinner for business leaders and wives in the First Minister's residence this evening, and she's asked me to chum her.'

'That's a nice way of putting it,' she said, as she ushered him inside. 'Is that how it's going to be from now on? Will we be seeing the two of you together at official functions?'

'Yes, and unofficial. We've been keeping the relationship low-key until now, to let the dust settle after my divorce, but we feel that we can move on now. We're not making any public announcements; we're simply going to stop being coy about it. For example, the Scottish Executive's press office will be issuing the guest list for tonight's event, and my name will be on it.'

Maggie chuckled. 'Yes, and on tomorrow's front pages. You can bet on that, sir.' She paused. 'Listen to me, Bob,' she exclaimed. 'It's going to take me a long time to get used to being a civilian.'

'I still can't believe that you are,' Skinner confessed. 'Honestly, Mags, I had your career all mapped out in my head. There'll be an ACC vacancy in Stirling in a couple of years and you'd have walked in there. Good preparation for an eventual move back to Edinburgh as chief.'

'You're kidding me.' She led the way into the kitchen, where a pot of coffee stood ready.

'No, I am not,' he declared, watching as she filled a mug for him, then took a bottle of water from the fridge for herself. 'That was my master-plan, and it still can come about. You've done nothing that can't be reversed.'

She rubbed the bump under her smock. 'Oh, no?'

'Why should motherhood hold you back? It can't be held against you at interview.'

'Get real, Bob; maybe it can't but it would be.'

He raised an eyebrow. 'With the First Minister looking on from a distance, and me from a hell of a lot closer? I don't think so.'

'Okay, maybe not, but you'd form a pretty big obstacle to any move back here.'

Skinner shook his head. 'No, I wouldn't. If I were to

succeed Jimmy . . . and it's IF in capital letters . . . I would not hang on for the duration. I'd do five years maximum, then I'd be out of there. I've been doing a lot of thinking on this sabbatical, Maggie; it's not just your career I've got mapped out.' He laid his leather case on a work surface as he accepted the mug from her.

'What would you do?'

'I'd be open to offers; I had a very big one a few months ago, but I turned it down because the time wasn't right, and because it would have been difficult for Aileen and me. If I was offered that again, when we were both ready for it, I'd maybe give a different answer. But if not, and if no other opportunities crop up, I'll write and teach. I've started both already.' He nodded towards the document bag. 'The paper I told you about yesterday: it's in there. I'd like you to read it . . .' he chuckled 'while you can still think professionally . . . and let me have your views, your frank and honest views, on my findings and on the thinking that's led me there.'

'I'm honoured; I really am. In confidence, I take it.'

'Please; if you're comfortable with that. It's rotten of me to ask you to keep a secret from your husband, but he's a serving officer.'

'I understand, and so will Stevie, I promise. Do you have a time frame?'

'Take as long as you like.'

'A couple of weeks, then. I'll have plenty of time: we're hiring a domestic, Ray Wilding's cousin. She starts on Monday.'

'Quite right too.' He followed her through into the sitting

room and settled into an armchair as she reclined on her couch.

'That was quite a thing,' she said, 'being asked to lecture by the FBI.'

'Yes, it was. Mind you, I've had a few dealings with them over the years.'

'What did you talk about?'

'The broad approach to integrity; the difficulty of holding on to it in the face of every situation, and the recognition that sometimes what might seem to be morally unthinkable can be the only possible moral choice we can make.'

'Were you speaking from personal experience?' she asked quietly.

'Oh, yes,' he murmured, 'all too personal, I'm afraid.'

'Maybe you could turn that into a paper too.'

'Not in a hundred years. It would be no use without specifics, and they're buried very deep. But I am writing, apart from that document. I've started working on a book about the difficulty of detection; it'll look at successful criminals and examine how they manage to get away with it over an extended period, and it'll develop the theory that none of us ever catches criminals, that ultimately they give themselves away. The perfect detective doesn't exist.'

'Are you going to describe the perfect crime?'

He smiled. 'How could I, Maggie? To my mind, the perfect crime is one that nobody even knows has been committed.'

'We could debate that for hours.'

'And maybe we will, now that you have the time at your

disposal. I know you've bumped into Aileen professionally, but I'd like you to meet her socially. You'll get on like a house on fire.'

'Is it the real thing this time, Bob?' she asked.

'Yes,' he replied, without hesitation. 'I love her; to be honest I have since the first moment I laid eyes on her, when she was deputy justice minister and she walked into a briefing at Fettes. But that's an admission I could only make to close friends, since I was still married to Sarah at the time.'

'I can't tell you how pleased I am to be included in that category.'

'You've been there for a long time. And now, close friend, are you going to tell me what's up?'

She looked at him, surprised, and instantly defensive. 'What makes you think that anything is?'

'I may not be the perfect detective,' he told her, 'but I'm pretty damn good. Your announcement last night was untypical. You don't make spontaneously emotional gestures, Maggie. I'm not questioning your decision to resign, but the way you sprang it on us: that was the act of someone with more on her mind than impending childbirth.'

She looked away from him. 'Bob . . .' she murmured.

'I'm sorry,' he said at once. 'I've touched a raw nerve. I'm being presumptuous.'

'No,' she assured him, 'you're not. As always, you're being perceptive. I'll tell you, on the same basis that you gave me that report through there. Yes?'

'Of course.'

She looked back at him, dead in the eye. 'I have a medical problem, one that's unrelated to my pregnancy.'

It was his turn to be taken aback. He inhaled deeply. 'Serious?' he asked.

'Potentially very serious.'

'Life-threatening?'

'Yes.'

'And are you being treated?'

'Not yet. While I'm carrying the baby I can't be, and I won't . . .'

'I understand. Stevie doesn't know, does he.' It was a statement, not a question.

'No, and he can't, not until she's been safely delivered. You will respect that, Bob?' she added anxiously.

'Of course. You have my word on it, I told you. I see exactly why you can't tell him, even though he is your husband and the father of your child. What was I just saying about the morally unthinkable sometimes being the only possible course of action? You're shielding him from such a choice. However, it will not stop me worrying like hell about you. That paper of mine, Maggie: forget about it.'

'Absolutely not! I'll live my life as normal; I have to. Bob, you may find this surprising but I feel . . . what's the word? Yes, that's it. I feel serene. With this wee girl growing inside me, I've done something that I never dreamed of achieving, something that's far, far more important than adding all the silver braid in the world to my uniform.'

'I can understand that,' he admitted. 'Fathers can feel that way too. We'll keep each other's secrets all right,

Maggie. And while all this is happening, I'll be there for you, if ever you need me.'

'I know you will, and that helps a lot, believe me.' She smiled. 'Now you'd better go and get on with your consorting duties!'

'Christ,' he exclaimed, as he rose, 'I never thought of myself like that.'

'It's a sort of a Stevie-ism,' she told him, accepting his hand to pull herself to her feet. She had just regained the vertical when his mobile sounded.

'Damn,' he said, 'I always forget to switch it off.'

'That's what they all say. Go on, answer it.'

'I'd better; it could be Aileen.'

She watched him as he walked to the window, his back to her as he answered the noisy summons.

'Mario.' He sounded surprised. 'Yes, go on.' As he listened, she could see his back straighten, his shoulders draw back. 'There is no doubt about this?' he asked. 'I see,' he said eventually, his voice as stiff as his posture. 'No, don't do that. I'll take that on board. I'm better placed than you to do it. I'm with her right now, in fact.'

He ended the call, and slowly turned towards her. Instinctively she held up a hand, as if to keep him at bay.

Fifty-nine

Stevie Steele was no newcomer to helicopter flight; in their short time together he and Dottie Shannon had gone on a clandestine winter break to Las Vegas and, rather than risk their spending cash on the tables, had splashed much of it on an excursion to the Grand Canyon.

Nevertheless he was surprised by the range and speed of the Metropolitan Police aircraft that picked him up from an open area in Regent's Park, less than twenty minutes after his call to Mario McGuire.

The pilot explained that he would have to make a stop at his depot but that, once fuelled up and under way, they would reach their destination in less than two hours. 'You've made our month, mate,' he added, jerking a thumb in the direction of the woman in the co-pilot's seat. 'We love to take this thing out of the city and really cut loose. Flying over bleedin' London, day in, day out, stops being fun after a very short while.'

He handed him a headset. 'You'll be able to hear us through that,' he told him, 'but nobody else. Mostly they're to stop you going deaf. Noise limitation is the one piece of chopper technology they haven't cracked yet.'

'That part I remember,' he replied.

The warning was well founded: throughout the flight Steele was content to sit strapped in, listening to the background chatter of the pilots and watching as England spread itself out below. The panorama was enthralling; for a while he concentrated on that and nothing else, until they crossed the Tyne and he forced himself to think once more of what might await him in Wooler.

The last part of the journey was over green countryside, flat at first, but gradually becoming more hilly, until they reached the Cheviots, the range that once served as a shield against pillaging Scots. 'We've been ordered to put you down on a flat area at the foot of Humbleton Hill,' the pilot told him through the headphones, as they approached their destination. 'You'll be met there by the local force.' Steele replied with a thumbs-up sign.

The landing was as smooth as the flight had been. The inspector checked his watch as he jumped out on to the grass, ducking instinctively under the rotors; it showed two minutes after six.

He was near the edge of a big field, mostly hillside, but with an area wide enough and flat enough for the chopper to put down safely. Not far away, there was a gate, where a Land Rover, bright with police markings, stood in waiting. As he made his way towards it a man jumped out; he was in his mid-fifties, big and red-faced, and wore a tweed jacket and grey trousers, tucked into black wellingtons.

'DI Steele,' he called out, above the aircraft noise. 'I'm Les Cairns, deputy chief constable. We're not far from the location: jump in and I'll take you straight down there.'

The Scot's ears were ringing as he climbed into the back seat of the big vehicle. 'Thanks, sir,' he said, a little more loudly than was necessary. 'Have you taken any action?'

'No, son, this is your investigation, so I felt it only right that you take the decisions. All we've done is secure the area, and keep the house under observation. Oh, yes, and we've secured the man Spicer and his associate too. We assumed that you'd need them for questioning.'

'That may depend on what we find in the house . . . or don't find, as the case may be. If it turns out that their failure to tell us about Ballester's hidey-hole as soon as they knew where it was has led to him getting away, then I'm going to take the biggest book I can lay my hands on and throw it at them as hard as I can. On the other hand, if we make an arrest, I'll probably thank the pair of them for their assistance and let them go.'

'That's what I'd be doing,' said Cairns. He tapped his driver on the shoulder. 'Let's go, Constable.'

The vehicle headed off down a narrow, twisty road until, after no more than half a mile, they came to a crossroads. Facing them was an even narrower road, little more than a driveway, with houses on either side. Two police people-carriers were parked on either side, and beyond, a silver Jaguar S-type.

'The Jag belongs to Spicer,' the DCC volunteered, as the Land Rover came to a halt. 'We've taken him and his mate to the local office. This is an armed operation, so we couldn't allow them anywhere near it. I've had the neighbours moved out too, discreetly. One of them told us that she's seen a man answering Ballester's description coming and going from Hathaway House.'

'When was the last time?'

'She told us that she thought she heard his car on the gravel yesterday, around midday. She can't swear to it, but she thinks it's been there ever since. How strong is your evidence against this man, Inspector?'

'At the moment, it's circumstantial, but it's very strong nonetheless. Amy Noone was killed in Edinburgh yesterday morning: if he did that, then drove down here, the neighbour's arrival time would have been about right. That fits the pattern. A single piece of firm evidence would wrap it up.'

'Such as?'

'First, there's the gun; the murder weapon. Also, items were taken from the first two victims; if we found any of those in his possession, it would seal it.'

'Yes,' Cairns murmured. 'The gun. I've got sharpshooters in position, front and back of the house. So far they've seen no sign of movement. The fire seems to have gone out, though; there's no more smoke coming out of the chimney.'

'Could he have seen your people? We believe that this is a resourceful man.'

'I doubt it. They're good. Plus, they can't actually see into the house themselves. It's in a gully, so they're well above all the windows. They're really waiting for him to come out. If he does, their orders are to let him climb up to the drive where his car's parked, unless he displays a firearm. I have more men there, waiting to take him down.'

'That's sound,' Steele conceded, 'but if there's been no

movement since you've been here, sooner or later we're going to have to take the initiative.'

'I agree with you,' said the Englishman, 'and I don't really want to wait till dark.'

'Can we get close enough to see inside?'

'That's where the risk will lie. Come on; let's get as close as we can and have a look.'

The two officers stepped out of the Land Rover. Cairns led the way down the narrow road until he came to a sign reading 'Hathaway House' fixed on a white-painted post. Beyond, a path, barely wide enough to take a car, led up to a circular area, where a garage faced them. To his left, Steele spotted the roof of what he knew was a blue Suzuki.

Quietly they approached the house, until they could just make out a chimney stack. Suddenly a man in a black assault uniform appeared from behind a hedge. 'No sign of movement yet, sir,' he murmured to Cairns, with a nod to Steele.

'This is Chief Inspector Roberts,' said DCC. 'He's based at our Berwick station.'

'I want to get closer,' the Scot told him, as they shook hands.

'Dodgy,' Roberts replied. 'However, there's a steep bank to the right of the cottage, as we're looking at it. You could get down from that side. We've pulled original drawings of the place from the local-authority office. They show that you can see into the kitchen and the living room . . . that's closest . . . from there. You have to go all the way around to access the bedrooms and bathroom. If the chief okays it, I'll send a man down to take a look.'

'I'll do it myself,' said Steele, at once. 'This is my shout. Can you give me a flak jacket and a weapon?'

'Yes, if you know how to use it.'

'I'm qualified.'

'Qualified and foolhardy,' Roberts suggested, 'from the sound of things.'

'Maybe, but do you want to wait him out for a day or two, only to find that he wasn't there after all?'

The chief inspector grimaced. 'Okay, if that's what you want to do, go ahead. I'll have two of my shooters give you cover from the top of the bank.'

'Sure,' Steele chuckled, with dark humour, 'and that way I'll be between them and the target if he makes a break for it. Thanks, but I'd rather trust my luck; it's been pretty good so far.'

'Fair enough.' Roberts eased off his own flak jacket and held it up for Steele to slip on, then took a revolver from his belt and handed it to him. 'Six shots,' he said.

'If I have to use it,' the Scot told him, 'I'll only need one.' He took the heavy weapon and flicked off the safety.

The chief inspector unstrapped his military-style helmet, and began to take it off. 'Here, you should wear this too.'

'By the book, yes, but if I do, it would just make it easier for him to spot me.'

'It's Kevlar, man: bulletproof. Are you sure about that?'

'Certain.'

'Even if I ordered you to wear it?'

'As DCC Cairns said, this is my shout.'

'On your own head . . .'

Stevie grinned. '. . . be it not.'

Roberts laughed. '*Touché*. Go on, then,' he said. 'Make your way round the edge of the circle, otherwise you'll make a noise on the gravel.'

'Where's your sniper on this side?'

'She's hidden over there in the trees, watching the door in the far gable. It's the only way in and out of the place.'

'Do you have a two-way?'

The chief inspector nodded, unclipped a transceiver from his belt, fastened it to the flak jacket, then flicked a switch. 'That's it on transmit.'

'Okay,' said Steele. 'I'm off.'

He felt his pulse quicken as he stepped carefully around the edge of the car park, then across, in front of the garage. As he looked around he had his first full view of the long, narrow cottage. The gully in which it sat was so deep that the ridge of its roof was at his eye level. He looked along the building's length and counted four windows. Below them ran a narrow walkway, no more than a yard wide.

Satisfied that he was out of sight of all the windows, he began to ease his way slowly down the bank. It was so steep that it was almost sheer, and he had to lean backwards to avoid slipping, and sliding noisily down to the foot. His shoes had corrugated soles, or the task would have been impossible, but finally he reached the path. He crouched there, until his breathing and his gun hand were both steady.

'Living room first,' he whispered into the transceiver, even though he was really talking to himself.

The window was around fifteen feet from the end wall of the house; it was set low, no more than three feet from the ground. He walked silently along, then crouched down, below the level of the ledge, until finally he held his breath and, literally, stuck his head above the parapet, as fast as he could.

A face stared back at him. Instinctively he threw himself to the side, more than half expecting a bullet to shatter the glass.

And then his brain finally registered what it was that he had seen. He stood to his full height, holding the gun in both hands, in a marksman's grip, and stepped back in front of the window.

The face that he had seen was black and distorted. Its owner was hanging from a hook set firmly in the ceiling to support a light fitting and, on that day, much more.

'Fuck it!' he yelled into the transceiver. 'He's topped himself. Marksmen, stand down, I'm going in!'

He sprinted along to the end of the house, and through a black wooden gate, which led to the entrance porch. As Roberts had said, the cottage had only a single door. He grabbed its handle and turned it, expecting to have to shoulder his way inside, but it opened under a single firm push.

In the second after he stepped inside, Stevie Steele knew that something was wrong. His heightened senses alerted him to one tiny shred of resistance as the half-glazed door swung inwards, and then to a metallic click from above his head.

He looked up at the ceiling, and saw the black round object that was taped there.

'Oh dear,' he whispered.

And then he saw the blinding flash.

He never heard the noise of the explosion that followed it.

Sixty

Ray Wilding gazed up at the ceiling. 'I've never seen anything quite like that,' he said, in a tone that was little short of awestruck.

'I don't imagine you have,' Becky Stallings conceded. Her face was slick with the perspiration of strenuous physical activity, and strands of her dark hair were plastered to her forehead.

From her bed, they were gazing up at a colour representation of the view across the treetops of the north embankment of the Thames, from Nelson's Column on the right to the Palace of Westminster on the left, a shot taken from a gondola at the very top of the London Eye.

'I'm very proud of that,' she told him. 'It was my own idea, from start to finish. A photographer mate of mine took the picture with one of those special lenses, then a girl I know who works in an advertising agency had it printed for me on about eight sheets, and finally I found a poster fixer-upper to paste it up there for me. It's got to be one of the sights of the city.'

'It beats a mirror, that's for sure,' the Scot admitted. 'My ex used to go on about wanting a mirror on the ceiling. I always reckoned it was so she could do her nails at the same time.'

'That's the usual reason, they tell me. I did think about a flat-screen telly, until I had this idea.'

'You're not your run-of-the-mill detective inspector, are you, Becky?' Wilding yawned contentedly.

'No, I don't suppose I am. But I'll tell you a secret, Ray. Since the poster fixer-upper fixed it up, you're the first bloke to have seen that.'

'How long's it been up there?' he asked. 'A week?'

'Cheeky bastard,' she exclaimed, the second word elongated by her slight Cockney accent. 'Nearly a year, since you're unchivalrous enough to force me to admit it. Shocked? Or surprised?'

'Amazed, more like. You're an attractive woman, working in a male environment, and, if you don't mind my saying so, you don't exactly hang about once you've made your mind up.'

'I don't mind at all. I'm pretty choosy about my blokes, but I've always believed in the unconventional approach. From fairly early on you and I both knew that this was going to happen. Much better that we got straight to it than that we edge around it all night and waste a nice meal by thinking about something else all the time we're eating. Do you agree?'

'With all my heart. What do we do now?'

'We go out and have that meal, and a nice bottle of wine, then come back here and get back to the action, with the ice well and truly broken.'

'Inspector, you are a bloody genius, if you don't mind me saying so again.'

'I don't mind that either,' she told him cheerfully, then sat up in bed. 'A quick shower before we go out would be in order, I reckon. It'll save time if we have it together.'

'In theory it will.'

'Let's chance it.' She swung her feet on to the floor and jumped up, just as her phone rang. 'Bugger,' she said. 'You know I can't just let it ring, Ray, don't you?'

'Am I a copper or not?'

She picked it up. 'Stallings.'

'Inspector,' said a thick voice, with a Scottish accent, a voice under stress, she recognised, a voice with a lot bearing down in it. 'My name's Tarvil Singh. I'm a DC and I need to contact my sergeant, Ray Wilding. Your office thought that he might have told you what hotel he's booked into.'

It did not occur to her for a moment that she might prevaricate, and tell him that she would contact Wilding and have him call back. 'He isn't,' she replied. 'He's here. Hold on.'

She offered him the instrument. 'It's DC Singh, Ray. Something's wrong, I think.'

She watched him as he took the call. She watched him as the colour drained from his face. She watched him as the phone fell from his grasp, and as tears began to course down his cheeks.

She picked up the fallen receiver and replaced it, without thinking.

He looked up at her, too stunned to speak at first, his mouth hanging open slightly. When he did find words, they came out in a moan. 'Stevie's dead.'

She sat down hard beside him, sharing his incredulity. 'The helicopter?' she asked. 'Did it . . .?'

'No. He got there all right. And when he did, Stevie being Stevie, he led from the front and went down there to have a look. Ballester had hanged himself; Stevie saw him through a window and went charging into the house. Only the evil motherfucker had booby-trapped the front door. When he opened it, he pulled the pin of a grenade.'

Sixty-one

Bob Skinner stood in the living room of Hathaway House, staring at the dead, darkened face of Daniel Ballester. Then, with neither word nor warning, he swung upwards and punched it, as hard as he had ever hit anything or anyone in his life.

'Hey!' Les Cairns yelled, and lumbered forward as if to restrain him, only to stop short as Mario McGuire stepped into his path, his expression as ferocious as any he had ever seen.

'Sorry,' said Skinner, grimly, as the body swung round, and back again, then round once more, in semicircles. 'Only I'm not. I wish I could have killed him myself, and that's all there is to it.'

'Still,' the Englishman protested, 'this is my patch.'

'Let's not get territorial about this.' The voice came from the living-room doorway. The three men turned towards it, and saw Chief Constable Sir James Proud, in full uniform.

'I'm very much inclined to do the same as Bob,' he said, 'but I'll defer to him, since he's much better at that sort of action than I am. I'm sorry I've taken so long to get here; I was out when Jack McGurk called to tell me what had happened. Maggie: what about Maggie? Has she been told yet?'

'She knows,' Skinner replied. 'By a miserable coincidence, I was with her when Mario rang to tell me what had happened.'

'How did she take it?'

'Jimmy,' the DCC snapped, 'how the hell do you think she took it? She wouldn't even let me say the words; she knew anyway, from my face. Eventually she asked if it had been quick. I told her that it was instantaneous.'

'Where is she now?'

'She's still at home. I called Neil; he came over straight away and he's with her now. So's Paula. She arrived with Mario when he came by to join me. I sent for a doctor too, as a precaution.'

'Of course. Let's hope the shock doesn't affect her pregnancy.'

'God forbid.'

'He doesn't seem to be in a very forbidding mood this week,' McGuire growled.

'Bob,' the chief began hesitantly, 'it really was instantaneous, wasn't it? He's under a sheet through there.'

'Yes, it must have been. If he'd taken the Kevlar helmet he was offered he'd probably have survived. The flak jacket he wore deflected most of the shrapnel from the grenade, but two large pieces, at least . . . maybe there were others the doctor couldn't see at a first examination . . . penetrated his skull. He'd no chance. He must have been dead before he hit the floor.'

'This swine here,' Sir James pointed at Ballester's body, 'did he leave anything behind him?'

'Apart from a booby-trapped door, rigged to take out the first person through it?'

'A note?'

Skinner's face twisted. 'Oh, yes,' he replied, 'but not the usual sort. This guy's high-tech. He left his on his laptop. Take a look: it's still switched on. But don't touch it: the local SOCOs are going to take it back to their lab to dust it.'

'Why?'

'Because the coroner would have their balls if they didn't, and so would I. They have to match the prints to the body for the inquest. Sorry, inquests: there will have to be one into Stevie's death as well.'

'I imagine so. Has anyone reported this to our procurator fiscal?'

'Yes, Chief,' said McGuire. 'I called him before we left Edinburgh. He's coming down to see for himself, but he lives in Fife, so it'll be a while yet before he gets here. That's why the bodies are still here.'

'I'll wait for him. You chaps should get back to Edinburgh to see how Maggie's doing. She may even want to talk to you.'

'We'll do that,' Skinner agreed. He turned to DCC Cairns. 'Les, when do you plan to start the full-scale search of this place?'

'Tomorrow morning, Bob. The light's going fast and I'm not having my people stumbling around in the dark in case this so-and-so's left us any more nasty surprises.'

'Absolutely not. If you have no objection I'd like to send down my chief technical officer, DI Dorward, and a couple of his people, to work with them. The findings here will be part of our report to the fiscal. That will have to be very thorough, so that the Crown Office can decide on how to proceed.'

'What options will they have under Scots law?'

'It could be they don't have too many: our system's a lot different from yours. Down here, your coroner will have full inquest hearings into Ballester's suicide and Stevie's murder. That should close your book. As for how we proceed, I'll need to consult with the fiscal on that one.'

'What does the note say?' said Proud, moving towards the sideboard on which the laptop lay. He peered at the screen, then took a pair of reading glasses from a pocket in his uniform.

'I can tell you, off by heart,' Skinner murmured. 'I've read it often enough since I got here. You'll find that it says, "*I, Daniel Ballester, confess to the executions of the two bitches who dumped me, of the lad who replaced me in Zrinka's bed, and of nosy little Amy who got too close. I die as I lived, unloved, and I leave you with a parting gift to those who have the misfortune to find my body. My last message is the soldier's salute, 'Farewell and fuck you all'. I'm on my way, Zrinka.*" Pretty comprehensive, you'll agree, Jimmy.'

The chief was still staring at the screen. 'Indeed,' he replied.

'I guess that was his motive after all,' McGuire mused. 'A murderous rage, flowing from rejection. Stevie was wrong.'

'Was he?'

The chief superintendent looked back at Skinner and nodded. 'He thought it was much more complicated than that. Deep down, even as he was going down that bank, gun in hand, I don't think he really believed that Ballester was guilty. When he found out that he was, he was reckless, for the first and only time in his police career, and it cost him his life.'

'And maybe not just his,' Skinner whispered.

'Sorry?' Proud enquired.

'Ah, nothing. Mario, let's get back to Edinburgh; I'll brief Dorward on the way, call in to see Maggie, then head for Charlotte Square. I promised Aileen I'd do that, whatever the hour . . . after the dinner guests have gone, though. She was going to call it off, you know, that big dinner of hers, but I wouldn't let her. The press office will have been busy, calling round everybody to tell them I wasn't there after all, but I have a terrible feeling that my name will still be on tomorrow's front pages.'

McGuire frowned, grief still written across his face. 'I'll need to brief the press tonight myself.'

'No, fuck 'em,' said Skinner, firmly. He looked at Cairns. 'Les, maybe your people could issue a holding statement tonight, no victim names, usual excuse, next of kin to be informed. We'll tell the whole sad story in the morning.'

'Sure,' the Englishman agreed.

'We?' the head of CID interjected.

'Yes, I'll do it with you. My sabbatical's on hold, for the moment. I'll tell Royston to set up the media meeting for midday. By that time, hopefully Les's people will have turned up the last piece of the jigsaw.'

'What's that?' the chief constable asked.

'The gun, Jimmy; we still need to find the murder weapon to tie it all up formally. But tomorrow we will; there's nothing surer, we will.'

Sixty-two

'Ray, you're upset: maybe you should stay with me tonight after all. You don't have to go back.'

'I do, Becky,' Wilding replied quietly. 'Thanks for breaking your neck to get me here, and thanks for pulling all those strings to get me on the last flight. I need to be back in Edinburgh tonight. I was Stevie's neighbour . . .'

'What?'

'You'd say "oppo"; it means the same. And it means that I belong in Edinburgh. You're a cop too: you know that. I was with him when he took the decision to go roaring off to Wooler, and I was involved in all the process that led up to it. I'm not just a police officer: I'm a witness to the events that led to his death.'

He was aware of the orange-coated air steward fidgeting nearby, waiting to check him on board, but he ignored him and took Becky in his arms. 'This has been a very different day,' he told her. 'I'd like to see you again, and to have another look at the view from the London Eye. Is that on, do you think?'

'Absolutely, but I'll probably see you in Edinburgh first.

Whenever Stevie's funeral is, I'm going to be there, and that's a solemn promise.'

'I'll let you know as soon as I do. And I'll make sure that Maggie knows who you are too.'

'Maggie?'

'His wife. Oh, fuck, his widow. And she's pregnant too.'

'Oh, she isn't! Jesus, that's awful.' She paused. 'You know, Ray, I'm thankful for just one thing. If you didn't get sick on helicopters, you'd probably have gone through that door alongside him.'

To her surprise, his eyes filled with tears once more. 'No, Becky,' he whispered. 'Don't be thankful for that. I'll have to live with that for the rest of my days. I've never been on a helicopter in my life; I just said that so I could be with you.'

'Okay, love, that's okay. It's done with, and you were.'

'The worst of it is, or maybe the best . . . I'm as confused as fuck and I don't know . . . Stevie knew it perfectly well, and he still went along with it. Because that's the sort of bloke he was.'

Sixty-three

'How does he look?' Her voice was flat, emotionless. 'Tell me, Bob, I need to know, and his parents will too. Will I be able to look at him in his coffin, or will the lid have to be closed?'

McGuire replied to her question: 'He'll look asleep, Maggie.'

'No, he won't,' she shot back sharply. 'He'll look dead.'

'Yes, he will,' Skinner conceded, intervening, 'but unmarked, and that's what you want to know. The grenade fragments that killed him went into his brain above the hairline; his protective jacket stopped the rest. Once an experienced undertaker's been to work on him, you won't see any wounds.'

'Thanks,' she said, 'for I'll have to look at him regardless, and I wouldn't want ever to remember him disfigured. He was such a lovely guy, in every respect.'

'He was that,' Paula Viareggio murmured. She looked as pale and shocked as Maggie.

'Ray Wilding called from London,' Maggie carried on, 'after you two left. Neil took the call, but I spoke to him. The poor guy was practically hysterical. He kept saying that he should have been with him, but that Stevie had let him stay down there.' Her face split into a strange, twisted smile. 'If I know him, he'll have pulled somebody, and Stevie's left him to get on with it.'

'He's on his way back up,' Neil McIlhenney told Skinner. 'He was still with their Met liaison officer when Singh found him. He told me later that she'd got him on to the last plane out of Stansted and that she was taking him there.'

'That's good. He'll need to do a report on what happened down there. I'll speak to him in the morning: Mario and I will need as much information as we can get for the press briefing.'

'Stevie saved my life,' said Maggie, from the couch.

'I remember,' McGuire told her, 'the time that low-life attacked you with a blade, and he took him apart.'

'I didn't mean that. I was talking about much more than that, when I was on the road to dying, only nobody knew. The job might have been going all right, on the surface at least, but away from it, I was lower than I'd ever been.' Her eyes darted to Paula. 'I'm not getting at Mario, or at you. That was meant to be, and I know it. But things happened to me.' She looked at McGuire and McIlhenney. 'You guys know what I mean.

'For a while I thought I'd never get over them. I'd go home, and some nights I'd drink myself to sleep, then be up next day as if everything was hunky-dory, only it wasn't. I began to develop a vision of getting in one night, turning on the gas and forgetting to light it.

'That would have happened too, sooner or later, but for Stevie. He was kind to me; he made me start to care about myself again. He was always a friend, before he was anything else. When he became more than that, it wasn't him that made the running, it was me, but when we did get together, completely, my life just lit up in a way it never had before. Even though he's dead, that'll never change,' she glanced down, at her lap, 'thanks to this wee one in here.'

Bob Skinner gazed at her and, inside, felt himself begin to buckle. 'Maggie,' he said, 'I don't suppose you're going to sleep, but you do need to rest. Mario and Paula are going to stay with you tonight.'

'That's okay, really. I'll manage.'

'Sure, but you don't have to,' Paula told her. 'A team of Clydesdales wouldn't drag me out of here.'

'That's settled,' Skinner went on. 'I'll be back in the morning, and I'll make arrangements with my opposite number in Northumbria for Stevie to be brought up here. When you speak to his family again, let them know that. The chief plans to visit them tomorrow, and you too.'

'That's good of him. Stevie's dad will be pleased. You know he was a police officer?'

'Superintendent Steele, Fife Constabulary? Of course I knew; I met him, years ago. See you in the morning, love.' He nodded his farewell to the two men and to Paula and was leaving when Maggie pushed herself to her feet and walked with him, through the unlit hall to the front door.

'Don't worry about me,' she told him quietly. 'Everything will be all right . . . or as all right as it can be.'

He was glad that it was dark, and that she could not see his eyes.

He left the big, handsome house, and slid into his car,

oddly grateful for its familiarity, and comforted by it. Finally, he switched on the engine, and drove out of Gordon Terrace, towards the centre of the city, and its Saturday-night bustle. He headed through Newington, across the bridges, past the Balmoral and the King James, then along the length of York Place and Queen Street, until finally he found the rear entrance to Bute House, the official residence of the First Minister.

As always, the door was guarded by armed officers. They saluted and let him in without a word; he could tell by their grim faces that word of the tragedy had spread through the ranks. For a moment he thought of calling Alex, who had known Stevie well, but decided against it. If Griff Montell broke the news, that was okay by him.

He climbed the back stairway, up to the private quarters; on the way he heard voices from the dining room, but carried on, in no way tempted to make a late entrance. Instead he went into the small kitchen and took a beer from the fridge, part of a private stock that he had put there.

He had almost finished his third, in the dark, staring through the window at the gloaming in the north, when the door opened behind him and Aileen de Marco slipped into the sitting room. 'How was it?' she asked him quietly.

'Awful, my love, awful,' he replied. 'It always is.'

Sixty-four

'You were right,' Maggie told him, as she handed him a mug of coffee, in the big kitchen. 'I didn't get any sleep. I did all I could to rest, but I spent most of the night padding about down here, with that line from Shakespeare running through my head, that voice crying, "Sleep no more! Macbeth doth murder sleep." It's weird, you know; I know that from now on every time I think of that man, that bastard, that Ballester, I'll think of William fucking Shakespeare. And I've always hated that bloody play.'

She had given him the coffee automatically, without asking whether he wanted it or not, from a filter machine. Skinner accepted it, though, and took a swig; it tasted as if it had been standing on the warming plate for hours. She caught his expression. 'Is that crap?' she asked. 'I made it for Paula and Mario. I'll do a fresh lot.'

'No, it's fine,' he lied. 'When did they leave?'

She glanced up at the kitchen clock; it showed ten minutes to eleven. 'About an hour ago. I made them go home. They must have had precious little sleep either. He looked like a zombie and I heard Paula crying well into the night. She went out with Stevie, remember, when we were all younger and I was married to Mario? Life's just so fucking random, isn't it?' She paused. 'Listen to me, Bob, swearing like a trooper. I must cut it out before Stevie's parents get here. His mum's very churchy and his dad can be a bit straight-backed too.'

'When are they due?'

'Mr Steele said they'd be here for lunch. He was going to bring it, but I told him not to: I've been cooking for hours, to pass the time. They're going to stay tonight.'

'Good,' said Skinner. 'When they arrive, you'll be able to tell them that I've spoken to Les Cairns. Stevie's body will be released tomorrow morning. You can countermand this if you like, but there's an undertaker we use on occasions like this; I've instructed them to go and collect him, early as they can, and to take him to their premises in Fountainbridge. When you're ready, their funeral director will come to you, and you can begin arrangements.'

'I'll go to them,' she declared. 'I want to see him.'

'In that case, I'll have a car collect you whenever you're ready: it'll wait for you and bring you home.'

She smiled. 'Bob, I've left the force.'

'You're a police officer's widow, and you'll have all the help we can give you. But, Maggie,' he said earnestly, 'I urge you to put that on hold. Everything is changed now. You may very well think differently in a while.'

'I've still got cancer, Bob. I can't put that on hold.'

He winced at her use of the word, for the first time, as he reached out and took her hand. 'Love, you're going to get through this, you and your daughter. I can work out why you're refusing treatment, but you must strike a balance.

Ensure her safe delivery, but listen to medical advice on that.'

'She's too small, Bob.'

'But she's growing. When they're sure she'll be safe, let them induce labour, and then start to look after yourself. Promise me you'll do what's best for both of you. That kid's going to need you more than ever.'

'I've been reading up on it,' she told him. 'The odds are not good.'

'Fuck the odds. The Maggie factor's at work here, and more. Do you know what I did this morning? I went to church with Aileen. She's Catholic; we went to mass at the cathedral at Picardy Place. I prayed for you, and so did she. Lass, you have no idea how many people are praying for you today, each in their own way.'

'I didn't realise that you were religious, Bob.'

'I don't shout about them, but I have my firm beliefs. They've been there since the time I was widowed. You talk to Neil McIlhenney, and he'll tell you much the same. You belong to the same club as us now. Nobody ever wants to join it, but eventually, one half of lifelong couples do; there is no happy ever after. For you and Stevie, and Olive and Neil, and Myra and me, that time came far too soon, but I tell you this, you'll find your own truths through it.'

She stood before him, laid the palms of her hands on his chest, feeling the hard muscle under his white T-shirt, and smiled up at him. 'Thanks, Bob,' she said, 'for caring so much. Far be it from me to reject your prayers. I will do everything I can to beat this thing, I promise you. When I've done that, I'll consider the future.

'By the way,' she added, 'you're not alone in knowing about this any more. I told Mario and Paula this morning; there was no reason not to, not any more. They both said the same as you. At this rate I'll have every priest in Edinburgh saying Hail Marys for me.'

She looked up at the clock once more. 'When's your press briefing? I wasn't really listening last night.'

'Midday.' He glanced down at the T-shirt and jeans, fresh from his overnight bag. 'Don't think I'll be dressed like this, though. I'll be in full dress uniform, and so will the chief.'

Maggie chuckled. 'Hardly anyone will know you.'

'They'd better. It's an occasion for formality, a time to show every respect for the service for which men and women give their lives.' He realised that, once again, he was on the verge of losing control of his emotions, and forced a smile on to his face. 'I'd better head off, though. It'll take me half an hour at least to shake all the mothballs out of the thing.'

'Afterwards,' she asked, as she walked him to the door once again, 'what have you planned for the rest of the day?'

'Afterwards, my dear, I'm going to do what I always do at times like these. I'm going to join Aileen out at Gullane and yield to a desperate need to be with my kids.'

Sixty-five

The chief constable, flanked by the stone-faced, uniformed figures of Bob Skinner and Mario McGuire, made the formal announcement to a respectfully hushed gathering. The journalists knew from the English force that an officer had gone down in an incident in Northumberland the day before, but no word of his identity had leaked, and so when Sir James Proud told them that Detective Inspector Steven Stuart Steele had been killed in the line of duty, there were several gasps of undisguised horror from Edinburgh men and women who had known him well.

He paused, then added that Detective Inspector Steele had gone to the scene with Northumbrian colleagues to arrest a man named Daniel Ballester, also known as Dominic Padstow, wanted for questioning in connection with several recent homicides in the Edinburgh area, and that he had been found dead there.

He closed by extending condolences to DI Steele's widow, Chief Superintendent Margaret Rose, and to the other members of his family, then sat back to allow his colleagues to take questions.

They came thick and fast, and were answered clearly, and as fully as legally possible, by Skinner and McGuire. Stevie Steele was thirty-four years old when he died, the victim, it appeared, of a trap set by Daniel Ballester before he committed suicide.

Yes, Ballester had left a note, on his laptop computer, confessing unequivocally to the four murders, and to rigging the grenade that had killed Steele. This had been given added authority by the discovery that morning of a weapon, a silenced pistol, and a quantity of soft-nosed bullets, hidden in a shed in the garden of Hathaway House. Other items had been found, including Stacey Gavin's sketch pad, three paintings by Zrinka Boras, and a brassiere that they believed had belonged to Amy Noone.

'What sort of grenade was it?' a man from the *Daily Telegraph* asked.

'We're told by munitions experts,' Skinner replied, 'that it was probably an Austrian-made fragmentation grenade, used by NATO and other military customers around the world, absolutely lethal at close range.'

'How was it triggered?'

'It was fixed to the ceiling. The pin was pulled by a wire attached to the inside door handle and led to the weapon through two eyelets. From the accounts of officers at the scene, it exploded within two or three seconds of Stevie stepping into the kitchen. He died immediately.'

'How easy would it have been for Ballester to get hold of one of these things?'

'Probably as easy as it was for him to get hold of a precision Sig Sauer handgun, and ammunition that's illegal in most countries. Regrettably, there have been so many armed conflicts in recent years that items like these are now falling into the wrong hands all too easily. Ballester was a journalist, with a record of going undercover. Who knows what contacts he had? Maybe, when we have a chance to go through his computer files, they'll lead us to his supplier, but then again . . .'

'Are you saying that we need tighter firearms control?' the *Guardian*'s Scotland reporter asked.

'Firearms control is already very tight,' the DCC replied. 'Unfortunately there's a snag. Fine, we made handguns illegal ten years ago, but criminals do not obey the law. All the legislation in the world isn't going to change that.' He glanced at the journalist. 'I'm sorry, Peter; I'm pontificating. My answer is a simple no.'

'Do you and the First Minister disagree about that?'

'The First Minister and I disagree about a number of matters; happily we agree about many more. And, ladies and gentlemen, that's the last time I will ever discuss her on this or any other platform, apart from telling you that she's as gutted by this as the rest of us. Now, is there one last question?'

Grace Pretty raised her hand. 'What about the million-pound reward that Mr Boras offered last week?'

'I'm glad you asked that, Grace,' McGuire replied. 'The three of us have been discussing that, and we're all agreed that it would be an excellent idea for Mr Boras to donate that money to the Police Dependants' Trust. We hope he shares that view.' There had been no such discussion, but the chief constable and his deputy nodded in confirmation.

'A nice closer, Mario,' Skinner murmured, as the three police officers made their way out of the briefing room. 'Stevie would have loved it. Let's see how the man wriggles out of that.'

Sixty-six

James Andrew Skinner had become used to his new lifestyle, and had adapted well to it. There were three other children from one-parent families in his primary-school class. Two of them never saw their fathers, and he knew that the third hated the weekends that he was forced to spend with his and his new girlfriend, who insisted on being called 'Auntie'.

Jazz, for all that he had just turned six, knew that he had the best of both worlds. He loved both of his parents equally, and when they had told him at the beginning of the year that they didn't love each other any more and intended to divorce, he had been sad, but sad for them more than for himself.

If he had been able to express it in such a sophisticated way, he would have said that the proposal they had put to him and to Mark, his adoptive brother, was ideal. They were able to stay with their dad in Gullane and go to school there, and three times a year go off with Trish, the nanny, on an adventure to America, to join their mum.

He liked America, where they had big cars and good weather. He had been there before, when he was younger, visiting his grandparents with his mum, before they had gone to Heaven. Jazz wasn't really sure about Heaven, but he went along with the concept, without asking awkward questions, to please his mum.

He understood that his dad was busy, being very important in the police, and that sometimes he had to be away during the week, and once or twice for longer. But most weekends he was home, and Jazz liked that, even when his new friend was there too. She was nice and, even though she was grown-up, he was allowed to call her 'Aileen', because that was her name.

Aileen had been different, though, when she had arrived that morning, on her own. Dad had explained that they were going to a very 'flash' . . . that was one of his special words, the kind he winked when he said . . . dinner, and would be away overnight, but he had expected them to arrive together, because Dad had promised him he would take him out on the golf course, on one of the big people's courses, when everybody else was having lunch and it got quieter. Aileen had explained that something had happened and that Dad needed to 'deal with it'. He didn't really understand the phrase, but he held himself back from asking what she meant, because she seemed sad, and because, well, she wasn't his mum.

Dad hadn't arrived until nearly two o'clock; and when he had, he had been sad too. He had told James Andrew that he was sorry, but the courses were getting busy again and that maybe they would just watch English football on telly instead, while Aileen did all the work that her office people had told her had to be done for Monday morning. Mark didn't bother: he didn't like golf, he didn't like football, he only liked his computer.

Dad had switched on the telly and then he had gone out again, to his office. Jazz had followed him, and because he'd left the door open he had seen that he was making a phone call. He heard him say, 'Sarah,' and realised that he was talking to his mum. He wondered why, because she had phoned them all the day before. Then he heard him say something about somebody called Stevie, and he heard him say, 'Yes, I know you liked him.' He hadn't done it at school yet, but he understood what a past tense was, and what, sometimes, it meant.

James Andrew watched his dad very carefully, while they were both supposed to be watching Manchester United thump some team in blue shirts. He saw that he was always frowning, and that wasn't like him, especially not at weekends. And sometimes, even when Wayne Rooney had the ball, his eyes were closed. Jazz knew when his dad was thinking, and usually he waited to be told about whatever it was. But this time he was . . . He didn't know what he was: 'anxious' had not yet found its way into his vocabulary, but he knew what it felt like, and that wasn't good.

Bob Skinner felt a small, strong hand close round two of his fingers, and squeeze them. 'What's the matter, Dad?' his son asked.

He blinked, pulling himself back into the room, taken aback by the question, and alarmed by the look in James Andrew's eyes. 'I'm not sure,' he replied slowly, making himself grin, 'but I think they're still missing Roy Keane.'

'I didn't mean the football. You're not watching it

anyway. Was it bad, the thing that Aileen said had happened?'

Bob was intensely proud of his son, and in particular of his inherent compassion. 'Yes, I'm afraid so. Somebody's died.'

'Gone to Heaven?'

'For sure.'

'Is it Stevie?' Jazz hesitated and then made an admission. 'I listened to you on the phone to Mum.'

'Yes, it's Stevie; a policeman, a detective like me.'

'Have I met him?'

Bob thought for a moment. 'As a matter of fact,' he said, 'you have, but you probably don't remember. Once, when your mum was working and before Seonaid was born, I took you with me on a stake-out. God, your mum gave me pelters when she found out.'

'And a man came into the car?'

He stared in his astonishment at the accuracy of the boy's recollection. 'That's right. That was Stevie.'

James Andrew's face grew solemn, as he tried to contemplate the end of the existence of someone he could picture in his mind. 'That's sad,' he said, squeezing Bob's fingers again. 'We can stop watching the game if you like.'

'No, no, it's important.'

'But you'd your eyes shut.'

'I know. I wasn't concentrating on it. I was thinking about something else, about Stevie. His death, Jazz, was a crime. You know what that is, somebody doing something that's against the law.'

'And it's your job to catch him.'

'Yup, and I like to think I'm good at it.'

'You are,' said a warm voice. Aileen had come into the room, unseen by either of them, She stood behind Bob's chair, put her hands on his shoulders and began to knead them gently, her slim fingers rippling his flesh. 'Go on,' she insisted, 'don't let me interrupt.'

'Okay. What I was about to say was that I believe that it's essential for a detective to have a picture in his mind of that crime, of how it looked as it was committed, from start to finish.'

'Like a film?' James Andrew suggested.

'Exactly. He has to be able to look at it, to play it back inside his head, and to see everything that happened, to understand every part of it. That's what I was doing when my eyes were closed.'

'And could you see everything?'

'Yes. I could see it all, as it was explained by the people who were there at the time, and as I saw it afterwards when I went there. It all fits together, every bit of it.'

'And now you know who the bad man is.'

Bob looked at his magic son and raised his eyebrows. 'This is the bit you might not understand,' he told him. 'Sometimes you look at a film in your head, and even though everything does fit, and everything's in place, leading you straight to the answer, and to the bad guy . . . you know that it isn't, quite, how it was.

'You can't see anything wrong, because there's nothing to see, but you know, you feel that there's more, there's something you haven't been shown yet, but it's there. It's what we call instinct. Can you grasp that?'

From the back of his ever-expanding mind, Jazz produced a word, one that he had heard his dad use in the past, one that he had filed away for the day when it would mean something to him. 'Yes,' he announced, 'you've had a hunch.'

Sixty-seven

'Where's Jack McGurk?' Skinner asked Ruth Pye, his secretary.

'He's on a temporary posting to Torphichen Place,' she replied. 'Mr McGuire needed someone there: they're short-handed in CID with Superintendent Chambers filling in for Maggie.'

'Fair enough. He could hardly have anticipated that I'd be back ahead of schedule.' He smiled. 'I can always borrow your husband from him, if need be.'

'Maybe not. Sammy was expecting to be sent down to Leith to help out there.'

'Somebody will need to go there, that's for sure. What's the latest on DCI Mackenzie?'

'I don't know, sir. We received another medical report last Monday, but those are confidential, so it went to ACC Mackie unopened.'

'Okay, I'll ask him, or Mario.'

'Ask me what, boss?' said the head of CID from the doorway.

'I could begin with the whereabouts of my exec,' Skinner replied, 'but Ruthie's filled me in on that. Come along to my office and tell me what the medics are saying about the Bandit.'

They walked along the corridor and into the DCC's room, overlooking the driveway that led up to the building. 'He's been signed off for another month,' said McGuire, as he closed the door, 'by Kevin O'Malley, no less. Severe post-traumatic depression, he calls it.'

'Prognosis?'

'Not good. I called Kevin after Brian showed me the report. He says that he's more or less collapsed in on himself. If he's ever ready to return to duty, it won't be to CID but to a no-hassle desk job. He's not far off recommending that we retire him on health grounds. I admit that I was sceptical about him for a while, but not any more. I'm convinced that he's genuinely sick.'

'That's two empty chairs down in Leith, then.'

'Sammy Pye's down there now sitting in one of them as acting DI, taking over from Stevie. If you agree I've got a mind to make it permanent.'

'I've got no problem with that; I'll attend to the formalities. What about Mackenzie's post?'

'Maybe we don't fill it. We can't bump Sammy up to DCI straight away, but he's a good operator, and capable of running the division, with Neil overseeing him.'

'Will Wilding be pissed off at being passed over?'

'If he is, he'll get over it, but I didn't get any hint of that when I called him to tell him that Sammy was on his way. He sounded relieved, if anything. He's still very upset. He thinks he should have been there, and that if he had he'd have held Stevie back.'

'Like hell he would,' Skinner exclaimed. 'He'd have been through that door half a second after him and we'd have two dead officers. Mario, I think you and I should take a run down to Queen Charlotte Street, pay a visit on them.'

'Let them see we care, you mean, boss?'

'Exactly. But more than that, I want to run my eye over the investigation, to see if anything jumps out at me. Come on, we'll take my car.'

The DCC slipped on his jacket and led the way downstairs. He drove smoothly out into Carrington Road, turning left at the end to avoid as much of the Monday-morning traffic as he could. They had cleared the second set of lights on Ferry Road when it occurred to him that McGuire had not spoken since they left Fettes. He glanced across at him. 'Something on your mind?' he asked.

'I think you know. Maggie.'

'Yeah. It's not good, is it? Not the sort of thing you ever need, but right now . . . But she'll get through it, Mario. You have to believe that, and let her see that you do.'

'Sure, and I will. It doesn't stop me being scared, though.'

'Me neither. But she isn't: as always she's positive, and ready to tackle it as soon as she can.'

'I know, but she's realistic too. Yesterday morning, before she made us leave, she took me to one side and said that if she doesn't make it, she wants Paula and me to raise the baby. She didn't tell you that, did she?'

'No,' Skinner admitted, 'she didn't; but that's just her being practical, dealing with the situation up front so that she has nothing to take her mind off her recovery. What did you say?'

'I told her that we would.'

'And Paula?' Skinner murmured.

'To be honest with you, we would both love a kid. Maggie knew that before she asked us.'

There was no more to be said, and so the rest of the short journey was spent in silence, until they drew up in the car park behind the old Leith police station, where they startled a middle-aged constable who was taking a cigarette break. At once, he crushed it underfoot, saluted and opened the back door for them.

They made their way unannounced to the CID suite. Pye was seated at the desk that had been Stevie Steele's; he stood as Skinner and McGuire entered. Wilding, Montell and Singh all followed suit, but the DCC waved them down. 'Relax, gentlemen,' he told them. 'This is an informal visit, to assure you of our support, and to make an announcement. Sammy's here as acting DI at the moment, but I can tell you all now that he will be confirmed in post very soon.' He looked at the new inspector. 'Do you have everything you need?'

'More or less, sir,' Pye replied. 'Ray's put a report on the file of his visit to London, and of the interview with the man Barker. The ballistics people have run tests on the gun recovered at Ballester's cottage, and confirmed it as the murder weapon. When I reported that to the fiscal, he said that's all he needs to wind up the investigation and make a recommendation to the Lord Advocate that he set up an FAI into the four shootings. The only thing I don't have yet is Ballester's computer. There was a small war over that, but a truce has been called.'

'What do you mean?' asked McGuire.

'Instead of taking it to their lab, the Northumbria technicians did the job on site, and left it there. When our procurator fiscal visited the scene, he picked it up and brought it back to Edinburgh with him. When the coroner in Berwick heard, he screamed bloody murder and said he had first call on it, and that we couldn't have it until he was finished.'

'Fuck that for a game of soldiers.'

'He's got a point, though.'

'So has Gregor Broughton. The coroner was entitled to hold it for fingerprint comparison, but once that was done it should be passed it to us.'

'But the coroner says that he'll need to produce it for the jury at his inquest, so that they can actually see the suicide message.'

'So what's the solution?'

'A simple one at the end of the day, thanks to the DCC down there; he wound up refereeing. The entire contents are being copied on to another hard disk. I'm keeping that and the original's going back down to England.'

'Thank the Lord for sensible old Les Cairns,' said Skinner. 'Sometimes these coroners think they're more important than anybody else in the whole wide world.'

He looked at the detective sergeant. 'Ray, how are you?'

'I'm all right, sir,' Wilding replied, 'but thanks for asking. I appreciate it.'

'That's good. No guilt, do you hear me? There's nothing you could have done, and there's nothing you can do that'll bring him back, so don't dwell on what might have happened.' He paused and smiled. 'Who was she anyway?'

The sergeant blinked. 'How did you . . .?' He glared at Singh. 'Tarvil,' he began.

'DC Singh is innocent.' Skinner laughed. 'Maggie's guess was right on the money, that's all.'

'DI Stallings, sir, Becky; she was our escort down there. She and I sort of made a date for afterwards, and Stevie let me keep it.'

'When did you get back, Ray?' Griff Montell asked.

'I caught the last plane out of Stansted on Saturday night. Becky got me on it.'

The South African smiled, and pointed a finger at Singh, who glowered back at him.

'She's going to be in demand,' said Pye, ignoring the exchange.

Wilding stared at him. 'What do you mean?'

'Like I said, there's going to be a formal inquest into Stevie's death,' the acting DI replied. 'It's English law. DI Stallings is a witness to the events that led up to it. She'll be called. Apart from that, though, there'll be our standard internal investigation into an officer fatality. For that she'll need to be interviewed, formally, and so will you.'

'That's absolutely right,' McGuire confirmed. 'And I'm not sending two officers down to London when I can bring one person up here.'

'Call her,' Skinner told Wilding, 'and explain the situation, although she may have worked it out for herself. Tell her I'll be requesting that she be seconded to us for a period to help us prepare for both inquiries.'

'She wants to come to the funeral.'

'I'll make sure that her secondment covers it.'

'Thanks, sir.'

'Don't thank me: it's necessary. It isn't about you: it's about proper procedure.'

He looked up as the door opened, and Detective Inspector Arthur Dorward stepped into the office, holding a bag in one hand and a big brown envelope in the other. His red eyebrows rose when he saw the DCC and the head of CID. 'Morning, gentlemen,' he exclaimed, as he crossed the room.

'Hello, Arthur,' McGuire called out in reply. 'Has the lab caught fire? I can't remember the last time I saw you in a proper police office.'

'They're usually too messy for me. I do all my work in sterile conditions, remember.'

'So what brings you to this smelly old rat-pit?'

'Two things.' He laid the bag down on Pye's desk. 'Those are Stevie's effects; his watch, his wallet, some change, his keys, his warrant card, and a minidisk that I found in his pocket.'

'That's the interview of Keith Barker,' said Wilding. He glanced at Montell and Singh. 'You guys should listen to it: it's a masterclass in how to sort out an awkward witness.'

'I don't know if I could,' said the South African.

'You'll have to,' Skinner told him sharply. 'It's relevant to your investigation.' He looked back at Dorward. 'What else?'

The inspector held up the envelope. 'A copy of my report on Hathaway House. I've submitted another to Mr Cairns, down in Newcastle.' He handed the document to Skinner.

'You should really give it to Sammy,' the DCC told him. 'He's the senior officer in this division, as of this morning.'

'If you say so, sir, but can I have a word with you first, in private?'

From out of nowhere, Skinner felt a tingle run down his spine. 'All right.' He led the way into the room that had been Bandit Mackenzie's. 'What is it, Arthur?' he said, when they were alone.

'It's something I want to talk through with you, before making an arse of myself in front of that lot. Can I have the report back for a minute?' Skinner nodded and returned the envelope to him, then watched as he opened it.

'I won't go through it all,' the technician said. 'I'll get straight to the point. Apart from Stevie's, on the front-door handle, and those left by the officers who went to his aid, the only prints in that house belonged to Daniel Ballester. They were everywhere, including, as you'd expect, on the laptop where he typed his suicide note.

'Now, take a look at this.' He took out the document and riffled through the pages until he found the one he sought, then held it out for Skinner to see. 'This is a photograph of the wire that pulled the pin on the grenade,' he said. 'You can see how it leads from the door handle, up through these wee steel eyelet things, and along the ceiling to where the grenade was taped.'

The DCC nodded. The area was blackened, and ripped by fragments, but despite the blast the tiny round conduits were still in place, two in the wood of the door and two in the ceiling. 'Yes, very efficient. So what's your point?'

'There are no prints on them. They're clean, all four of them, absolutely. The things are so small you wouldn't expect to lift anything usable from them, but at the very least, there should be smudges on them. There aren't, though. There's nothing. They were put in place by somebody wearing gloves.'

'And you're wondering why Ballester would bother to wear gloves if he was about to top himself?'

'You said it, sir. But he couldn't have, even if he'd been so inclined. We went through that house like a dose of Andrews: there was no sign of a pair of gloves anywhere.'

'Could he have used a handkerchief? To gain purchase on the things, maybe.'

'In theory, but he didn't have one of them either. There was hardly anything in the place: shirt, socks, shoes, underwear, a second pair of jeans and an outdoor jacket. That was all.'

A thin smile creased Skinner's face. 'Let me get this right, DI Dorward. You're suggesting, on the basis of no concrete evidence, indeed on the basis of a complete lack of such, that Daniel Ballester's apparent suicide was staged, and that the person who killed him then rigged the grenade that Stevie walked into. Does that sum it up?'

'Either that's what happened or, rather less likely in my opinion, especially in view of what was said in the suicide message on the laptop, somebody went into the place after he had strung himself up and did it. Now maybe you see why I wanted to bounce it off you before trying it on the rest of them out there.'

'You're crackers, Arthur,' Skinner declared. 'You're the

conspiracy theorist to end them all . . .' he laughed '. . . or you would be if I didn't exist, because I'll go along with what you're saying. There's just one drawback, though. How did this person wire up the grenade from the outside?'

'He didn't, not completely. He ran the wire through the keepers, then he closed the door, reached through the letterbox and hooked it round the handle.'

'The letterbox is big enough?'

'Just. I did it myself, and if I could . . .' The inspector held out a ham-sized right hand. 'In the process, I scratched myself on a rough bit on the brass frame. I took a wee piece of skin off. But you'll never guess: when I looked for it, with a magnifying-glass, I found two pieces there.' He took two small clear plastic cases from his pocket and held them up. 'One of these is mine. The other isn't. I don't know which is which, but DNA comparison will tell us soon enough. If you can find this bloke, sir, he might just have signed his name for us.'

For the first time in almost two full days, Skinner was beaming as he stepped back into the main office. He laid the report on Pye's desk. 'Read that, all of you,' he said. 'Read it and learn from the mad genius Dorward. Sammy, have we taken steps to acquire the autopsy report on Ballester?'

'I've got it, sir,' Wilding volunteered, 'and the one on Stevie. I had them e-mailed to me an hour ago. There's the Ballester printout.' He handed over a folder. 'It's straightforward: death by strangulation.'

'Sure, but . . .' Holding the document in his left hand he flipped it open and scanned through it. 'Obvious suicide,' he murmured, 'so how thorough was the pathologist?' Suddenly his right index finger stabbed at a paragraph. 'Very thorough,' he exclaimed, then began to read aloud: '*One other injury was apparent on the body, a depressed fracture of the left zygomatic and temporal bones. This was peculiar in that it was certainly sustained* post mortem. *I can only speculate that it was caused by the body being dropped by the officers who cut it down* . . . Sorry, lads . . . *Within this area there were two small marks on the surface of the skin, seven and a half centimetres apart, which appear to be burns. It is not possible to say whether these were inflicted before or after death.*'

He turned to another part of the report. 'It says here,' he continued, 'that Ballester was one metre eighty-two centimetres tall, about six feet, weighed eighty-three kilos, thirteen stone, give or take, and that he was in good physical condition. Mario, how would you subdue a big guy like that?'

McGuire held up a massive fist. 'Same way as you would, probably. If you two were concluding in there that Ballester's suicide was assisted, to put it gently, then somebody bigger, or harder, banjoed him, I guess. Maybe when you lost it in the cottage and walloped him you covered up something that was there already.'

Skinner shook his head. 'There were no signs of a fight, in the kitchen or anywhere else.'

'Then what about a stun gun?'

'That's what I'm looking at. The picture in my head is showing me Ballester answering a knock at the door.'

'Why would he do that? He was on the run.'

'Then, whoever it was, he knew him; the door had glazed panels, remember, so he'd have been able to see who was on the other side. Either he knew the caller, or he reckoned it was one of us, knew he was trapped and was prepared to give himself up. He didn't have the gun to hand, remember: it was stashed in the shed, so shooting his way out wasn't an option. My thinking is that he let his guard down and the newcomer zapped him and, yes, probably with a stun gun. That would have been quick, effective, and afterwards virtually untraceable.'

'Too right, sir,' said Montell. 'I've used one in South Africa. You shoot three-quarters of a million volts into somebody, it fucks up his nervous system big-time. He's helpless, all yours.'

'Why doesn't it fry him?' asked Singh. 'That's what I've never understood.'

'That's because you spell "physics" with an F, Tarvil. A stun gun delivers a huge voltage, but it has very low amperage, so it's entirely non-lethal.'

Skinner looked at him impatiently. 'Thanks for the lesson,' he said. 'But that's my scenario. Ballester was knocked down so efficiently that his assailant or assailants . . . it might not have been the Aeron guys, but there may very well have been more than one attacker . . . were able to hang him, unresisting, from the hook in the ceiling.'

'But how did they know the hook was there, sir?' asked Montell.

The DCC frowned. 'You know, Griff, there's a fine line between being a devil's advocate and being a smartarse, and you want to be sure that you never step over it when you interrupt me.' The detective constable gulped. 'Happily, this time you're just about all right,' Skinner continued. 'Have you ever seen a suicide by hanging?' he asked.

'No, boss,' Montell confessed, 'I haven't. A couple of lynchings, in my early days on the job back home, but that's all.'

'Yeah, well, I've come across a few, and quite recently I saw one that was supposed to be a suicide, but wasn't. If you want to do yourself, you don't need a hook, or a tree branch or anything other than a ligature. In the case I'm talking about, the guy was on his knees, but if circumstances hadn't proved it otherwise, it would have been accepted that he'd topped himself.

'So the hook's irrelevant; it was handy, that's all. He was strangled by the rope, as intended. Once he was, the message was typed on the laptop, by someone wearing gloves, so that nobody could ever prove that the dead man hadn't done it, and the grenade was put in place.'

'I don't get that part, sir,' said Pye. 'Why do that?'

'I don't get it either, Sammy, not at the moment. But let's not get sidetracked by it. Who are we looking at? Who are our potential suspects?'

'Surely the two guys from Aeron,' said Wilding, emphatically. 'Spicer and his mate. They have to be first on the list.'

'Correct me if I'm wrong, Ray, but didn't the man you and Stevie spoke to say that they left for Wooler around midday?'

'Maybe he lied.'

'You were there. Is that what you thought at the time?'

The sergeant shook his head. 'So let's assume that he didn't. When does the pathologist reckon Ballester died?'

'She says around eleven o'clock, but she can't be precise about it, since there was a fire burning. The place doesn't have central heating, and it had been a cold morning in Wooler. Ballester must have lit it when he got up, but as the sun got higher the room must have got a lot warmer.'

'Yes,' McGuire agreed. 'It was still pretty warm when we were there, even though the fire had burned itself out a while before. But even at that, he must have been killed well before Stevie spoke to the man Spicer on his mobile.'

'Precisely,' Skinner continued, 'and they were still there. According to your statement, Ray, they were even prepared to keep the place under observation until the police arrived; in fact, they did just that. If they'd just rigged a lethal trap they'd hardly have hung around to watch it sprung, would they? Let's agree they're in the clear. So . . .' He paused and looked at each officer one by one. '. . . that points us straight at one man, the man who gave them their orders, the man whose daughter is one of the murder victims, the only other person who knew where Ballester was, and the man who put a price on his head: Davor Boras. It's time that he and I had a conversation.'

'Boss,' said Wilding, 'we're not allowed to go near him. Becky told Stevie and me that she'd been specifically ordered not to bring him into the Barker investigation, by one of her big bosses. And that woman from the Home Office was all over our interview. He's got protection, from political contacts, Becky reckons.'

'Ray,' the DCC replied quietly, 'we're investigating the

murder of one of our colleagues, one of our friends. If Boras knows something about that, there is no power in this land that will protect him from me. Have you spoken to DI Stallings yet?'

'Yes, boss, while you were in there.' He nodded towards the now empty room.

'Well, call her back, and tell her that her secondment starts this afternoon. Mario, you and I are going to see Boras, and Inspector Stallings can come with us.' He looked back at Wilding. 'Tell her not to worry. By the time we get there, all the arrangements will have been made. I'll send her flight details as soon as I have them.'

'What if the Home Office try to get in the way, sir?'

'Then somebody's getting arrested for obstruction. Sergeant, I'll lift the Home fucking Secretary if I have to.'

Sixty-eight

'You realise, boss,' said McGuire as he and Skinner strode along the air bridge at Heathrow, 'that we have no legal right to be here. We're investigating two homicides; everybody but us thinks that one was a suicide, and that the other is a closed case. But neither of them took place within our area. By the book, we should be reporting what we believe to Les Cairns and letting his CID take it from here.'

The DCC smiled. 'It's not too often I say this, Mario, but bugger the book. Les Cairns and his people have got access to the same information as us, and they yet don't see anything in it to contradict their assumptions. We've found Ballester and you and I are happy to sign off on him as the guy who killed the three girls and Harry Paul, on the basis of motive, weapon and everything else.

'They've got him dead as a suicide, killing Stevie Steele in a last, bitter, random act of violence, and they haven't looked beyond that. They'll have read Arthur's report, and they've either missed or ignored the significance of the eyelets.

'I'm not bloody prepared to trust this investigation to them. Now I'll admit, privately, that Arthur was a wee bit naughty bringing those skin fragments back to Scotland and leaving that out of his findings, but what the hell? One of them was his own!'

He looked at his colleague. 'Are you nervous about this? Because if you are, we'll collect DI Stallings and take the first plane back home.'

McGuire snorted. 'Did I say I was nervous? I'm sure Les Cairns will welcome our assistance at the end of the day.'

'That's the spirit. But if you want justification, what are we doing? Officially, we're going to see a bereaved father, a man who has just announced the donation of a million sterling to the Police Dependants' Trust, to advise him that the man who killed his daughter is dead himself. That's common courtesy, man, and to prove it, when we get back to Scotland, we'll pay similar visits to the parents of Stacey Gavin, Amy Noone and Harry Paul.'

'You really do think that Boras killed Stevie, don't you?'

'Or had him killed. I'm absolutely certain of it, not that I believe he was trying to. The trap was set for someone else, but I'm a way off knowing why.' As he finished, they reached the end of the arrivals corridor, to see a tall, attractive, dark-haired woman, walking purposefully towards them, against the flow of disembarked passengers.

'Now I know why Ray stayed over,' McGuire murmured. 'But I'm wondering what the hell she saw in him.'

'When you can answer that,' said Skinner, 'you can chuck the police and start the dating website to end them all. DI Stallings?' he asked, as she came within hailing distance.

'Yes, sir. Deputy Chief Constable Skinner?'

'That's right, and this is DCS McGuire, my head of CID. You'll be reporting to him during your brief secondment to us. Do we have transport?'

'Nearby: I'm in the short stay.'

Stallings led the way out of Terminal One and into the car park. She showed her warrant card at the exit booth and the barrier was raised.

'Where are we headed?' said Skinner, in the front passenger seat.

'We're going to the Continental IT office, in central London. I checked with them to confirm that Mr Boras would be there all afternoon, and made an appointment for both of you to visit him.'

'All three of us: you're coming too. You're playing on my team for the present.'

'When are we going back north?' she asked. 'If it's today, I'll need to make time to go home and pack.'

'That'll be okay. If we go back tonight, you can fly north tomorrow morning. But we're flexible; it depends on how we get on with Boras. As you saw when we met, we've both brought overnight bags, just in case.'

'Ahh.' Stallings fell silent as she drove out of the airport and picked up the M4.

The DCC glanced at her. 'Something on your mind, Inspector?' he said quietly.

'No, sir.'

Skinner grinned. 'Did nobody tell you I'm a mind-reader? Out with it.'

Hesitantly, she risked a quick look at him. 'Well, sir, it's what you said about Mr Boras, that the length of your stay depends on how you get on with him. I thought that this was a courtesy call, to advise him of the conclusion of your investigation into his daughter's murder.'

'You forgot about us thanking him for giving a million to the PDT.'

'Yes, and that.'

'It's all true, all of it. However, my big friend here and I have a couple of questions to ask him. The way that he answers them may determine how courteous we are.'

'I see.' Nervousness replaced hesitancy in Becky Stallings's voice.

'What did you think of our boy Stevie?' the DCC asked her suddenly.

'In our very brief acquaintance,' she replied, 'I thought he was a very nice guy. I also saw that he was a brilliant police officer. The way he handled Keith Barker was as good as anything I've ever seen.'

'Yeah. Stevie was all that. He'd have gone all the way in the force; I'm in no doubt about that.'

'How's his wife bearing up?'

'She's also an exceptional police officer, and an exceptional person. She's dealing with it.'

'Would she mind me going to the funeral?'

'Becky, I think she'll insist on it. In fact, while you're with us, I imagine she'd like to meet you.'

'I'd be . . .' She paused.

'I know, it'll be awkward, but it'll be good for both of you.'

'In that case, I'd be happy to visit her; maybe with Ray.'

'Of course.'

'How is he?'

'DS Wilding is like the rest of us, bereaved but continuing to function professionally. Don't worry about him. He's a good lad; he's one of mine, but don't ever tell him I said that. It would go to his head.'

'One of yours?'

'Mario knows what I mean. Don't you, mate?' He glanced over his shoulder, then back at Stallings. 'I cherish every police officer, every man and woman who carries a warrant card, plain-clothes or uniform. But some I cherish even more than others, because I see a bit of me in them.'

He smiled grimly. 'Be in no doubt, Becky, I wasn't out of the room when they were handing out egos. I was at the front of the queue and I got first pick.'

He paused. 'Every so often, though, something happens that reminds me that I'm not infallible. A few years back, one of mine went very bad. More recently, I put another in a situation that I thought he could handle. He couldn't, and maybe he'll never be the same again. I'm going to look after him, mind you. I'm going to keep him on the force and I'm going to help him get back his self-esteem.' He glanced backwards again. 'That's a decision I've made since Saturday night, Mario.'

'Bandit?'

'Yes.'

'How are you going to do it? That report didn't make good reading.'

'I'm going to keep him close. He'll replace McGurk, but with a bigger job, as executive officer not just to me but to everybody in the Command Corridor. Sorry, Becky,' he exclaimed. 'Digression.'

'And Stevie was one of yours as well?' she asked.

'Oh, yes. Top of the class.' Skinner sat in silence for a while, staring ahead through the windscreen as the motorway bore into the city, and as world-famous landmarks came into view. They were heading through Holborn before he spoke again.

'We think Boras killed Stevie, Becky.'

'What?' The shout escaped before she had a chance to choke it off, but she managed to keep the car under control.

'I'm sorry,' he said. 'Sorry to startle you. I said that we believe that Boras may have been responsible for Stevie's murder. We do not buy Ballester as a suicide. All the evidence points to him having shot Zrinka and the others, but we reckon that when Boras learned this, and discovered where he was hiding out, he either went up there and killed him or, more likely, he ordered it done.'

'You mean that you're going to interrogate him as a murder suspect?'

'No. I'm telling you that we're going to play it by ear, but advising you that the conversation might take an interesting turn.'

Keeping her eyes on the road, she smiled. 'That sounds like fun. Mind you, sir, the Home Office will not like it when they find out.'

'Does that bother you?'

'Not one small piece.'

'That's the lady.'

The office of Continental IT was in a green square, near the junction of London Wall and Aldersgate Street. As she had been directed, Stallings drove into a basement car park, where she chose a vacant 'visitor' space.

'Sir,' she said, as they stepped out of the vehicle, 'you should be aware that Boras is very security-conscious. Barker said that he has his office checked for bugs every day, and that he does all his important business in there.'

'I know. We listened to his interrogation by Stevie before we left. Don't worry: I'm going to assume that he has bugs of his own installed and that he tapes everything that's said in there.'

'Won't that make it risky, if you plan to accuse him?'

'Maybe, but I'll play it by ear . . . almost.' He took a palm-sized black box from his pocket and showed it to her. 'Before we left, I got this from my technical people. It detects transmitters and hidden cameras. It's a clever wee bugger . . .' he chuckled '. . . or de-bugger, I should say. The warning is set to "vibrate" so it can be used as discreetly as the things it's picking up.'

He concealed it and they headed towards the garage exit door, past a shirtsleeved man, in his late twenties, who was busy removing splattered insects from the windscreen of a new silver Rolls-Royce Phantom. A uniform cap lay on the roof. 'Nice motor,' said McGuire, casually. 'The boss's?'

'Yes, sir,' the chauffeur replied, in an accent that was not from anywhere in London. 'I don't care what anyone says, this is still the finest car in the world, and it deserves to be kept immaculate.'

'He's not kidding,' the chief superintendent murmured, as they stepped through the door and found themselves facing an elevator.

Skinner pressed the button to summon it. 'Why don't you work on Paula to buy one?' He suggested. 'I'm sure that the shareholders of Viareggio PLC wouldn't mind the chief executive having a vehicle worthy of her status.'

'Sure, and the customers of the Viareggio delis would be really impressed too, to see one of those doing the rounds of our shops. Besides, she loves her Mini.'

The lift took them up to the foyer. The three officers stepped out, and Stallings walked over to the reception desk to announce their arrival. A middle-aged woman sat behind it. 'Ah, yes,' she replied, in cut-glass tones. 'Mr Boras is ready for you. If you go up to the top floor, I'll let him know you're on the way.'

They did as they had been instructed. As the lift doors closed on them, and Stallings pushed the button, Skinner said to the head of CID, 'When we get up there, you make the running.'

The building had fifteen floors; when they emerged on the top level, they found that its partitions and outer walls were made entirely of glass. Davor Boras was waiting for them, a cool smile on his face, his stocky frame encased in a powder-blue suit that shone like silk. 'Mr McGuire,' he exclaimed. 'I'm pleased to see you again, especially since you bring such, er, satisfactory news of your investigation . . . although,' he added at once, 'I was devastated to hear of the death of your colleague.'

'We appreciate that, sir. Please let me introduce Deputy Chief Constable Bob Skinner, and Detective Inspector Becky Stallings, who's our liaison officer with the Met.'

'My pleasure,' he replied, as they shook hands. 'Come

with me; let's go into my hospitality suite. My office is far too formal.' Skinner was taken by surprise, but he nodded; he was last in line as they followed Boras into a big square room, set on a corner of the building so that two of its sides offered a spectacular view across the rooftops to the Tower of London and the bridge beyond. As Boras closed the door, the DCC activated the box in his trouser pocket, and almost immediately felt it vibrate strongly against his thigh.

Their host looked towards a drinks table, with a laden ice-bucket sitting on it, and a small fridge beside it. A waiter stood ready. 'Ms Stallings, gentlemen: may I offer you a drink?' He laughed lightly, 'Or don't you do that on duty?'

'Only when it's formal,' McGuire told him. 'The inspector's driving, so hers will have to be soft, but if that's a bottle of Sancerre open in the bucket, the DCC and I will be very happy to join you.'

They stood in silence while the waiter poured the drinks, a Pepsi Max and three glasses, and handed them round. 'Thank you, Neville,' said Boras. 'I'll call you when we need refills.' As the man left he showed his guests to a seating area, where leather armchairs were arranged to take maximum advantage of the view. As she settled down, it occurred to Stallings that it would make a very fine ceiling, if the building was just a little higher.

'Well.' The businessman fixed his gimlet eyes on McGuire, and gave another thin smile. 'I'd have done it anyway, you know,' he murmured, his voice barely carrying to the inspector who was placed furthest from him.

'What's that?' the chief superintendent asked.

'Make the donation to the Dependants' Trust. You

anticipated my announcement, although some have said that you forced my hand.'

McGuire beamed at him. 'There will always be mean-spirited people like that, sir. Just as, happily, there will always be generous people like you. I was asked a straight question, and I gave a straight answer. You're right, I anticipated your announcement, but I never had any doubt that in the circumstances you'd make your gift, if not to that charity then to another worthy recipient.'

'Of course, I am aware of that, really. *Samo vas zavitlavam*, to use my native tongue. I was only swinging with you; pulling your chain, as we say in English. It is over, then?'

'I believe that we can say that the investigation into your daughter's murder is over. Our Crown Office, the Scottish prosecution service, is about to announce that, with Ballester's death, we are no longer looking for anyone else in connection with the four homicides.'

'Then I thank you, and I congratulate you. Again, though, I must express my sorrow at the needless death of your colleague, Inspector Steele. I was shocked by it, shocked; he was such a fine, dedicated officer.'

Skinner gazed at the man, looking for the faintest sign of insincerity in his eyes. Over the years he had stared down many guilty men, and he had been able to read their secrets as easily as if they had confessed them, as eventually virtually all of them had. Boras's expression told him nothing, nothing at all. He had a strange feeling that what the man was saying was literally true. 'Thank you for that,' he said, addressing him for the first time. 'I'll convey it to Stevie's widow.'

'Thank you, sir. If there is anything I can do for her, anything at all, you or she simply has to ask.'

'That is also kind of you, but in my force, officers' widows want for nothing.'

'I'm sure. Will there be a court proceeding of any sort, Mr Skinner? A public inquiry into Zrinka's death, and the others?'

'There's no statutory provision for it in Scotland,' the DCC told him. 'Formal hearings into fatal accidents and sudden deaths are only mandatory when a person is killed at work, or dies when in custody. Murder investigations result in prosecution when they're concluded, but in this case, the Crown has nobody to prosecute. There is no suspect, other than Ballester, and he's dead. He had motive, opportunity, everything, and we found the murder weapon in his house. We also found personal possessions that he had taken from three of the four victims. He did it.'

'There is no chance that he could have been framed by someone else?'

'If you don't mind my saying so, that's a strange question, coming from you.'

'I need certainty, sir, that my daughter's killer is dead.'

'Then you have it for, I promise you, that evidence simply couldn't have been planted. Nobody knew where Ballester was, other than your guys, and neither of them could possibly have killed Zrinka, Stacey, Amy or Harry. Okay, you knew too, but you didn't murder your daughter, Mr Boras, you loved her.' The businessman's mouth opened, then closed, then opened again, but Skinner held up a hand.

'The irony is that although Ballester was murdered himself, he was our man all right, not a serial killer as my officers suspected at first, but a rejected lover with a grudge, and into the bargain, a previous conviction for violence against a woman.'

Boras glared at the DCC as he finished, and their eyes seemed to lock in unblinking conflict. 'My guys knew, you say. I knew?'

'Your former employee,' said Skinner, 'Mr Barker, has been talking, in the wake of his arrest for bribing a civil servant, using money which he says came from you. He says that three years ago you commissioned a firm called Aeron to make enquiries about a journalist who had been making unwelcome enquiries into your company. They identified him as Daniel Ballester, in a report that Barker claims to have seen in your possession. He alleges that you instructed Aeron to discourage Ballester from making further trouble. However, shortly afterwards he was professionally disgraced, after being tricked into doing a silly story about Princess Diana's death.

'When Dominic Padstow's name was mentioned that was news to you, Barker says, and you instructed him to trace him through the Passport Office.' Skinner's eyes narrowed a fraction. 'My guess is that you didn't suspect at that stage that Padstow was Ballester; I reckon you simply wanted to get to him first. But when our clever detective constable came up with his portrait, you certainly knew who he was even before we identified him, because you set Aeron on to finding him. They were good; we'd have found him eventually, but they did it first and again you were one step ahead. This we know from Aeron, rather than Barker.' He paused. 'At this stage,' he asked, 'would you care to comment on anything I've said so far?'

Boras continued to look back at him, his little dark eyes impassive. He sipped his Sancerre. 'No,' he replied. 'Please carry on, unless your story is over.'

'Oh, it isn't,' Skinner exclaimed, 'because we found Aeron ourselves at that point. DI Steele and DI Stallings went to their office on Saturday afternoon. After some persuasion, they were put in touch by telephone with the company's chief executive, Mr Michael Spicer. He had just arrived at Hathaway House, with his associate Mr Ivor Brown, having gone there, on your instructions, to locate and apprehend Daniel Ballester.

'At least, that's what they said your orders were, but even if they were a little more extreme it wouldn't have mattered, because when they got there, the man was dead. And if Stevie Steele had phoned them ten minutes later, they'd have been dead too. They'd have gone into that house and they'd have walked into the grenade trap.'

'Indeed?' The voice was as cold as the ice in the bucket.

'Oh, yes. You had Ballester killed, Mr Boras. You had him executed. I don't suggest for a moment that you did it yourself: I'm sure that any investigation would show very quickly that you were at home with your wife all day on Saturday, continuing to make arrangements for your daughter's funeral.

'No, you had him killed,' the DCC repeated, 'and Spicer and Brown were meant to die too. They were your only contacts with Aeron; they were the only people who could prove that you had prior knowledge of Daniel Ballester, and that you identified him as your daughter's killer before the police did.'

'And what about Barker?' Boras asked. 'If your fanciful theory is correct, why is he still alive?'

'Hey,' Skinner retorted, 'it's never a good idea to offer a defence before you've been accused, and as we keep on saying, this is an informal visit. But since you ask, Barker's nothing. He has no evidence that you ever knew Ballester. The Met have got him by the balls for bribing a public official and he's singing like George Michael to try to get out of it. They've also got him for tax evasion, thanks to a slush fund, under the rather frivolous name of Jack Frost, set up with money that will never in a million years be traceable back to you.

'So you're not worried about him at all. Mind you, that may not prevent him having a fatal accident in the near future: time will tell.'

He leaned back in his chair. 'You're not worried about Spicer and Brown either. My colleagues in Northumbria had no grounds to hold them on Saturday, so they sent them on their way. In hindsight, that's a pity, for . . . and this will surprise DI Stallings, who doesn't know about it . . . when I pulled a couple of strings this morning and had Special Branch officers sent to their place to hold them for questioning, they discovered that they were gone. Not just the two of them either, the whole Aeron operation, vanished as if it had never existed.'

He tilted his glass in a gesture that could only have been a salute. 'My congratulations, Mr Boras: you've done what you told a whole roomful of people last Thursday that you would do. You've had your revenge on your daughter's murderer. And nobody will ever lay a finger on you for it.'

Finally, Boras broke eye contact with Skinner, as he bowed his head to him, briefly. 'Remarkable, quite remarkable,' he exclaimed. 'Your picture is as clear as any my Zrinka ever painted, and just as imaginative. And, of course, you could not resist coming here to set it out for me. I am flattered, sir.'

Skinner let out a sound that was somewhere between a laugh and a growl. 'You know, that's the first silly thing you've said. I'm not flattering you, man. I'm not even addressing you. All along I've been talking to whoever is monitoring this meeting, to whoever is looking and listening in.

'I'm not sure who it is, but it's not the *Sun*, that's for sure. You have your office swept every day; that's secure, so why bring us in here, unless you actively want somebody to hear what's being said.' He took the small box from his pocket and held it up as he twisted half-way round in his seat to gaze at the back wall, at a point above the drinks table.

When he turned back to face Boras he saw a teeth-baring grimace on the man's face. Instantly, it vanished, but the look that replaced it was thunderous.

'You may think,' Skinner told him, 'that what I've just done was a bit risky. But it wasn't. It doesn't matter who's watching us, I'm too high-profile to vanish off the face of the earth, and so is Mario. On top of that,' he added, with a smile, 'we're both extremely dangerous. I came into this building with a purpose, and I still have it. So what I'm saying to the boys and girls in our audience is this.

'I know that your man Boras is fireproof, but I want the man who killed Stevie, and I'm going to have him. The best thing you can all do is give him to me. The second best is stay out of my way while I find him.' He pushed himself violently to his feet. 'Come on, you two. We're finished here.' He drained his glass and looked down at the blue-suited figure, into his furious eyes. 'Not bad,' he said, 'but I've tasted better.'

Sixty-nine

It should have been the best day of Sammy Pye's career. He had been sure that he would move up, one day, from being Mario McGuire's sidekick, having followed him, as a sergeant, through two divisional commands and finally into the head of CID's office.

For some time it had been a matter of when, not if, he would make detective inspector and occasionally he had let himself wonder where that might be. He had been a little hurt when McGuire had told him that he was moving Jack McGurk temporarily to Torphichen Place, with George Regan as acting DI, and it must have shown, for his boss had been moved to tell him in confidence that he was simply waiting for the Bandit Mackenzie situation to resolve itself, before sending him down to Leith.

The promised move had come about, but not in a way that anyone could have foreseen. Pye had felt uncomfortable from the moment he had settled in behind Stevie Steele's old desk, as if there were two of them in the chair. The other three guys had done their best to make him feel welcome, but still the atmosphere had been awkward.

Finally, after Skinner and McGuire had visited and

departed, Wilding had pulled his chair over towards him. 'Listen, Sammy,' he had said, 'this is going to be a tough day for all of us, but it would be better for you if you moved into the DCI's room. Stevie never did, because he didn't want it to seem that he was jumping into Mackenzie's shoes. But you never worked with the guy, so there's no reason for you not to.'

Sometimes, Pye thought, as he looked through the Perspex wall, when he took off the 'hail fellow, well met' guise and turned serious, Ray Wilding was a pretty impressive bloke. He decided that it would be his practice to encourage him to do so more often.

His musing was interrupted when he saw Griff Montell rise from his chair, and head towards him. 'Boss,' said the South African, as he opened the door, 'I'm into that disk that the fiscal's office sent up, and there are some things on it you should see.'

'Show me,' Pye replied, rising to follow him back to his work station. A screen saver was active on the DC's monitor; as soon as he touched the mouse it vanished and a folder headed 'my documents' appeared. 'How does the calendar look?' asked the inspector.

'It has him in Edinburgh on the days of all three murders, but that's not what I wanted to show you. Wait a minute.' He clicked on a subfolder. It opened another series: Montell moved the cursor on to an icon marked 'Les Girls' and opened it. A strip of small images appeared. 'Watch,' he said, then hit the 'view as a slideshow' command. The screen went black for a second, and then was filled with a clear, sharp photograph of a woman, lying on her back on stony ground. 'Stacey Gavin,' the detective constable announced unnecessarily, as Pye had found himself gazing at her image on the wall, with the rest, for much of the morning since his arrival.

'Jeez,' he whispered.

The frame held for a few seconds until it was replaced by another, taken from a different angle, then by another, of Stacey's pale face. The location moved, to a yellow beach, and another dead girl, the same sequence repeating until the naked form of Amy Noone was revealed. As they realised what was happening, Wilding and Singh stopped what they were doing and moved across the room to watch the display as it completed, then repeated, then ran again. There were no photographs of Harry Paul, only the three young women.

'He loved them,' said Pye, quietly. 'Look at the way they're photographed: it's perfect, they're beautiful. He killed them and yet he loved them. He loved them . . . and yet he killed them.'

Seventy

Bob Skinner did not believe for a second that his confrontation with Boras might have endangered himself or either of his companions but he did read anxiety in Stallings as she sat down to dine with him and McGuire in an Italian restaurant near Covent Garden, after she had dropped off her car in the park behind her office.

'It's okay, Becky,' he assured her, as they scanned the menu. 'Relax, have a couple of drinks with your meal, then get a car to take you home.'

'You know, I think I might,' she said. 'That was a very scary scene, especially when you said that the room was under surveillance.'

'It had to be. Why else would he have taken us there, rather than to the security of his office?'

'If what Barker told us was true, why does he have that screened every day?'

'Because it suits him. He operates a very high-level business; plus, he's a very dodgy guy. He has to have somewhere he can function in absolute secrecy. But if he's involved with the intelligence community, as I reckon he is, he has to accept a degree of surveillance. Boras knew damn well that a deputy chief constable doesn't travel four hundred miles just to have a drink with him and tell him something that he and the rest of the country heard on telly the day before. That room's his security blanket.'

'You're certain it was bugged?'

'One hundred per cent.' He took the device from his pocket and handed it to her. 'Did you see any cameras or mikes in Boras's eyrie?'

'No.'

He pointed to a corner of the restaurant, where a CCTV camera, mounted on a pivot on the ceiling, silently scanned the area. 'Do you see that?'

'Yes.'

'Then hold on to that box, and press the "activate" button.'

She did as he said, then yelped. 'It's vibrating.'

'Just as it did in my pocket earlier on. Right now, it's telling you about that camera up there.'

'Couldn't it be something else?'

He laughed. 'I like healthy scepticism in a police officer. Yes, it could, if this place is bugged as well, but regardless of that, it's picking up that camera.'

'If you're right, what's going to happen?'

'Maybe nothing; maybe they will just stand back and let me get on with it. If not, somebody will get in touch with me, very soon.'

'Do you know who that will be?'

'I suspect it may be someone I know, under orders to persuade me to be a good boy, but I'll find that out in due course.'

Stallings frowned. A waiter approached, but Skinner waved him away. 'Sir, what makes you so sure that Boras is involved in something covert?'

The big Scot grinned. 'Do you think I've got a spook complex?' he said quietly. 'Becky, I am a bloody spook. Up in Edinburgh I have a Special Branch unit reporting directly to me. I have served time as security adviser to the government in Scotland, and I have done a few other things that I can't tell you about.

'If you want specifics, very well, let's look at Aeron, Boras's so-called security consultant. It was there on Saturday, as you know first-hand, and today it's gone. That business had to be a front, with legitimate clients, I'm sure, but involved also in intelligence work and covert activity.

'It was blown yesterday, in the aftermath of what happened in Wooler. If you look, you'll probably find the man you and Stevie and Ray met in that office on Saturday sitting at home right now, and he'll tell you that Spicer, his boss, came to see him on Sunday, gave him a big severance cheque and told him that he was out of a job, him and all the other operatives. But you try and find Spicer now. Not a chance.

'Here's some more evidence: when Boras first learned about Ballester, three years ago, he reported him to Aeron. They identified him and what happened next? The guy was hopelessly compromised by that story on the so-called assassination of the People's Princess, fed names and everything, which he published; that was a classic security service sting.'

'A lot of people still believe that happened,' Stallings pointed out.

'Then they're daft. Princess Di and her friend had just flown into Paris on his father's jet. If anyone had wanted to kill them it would have been far easier to arrange for that to crash. It would have been accepted as an accident too.' He chuckled darkly. 'Tell me: how many Buddy Holly conspiracy theories have you heard?'

The inspector held up her hands in a gesture of mock surrender. 'I give in,' she exclaimed.

But Skinner was no longer looking at her. Instead he was gazing over her shoulder, towards the circular entrance area. 'That's just as well,' he said, 'because once again Magic Bob has been proved right. That person I mentioned a minute ago, that someone who knew me, and who might contact me; I wasn't expecting this one in particular, but she's just come in, and she's just given me a very meaningful look. I'm sorry, folks, but I'm not going to be able to eat with you. Mario, look after Becky; I'll see you later.'

He rose from the table and walked away. McGuire and Stallings looked after him, and beyond, towards the entrance area. It was empty. He did not look back as he stepped out of the restaurant and into the street. Through the glass door, they saw him lay his hands on the shoulders of a middle-aged woman, and kiss her lightly on the cheek.

Seventy-one

'Fancy seeing you here,' said Skinner, quietly, as the woman linked her arm through his and they walked away down King Street, like old friends reunited, as indeed they were. 'You've changed since the last time I saw you.'

'Do you mean,' she asked, 'that I look better or worse? Do you mean that I look younger and refreshed, or that I'm ageing under the burden on my shoulders, the one you placed there when you turned down my job? Before you reply, the second answers to each question are correct.'

'No, they're not. You look about five years younger than you did. Your hair's longer, you're dressed differently, and you're walking taller than you did.'

'That's just the heels,' she replied. 'As for the rest, I've changed the dress code, found a new hairdresser and . . . it's amazing what a little makeup can do.'

'Oh, yes? And what did you spray in your eyes to make them sparkle?'

Amanda Dennis smiled. 'There's no fooling you detectives. Very well, I admit it. I have a new interest in my life, apart from the job. He's the father of one of my son's friends . . . Oh, shit, let me abandon all subterfuge, he's the older brother of one of my son's friends.'

'How long has this been going on?'

'About three months.'

'Good for you, Mandy. Does he know what you do?'

'My son's been describing me as a civil servant for years and getting away with it, because we do still remain largely anonymous within our department, but these days, when you rise to the top job, even if it's only on an acting basis, you become visible. So I told him, before he looked me up on the Internet and found out for himself.'

'And he came though his vetting with flying colours, I take it.'

'Before our first dinner date. It's nice to go out with someone who has nothing to do with the department,' she confessed. 'It's the first time I have since I joined.'

'What does he do?' As Skinner asked the question he was aware that they were walking towards a black Vauxhall, parked on a yellow line.

'He's a jeweller. This is us,' she said, her tone suddenly brisker. 'Your dinner's postponed, I'm afraid. I'd like a chat back at the office. Did you tell your colleagues where you were going when you left them?'

'Why? Am I not coming back?'

'Don't be silly. I meant are they expecting you?'

'Not any time soon. But they understood what was happening this afternoon, in Boras's building. They know my departure is related.' He paused, as the car pulled away from the kerb. 'So you're not denying it?'

'Of course not.'

'How did you know where we were? Have you been tailing us since Heathrow?'

'No. We traced you through Stallings's office,' Dennis replied, as they turned into the Strand, heading for Trafalgar Square.

'God, this place is never quiet,' Skinner exclaimed as the car cruised along Whitehall.

'You get used to it.'

'I couldn't.'

'Is that why you turned the job down?'

'No, I turned it down because it didn't suit a guy with three young children and a high-profile relationship.'

'Plus, you knew you'd be too hard for our Establishment to handle.'

He grinned. 'There is that.'

They reached their destination in less than ten minutes. The car stopped in front of Thames House, the headquarters of MI5, the security service, and Dennis led the way inside. Skinner knew the building well: he had spent some time there, brought in to conduct an internal investigation. He said nothing as the lift rose up to the director general's floor, as the doors opened and as he followed his escort into her office. They sat at a small conference table, and once again, she was all business, the woman he had always known.

He took the box from his pocket, laid it on the table, activated it and watched it vibrate. Dennis shrugged her shoulders. 'Don't worry,' she said, 'they're all ours.'

He was about to remark that that made a change, but he held it back: some wounds were still recent and raw.

'I'm sorry I had to bring you back here,' the acting director general began. 'What I have to tell you is too sensitive for my driver to overhear.'

'I know.'

She allowed him a small smile. 'Indeed. Well, Bob, as you see, your grandstanding performance with Boras has paid off. You had barely left the building before I had a visitation from two people who knew of our acquaintance and of your recent history with Five. They've asked me to explain things.'

'They don't have to. I don't care about the detail, I just want to get my hands on the man who killed my officer. He and Boras could have hung Ballester up by the nuts and I wouldn't care; they could have taken out Spicer and his mate after the event and I wouldn't care. But there's a widow up in Edinburgh, and I do care about her, oh, God, do I care.'

'Nevertheless, let me tell you about Boras.'

'If you insist.'

'Thank you. It is widely believed, even by his own son, that Davor Boras left Sarajevo because he foresaw the chaos that the sundering of Yugoslavia would bring, and that he wanted no part of it. It's true that he wanted to get his children out of there, and that he was ambitious in his business life, but in fact he is a patriot.

'By the time the Bosnian war started in 1992, Boras's first business in the UK was successful and he was a wealthy man. Not only that, but he had retained many contacts in Sarajevo, Belgrade and other cities; he had continued to do business there, and was a regular visitor. He cared about the place, for emotional and commercial reasons. A year before hostilities erupted, Boras contacted the Central Intelligence Agency through the American Embassy in Grosvenor Square. He offered his services in any way they thought fit.'

'Why didn't he go to our intelligence service?' Skinner asked.

'He wasn't sure whose side they'd be on, simple as that. The Americans, on the other hand, had caught on to Milošević at an early stage, and knew what he was capable of. He was also a Communist, and that crystallised their view of him.

'When Boras came to them, the CIA people rolled out the red carpet; they had actually been considering trying to recruit him. Ever since then, he's been their guy. If you were to look at the records of Bolec, his company at that time, you'd find people listed as employees whose jobs were never phoney but who had other functions. Throughout the war he infiltrated personnel into the region, intelligence-gatherers, saboteurs, assassins. They were very effective, and never detected. Several Serbian paramilitary figures were eliminated by people who were officially employees of Bolec plc.'

'The war's been over for a long time,' Skinner pointed out.

'Not for some people, including the CIA. Boras has continued to be an asset of theirs. When he sold Bolec it was with their approval. They felt that they had run enough through it and that, sooner or later, the increasingly effective intelligence services in the new countries would catch on.

'So Boras allowed himself to be bought out, and

promptly started another business, Continental IT, in a slightly different sector, but still with a presence in the region, albeit lower profile. Its principal use to the CIA lies in the apprehension and, where necessary, elimination of war criminals. Several people on trial at The Hague have Davor Boras to thank for it, or rather Continental IT; several others have simply disappeared, including one or two alleged criminals on his side, who have been given safe haven in the US.'

'And he's still active?'

'Whenever necessary; that was why there was a small alarm when Ballester first surfaced. Boras's first thought was that he was a Serbian spy, but the Americans, through their UK front organisation Aeron, soon established the truth, that he was a radical, slightly crackpot journalist, with a penchant for bringing down big names.

'He wasn't after Boras the spy; he was after Boras the businessman, whose dealings in that sector were not always kosher, as witness Mr Barker's "Jack Frost" account and his dealings with the man Dailey, and several others. When this was uncovered, Ballester was set up by CIA operatives in Paris, with the assistance of MI6, who owed somebody a favour at the time.

'After his public humiliation, he dropped out of sight for much of the time. In truth, he was almost forgotten, until Dominic Padstow's real name came out, through your investigation. The CIA believe that his involvement with Zrinka, and finally, vicariously, through her friend, was a last attempt to get to Boras. When it failed . . . well. The man had a kink, and a history of violence; poor girls, poor lad, poor Stevie.' She looked across the table. 'There's no doubt that he did it?' she asked.

'Not a shred. There is no way this could have involved the people you're talking about, or anyone other than him. Items were recovered at the scene that only the killer could have possessed. Skinner frowned. 'So who did it?' he asked abruptly. 'Boras sent Spicer and Brown up there to be killed. Did the CIA sanction the murder of two of their own, as a favour to Boras?'

'No: Boras has been operating independently. They're not pleased about it, but there's nothing they can do. As I gather you know, they've made the two men, and the entire Aeron operation, disappear already.'

'Have you known about Aeron all along?'

'Of course. We live with these things, as long as they observe certain niceties.'

'Such as?'

'Not killing British citizens, for a start. That's why eliminating Ballester permanently wasn't an option for them. Bob, the CIA do not know who killed the guy.'

Skinner shook his head. 'That's why I don't rate them, when it comes down to it. Boras is very clever: he was fireproof, and he wanted to stay that way. He was determined to execute his daughter's murderer, as soon as the Aeron people told him where he was. But when they did, that made them potentially dangerous to him. So he sent somebody outside the intelligence community, someone he could trust absolutely, to take care of the whole situation.'

'Who?'

'Somebody who'd be just as intent on killing Ballester as he was; I reckon he sent his son.'

'Dražen? But he and his father barely speak.'

'The man loved his sister; her death would have brought them together, even if it was only a temporary truce.'

'That's possible, I'll grant you.'

'Anyway, whose word do we have for their rivalry? Theirs, and second-hand confirmation by the desperate Keith Barker, that's all. If I was in Boras's situation, running a business that was tied into the intelligence community, and I had a son that age, I'd want to protect him by keeping him well away from it.

'Dražen, or David Barnes, as he calls himself now, has no connection with his father's company; in fact, he's one of his rising competitors. There's even talk of Davor feeling the pinch, thanks to him, and looking to sell out again. That may be a family at war, but it's also a bloody good cover story to protect the son, if his father is ever exposed.'

'Why should you doubt them?'

'Because I've got twenty-five years' experience in this business and when I'm investigating I doubt everything until I see unshakeable proof that it's true.'

'Bob,' she began, then paused, like someone risking a trump too early in the game, 'even though Boras was acting outside the intelligence community, the Americans still have to protect him, because of their own involvement with him, and they would not like you going after his son.'

'How do you know?'

'Because they told me so,' she murmured.

'Are you telling me that he's a CIA asset too?'

'They didn't say that, not outright, but the implication was clear.'

'Why else would they even mention him? Jesus,' Skinner exclaimed, 'of course he is: stun gun, grenade, that's not stuff your ordinary yuppie businessman can get his hands on too easily.'

Dennis shrugged her shoulders. 'Bob, the bottom line is this. These people are valuable to the Americans, and I've been asked to persuade you to call it a day. I've even been asked to have someone order you, if necessary.'

Skinner threw his head back and laughed. 'But you're not going to bother, are you. Because I'm Scottish, and outside Home Office control, only my chief constable can give me that order, and you know he won't. Let me ask you something, Amanda. If this was an MI5 operation, in your home country, and the Yanks were telling you to pack it in, what would you do?'

Dennis drew a long, deep breath. 'I'd tell them to piss off,' she admitted.

'Then will you tell them that for me, please? If I can prove that Dražen Boras killed Stevie Steele, I'm going to have him.' His smile vanished. 'However, if you want to give them some comfort, you can tell them that I'll have a real problem doing that.'

'Why?'

'Because right now I've got two detective constables giving him an alibi.'

Seventy-two

Maggie settled into her chair and breathed a sigh of relief. For much of the day, Stevie's father had been declaring that he and his mother would stay for another night, to look after her, as he had put it. 'Stevie would have wanted us to,' he had said more than once, until finally she had taken him aside and had told him that a house could only hold so much grief, and that in fact Stevie would have told them to go back to Dunfermline and allow her some space.

Margot Wilding had phoned her at eight thirty, expecting to be told that the start of her new job would be postponed, but she had asked her to come as agreed. Her bright presence had brought some light into the morning, but Maggie knew that it would be only a brief respite before the things that had to be done.

Mr Steele . . . she rarely called him anything else . . . had come with her to the undertaker's in the patrol car that had called for her at noon. She had felt a sense of intrusion then too, but she could not have forbidden him.

Bob Skinner had been right: Stevie's body had been unmarked, when she had seen him lying there in his coffin.

But he hadn't looked like Stevie either, only a pale likeness of someone very young, a waxen model, in his cremation garb. Of course she had broken down, and at that time she had been grateful for her father-in-law's strong support, glad that she had let him come.

Once that desperate part was over she had to put some purpose into her day, by discussing funeral arrangements with the undertaker, settling for Friday, at Mortonhall Crematorium, the easiest for Stevie's family and friends to access from Fife. There had been a reception to arrange at the Braid Hills Hotel, and she had done that too, ready and willing to use police transport to get there and finally to return home.

Her father-in-law, a good man, no doubting that, had made an evening meal, since his wife was still incapable of anything. They had eaten together, and then the Steeles had left, still a little reluctantly. 'Are you sure now?' Stevie's dad had said, even as she was closing the door on him.

As the day had worn on it had begun to worry her that she did not feel exhausted. But as she sank down into the soft upholstery, and the last of the adrenalin had worked itself out of her system, tiredness caught up with her. She put a hand on her bump and whispered, 'Just you and me now, kid,' as her eyes grew heavier.

She had dozed off when the phone rang. She blinked herself awake and picked up the cordless handset from her lap, then pressed the receive symbol. 'Hello,' she said drowsily.

'Margaret, is that you?' The voice was strained, urgent.

'Yes.'

'Margaret, it's Bet. I don't know how to ask this . . .'

She was wide awake now. 'It's true,' she said. 'How did you find out?'

'From the BBC website; it's one of the things I check first thing in the morning, before I start my day. Normally I look at the world version, but today I clicked on the UK edition as well, and I saw a news item about a policeman being killed. When I saw the name . . . Oh, Sis, it's terrible. Why you?'

'Why anyone?' She felt the tears threaten again and bit her lip. Yet in the same moment she felt an enormous wave of something that she could describe as relief, at this reminder that she was not alone in the world, that she still had blood out there. 'It's the fickle fucking finger of fate.'

'Well, it should have pointed somewhere else.'

Maggie made a decision. 'Bet,' she said, 'I hardly know you as an adult. Are you a strong person?'

'I reckon,' her sister replied.

'Then let me tell you everything.'

Seventy-three

As soon as McGuire stepped through the door of the old pub, he saw two familiar faces, sitting at a tiny table near the bar, the only people in that small area. They recognised him at once, but that was no compliment for their special skills included instant recognition of almost everyone they had ever seen. Their names were Queenstown and Strivens, and they were fellow police officers, but he had no idea of their rank because that was irrelevant on the Prime Minister's close-protection squad.

'Bloody hell,' said the fair-haired Queenstown, the taller and slimmer of the two, 'are the Scots invading?'

'We control this place already, man,' the big Scot replied, 'you know that. From the top down, starting with the guy you work for.'

'Yours is in the back bar,' Strivens told him. 'He came in ten minutes ago, bought us a pint and then went off in search of food. Good luck to him: it's just gone nine so the pies will be pretty solid by now. It must be heavy stuff.'

'The pies?'

'Nah!' Strivens laughed. 'Whatever brings you two down here together.'

'Rollover from an investigation, that's all. The gaffer had to go off and see a mate; he called me and told me to meet him in the Red Lion, Whitehall.' He glanced around. 'I've never been here before. You won't find too many places like this left in Edinburgh.'

'None at all. We're half-way between Downing Street and the Palace of Westminster. Everyone in here's a face of some sort or another; the place is an unofficial safehouse for coppers and politicians.'

'Sorry about young Stevie,' said Queenstown, quietly. 'What the hell made the guy rig the place after he croaked himself?'

'Nutter,' McGuire growled. 'Blaze of glory, they reckon. It didn't happen on our patch, so it's Northumbria's job to figure it all out.'

'God help them, then, with Mr Skinner looking over their shoulders.'

'Through there, you said?'

'Yes.'

'Thanks. Maybe see you next time your man's up north.' He pushed his way through a swing door and found himself in a much bigger area, long and narrow, with a wooden-topped bar taking up most of its space, and with its own entrance. His way was blocked by four people, two of whom were high-profile television journalists. Their companions' faces were familiar also; he knew that they were junior government ministers, but failed to put a name to either. They fell silent and stood aside quickly at his 'Excuse me, please.' He guessed that dark, muscular strangers always had that effect on conversations in the Red Lion.

Skinner was sitting at the far end of the room. There was a plate in front of him, clean but for a smear of tomato sauce, and an almost empty glass. McGuire pointed. Skinner nodded. 'Adnams,' he said.

'Two of them, please,' he told the barman.

When they were filled, settled, topped up and paid for, he carried both pints across to the DCC's table and joined him. 'Pies okay?' he asked.

'Yes, but not as good as that fucking restaurant I left you in. I was expecting to be taken to Lockett's, but my friend had a date.'

'Your friend?'

'Amanda, Thames House, top floor.'

McGuire whistled. 'Your message really got through. Who was looking in on us?' He paused. 'Can we talk here?'

'Yes, it's clean. I checked it with my wee box.'

He glanced at the journalists and their friends. 'So it really is a safehouse,' he murmured.

'What?'

'Nothing; just something the guys next door said.'

'Cerberus?'

'Eh?'

'The three-headed dog that guards the entrance to Hades . . . or, rather, the exit, for who would want to get in? It's what I call Queenstown and Strivens, because they're such a unit. Okay, I know, they're one head short, but it fits.'

'Hell, boss! What sort of a mood are you in?'

'The sort that comes over me when I'm trying to figure out how somebody could have been in two places at once. To answer your question, when we were with Boras, we were talking to people he's been involved with for over fifteen years. On Saturday, he was acting on his own, but he's still under their umbrella.' Succinctly, keeping his voice low, he summarised Amanda Dennis's message.

'We're being warned off by them? Does that mean we have to start checking under our cars every morning?'

'No. It's a bluff. But it might as well have been a warning. If Dražen didn't kill Stevie, although I'm damn near certain he did, then we will never know who did.'

'Boss, I met the man myself. He walked into our office in Queen Charlotte Street at around two fifteen, and the boys took him round to the Waterfront, where I saw him. You've read Montell's report of their discussion in the investigation file. He got back from Los Angeles that morning, found out what had happened to his sister, went to see his folks, and caught a BA flight up to Edinburgh. He checked into the George, then took a taxi down to Leith. The pathologist has Ballester dying at half past twelve, in Wooler. He couldn't have done it.'

Skinner frowned. 'There's flexibility in the time of death. Suppose he killed the guy an hour earlier? He could have got to Edinburgh from Wooler by road in that time.'

McGuire shook his head. 'But not from London to Wooler by road, no way.'

'Fly to Newcastle, hire a car?'

'No time and eminently traceable.'

'Fuck it!' Skinner snapped. 'Private plane? Davor has one.'

'It's a jet. Brian Mackie's a plane anorak; he met it at Turnhouse. He told me the thing could cross the Atlantic.

You won't land that in the fucking Cheviots and take off again.'

'No.' The DCC looked down at his glass, and realised that his second pint was almost gone. 'Mario, I need to shut my brain down for a while. I'm in danger of becoming obsessive. I've promised Maggie that I'll find Stevie's killer; if I can't . . .'

'Then you can't, big man, and that'll be an end of it. Nobody will ever blame you for not trying.'

Skinner rose to his feet. 'I will, son,' he said. 'Two more, please,' he called to the barman.

Seventy-four

'Thanks, Griff.' Sammy Pye took the report from Montell. The new DI had arrived in the office at five minutes past eight to find the South African already there.

'I finished that last night,' the detective constable told him. 'I've been through every file and every folder on that disk. I can tell you just about everything there is to know about the personal and business life of Daniel Ballester, and I'm glad the bastard's dead.'

'Me too. I'll read through it.' As the door of his office closed once more he began to read. Montell's paper was well structured: it began with a printout of Ballester's diary entries over a three-year period. There was no detail, only times and venues of appointments, with individuals identified by initials. His involvement with Zrinka Boras was identifiable on that basis, as was his liaison with Stacey Gavin. On the day of her death, there was a single entry: 'SQ'. Then on the day before Zrinka's murder, another, 'NB'.

'South Queensferry, North Berwick,' Pye murmured. He moved on to the descriptions of each of the folders on the disk, beginning with 'My Pictures'. Montell's summary revealed that there were few. There were some from

Ballester's youth and childhood, but the main concentration was in the folders marked 'Zrinka' and 'Stacey'. They included intimate shots of both women, and in Stacey's folder was a nude shot of Ballester himself, taken by Stacey while he posed for her portrait, for the next image was one of the young artist, partly hidden by a canvas on an easel, brush in hand.

From 'My Pictures', Pye moved on to a group under a one-word heading, 'Business'. He read through printouts of each one; each contained detail of a story on which the journalist had been involved, with notes, interview summaries and frank opinions, which, to Pye, revealed much more about the author than about his subjects. As he progressed, he understood why Montell had found the man repellent: the notes showed the man inside, and not, he was sure, the Ballester that Zrinka and Stacey had thought, at first, that they knew. As he read, he was certain that Zrinka must have come upon these files, and that they had brought their relationship to an end.

And yet: Pye checked the list once, then again. He reached across his desk and found a pad on which was scrawled the number of the Royal Horseguards Hotel. He picked up his phone and dialled. The receptionist answered on the second ring.

'Good morning,' he said. 'I'm trying to contact one of your overnight guests, Mr McGuire.'

There was a pause, and then, 'He hasn't checked out yet. I'll try his room.'

He waited, until a familiar voice answered, a shade gruffly.

'Morning, boss, it's Sammy. How are you?'

'Never go on the piss with Bob Skinner. What's up, Sam?'

'Maybe nothing, but I thought you should know. Montell's done a full analysis of Ballester's computer. Most of his sad life's there, all his seedy stories, even the Diana nonsense, but there's one thing that isn't. There is nothing relating to Davor Boras or his company. Yet he spent a whole chunk of his life digging into it. Does it strike you as passing strange that there's nothing about it?'

McGuire was fully awake in an instant. 'It sure does. And I'm afraid it's going to give the bloke along the corridor a whole new lease of life.'

Seventy-five

'He's sure about that?' Skinner exclaimed. 'There are no entries on Boras?'

'Montell's thorough,' McGuire told him. 'Sammy wouldn't have called me if he'd been in any doubt.'

'And here was me ready to give up. I've lain awake half the night thinking that I'm an impressionable fool, down here because of a flight of Arthur Dorward's fancy. You know the techs. They always want to show they're the cleverest kids in school. But now . . .'

'Arthur only deals in fact. He told you what was and wasn't there and you drew conclusions, which I support.'

'So what are your conclusions from the fact that while Ballester's entire career as a journalist can be traced through his computer, there's nothing at all on the one that ties him to Boras?'

'They were wiped by whoever killed him. And that brings me back to Dražen, the only person we know of that his secretive father might trust with the task.'

'Yet he was flying at the time Ballester was killed,' Skinner pointed out.

'That's if he was the man who got on the plane,' said

McGuire. 'I've been doing some after-midnight thinking as well. What if a substitute caught the flight to Edinburgh?'

'That still leaves Dražen with the seemingly impossible task of getting to Wooler in time to kill Ballester, then get up to Edinburgh.'

'He's a rich man too.'

'Another plane? Mario, get Sammy on line, please.' He waited as McGuire called Pye on his mobile, then took it as it was handed over.

'This is the DCC,' he said. 'I want your team to get on to the Civil Aviation Authority and check their records for all aircraft owned personally by Davor Boras, his son Dražen, also known as David Barnes, and by any companies they might control. I know of one, a jet belonging to Daddy, so disregard that. If you get any other results, find out where those planes are based, and when their last recorded movements were.

'Also, I want to know if Dražen, or David Barnes for that matter, has a pilot's licence. Finally, I want you to check flight arrivals from JFK at Heathrow on Saturday morning, looking for Dražen, under either of his names, and departures from there to Edinburgh at midday.'

'Yes, sir. Do I call you back on this number?'

'No, you won't be able to. DCS McGuire or I will call you, when we can.'

'I'd better get on with it, then, boss.' The line went dead.

'That's under way,' said Skinner, reaching for his jacket. 'Let's book ourselves in here for another night, just in case.'

'We're not going straight home?'

'Hell, no. We're going back to where I was last night.

You've done your Special Branch stint, now it's time you saw where the real game's played. Let me stretch that memory of yours. When you saw Dražen on Saturday, can you remember how he was dressed?'

'Yes, I can. No way could I have forgotten it.'

Seventy-six

'I am not comfortable with this, Bob,' said Amanda Dennis. 'You giving two fingers to the people in Langley is one thing, but my being seen to help you do it, that's quite another.'

'Mandy,' Skinner cajoled, 'we both know that you're as annoyed with them as I am. Besides, eventually I'll get what I'm looking for; all I'm asking you to do is save me some time.'

'You are a persuasive old sod,' she exclaimed. 'On second thoughts delete the "old": you're younger than me. Come on.'

She led Skinner and McGuire, the latter unusually silent, out of her office and across to the lift. They took it down to the third floor and stepped into a corridor with a door at the end. She entered a code into a keypad on the wall then swung it open. 'This is our counter-terrorist section,' she said, for McGuire's benefit. 'Not nearly as flashy as you see on the telly, but the job is much the same.'

Heads turned as they crossed the floor; Skinner recognised one or two faces from previous visits. They stopped at a desk the size of a dining table where a man was working at a computer terminal. He was in shirtsleeves, wore glasses and was totally bald; whether by nature or design, neither visitor could tell. 'Adrian,' she murmured, 'these are two friends of ours from the north, Bob and Mario. They're working on something very sensitive and need your help; give them what they need, please. Gentlemen, come back up when you're done.'

'Thanks, Amanda.' Skinner turned to Adrian as she left. 'Before we start I need to make a phone call. May I use yours?'

'Sure,' the man replied affably.

'Mobiles are a last resort in here,' the DCC explained to McGuire, as he dialled. 'They give too much away. Sammy, how goes?'

'So far so good, boss. David Barnes was a passenger on a flight to Heathrow Terminal Three on Saturday morning, from JFK, onward from Jamaica. He then caught the twelve-fifteen shuttle to Edinburgh, and returned on Sunday. The last part I knew because Griff picked him up and took him to the airport.'

'What about the rest of it?'

'Neither David nor his company owns an aircraft. However, Continental IT does. The Embraer is Davor's personal property, but the company owns a Beechcraft Bonanza. It's kept at its depot in Surrey. There are no flights logged for Saturday, but that doesn't necessarily mean anything since the depot has its own landing strip.'

'Is Dražen licensed to fly it?'

'Not under that name, but I can't say for sure. There are three qualified civilian pilots in Britain with the name

David Barnes. I'm trying to get hold of file photos for each of them, but I'm getting Data Protection Act resistance from the Department of Transport.'

'Tell them we're investigating the carriage of illegal armaments, and that you can arrange to have the security service shit on them but that you'd rather not do that. If you have any further problems I'll attend to them myself. Sammy, I want you to find out all you can about the performance limits of that type of aircraft, then see if you can find a small airfield in Northumberland where it could have landed.'

'Understood.'

'Cheers.' Skinner hung up and turned back to their helper. 'Adrian, I want you to access camera footage from Heathrow early Saturday morning, showing passengers disembarking from the American Airlines flight from JFK. We need to see them all. Can do?'

'Give me about two minutes.'

'I'll give you a clue,' said McGuire. 'We're looking for a man, late twenties, possibly wearing a denim jacket with a big coloured logo on the back, and with a baseball cap covered in parrots.'

'They're pretty tight search parameters.' Adrian chuckled, and set to work with mouse and keyboard. The monitor screen flashed as it ran through a jerky series of choices, until finally he found the one they sought. The two detectives watched intently a line of people walking along a narrow, tube-like corridor; it was covered by two cameras giving a full frontal, then a back view.

Skinner had expected a wait, but after only three

disembarking passengers had passed under the camera's eye, Adrian called out, 'How about him, then? As described, plus a pair of wrap-round shades.' He froze the back view and enlarged it, until they could read the logo on the jacket 'Margaritaville, Jamaica'.

'That's the man,' McGuire exclaimed. 'It looks like him, even with the shades, and anyway, I could not miss that jacket or that cap.'

'Good lad,' the DCC told Adrian. 'Now, get the images as sharp as you can, then print them out as big as you can. We'll still have to look at the lot, just in case there is someone else on that flight who's been to the same bar, but I don't expect to find him.'

It took twenty minutes to print the images, then to run fruitlessly through the remaining passengers; to the Scots it seemed like much longer, but finally the line ended, and the aircrew were seen to leave, rolling bags behind them. 'Thanks,' said Skinner. 'Now I want to see everybody embarking for Edinburgh, same day, on the twelve-fifteen BA shuttle. Can you do that?'

'On an internal flight, probably not, but I should be able to find something from the security area.' He exited the tape and entered a 'search' command, with date and time. Seconds later a new location appeared, showing passengers stepping through a metal detector as their carry-on luggage was X-rayed. 'I'm starting two hours before flight time,' Adrian explained. 'Generous, but now that I know who I'm looking for I can run it through fast. Go and get yourselves coffee from our filter, if you like.'

'I could use somc,' McGuire admitted. 'Where is it?'

'In the kitchen, just round the corner. Leave twenty pence in the saucer, like we do.'

'Leave forty pence and bring me one,' said Skinner.

'Actually . . .' Adrian called out, as McGuire left.

When he found the coffee-maker, the jug was empty, and so he had to brew a fresh batch. There was no change in the saucer, and so he left a pound coin: being Scottish, he poured five cups and carried them back to the work-station on a tray. 'I put milk in yours, Adrian, okay?'

No reply came: he looked up and saw Skinner and the technician staring at the monitor, at a still figure framed there, clad in a denim jacket and a garish baseball cap, with half of his face hidden by a pair of wrap-round sunglasses.

'Bugger,' the DCC whispered.

McGuire laid down the tray and peered at the screen, for thirty seconds or more. 'Let me see him move,' he said eventually. Adrian rewound the recording and played it, at normal speed, until the man had moved out of shot, with a flight bag over his shoulder. 'Again.' The recording was repeated.

'What are you thinking?' Skinner asked.

'There's something wrong. I don't know what it is; maybe it's the way he moves. Have you called up prints?'

'Not yet.'

'Let's have a look at one; front view only this time.'

Again they waited as Adrian went back to find the best available image of the man, then sharpened it and sent a command to the networked printer. When the picture was ready, he picked it off the output tray and laid it on the desk beside the others.

'Same build,' McGuire admitted, 'same height, same overall appearance. If only he wasn't wearing those fucking sunglasses.'

'Exactly,' said Skinner. 'It never gets too bright in the departures hall, as I recall.' He gazed at the images, until . . . 'Hey,' he exploded suddenly. 'Do you think that, between calling in on his folks and going to catch the Edinburgh flight, Dražen had time to get married?'

'What?'

'Look at the pictures. The Dražen who got on the shuttle is wearing a wedding ring; the other one isn't. That's not an item you wear as costume jewellery, is it?'

'No, and Dražen isn't married. We've got him,' McGuire exclaimed.

'Not quite,' the DCC replied, bringing them both down to earth in a hurry. 'That isn't enough to put to a jury. We haven't proved anything, until we find out who this man is, and get him to admit being Dražen's double on the Edinburgh flight.'

'Damn it, you're right,' the chief superintendent conceded. He stared at the second image, as if willing himself to recognise the man; for a moment, he felt a click in his memory, but just as quickly it was gone.

'It's a step forward. We do know for sure now, even if we can't take it forward. Let's see if Sammy has any more for us.'

He picked up Adrian's phone once more and dialled Pye; this time he switched on speaker mode so that McGuire could hear. 'Anything fresh?' he asked, without preliminaries.

'Department of Transport have coughed up those photos, sir. Griff and Tarvil both say that one of them is Dražen Boras.'

'Sammy,' the head of CID interrupted, 'I'd like you to forward them to my e-mail. I can log on from down here.'

'Okay, sir. I'll send it right now.'

'Not it, all three.'

'Okay. I'm still working on those airfield locations. The plane has the range to make it to Northumberland and back, no problem.'

'Carry on with that,' Skinner told him, 'but send those images first. So long for now.'

They sat for a few minutes, drinking their coffee. As the DCC picked up his second cup, he realised that Adrian was looking at him. 'I've seen you before,' said the MI5 officer, quietly.

'I'll bet you see a hell of a lot of people in the course of your working day.'

'I mean that I've seen you in here, a few months ago, around the time of that business with Rudy Sewell.' He sighed. 'Poor old Rudy.' Skinner looked at him impassively. 'He was well liked in here, you know.'

'I'm sure he was,' the Scot replied. 'I met him once up in Edinburgh; decent guy. What happened to him?' His question was a warning and the other man read it correctly. It meant 'subject closed'.

'Adrian,' said McGuire. 'I'd like to log on to my internal e-mail from here. You can do that, can't you?'

'If you give me the IP address I can call up your system, then you can enter your own password.'

The head of CID knew the sequence of numbers off by heart; he recited them then watched as they were keyed in and the force Intranet homepage appeared on screen. The technician rolled his chair back from the desk. 'It's all yours,' he said.

McGuire entered his user name and password, then went straight to his mailbox. It contained several new items, but he went straight to the most recent, from Sammy Pye, at the top of the list, and clicked on it. There was no text, only an attachment, named as 'Barnes.MOT.zip'. He opened it and saw three small images in a strip. 'Adrian,' he asked, without looking round, 'how do I blow these up to workable size and display them side by side?' He followed the instructions as they were given, one by one, until three faces, all clearly recognisable, appeared on the big widescreen monitor.

The David Barnes on the right wore a beard, and looked to be at least forty. 'That's Dražen on the left,' said the chief superintendent.

'Yes,' Skinner whispered. 'He's not a lot like his father, but the look in his eyes gives him away. And what about the one in the middle?'

McGuire looked at the third image, and his mouth fell open. 'Jesus, we know him! That's Davor Boras's driver. And do you know what, boss? He was polishing that windscreen left-handed, and he was wearing a wedding ring. I can see it, clear as a bell.'

Skinner laughed, shattering the library quiet of the room and causing heads to turn. 'How fucking cute can you get?' he exclaimed. 'When Dražen anglicised his name, everybody must have assumed that he chose one with the same initials. But that wasn't what he was doing. He was taking a new identity that would prove useful to him, copied from someone he knew and who could act as his double when necessary. Adrian,' he pointed at the centre of the screen, 'I want to know everything about this David Barnes, family background, address, the lot. I want all his secrets, all his weaknesses.'

'That's not what I do, Bob.'

'But can you do it?'

'Yes.'

'Then help us with this, please. Call Amanda for authorisation if you must, but do it.'

'It's all right. I have the clearance. Leave it with me.'

'Good lad.' He turned to McGuire, as Adrian resumed his place at the keyboard. 'We're getting there, mate.'

'Could it have been him?' asked the chief superintendent. 'Could it have been this guy who went to Wooler?'

'What about the ring?'

'You said yourself, that's not conclusive. Maybe Dražen is into wearing gold knuckledusters.'

Skinner frowned, then leaned across the desk, picked up the phone, dialled and waited. 'Arthur,' he exclaimed, 'DCC here. Remember that letterbox in Wooler? The final part of the set-up, looping the wire round the door handle: how difficult was that when you did it? . . . Very? That's what I hoped you'd say. So, in your opinion, could it have been done by someone who was naturally left-handed? . . . Hah! Thanks.'

He hung up and turned back to McGuire. 'I quote the mad Dorward: it would have been impossible to do it left-handed unless you were standing on your head: you'd have had to reach too far through the letterbox.' He shifted impatiently in his seat, then stood. 'Get back on to Sammy: see how he's done, whether he has anything fresh. I'm going upstairs. Adrian, what's the pass-code to get back in?'

'That's classified.'

'Son, it's changed every fucking week. I know that.'

The man sighed. 'Okay. It's one seven zero eight.'

The DCC left the unit and took the lift back to the top floor, where the director general's imperious secretary, a holdover from her predecessor's time, granted him admission to her office. 'Do you have what you need?' Dennis asked.

'Most of it. I'm on the way to knowing how Dražen killed Ballester and Stevie, and why. It wasn't just about revenge: he also wiped out any information he might have had on Boras's operation.'

'Knowing is one thing, Bob. Proving . . .'

'Teach your granddad, love,' he said, and winked. 'I'll bet you have this conversation wiped from the tape. To prove it, I need to lift someone; I could use the Met to do it, but that would get messy. I'd need to take him to one of their stations, but that would be on the record and all sorts of questions would be asked.'

She laughed. 'You are a master of manipulation,' she exclaimed. 'What's the man's name?'

'David Barnes.'

'David . . . Isn't that . . .?'

'Dražen's alias; that's right. The other David is Boras's driver. It's a nice arrangement, I'd guess, if Dražen ever needs to be in two places at once. Wherever Davor is, his driver will be, and since he never seems to stray far from his inner sanctum in the City, you should be able to pick him up from the garage below it. He'll probably be polishing the boss's Roller.'

'Okay. There's a house we use in Clapton; you can interrogate him there, but please leave him in one piece.'

'We'll have to; with a bit of luck his boss will never know he's been gone.'

'I'll get it under way.' She smiled as he rose to leave. 'About the tape: one thing that people in intelligence learned from Richard Nixon was to be sure you have an off switch.'

Skinner was still smiling as he made his way back to Adrian's desk. 'There you are,' said the operative, holding out a two-page document. 'David Barnes, his life and loves. Memorise it, then shred it, please. It can't leave the building.'

'I know. Thanks.' He turned to McGuire. 'Any more from Sammy?

'Well, he says that Ray Wilding's a happy boy: he's just arrived back from the airport with Becky Stallings. He tells me she's looking pretty pleased with herself too.'

'Which flight did she catch?'

'The first one. It's taken them two and a half hours to get back to the office.'

'I don't want to know. Apart from that?'

'He's found an airfield. It's just west of the A1 north of

Newcastle; it's a wartime RAF place that reverted to the farm from which it was requisitioned. It was kept in operational condition and the present owner runs it commercially. It's called Walkdean.'

'How far from Wooler?'

'Forty-five minutes by car, Sammy says.'

'Would the Beechcraft be able to land there?'

'Easy.'

'But how the hell would he get a car? They didn't have time to get one there, and a hire vehicle would be traceable.' Skinner scratched his chin. 'You know, Mario,' he murmured, 'I reckon it's time to let our friends in the north in on a bit of what's happening.'

Seventy-seven

Deputy Chief Constable Les Cairns smiled as the Land Rover edged along the narrow road. He was a countryman at heart, and so he snapped up any excuse to escape from the city, and from his office in Ponteland.

He liked a bit of mystery too. Much earlier in his police career, he had been a detective constable in Special Branch, and he had enjoyed the cachet that the posting gave him among his professional peers. Since attaining command rank, he had been confined to the office; he was envious of people like Bob Skinner, mavericks who had the balls to write their own job descriptions once they had made it to the heights.

Actually, when he thought about it, there was only one Bob Skinner. Even in England he was legendary, although in some eyes notorious, for his ability to delegate and yet still manage to stay involved. Cairns had seen the man for himself a few days before, and he had to admit, he had an air about him, a compelling friendliness, yet with menace close to the surface.

His call had come entirely out of the blue, and it had been intriguing. His request was simple, investigate and report, to be carried out by someone with Special Branch clearance, with nothing on paper. The temptation had been too much to resist and, anyway, the place was not all that far from HQ. He had called up his favourite car and driver, harbouring a strong feeling that Skinner had guessed he would.

He gazed ahead until, around a slow right curve, he saw an old finger-pointing road sign that read 'Walkdean'. 'That's us,' he murmured.

His driver turned off the road and into a track that led through a copse and opened out into flat countryside. Around half a mile away, Cairns could see a line of grey wooden huts, two tall hangars and what appeared to be a parking area for cars and microlight aircraft. Beyond, rising above them all, there was a control tower, and to the right, on the other side of the landing strip, two squat round tanks, which he assumed contained aviation fuel. 'Find the office,' he instructed.

It was easy enough. As they drew closer he saw a sign fixed to the side of the first hut: 'Walkdean Airfield. Leisure flying and general aviation. Enquire within.' They pulled up at the door, and the deputy chief stepped out, buttoning the tweed jacket that he had picked up on the way out to disguise what was clearly a uniform shirt.

Two steps led up to a door marked 'office'. He opened it and went inside.

'Morning,' a woman greeted him brightly. 'Welcome to Walkdean. I'm Chloë Ritter, proprietor. How can I help you?'

'Les Cairns,' he said, shaking her hand and finding her grip as strong as his. 'Northumbria Constabulary.'

'What have we done?'

'Nothing, I hope,' he replied, the police–punter cliché conversation. 'I'd like to ask you a couple of questions, that's all.'

'Fire away.'

'Thanks. What sort of traffic do you get through here?

'It varies; it's mostly hobby flying, but we do get some commercial landings. There are a few swish resort hotels in the area and they use us when guests want to fly in, for golfing weekends or whatever. I keep hoping that a helicopter firm will decide to base itself here but, to be honest, I think we're on the wrong side of Newcastle for that.'

'Did you have anyone land last Saturday?'

She nodded. 'The usual swarm of microlights, Mr Alexander in his Piper and, oh, yes, the Beechcraft.'

'What was that?' Cairns asked.

'A Beechcraft Bonanza, twin-prop; a cracking little plane, although it's bigger than it looks in terms of payload.'

'Were you expecting it?'

'No, it wasn't booked in. He came on radio asking for landing clearance and my husband gave him the okay; he was in the control tower at the time.'

'Family business?'

'Yes. We own all the land around here, but the farming operation is all tenanted now. This is what we like doing.'

'Did you see the pilot?'

'Yes, I did. As soon as he had parked and offloaded his motorcycle he came across, paid his landing fee, and roared off. We're a cash-only business,' she added.

'His motorcycle?'

'Yes. I've seen that before. People fly in from other cities, land here and then bike it into Newcastle. Some even use pedal cycles.'

'Can you describe him?'

'I'm afraid not. I never saw his face close up. He was wearing his crash helmet when he came in here, and when he came back, it was my turn to be up in the control tower, shepherding the microlights.'

'Would your husband have seen him?'

'I doubt it. The guy rode straight up to the plane, loaded the bike, up its little ramp, then climbed inside. He had to wait for take-off clearance, in the queue with the flying sewing-machines, but he got off all right.'

'He didn't refuel?'

'Obviously he didn't need to. Bonanzas have a range of around eight hundred miles with a low payload, as this chap had.'

'Right,' said Cairns. 'That'll be all, Mrs Ritter. You've been very helpful.'

'My pleasure, but can you tell me what it's all about? Has he crashed, or was he doing something illegal?'

He would have answered her question, but he knew no more than she did, and so instead he shook his head and fed her another cliché. 'No, no, nothing like that; purely routine.' He gave her a brief salute and stepped outside.

Seventy-eight

The security service safe house was in Millfields Road, a quiet thoroughfare well away from congestion zones, cars parked outside houses with the security of traffic-calming bumps, which prevented them being driven away at high speed.

David Barnes was waiting for Skinner and McGuire at a table in an upstairs room when they arrived just after two p.m. He was handcuffed and his ankles were secured to the legs of his chair. He glared at them as they entered and sat opposite him. 'What the 'ell is this?' he barked, in broad Mancunian. 'Who are you barstards?'

The two detectives produced their warrant cards. 'That's who we are,' said McGuire, as Skinner leaned back and stared coldly across the table. 'And this is about you being done for the murder of two men, one of them a police officer.'

'You're crazy!' Barnes screamed. 'I never murdered anyone in my life.'

'Of course you did,' the chief superintendent told him. 'You were in the army, a sergeant on duty with KFOR in Kosovo, about seven years ago. You were part of an interrogation team that interpreted its orders very broadly. You killed three prisoners under questioning in separate incidents, but the third one went public and you became an embarrassment. Consequently your death in action was reported, and you were quietly made to disappear, with the help of Mr Davor Boras, a facilitator with links to the CIA. You went to work for him as his chauffeur-cum-bodyguard. Your duties also included piloting the company's light aircraft on occasion.

'A few years ago, Mr Boras and his son decided that it would be a good idea if they appeared to be at odds, and so Dražen was seen to leave his old man's business, set up on his own and take an English name . . . David Barnes, on the basis that it might be handy to have two of you around.'

McGuire leaned forward. 'Are you going to dispute any of that?' he hissed. 'Because my boss and I would love to interrogate you, just like you used to in Kosovo, only we're better at it than you were. We won't kill you, we won't mark you, but we will fucking well waste you, in memory of our dead colleague.'

Barnes looked, and believed. 'You've got all that right,' he murmured, 'but I never killed no copper.'

'No,' said Skinner. 'This is what you did. On Saturday morning Davor Boras called you to see him. He gave you a return e-ticket for the Edinburgh shuttle out of Heathrow at twelve fifteen. He also gave you clothes, specifically jeans, a T-shirt, a very garish denim jacket and cap, and a pair of Oakleys. He ordered you to fly north, in that gear, and to meet the other David Barnes at a location in Edinburgh.

'You did just that. You met Dražen, you changed clothes,

and you gave him the return ticket. Then you rode his motorbike back to Walkdean Airfield, near Newcastle, where Dražen had parked the company Beechcraft, and flew it back to the depot in London, returning to London in transport he had left there.

'While you were engaged in this pantomime, Dražen went to Wooler, in Northumberland where he killed a man named Daniel Ballester and, in mistake for two other people, Detective Inspector Steven Steele, a colleague and very good friend of ours.'

Barnes paled. 'I read about that. He did that? Christ, mate, I never knew.'

'I couldn't give a shit what you knew,' the DCC growled. 'Tell me, David, do you love Sharon, your wife?' Barnes nodded. 'And do you love Wendy, the girl you've been shagging on the side in a flat in Victoria Park for a year now?' The man gasped.

'Actually, I don't care about that,' Skinner continued. 'But I would like to know whether you would like to see either of them again, or whether you're prepared to have your body fed through an industrial-sized tree-shredder, maybe before you're quite dead. Because, mate, as you will have gathered from the depth of our knowledge, and because of the unconventional nature of your arrest, we are in a position to make that happen.'

He laid two sheets of paper on the table. 'That's your admission that everything within your sphere of knowledge happened as I have described. Did it?' he snapped. 'Yes or no?'

'Yes!' Barnes screamed again, but this time out of pure

terror, as he stared at the nightmare across the table, pointing a pen at him like a dagger.

'Then sign that, both pages, within ten seconds or Mario will start breaking your fingers.'

Barnes snatched the Pentel from Skinner, with both manacled hands, and scrawled his name, twice.

'Thanks,' said McGuire, amiably, as he pocketed the signed statement. 'We'll have you taken back to work now, hopefully before your boss notices you're missing. But breathe just one word to him, and I promise you, the best that'll happen is that your wife will hear about Wendy.'

Seventy-nine

'You know,' said Skinner, 'I thought Barnes would have been tougher than that.'

'Me too,' McGuire agreed. 'But I have to confess you scared me a wee bit, so Christ knows what he must have felt.'

'Maybe we're getting too good at it.'

'Maybe, but I'd like to think that there's still room for improvement when we get our hands on Dražen. He'll be a harder nut than his namesake, I'm sure of that.' The head of CID's eyes narrowed. 'I wish we could go in there first.'

'So do I, but that was never on. Amanda helped us as far as she could, and probably further, by having her people snatch Barnes for us. But when it comes to making a proper arrest, we've got no locus down here. We had to bring the Met in on it.' He broke off as a tall figure came towards them, down the corridor in which they stood.

'Gentlemen, we're ready upstairs,' said Deputy Assistant Commissioner Davies, head of Specialist Crime operations in the Met. He wore the air of a man who was doing something that had been forced upon him and did not like it.

'I hope to God you're right about this. Right or wrong, I'm going to catch Foreign Office flak for this. That damn woman Weiss has been bending my ear since last Saturday when your man threw her out of an interview.'

'I thought she was Home Office,' Skinner remarked.

'That's what I allowed Becky Stallings to believe.'

'Christ,' the Scot gasped, 'you lie to your own officers.'

'I wouldn't put it quite like that.'

'I would. Now don't lie to me. I want Dražen alive, to stand trial; if you're under orders from anybody to put a bullet in him to keep him quiet you'd better tell me now.'

'I'm not, I assure you.'

'Then make fucking sure that nobody does.'

'My men will meet force with force.'

McGuire took a twenty-pound note from his breast pocket and held it up. 'This says they won't face any. Dražen Boras is anything but stupid: he's not going to keep firearms in a luxury penthouse that's pissing distance away from Chelsea Bridge. You could ring the fucking doorbell and he'd answer it and invite you in, yet you've got a squad of commandos up there. God bless Harry Stanley, may he rest in peace.'

The taunt, about the man shot dead by armed officers while carrying nothing more lethal than a table leg, struck home hard. Davies turned on his heel and stalked off.

'You shouldn't have said that, you know,' Skinner murmured. 'That's the sort of guy that might apply for Jimmy's job.'

'The day he gets it, I'm going into the family business with Paula.'

'He'll have to get past me first.'

McGuire stared at him, but said nothing, as the sound of indistinct shouts drifted down from the floor above. They waited for ten minutes until, finally, Davies reappeared. 'You can come up now,' he said coldly.

They followed him, up one floor and through the open door that led into Dražen Boras's penthouse. As with his father's office, the living-room wall was made almost entirely of glass, framing Chelsea Bridge like an enormous picture postcard.

The furniture was 1960s retro, the kind that had once made Paula Viareggio stick two fingers down her throat when Mario had suggested buying a piece. Slowly, a vast white egg-shaped chair began to turn towards them on its base. Settled deep into it, and smiling like a demon, was Davor Boras.

'I regret,' he said, 'that my son is not here to receive you. Nor will he be for quite some time, not until these silly allegations against him are shown to be unprovable and the Attorney General has exonerated him. In the process, you will, of course, be excoriated.' He leaned on the last word as if he was proud of it.

McGuire took the chauffeur's statement from his pocket, and waved it in the air. 'The other David Barnes doesn't agree with you.'

'Come, come, Chief Superintendent,' the millionaire laughed, 'would you care to explain how that was obtained? Even now, Mr Barnes is recovering his courage.'

Skinner ignored him and turned to Davies. 'I want this place searched under your warrant; look for passports. I bet you'll find two: a guy like this, he'll have had a third identity ready, in case of emergencies. Or . . . What's the range of an Embraer jet? Transatlantic, you said, Mario? He's gone west, hasn't he, Davor? And when he lands he'll be welcomed in Virginia.'

From the depths of the chair, Boras winked at him.

Skinner turned on his heel and walked out of the room, through the apartment until he found the master bedroom. He went into Dražen's en-suite bathroom and started to open drawers. In the third, he found a Philishave electric razor. He flicked it open, and saw that the chamber below the blades was full of beard residue. Very carefully, he closed it again, and returned to the huge, curved living room.

Boras was still in the chair, watching the proceedings with evident amusement. He turned as the DCC re-entered and held up the shaver.

'Is this your son's?'

'Of course. A gift from me, in fact; top of the range, best in the world. He has another in his travel kit.'

'I'll borrow it for a while. Mr Davies, have it bagged it for me, please. That's okay with you, Davor, isn't it?'

Boras's smile, and his eyes, narrowed just a little, but he nodded, and replied, 'Of course.'

Skinner and McGuire stayed silent until they were clear of the building, and half-way across Chelsea Bridge. Finally, the chief superintendent exploded: 'The shaver: Dražen's DNA?' he exclaimed.

'Chock full of it, and his father's witness to the fact.'

'Yes! We've got the sod.'

'If the lab does the business.'

'Too bad about that confession, though.'

'Yeah,' Skinner grunted. 'I suspect that Boras noticed that Barnes was absent and, in the circumstances, put the screw on him when he got back. "Courage," he said; money can buy that too. Anyway, that statement was useless in court: the eedjit was too scared to notice that he'd never been formally cautioned.'

The head of CID stopped in his tracks. 'Earlier on,' he asked, 'did I see you log Barnes's phone number into your mobile, before you shredded Adrian's note?'

'I'm afraid so,' said Skinner, cheerfully, 'and his address too. Wicked, eh?'

'Can I borrow it?'

'Sure.' He took the cell phone from his pocket and handed it over.

McGuire opened it, found the number, and pressed the green button. 'Is that Mrs Barnes?' Skinner heard him say, as they resumed their walk across the bridge. 'This is a friend, one of yours, not your husband's: there's some stuff about him that you should know.'

Eighty

'Nice place you have here, Les,' said Skinner, as he looked round his opposite number's office. 'There are times when I don't like being stuck in the city centre. I hope you don't lose this under the force amalgamation.'

'It'll see me out,' Cairns assured him. 'Is that why you're here, sizing up this office in case they make you head of the new regional force?'

'Nothing could be further from my mind,' the Scot assured him sincerely. 'No, I'm here to apologise for the most unprofessional thing I've ever done in my life.'

The Geordie's heavy eyebrows came together. 'Thumping Ballester, you mean? On reflection, I should have done that myself. It isn't against any law I know of to belt a dead man.'

'Thanks, but that's not what I meant.' He opened his briefcase, took out a thick folder and pushed it across Cairns's desk. 'I want to give you this, and to say sorry for having kept you in the dark all the way through its compilation.'

'What is it?'

'It's the documentation of a very private investigation

into the murder of Daniel Ballester and Stevie Steele.'

'Ballester? Murder?' Cairns exclaimed.

'I'm afraid so. And it was on your patch, which made it your business. But it started in Scotland, which made it mine. That's my excuse, anyway. Read that, and you'll find that you have overwhelming grounds for seeking a warrant for the arrest of a man called Dražen Boras, and his extradition from America, where he's believed to be hiding.

'Play it right, Les, and your knighthood could be in there. I want you to give it to the Crown Prosecution Service. They may come under pressure from upstairs not to take it further. If they do, I'd like you to let them know that I have another copy that I will not hesitate to leak to the newspaper for which Ballester used to work, and to a few others as well.'

'This is unshakeable?'

'Cast-iron,' said Skinner. 'I got the clincher this morning: the DNA of Dražen Boras, legally obtained, with his father Davor's consent, given before a DAC in the Met, matches a sample of skin taken by my guy, DI Dorward, from the letterbox at Hathaway House.'

'And you did all this without reference to me?'

'I'm afraid so. Apart from that call you made for me on Tuesday, that is; it was part of the investigation, although I chose not to burden you with it at the time. I'm sorry, mate; I had to use some heavy contacts. If I'd done it by the book . . .'

'. . . I might have made a balls-up of it.'

'Les, I'm not saying that for a second.'

Cairns laughed. 'No, but I am. Man, you're playing by

the book now, when it really matters, and you've saved me a shedload of grief. My biggest problem now will be to explain to the coroner how Ballester's suicide is suddenly a murder, but I can deal with that. Bob, I'm happy to steal your glory any day of the week . . . and your bloody knighthood, if it comes to that.'

'You can have my seat in the Lords as well, if you want.'

'Red's not my colour.' Cairns turned serious once again. 'Look,' he asked, 'for me, presenting a solid case is enough, but what are my chances of landing this Dražen bloke?'

'In truth, somewhere between slim and non-existent,' Skinner told him. 'Especially if I find him first.'

Eighty-one

Although he was in the second rank of mourners at Stevie Steele's funeral, stiff in his uniform, with Aileen and Alex, both in black, on either side of him, and Sir James and Lady Proud beyond his daughter, Skinner stayed in the background during the reception at the Braid Hills Hotel. He felt that that time belonged to families, and so, after no more than fifteen minutes, he left, dropping the First Minister at Holyrood, and heading for Fettes to sign off, before resuming his sabbatical.

But when he was finished, and when he knew that she would be there, he headed home, by way of Gordon Terrace. When he rang the bell, the door was opened by a red-haired woman; she had been by Maggie's side at the crematorium, and again at the reception. 'You're Bet,' he said.

'And you're Bob,' she replied. 'I guess Margaret's told each of us about the other. Come on in; she's been half expecting you.' She led him into the 'playroom' where Maggie was waiting, then left them alone.

'Hi,' he said quietly. 'How're you doing?'

'I'm fine; I suppose that's because the worst part's over.'

'It's not. All other things aside, the worst part begins after the funeral, when there's no more we can do for them, other than miss them, and go quietly crazy. In a way it's a blessing that you have things to distract you. I had Alex and the job; you've got the baby, and then your treatment.'

Maggie laughed softly. 'And my sister; she's quite a distraction too. She says she's staying for as long as I need her. She works mostly on computer and she can keep in touch with her clients by e-mail. It's great; it's like finding someone completely new.'

'That's good.' His head dropped. 'Maggie, there's something I've got to tell you. I've failed you. We had him, the guy who . . . did it but he got away. Not for ever, though: he will always be on my personal Wanted list, and when I catch up with him . . .'

She held up a hand, then reached out and took his. 'Bob,' she whispered, 'stop. I've already had Mario here, telling me about it and promising the same vengeance you are. I want you to put it on hold for now. You guys say you're praying for me, and as long as you are I'd prefer it if you were in God's good books. I need you both to focus on me, not him.'

He looked at her, but her smiling face was hazy to him.

'Things have moved on since I saw you last. Mr Fine has taken another opinion: they're both agreed that Stephanie Margaret . . . that's her name by the way . . . is growing at such a rate that she can be safely delivered in two weeks' time. She'll weigh around four pounds by that time, and they'll be happy with that. I'll get to see her, and then they'll go to work on me. Mr Ronald, the new guy, sounds optimistic. So please, if you want to do something for Stevie, then concentrate, for now, on helping his daughter and wife get through this experience together. Okay?'

He smiled, a little mistily, and squeezed her hand. 'Promise,' he whispered.

'Good,' she said grimly, as her eyes tightened, showing creases that he had never noticed before, 'but be in no doubt of this, just in case you think that the Maggie Rose you knew has gone beyond recall. When we've done that, the two of us, and I'm back to full strength, I'll be ahead of you and Mario in the queue to track down Mr Dražen Boras.'

For The Death Of Me

Quintin Jardine

It's summertime in Monaco and Oz Blackstone, now an international film star, is idly gazing at Roman Abramovich's luxury yacht as it gently cruises into the harbour. Life doesn't get much better than this.

But when a struggling author sweet-talks him into buying the movie rights to his latest novel, a shocking trap is laid.

Oz travels all the way to Singapore to track down the owner of some incriminating photographs but he's in grave danger of over-exposure. And when organised crime muscles in on the picture, Oz is getting perilously close to losing a lot more than his wealth and reputation . . .

Praise for the Oz Blackstone series:

'Perfect plotting and convincing characterisation' *The Times*

'Jardine's plot is very cleverly constructed, every incident and every character has a justified place in the labyrinth of motives' Gerald Kaufman, *The Scotsman*

978 0 7553 2107 0

headline

Dead and Buried

Quintin Jardine

Murder is rarely cut and dried. Usually it follows its own unique, twisted logic . . .

Deputy Chief Constable Bob Skinner has a failed marriage on his hands, and a death on his conscience. He faces the biggest challenge of his career within the secret corridors of Westminster, where dark power is wielded.

Meanwhile, back in Edinburgh, Skinner's daughter is being harassed by a stalker. Can he protect her?

A bookmaker has taken one gamble too many and paid his debt in a gruesome fashion. Is it an underworld vendetta, or something more sinister?

Alongside it all a casual call to the Chief Constable sets him on a personal crusade which quickly points to a bigamist at work. Or is it worse?

Four crimes, four crises: can Skinner and his people solve them? Indeed, can they survive them?

Praise for Quintin Jardine's novels:

'A triumph. I am first in the queue for the next one' *Scotland on Sunday*

'Well constructed, fast-paced, Jardine's narrative has many an ingenious twist and turn' *Observer*

'Deplorably readable' *Guardian*

978 0 7553 0410 3

headline